Black Consciousness

Steve Biko

Black Consciousness in South Africa

Millard Arnold, ed.

Director, Southern Africa Project,
Lawyers' Committee for
Civil Rights Under Law

**Random House
New York**

Library of Congress Cataloging in Publication Data

Biko, Stephen Bantu
Steve Biko: Black Consciousness in South Africa.

1. Cooper, Sathasivan.   2. Trials (Terrorism)—South
Africa—Pretoria.   3. Biko, S. B.   4. South Africa—
Race Relations. I. Arnold, Millard, ed. II. Title.
Law   345'.68'0231   78–10118
ISBN 0–394–50282–5

MANUFACTURED IN THE UNITED STATES OF AMERICA

2 4 6 8 9 7 5 3

First Edition

Designed by Carole Lowenstein

We are looking forward to a nonracial,
just and egalitarian society
in which color, creed and race shall form
no point of reference.

—Stephen Biko

ACKNOWLEDGMENTS

My sincerest appreciation to the following individuals, whose advice, help and comfort made the book possible: Anthony Lewis, Mike Davis, Mike Peay, Marcia Ellis, Emmitt Roberts, Carol Eby, Bob Bernstein, Dean Louis Pollak, Carol Simkin, Bill Pollard, Bob Halper, Charlie Runyon, Grant Ujifusa, Cordelia Jason, Jeff Baqwa, Gail Gerhart, my special friends in South Africa, and most particularly and lovingly, Miriam.

M. A.

Contents

A List of Acronyms

AFECA   Association for the Education and Cultural
           Advancement of the People of South Africa
AICA   African Independent Churches Association
ANC   African National Congress
ASA   African Students Association
ASUSA   African Students Union of South Africa
BAWU   Black Allied Workers Union
BCP   Black People's Convention
CENBAD   Central Bureau for African Development
CRC   Coloured Representative Council
FNLA   National Front for the Liberation of Angola
GSC   General Students' Council
IDAMASA   Interdenominational African Ministers Association
           of South Africa
MPLA   Popular Movement for Liberation of Angola
NIC   Natal Indian Congress
NUSAS   National Union of South African Students
NYO   National Youth Organization
PAC   Pan-Africanist Congress
PRP   Progressive Reform Party
SAIC   South African Indian Congress
SASO   South African Students Organization
SPRO-CAS   Study Project on Christianity in Apartheid Society
SRC   Students Representative Council
TECON   Theatre Council of Natal
TRYO   Transvaal Youth Organization
UBL   Union of Black Labourers
UCM   University Christian Movement
UNB   University of Natal Black Section
UP   United Party

Introduction

I

On May 2, 1976, David Soggot, senior counsel for the defense in the trial of Sathasivan Cooper and Eight Others in Pretoria, South Africa, called to the witness stand Stephen Bantu Biko. A low murmur rolled across the crowded courtroom. Anxiety and anticipation caused most to squirm slightly in their seats. Steve Biko was to testify. No one knew it at the time, but it was to be the last public appearance Biko would ever make.

For nearly three years Biko's voice had been silenced. The founder of the South African Students Organization (SASO) and honorary president of the Black People's Convention (BPC), Biko had been banned or restricted to the magisterial district of King William's Town. In South Africa, a banning order, among other things, forbids a person from being in the presence of more than two people; addressing an audience; being quoted by the media or having anything he had written, whether before or after his banning order, published or disseminated. Now, after three years of near total ostracization, Steve Biko was being allowed to speak in public.

Biko's appearance and testimony at the trial were critical. The defendants in the case, all members of either SASO or BPC, were accused of "endangering the maintenance of law and order in the Republic," or alternatively, of conspiring to "transform the state by unconstitutional, revolutionary and/or violent means"; to "create and foster feelings of racial hatred, hostility and antipathy by the Blacks toward the White population group of the Republic"; and "to discourage, hamper, deter or prevent foreign investment in the economy of the Republic." The charge sheet had nine annexes and totaled eighty-two pages, which consisted of three pamphlets, one SASO resolution, one poem, and four statements, one written by Steve Biko. That material constituted the evidence. The defendants were charged with the crime of terrorism and faced the possibility of death by hanging.

Of the numerous witnesses called by the defense, none was as important as Steve Biko. SASO and BPC, the organizations which were in effect on trial, sprang from an ideological concept conceived by Biko that became known as "Black Consciousness." To Biko, there was a fundamental disorder in a society where Blacks outnumbered Whites four to one, yet were subjected by the White minority South African government to the most extreme forms of social, political and economic suppression with no aspect of Black life escaping regulation. The legal system, for instance, makes it illegal for Blacks to live in certain parts of South Africa, or to live together as husband and wife without special permission—social engineering backed by the awesome military and police strength of the South African government.

For generations, South African governmental suppression and subversion of basic human rights had led Blacks to believe that their condition was hopeless. But it was clear to Biko that while the government's presence was very nearly overwhelming in concrete physical terms, the more damaging oppression was occurring psychologically. Blacks in South Africa had unconsciously resigned themselves to the malaise engendered by the ruling White minority. Recognizing this, Biko saw the immediate need for consciousness-raising. And from that recognition was born his concept of Black Consciousness. In essence, Black Consciousness represented a liberation movement of the mind. A psychological revolution aimed at forging Black thought and feeling into an amalgam of Black pride and ultimately Black unity. In South Africa, such is the stuff of terrorism.

In Biko's four and a half days as a defense witness, he provided the court, the state and the world the opportunity to understand the philosophy of Black Consciousness. This book is Biko's testimony. It is an exposition of the political and psychological movement of Blacks in South Africa. It lays out the rationale and basis of Black Consciousness and describes the origin and history of the organizations that espoused the ideology. But most important, the testimony provides us with a first-person account of the mind and personality of Steve Biko —his thinking, his feelings, his humor, his vision of a future South Africa.

In setting forth the nature and evolution of his political thinking, Biko affords the reader an opportunity to understand fully the ongoing struggle for human dignity in South Africa. While much has been made of the similarities between the civil rights movement in this country and events in South Africa, Biko's testimony explores the differences. Those differences include the political environment of South Africa, in which any form of dissent is considered an activity "which endangers or is calculated to endanger the security of the state or the maintenance of public order." Those differences include a government firmly committed to denying Blacks participation in the mainstream of South African life, and those differences include a legal system once grounded in a stalwart Anglo-Dutch tradition, but now virtually incapable of providing Blacks with a legal remedy to redress obvious wrongs. Nevertheless, the book is a compassionate appeal to reason. In the often eloquent words of Steve Biko, it offers a comprehensive view of the range and depth of Black thinking. It explores virtually every issue that has been raised in contemporary South Africa: education, trade unions, religion, foreign investments, Black attitudes toward Whites, revolution and violence, and all told by the most important Black leader to appear in South Africa in the past decade.

In the continuing battle for human decency in South Africa, the name Steve Biko will not be forgotten. Yet there was no indication in his childhood or early background that Biko possessed the political genius that would lead him to develop an ideology and a mode of action that would irreversibly change the course of history in South Africa. Born in 1946 in King William's Town, Biko came from a family of ordinary means. His father worked as a clerk and his mother did domestic work for White families in and around King William's Town. His first known involvement with politics came when he was seventeen years old. It was 1963 and the police were crisscrossing South Africa arresting hundreds of young political activists. Biko's older brother was one of those jailed. Perhaps because of his own activities, or perhaps because his brother had been arrested, Biko was expelled from Lovedale High School. In 1963 Steve Biko became politically aware.

In 1966, following his graduation from St. Francis College at

Marian Hall, a liberal Catholic boarding school in Natal, he entered the University of Natal Medical School. His secondary-school training had left him with an appreciation of Christian principles and the ideals of an integrated, multiracial society. Yet, as Biko began to think more and more about the plight of Blacks in South Africa, he began to question the virtues of a society in which Blacks, regardless of talents and skills, suffered the indignities of patronizing Whites.

Once at the University of Natal, in an environment that fostered serious intellectual inquiry, Biko soon lost interest in medicine and began to concern himself with the daily oppression that Blacks faced. Following the death of sixty-nine Blacks at Sharpeville in 1960, the rest of the decade had seen the virtual elimination of all Black criticism of apartheid. A sullen frustration was pervasive, but almost no political activity.

At the universities, the predicament of Blacks was only slightly improved. They participated in student government organizations, but the expression of most political grievances was aired by Whites. Blacks were resentful, but seemingly powerless to focus attention on Black demands as viewed and analyzed by Blacks.

Soon after entering the university, Biko was elected to the Students' Representative Council (SRC), and through it became involved with the multiracial National Union of South African Students (NUSAS). The membership and leaders of NUSAS were largely drawn from the liberal English-speaking universities. It had long championed the cause of Blacks, and was so outspoken that Prime Minister John Vorster, in May of 1963, referred to NUSAS as a "cancer in the life of the Nation."

Until 1968, Black students saw NUSAS as their one and only meaningful vehicle to change. Disillusionment began to grow, however, as NUSAS seemed to confine itself to symbolic multiracial activities and protests after-the-fact against government infringements on academic freedom.

It was perhaps inevitable, then, that a schism would develop between Black and White students. It was Biko, however, who first grasped its necessity and articulated its reasons:

The people forming the integrated complex have been extracted from various segregrated societies with their inbred complexes of superiority and inferiority and these continue to manifest themselves even in the "non-racial" setup of the integrated complex. As a result, the integration so achieved is a one-way course, with the Whites doing all the talking and the Blacks listening.

In assessing the situation it was clear to Biko that the entire issue of Black suppression, and in turn the future of Black survival, hinged on the psychological battle for the minds of Black people.

To Biko, NUSAS and, indeed, Whites in general possessed a flawed interpretation of what constituted the problem of Black-White relations in South Africa. The accepted argument was that if apartheid, the South African government's policy of separate development, could somehow or another be dismantled, then cordial race relations would result. The method advanced as the best means of destroying apartheid was a coordinated, multiracial effort. Biko had no difficulty in accepting the premise that apartheid had to be demolished. But he did have problems with the method advanced by Whites.

In a nation where Blacks were the clear majority (twenty million to four million), apartheid existed because it possessed an overpowering psychological grasp on the minds of Black people. For centuries, Blacks were led to believe that they were an inferior people incapable of development and that Whites intrinsically possessed all that was good and all that was superior. Biko perceived the problem as a twofold psychological phenomenon. On the one side, following generations of exploitation, Whites actually believed in the inferiority of Blacks. On the other, Blacks had developed an ingrained dependence fostered by White domination. Thus, to Biko, while multiracialism made for an interesting theoretical exercise, it was an approach without operational value.

Biko felt that the existence of multiracial organizations in South Africa posed a contradiction: within them, as always, Whites tell Blacks how to respond to Whites. This, like the social and economic system of apartheid, mirrors and embodies White racism. To break the chains of oppression, and to escape a continuing sense of frustration, Biko advocated solidarity among Black people. In short, Black people needed to identify with themselves completely.

So to overcome racism, Blacks had to overcome a negative sense of self and the psychological paralysis and erosion of Black will that stemmed from a systematic manipulation of Black minds by a government and a society that had long recognized the value of thought control. As Biko pointed out, "We must realize that our situation is not a mistake on the part of Whites, but a deliberate act and that no amount of moral lectures will persuade the White man to 'correct' the situation."

The task confronting Biko was formidable—to reverse years of negative self-image and replace it with a positive and dynamic identity that would permit Blacks to move on to the next stage of their liberation. What was needed was an "attitude of mind, a way of life" that would liberate Black aspirations and Black people. For Biko, the first step was to sever relationships with White liberals. For years the liberal had been the spokesperson for Black demands, and Blacks had become dependent on that relationship. Consequently, Biko, still a student and barely twenty-one years old, encouraged Black students to divorce themselves from White student organizations. Blacks needed to commit themselves firmly to Blackness—to each other—in order to change their destiny. Moreover, Biko knew that in the long run the mass of uneducated Blacks could not trust and therefore would not identify with a movement containing Whites and White spokespersons, however good their intentions.

It was clear to Biko that given a rigid caste society based on race, Blacks and Whites had divergent interests in South Africa. Despite some overt sentiments to the contrary, Whites were, by and large and in the final analysis, satisfied. Of course, tinkering, revision and repair were necessary, but all in all, multiracial activity could achieve an integrated and harmonious society. However, as Biko saw things, integration was "based on exploitative values in a society in which the Whites have already cut out their position somewhere at the top of the pyramid. It is an integration in which Blacks will compete with Blacks, using each other as stepping stones up a steep ladder leading them to White values. It is an integration in which the Black man will have to prove himself in terms of these values before meriting acceptance and ultimate assimilation. It is an integration in which the poor will grow poorer and the rich richer in a country where the poor has always been Black."

In 1968, Biko and his confederates formed SASO, with Biko's philosophy of Black Consciousness at its core. The new organization and its ideological underpinnings struck a hugely responsive cord in young Blacks, and the movement spread rapidly. As Biko explained SASO, its importance was not that it existed, but "rather it is to be found in the fact that this new approach opened a huge crack in the traditional approach and made the Blacks sit up and think again. It heralded a new era in which Blacks are beginning to take care of their own business and to see with greater clarity the immensity of their responsibility."

It is the concept of Black Consciousness, Black awareness, that will stand as Biko's most lasting contribution to the liberation struggle in South Africa. It, like no other doctrine before it, uplifted a mass of people, inspired hope and gave direction and purpose to Black lives.

Black Consciousness was then a battle for the mind—war waged in the subconscious. In 1972 Biko emphasized this point by writing that

> The call for Black Consciousness is the most positive call to come from any group in the Black world for a long time. It is more than just a reactionary rejection of Whites by Blacks. The quintessence of it is the realization by the Blacks that, in order to feature well in this game of power politics, they have to use the concept of group power and to build a strong foundation for this. Being an historically, politically, socially and economically disinherited and dispossessed group, they have the strongest foundation from which to operate. The philosophy of Black Consciousness, therefore, expresses group pride and the determination by the Blacks to rise and attain the envisaged self. At the heart of this kind of thinking is the realization by the Blacks that the most potent weapon in the hands of the oppressor is the mind of the oppressed.

The concept of Black Consciousness held that it was necessary to first effectuate "mental emancipation as a precondition to political emancipation," that to sever the deadly relationship between White control and Black fear, Blacks had to overcome the alienation created by fear —something they could do by themselves, for themselves. For a people long shorn of dignity, Black Consciousness easily fanned the rising tide of Black nationalism.

While Biko's brilliant and perceptive analysis of conditions in South Africa led to the development of Black Consciousness, the idea succeeded because it was first introduced to an almost captive audience, Black university students. While it ultimately spread to include all levels and facets of Black life, it was initially designed to meet the indifference of White students to Black problems. Idealistic Black students became the first and strongest adherents to the concept of Black awareness as embodied in Biko's philosophy.

It is also important to note that while Black Consciousness has become a way of life to most Blacks in South Africa, it never really constituted a political movement. It was Biko's genius to understand that the South African environment dictated Black policy, and in turn Black politics. Not a soaring philosophical visionary, Biko was a pragmatist who could bring immediacy to theory. Black Consciousness was, in a sense, nonpolitical politics. It appealed to the masses of poor, semi-illiterate Blacks precisely because it was able to cast theory in terms of the day-to-day frustrations that most Blacks experienced, and therefore readily understood. Biko's philosophy was an easy marriage between political thought and psychological reality.

Unaware of the significance of the Black Consciousness Movement, the South African government failed to take seriously SASO and BPC, the latter the political wing that operated beneath the Black Consciousness umbrella. By 1973, when the government became aware of the political threat that SASO, BPC and Black Consciousness posed, the damage had already been done. By then, the idea of Black pride had ingrained itself in the minds of young Blacks and, indeed, in the minds of most Blacks.

It was with this as a backdrop, that the Sathasivan Cooper and Eight Others Trial took place, by which time Biko had been banned to the magisterial district of King William's Town. The banning order was the first in a long line of harassing methods that the South African government employed against Biko in an effort to lessen his influence.

Biko had been banned for almost a year when the transitional government in Mozambique, South Africa's neighbor to the east, came to power. The government consisted largely of members from the Front for the Liberation of Mozambique (Frelimo), and was the culmination of that organization's efforts to achieve independence, following a ten-year war against Portugal. Frelimo and Mozambiquian independence had an enormous impact on Blacks in South

Africa. Both BPC and SASO organized rallies to take place in the cities of Durban, Cape Town, Port Elizabeth and Johannesburg to coincide with the introduction of the Mozambique transitional government, "and to show our solidarity with the people of Mozambique who have been freed by Frelimo."

Days before the rallies were to begin, a White Durban businessman, Cornellius Kockemoer, telegraphed the Minister of Justice, Jimmy Kruger, demanding that he ban the rallies or be confronted with thousands of Whites in Durban who were willing to take it upon themselves to see that the rally did not take place.

The evening before the rallies, Kruger announced in Parliament that all gatherings organized by SASO or BPC would be banned immediately and that the ban would continue in effect until October 20, 1974. SASO and BPC responded by issuing a press statement that appeared in the September 25 edition of the *Daily News:* "This afternoon's rally will go ahead as scheduled . . ." Thousands of pamphlets and several bill posters announcing the rally had been posted in Durban, so that it was unlikely that SASO or BPC could have prevented the Black community from gathering even if they had wanted to do so.

On the day of the rally and despite the banning notice, nearly 5000 people gathered opposite the entrance to the Curries Fountain Stadium. The police had cordoned off the area around Curries Fountain and were preventing anyone from entering the stadium. As more and more people arrived, the crowd surged forward; there was some jostling; a *Daily News* report claimed that the District police commander for Durban West, Colonel A. Fordaan, had tried to address the shouting crowd through a megaphone. Apparently the crowd took no notice. An order was given to unleash the dogs. Panic ensued as people began to flee from the dogs and the charging police. Many were arrested; many more were injured.

The Durban experience triggered a country-wide sweep of all Black organizations. By the end of October 1976 the homes and offices of SASO and BPC members had been raided and numerous people detained. The police announced that the detainees would be held under Section 6(1) of the Terrorism Act, which permits indefinite incommunicado detention.

The Terrorism Act stands as the centerpiece in South Africa's awesome arsenal of security legislation. Since 1950 and the enactment of most of the security laws, more than 40,000 South Africans are believed to have lost their freedom or had their civil liberties curtailed under this panoply of legislation designed to protect the security of the State.

None of the laws, however, are as draconian as the Terrorism Act. In addition to the usual definition of terrorism, under the provisions of the Act, terrorism is also defined as an act which embarrasses the South African government; or which would bring about any social or economic change; or which would "cause, encourage or further feelings of hostility between the White and other inhabitants of the Republic." It is this latter language that forms the basis for most of the prosecutor's questions of Biko during the trial.

Of the many charges alleged against the defendants in the case, most of them focused on the activities of the accused relating to encouraging Black Consciousness, and the distribution and preparation of other documents and newsletters. The government's case rested principally on documentary evidence rather than oral testimony.

Indeed, the Johannesburg *Star* in commenting on the case pointed out that "the trial has become recognized as the 'Trial of Black Consciousness' rather than of the nine accused, and has a particularly novel aspect. There are no physical acts of terrorism or recruitment alleged in the 82 page indictment apart from charges of writings, allegedly composed or distributed by the nine accused. Instead the charges relate to the September 1974 'Viva Frelimo' rallies, SASO and BPC documents and speeches, and the very concept and theory of the Black Consciousness philosophy."

Aware of the gravity of the charges against the defendants and aware that by being called as a witness he would be able to reach far more people than he normally could because of his banning order, Biko volunteered to testify. His task was extremely difficult. He had to be at the same time unflinching in his defense of Black Consciousness while mindful that the slightest miscue could result in harsh penalties for the defendants.

Biko proved to be a striking witness. During his four and a half days of evidence, he gave a comprehensive and detailed analysis of Black Consciousness, its principles and objectives, while doing all that he could to aid the cause of his compatriots.

Despite Biko's outstanding testimony, the defendants were all found guilty on either one or two counts of the indictment. Efforts were made to appeal the convictions on the basis of various irregularities in the trial, but the defendants' application for leave to appeal were denied. It was unfortunate for Biko that he was not a defendant. Had he been, he would just have been another statistic languishing in a South African jail. Instead, he became a statistic of a different sort. On September 12, 1977, Biko became the forty-first person detained under South Africa's security legislation to die while in police custody.

News of Biko's death stunned the world. From all over there came an enormous outpouring of sadness, grief and anger. The United States Ambassador to the United Nations, Andrew Young, said that "the sudden and tragic death of Mr. Steve Biko will prove to be a major loss for the future of South Africa. No nation can afford to lose its most dedicated and creative leadership and yet prosper."

Chairman of the UN's Special Committee against Apartheid, at the UN, Ambassador Leslie O. Harriman, called Biko "one of the best sons and great patriots of Africa," saying, "he has joined the great martyrs of the African renaissance and revolution in this generation —men like Amilcar Cabral, Eduardo Mondlane and many others."

The government of the Kingdom of Lesotho said that "Mr. Biko is one of the gallant sons of South Africa who have fallen victim to the ever-widening selective elimination that the South African Government serves on its opponents."

Writing from Johannesburg, a *New York Times* correspondent pointed out that "a week after the event, it is clear that the death of Stephen Biko has shaken South Africa more than any single event since the police opened fire at Sharpeville in 1960, killing 72 [sic] Black demonstrators."

Biko's funeral was attended by more than 15,000 mourners, and this despite police action that kept thousands more away. Thirteen western states sent senior diplomatic representatives to the funeral to pay respects.

Following his death, many, both in the press and in governmental circles, referred to Steve Biko as a "moderate." Biko was an extremely sensitive, compassionate man filled with a sense of humanity that made him a fierce foe of apartheid, but he was not a moderate. His ethical and moral commitment to decency and dignity was total, a commitment that cost him his life. He once said that "in a real bid for change we have to take off our coats, be prepared to lose our comfort and security, our jobs, and our positions of prestige, our families; for just as it is true that 'leadership and security are basically incompatible,' it may well be true that a struggle without casualties is not worth its salt."

Historian Gail Gerhart writes that:

> The only accurate label for Biko is revolutionary—ironically the label which all his lawyers (and the lawyers for all his lieutenants convicted under the security laws) have at all times assiduously tried to deny. Now that he's dead and all the organizations he inspired are banned, I see nothing to be gained or protected by avoiding this label anymore. The sooner the outside world begins to take the South African revolution seriously the better. The fact that Biko was willing to hold discussions with Whites and to concede Whites a place in a future Black-ruled South Africa doesn't constitute grounds for calling him a moderate in relation to people of supposedly more radical views; he was just a smarter radical, one with a fine-tuned sense of what tactics would best promote his cause under the conditions prevailing in South Africa.

The truth of the matter is that Black Consciousness, Biko's legacy to his followers in South Africa, can be called nothing but revolutionary. For one, it changed not only the way that Blacks in South Africa saw themselves, it changed the political vocabulary as well. "Black," as defined by Black Consciousness, was now more a state of mind than an expression of origin. The use of the word was a deliberate attempt to lay both the intellectual and emotive base for ultimate political unity between the Africans, Coloreds and Asians of South Africa. Relying in part perhaps on Frantz Fanon's writings, Biko perceived that the "redefining of all Whites including liberals as oppressors also required the conceptual regrouping of all Non-Whites into the single category of 'Black.' "

Far more, Blacks of whatever persuasion saw the pride and fearless-
ness that imbued the followers of the Black Consciousness Movement.
This daily reminder had a pronounced effect on Blacks everywhere.
Biko's movement had succeeded, freeing Blacks from the shackles of
mental oppression. In June of 1976 Soweto exploded. The youth of
that sprawling Black township outside Johannesburg armed with but
stones and pride clashed with police and dogs. When finally the
rebellion in Soweto and other Black townships was put down, nearly
700 Blacks had died.

To many, the revolution in South Africa had begun. On the one
side the South African government stands poised with the strongest military and police force in all Africa. On the other side stand
twenty million people with no weapons, no political organizations
and all of their leaders incarcerated or dead. And yet, the struggle
will go on. For Blacks in South Africa have won the most important battle of many yet to come—the battle for control of their
own minds.

II

Courtrooms are often the place of high drama, intrigue and subtle
legal maneuverings. The trial of Sathasivan Cooper and Eight Others
was no exception.* The case juxtaposed the South African government's need to suppress internal dissent with the defendants' attempts
to encourage political and human awareness. Biko's testimony was a
focal point in the efforts of lawyers for both the state and the defense
to prove their respective cases. As important as Biko's testimony is
in understanding the concept of Black Consciousness, it also drama-

---

*In addition to Cooper, the other defendants were: Justice Edmund Lindane Myeza,
Mosioua Gerard Patrick Lekota, Maitshe Nchaupe Aubrey Mokoape, Nkwenke Vin-
cent Nkomo, Phandelani Jeremiah Nefolovhodwe, Gilbert Kaborane Sedibe, Absolom
Zitulele Cindi and Strinivasa Rajoo Moodley.

Since this book is based directly on court transcripts, we apologize for any misspell-
ings that might have occurred due to the court reporter's phonetic spelling of some
South African names.

tizes the struggle between the State's advocate, Mr. K. Attwell, and the defense counsel, Mr. David Soggot.

To comprehend the legal issues it is perhaps useful to set forth a summary of the charges against the defendants together with a brief description of the law under which the charges were brought.

A. INDICTMENT

The indictment against the nine accused contained thirteen counts. It alleged a conspiracy arising out of the activities of the accused as officers and members of SASO and BPC. The conspiracy count stated that the accused sought to bring about a revolutionary change of the political, social and economic system of South Africa by unconstitutional or violent means and to "cause, encourage or further feelings of hostility between the White and other inhabitants of the Republic."

Specifically, the indictment alleged that the accused recruited individuals to form a "Black Power Bloc hostile to the State," "acted to instill and foster in Blacks a spirit of aggression," acted "to oppose and denigrate Black homeland leaders," and acted to support and eulogize persons who had been convicted previously of various offenses. Also alleged were acts to "undermine the economic system of the South African government," acts "to isolate the Republic in the political, economic and sporting spheres from the international community," and acts to "cooperate with and maintain communication with foreign-based organizations and persons hostile to the Republic."

Other counts charged certain of the accused with organizing the "pro-Frelimo Rallies" and with holding of a "Sharpeville Commemoration Meeting" at which some of the accused recited a poem and delivered a speech. The remaining counts alleged that the accused encouraged Black Consciousness and the distribution and preparation of literature espousing Black Consciousness.

B. THE TERRORISM ACT

The charges were all brought under the infamous Terrorism Act, Section 2(2) of Act No. 83 of 1967. Before going into a description of the Terrorism Act, it is important to point out that the South African constitution contains no Bill of Rights which protects the fundamental freedoms and civil liberties of the individual. Thus, the highest appeal court in South Africa stated in the case of *Sachs v. Minister of Justice* 1934 AD II, at p. 37, that Parliament "may make any encroachment it pleases upon the life, liberty, or property of any individual subject to its sway, and it is the function of courts of law to enforce its will."

With but two highly technical exceptions, the power of Parliament is absolute. Indeed, the principle of legislative supremacy is entrenched in the South African Constitution. "No court of law shall be competent to inquire into or pronounce upon the validity of any Act passed by Parliament . . ." [Republic of South Africa Constitution Act, Sec. 59 (No. 32 of 1961)]. Moreover, Parliament has conferred broad discretionary power on the State President to introduce legislation with far-reaching consequences, which is inevitably passed. In an effort to insure the maintenance of White economic and political supremacy, the Terrorism Act was enacted.

Under the Act, a person is guilty of terrorism if he "with intent to endanger the maintenance of law and order in the Republic or elsewhere, commits any act or attempts to commit any act." As far as the kind of act that constitutes terrorism is concerned, there is no restriction whatsoever; the definition covers, literally, *any act.* The intent to endanger the maintenance of law and order is presumed if the act committed by the person is one that would have any of twelve possible results.

Paraphrased, these, as listed in subsection 2(2) of the Act, are:

—to hamper or deter any person from assisting in the maintenance of law and order;

—to promote the achievement of any object by intimidation;

—to cause or promote general dislocation, disturbance or disorder;

—to cripple or prejudice any industry or undertaking or the production or distribution of commodities or foodstuffs at any place;

—to cause, encourage or further an insurrection or forcible resistance to the government;

—to further or encourage the achievement of any political aim or of any social or economic change by force or violence or under the direction or guidance of or in cooperation with any foreign government or foreign or international body or institution;

—to endanger or cause serious bodily injury to any person;

—to cause financial loss to any person or to the State;

—to cause or encourage feelings of hostility between White and Non-White South Africans;

—to endanger, damage or destroy the supply or distribution of essential services;

—to obstruct land, sea or air traffic;

—to embarrass the administration of the affairs of the State.

As a result of the broad and indefinite language found in the Act, the burden is placed on an individual to prove beyond a reasonable doubt that he did not intend any of the twelve listed results. If he is unable to do so, he is presumed to be a "terrorist."

But it is not just this that makes the Terrorism Act so onerous. Under the Act, any police officer with the rank of lieutenant-colonel or above can order the arrest without warrant of any person he *suspects* of being a terrorist. Such a person is held for the purpose of interrogation by the police for as long a period as it takes for the person to reply "satisfactorily to all questions of the said interrogation." Detainees have been held for as long as 513 days without being charged.

While detained, an individual may not receive visits from his family or friends, clergy or counsel. There is no right of *habeas corpus* and no recourse to the courts. Indeed, no court of law may pronounce upon the validity of any action taken under the provisions of the Act, or order the release of any detainee. For one found guilty under the Act, the minimum sentence is five years imprisonment and the maximum is death.

C. BACKGROUND TO THE CASE

After the violence in Durban and following a country-wide security sweep, scores of individuals were detained, nine of whom were the defendants in this case. Initially, twelve people appeared in court on January 3, 1975. On February 11, 1975, one other person appeared in court and was remanded to March 14, 1975, to appear with the other twelve. The accused were represented by exceptionally able counsel in Messrs. Roy Allaway, Harry Pittman and David Soggot. They were in turn instructed by Mr. Shun Chetty. Mr. Cecil Rees and Mr. K. Attwell appeared for the State.

The defense managed to secure a series of continuances and postponements as they argued for clarification and more particulars regarding the indictment. In June of 1975, having sought further information with regard to the charges, and getting inadequate responses, the defense filed an application seeking to quash the charges against the thirteen on the grounds that the indictment against the accused was vague.

Two weeks after the defense's application, the State withdrew all charges against two of the accused, Sivalingham Moodley and Solly Ismail. Four days later, the indictment against the remaining eleven accused was withdrawn and a new indictment issued against nine of the defendants. Individual indictments were served against Rubin Hare and Sadecque Variaun. Finally, six and a half months after their first appearance and eleven months after the rally, the accused were asked to plead. The trial was then remanded to August 4, 1975. By the time of its conclusion on December 15, 1976, it had become the longest Terrorism Act trial in South African legal history.

As the trial ground on, the tactics of both the defense and State counsel became readily apparent. The defense had the unenviable task of convincing the court that all of the activities of the accused were within the limits of the law and did not constitute acts that could be considered "terroristic" under the broad definition given the term under the Terrorism Act. Justice Boshoff, the trial judge, pointed out that in seeking a conviction, subsection (2) of the Terrorism Act helped the prosecution prove the men had intention to endanger the law and order of South Africa. As noted above, that subsection listed a series of "likely results" which if not disproved by the defense presume the defendants to be guilty of terrorism.

Thus the defense had the burden of proving beyond a reasonable doubt that the acts that the defendants were charged with did not, or were not likely to, among other things, embarrass the administration of the affairs of state, cause further feelings of hostility between Whites and other inhabitants of the Republic or promote general dislocation, disturbance or disorder.

For the State, things were far more simple. All that it needed to show was that SASO and BPC were organizations which had as their purpose revolutionary or subversive intentions, making them implicitly, if not explicitly, "terroristic." Of course, the State's case was aided by the definition of terrorism under the Act. It should also be noted that in South Africa, jury trials have been abolished. All arguments are made before a judge who renders a decision.

The tactics of both the defense and the State were never more obvious than in their respective handling of Steve Biko, the key defense witness.

D. DEFENSE APPROACH

David Soggot, who led Biko through direct examination, started slowly. He began with the traditional approach of establishing the witness' credentials, and presenting him in a most favorable light. Soggot then set out to give a chronological progression of the development of SASO, and the reasons behind that development, and in turn the break from NUSAS.

In this stage, Soggot got Biko to give rather detailed accounts of events that precipitated the break from NUSAS and the thinking of Blacks that led to SASO. At one point, Soggot asked Biko to tell the court of various decisions taken by the executive meeting of SASO. The court intervened and instructed Soggot to give Biko the minutes of the meeting to refresh his memory. Soggot was forced to admit the minutes did not exist. Before the court could make a ruling on the admissibility of the evidence, Biko rushed in with his recollection of critical events that went to the heart of one of the counts in the charge sheet, namely the holding of a Sharpeville Commemoration Day. It was an instructive and critical move on the part of Biko that greatly aided Soggot in laying the foundation to refute that particular charge. Soggot later comes back to that point with the clear intention of demonstrating that the Sharpeville Commemoration Day was an attempt to develop social consciousness and not to inflame racial hostility.

Soggot next sought to disarm the charge that SASO and BPC sought to instill or foster in Blacks a spirit of aggression. Through his questioning, Biko pointed out that Blacks experienced a feeling of inadequacy that led to unverbalized Black frustrations. This frustration was in turn taken out on other Blacks, starting a vicious cycle of insecurity that stemmed from a feeling of incompleteness of self.

Biko then showed that in everyday language Blacks constantly spoke in rather harsh terms of their frustration and oppression. Soggot used that to establish that what SASO and BPC did was to crystallize Black thinking on the reason for their oppression and to provide some insights into what it took to change their condition. That was a far cry from instilling a spirit of aggression.

Soggot's next step was to deal with the question of foreign investment. Here, his questioning was designed to demonstrate that SASO policy was not aimed at weakening the South African economy as charged in the indictment. As a result of the questioning, Biko outlined the role of foreign investors in South Africa as being either to aid in the "building of the humanity of the Blacks" or else "they might as well get out."

Throughout his questioning, Soggot attempted to show that SASO and BPC were essentially a platform from which Blacks could articulate their grievances to the government. That consciousness-raising was nothing more than a method of building hope in Blacks. The court, however, asked the telling question: "Can it not be said that you are trying to achieve your end in such a way that you are building up a hostile power bloc, which is sort of oriented for action, and if you don't get your—if you are not satisfied when it comes to, well, bargaining, that your power bloc will then react and then you will have no control over the power bloc?" Biko gave a fair reply to the question, but it may have been one of the most critical questions the court asked. Soggot never fully responded to the question in an attempt to mitigate or to repair any damage done by the inquiry. Perhaps it was because of the adjournment which followed, or perhaps it was a belief on the part of Soggot that Biko had answered the question fully and had not been hurt by it.

Further in his questioning, Soggot sought to put some distance between SASO and BPC, which he attempted to show as programs and not political parties, and the banned African National Congress (ANC) and the Pan-Africanist Congress (PAC). Both had stated that SASO and BPC differed from ANC and PAC, in that the former entities did not seek confrontation. His rationale was superb, but he was nearly trapped on this point much later by the prosecution.

Finally, Soggot established that at no time did SASO or BPC push itself or the doctrine of Black Consciousness as one aimed at fomenting revolution. He spent a great deal of time attempting to defuse the strong language found in various SASO and BPC documents, fully aware that in large part the State's case rested on the language used by SASO and BPC.

E. PROSECUTION'S APPROACH

The prosecution, relying solely on the charges and their relationship with the Terrorism Act, focused much of their cross-examination on three main points. The first of these was that, from the very beginning, SASO was imbued with the idea of fomenting revolution. The second was that SASO's language got progressively more militant as the organization became more secure. And the third attempted to show that SASO and BPC indeed sought confrontation.

Perhaps in his haste to demonstrate that SASO, BPC and the concept of Black Consciousness were all aimed at "bringing about a revolutionary change of the political, social and economic system of the Republic," Attwell early on tipped his hand as to the line of thinking his cross-examination would take. In one of his questions to Biko, Attwell referred to past organizations which had been described in various SASO documents as those "which stood high in the defense of Black dignity and righteousness which were banned during the sixties."

"I gather that is a reference to the banned African National Congress and the Pan-Africanist Congress?" Attwell asked of Biko. Implicit in that question and subsequent ones was an attempt by Attwell to show that SASO and BPC, far from being a spontaneous outgrowth of student disenchantment, were in fact part and parcel of the ANC or PAC. The question was a rather clumsy effort to link SASO and BPC with the ANC or PAC which had been banned as "communistic." In the minds of most White South Africans, "ANC and PAC" were inflammatory code words for Black revolution. At one point Attwell offered: "I gather primarily the PAC and ANC had created a void which SASO and BPC were designed to fill." Much later, Attwell would come back to this point by asking Biko about Robert

Sobukwe, the founder and banned leader of the PAC. Here again, Attwell sought to demonstrate a connection between SASO and the PAC.

As Attwell warmed to his task, the exchanges between him and Biko became more heated, leaving the issue of SASO and BPC as revolutionary organizations. Attwell then focused his attention on the language found in SASO and BPC documents. The indictment, of course, had stated that the defendants were guilty of instilling and fostering in Blacks a "spirit of aggression and a desire for revenge against the State and the Whites," as well as encouraging or furthering the feelings of hostility "between the Whites and other inhabitants of the Republic."

Attwell's next series of questions were couched in terms of the charge sheet:

ATTWELL: Now, you know the accused are charged with causing or encouraging or furthering these feelings of hostility?

BIKO: I have heard this, yes.

ATTWELL: And do you consider there is a difference between causing something, encouraging something or furthering something?

BIKO: Oh well, I am sure there is a difference because they are words with different meanings.

ATTWELL: What do you understand the difference to be? The difference between . . . Let us start with cause and then encourage and then further—what is the difference?

BIKO: To cause racial feeling, racial hostility, I would understand it to be exactly what, for instance, the System does to us. You know, they constantly knock against your head so that you can respond. I mean, you can adopt an attitude to them.

ATTWELL: Is it to create something which does not already exist, to cause?

BIKO: That is right.

ATTWELL: To encourage?

BIKO: To encourage would be to further it.

ATTWELL: So encourage and further you see sort of synonymous?

BIKO: Right.

ATTWELL: They would be something which already exists in some form or other which you carry further?

BIKO: That is correct.

ATTWELL: Now, would this type of—call it propaganda, language, call it what you like—would it not encourage or further feelings of hostility . . .

Attwell continued to posit arguments aimed at showing that through the use of the language in various documents, SASO and BPC were far from being benevolent, community-oriented organizations, but were instead bent on an overthrow of the State.

Attwell later turned to the issue of confrontation which Biko said that SASO and BPC avoided. During an exchange between Attwell and Biko, Biko stated that SASO and BPC had helped students get food while the students were carrying on a strike. Attwell seized the opening:

ATTWELL: So in effect your action was helping to perpetuate that strike?

BIKO: That is not correct. We were helping to give food. We were asked to give food and we gave food.

ATTWELL: Without that food they would have either to go back or leave the university or something?

BIKO: Well, this is a postulation, you know, that you can make.

ATTWELL: What other postulation is there? If you don't feed them and they had to get their food . . . ?

BIKO: They would have gone out to eat, they probably wanted to continue sitting where they were sitting.

ATTWELL: And you aided the striking students?

BIKO: This is your conclusion.

ATTWELL: Was that a situation of confrontation?

BIKO: Which one?

Rather than pinning Biko down on this critical point of confrontation, Attwell allowed Biko room to maneuver. Biko gave a rambling reply as to how SASO had gotten involved, and by the time he finished, Attwell had lost the momentum of the question.

F. VERDICT

On December 15, 1976, Justice Boshoff rendered a 260-page decision that found all the defendants guilty on either Count One or Count

Two of the indictment. Count One alleged a conspiracy to commit acts to cause, encourage or further feelings of hostility between the races. Count Two alleged that the defendants arranged for the holding of the "pro-Frelimo" rallies in various cities within South Africa. The defendants were found not guilty with respect to Counts Three through Thirteen in the indictment. The exoneration of the defendants from the charges laid out in Counts Three through Thirteen of the indictment was due in significant part to the court's finding that SASO and BPC were not revolutionary organizations.

The defendants were all sentenced to either five or six years' imprisonment and are at present incarcerated on Robben Island.

—Millard Arnold

Day One

The Morning of May 3, 1976

This direct examination of Biko by Advocate Soggot traces the evolution of Black student thought from a criticism of the predominantly White National Union of South African Students (NUSAS) to the formation of the South African Students Organization (SASO), which sought to embody Black experiences and to promote Black ideals. Biko relates the development of SASO and provides a definition of Black Consciousness.

Soggot was well aware that the charges against the defendants centered on the purported attempts by leaders of SASO and the Black People's Convention (BPC) to "create and foster feelings of racial hatred, hostility and antipathy by the Blacks toward the White population group of the Republic"; the advocate therefore begins to establish his argument that "Heroes' Day" and "Sharpeville Day" were, in fact, commemorative events and not intended to incite racial hostility. Biko then creates a vivid picture of life for a Black person in South Africa. Near the end of this session, the question of foreign investment is introduced, followed by a discussion of how Blacks regard such investment in a restructured South Africa.

STEPHEN BANTU BIKO DECLARES UNDER OATH

EXAMINATION BY MR. SOGGOT: *Mr. Biko, the acoustics are not very good, and if you would address His Lordship and please speak up, then we would be able to hear. Mr. Biko, I think we should first go through the essential elements of your personal history. You were born in 1946 in King William's Town, is that correct?* —— Yes.

And you matriculated at Marian Hill which is near to Pinetown in 1965? —— That is correct.

Now, would you tell His Lordship . . . From 1966 you went to the medical school at U.N.B. as a medical student—apparently your answers are not clear, perhaps if you will stand nearer to the microphone and raise your voice, please. You were a student till what year? ——

I entered the university as a preliminary year student in 1966 and I stayed on up to 1972, June, when I was expelled from the university. I was then doing third year, I was repeating third year.

Third-year medicine? —— Yes.

And you were then expelled? —— That is correct.

Can you tell us why you were expelled? —— Well, the reasons given by the administration were those of inadequate academic performance.

And what do you say about those reasons? —— They were challengeable—that is all I am prepared to say.

Were you interested in medicine? —— By the time I was expelled I had already made up my mind in fact to leave.

And you left, I think you said, in 1972. Is that correct? —— That is correct.

And what then did you do? —— I worked for the Black Community Programmes for . . . [Mr. Soggot intervenes]

The BCP? —— The BCP, yes, as from the beginning of August 1972.

Where did you work? —— I was stationed in Durban at the time.

And how long did you last in Durban? —— Well, I lasted until I got banned, which was the beginning of March 1973.

The beginning of March in 1973? —— That is correct.

And then where did you go? —— I then went to King William's Town, where I was requested by the . . . [Mr. Soggot intervenes]

I am sorry, Mr. Biko, my apologies, when you say you were banned, I know it was a favorite phrase—you mean you were restricted in terms of the Suppression of Communism Act? —— That is correct.

And you then migrated to King William's Town? —— Well, I was directed to go to King William's Town.

And did you then take up employment in King William's Town? —— Yes, I was asked by the Black Community Programme to start a branch of the same organization in that town.

And you then started working for them? —— That is correct.

Is that from February 1973? —— Well, effectively from April 1973.

And are you still working for them? ——— Well, I worked up to the 9th December 1975.

Why did you cease working for them in December 1975? ——— I was directed by a variation to my restriction order.

Now, apart from your Community Programme's work, have you become interested in the study of law? ——— Yes, I have.

When did that start? ——— I registered for the first time in 1973.

With the university of . . . UNISA? ——— With the University of South Africa.

And are you still continuing with that? ——— I am still pursuing that.

And are you contemplating taking articles? ——— That is correct.

I think you mentioned that you are doing your B. Proc. ——— That is correct, yes.

I want to come back to the Black Community Programme and your experience there, but perhaps it might be opportune if we reverted back to the university of U.N.B., and if you were to tell His Lordship the circumstances surrounding the formation and rise of SASO. Now, when you got to the university was NUSAS the dominant student body there? ——— That is correct.

Would you tell His Lordship how the Black students fitted in to the NUSAS framework? ——— Where do I start? Do I start from the differences with NUSAS?

I think that might be appropriate. ——— Right. Well, when I got onto the campus I got interested initially in NUSAS, and I accepted fully their nonracial approach to the solution of the problems we experience in this country. I then began to debate in favor of this with people who were of other views, who were very critical of the kind of allegiance that Whites in general have to the same nonracialism that I am speaking about.

Can you just elaborate on that a little bit? Who were these other people who had that view? ——— Well, there were several students on the campus. Some of them were my friends, like Dr. Mokoape, and others were not friends of mine but they were politically motivated people on the campus.

When you say Dr. Mokoape, do you mean accused number 4 sitting there? ——— I do not know his number. Yes, he is that man.

What was their attitude? —— Well, their attitude was one of a very deep level of distrust of the attachments of Whites to the concept of nonracialism. They felt that this would always be propounded as an idea only, but that in effect Whites in general are satisfied with the status quo as it exists now, and are not going to assist completely in moving away from this situation to one of nonracialism. My view was that I do not believe this. I believe that there are equally committed Whites who want the situation changed—who would like to share with us everything that the country can produce.

Now, this may be of some importance, this first view which criticized NUSAS—perhaps when I say the word first I am wrong—this view which criticized NUSAS . . . Did it fix on any specific examples as demonstrating their thinking of the White students' role? —— Well, I cannot remember now specific examples quoted then, but it was common cause amongst students that in the history of the students' organizations, certain of the NUSAS leaders had done things that Black students looked at with contempt.

Such as? —— I cannot remember specifically. Sometimes they would mention a statement by a particular NUSAS president in a situation where he did not suspect that he was being overheard. Sometimes they would talk about segregation. For instance, during NUSAS conferences there would be private student parties in the residences, where Blacks were not allowed to come in, and there you would find officials of NUSAS, and these were the things that made Blacks begin to feel that the attachment of liberal students to this tag of nonracialism was shaky.

THE COURT: *Was that the policy of the university, or was there social equality at the university—the official policy?* —— Well, the official policy of the university was that in most instances Blacks should not come into the residences, but then the officials were free to decide where to throw their parties, and in many instances they were known to hold their parties in the White student residences where they knew Blacks could not come.

MR. SOGGOT: *And now what I want to ask you is this: Was there ever an occasion where there was a NUSAS conference and any dissatisfaction was expressed as to the accommodation of Black students?* ——
This is correct. It was the 1967 conference at Rhodes University. We

had been given to understand at that particular moment that residences would be completely integrated for the first time at a NUSAS conference, and on our way to the conference in the train we had a discussion as a delegation from the Natal University, Black section, to the effect that if this condition is not met, we should in fact register our protest, withdraw from the conference and go home. It so happened that when we got to Rhodes University in the first instance the conference organizer could not quite say where we were going to stay. We were all put out at the hall in different places, and we eventually noticed that all the White students first went, then some of the Indian students, then eventually he came back to us to say he had eventually found a church where we could stay. At that moment I felt we had ample reason to stick by our decision in the train. So that evening . . . I think we were outwitted by the executive of the organization in that just as we started to sit for the session, the executive brought in a resolution spearheaded by them condemning the Rhodes University Council for not allowing them to have Blacks in the residences. Now, I think this tended to split the attitudes of some of the Black students to the whole question, because they felt that the blame devolved not on the NUSAS executive but more on the University Council. My view was that NUSAS had known for a long time that this is a very difficult aim to achieve, and that they should have made much more in-depth preparations, and that anyway the time had come where if they could not get an integrated venue, they should simply postpone the conference. Now, we debated this with my delegation, and eventually there was no agreement. I had to move a private motion to that effect—which was supported by quite a few of the students—saying that the conference must adjourn from that time until we could get a nonracial venue. I think the motion was introduced at 12 o'clock at night and the vote was finally taken at 5:30 in the morning, and during the intervening . . . [Mr. Soggot intervenes]

Well, that effectively solved the accommodation problem for that night. [Laughter] —— During the intervening debate I think a lot of attitudes became clear, and new ideas came to my mind specifically. I think I realized that for a long time I had been holding on to this whole dogma of nonracialism almost like a religion, and feeling that it is sacrilegious to question it, and therefore not accommodating the

attacks I was getting from other students. But in the course of that
debate, I began to feel that there was a lot lacking in the proponents
of the nonracial idea—that much as they were adhering to this very
impressive ideology or idea, they were in fact subject to their own
experiences back home. They had this problem, you know, of superiority, and they tended to take us for granted and they wanted us to
accept things that were second-class. They could not see why [we]
could not consider staying in that church, and I began to feel therefore
that our understanding of our own situation in this country was not
quite coincidental with that of the Whites.

*Yes, and subsequent to this NUSAS gathering can you tell us what
further developments there were?* —— Well, firstly, one must mention that I began to share some more of the Rhodes experience with
a number of Black students, first on my campus and then elsewhere,
and I think at that time there began to emerge some kind of creative
thought, to say, Well, we cannot blame your White students for
what they do—they have got their experiences in their homes. We
have to look positively at what we have to do as Black students, and
we began to feel at that time that perhaps there was a need for some
kind of consultation amongst Black students which focused on their
problems as Black students on the campuses, and which allowed
NUSAS to continue as it did, but operated specifically for Black
students.

*And this group of people who were opposed to NUSAS, did it become
greater or fewer as time went on?* —— I think it became greater. I
think more and more Black students began to [move away] from the
hard-line support for NUSAS to accommodate, you know, the new
thoughts that were beginning to crystallize.

*And can you tell us, there was a UCM—that is, a University Chris-
tian Movement conference in 1968?* —— That is correct.

Was any expression given to new thinking then? —— That is correct, yes.

Can you tell us about it? —— We had decided—when I say "we"
now, I am referring to the students who were beginning to think more
in terms of Black dialogue amongst the relevant Black universities—
were beginning to think that we should sound this idea a bit more, and
a number of us went to several conferences. We went to the NUSAS

conference in 1968, which was here at Wits, but found very few Black
students were participating at that conference. We then went to UCM
which was at Stutterheim, also in July following the NUSAS conference, and at that conference there were a number of Black students
from all over, you know, the country, from universities and colleges,
and in fact they were in the majority at that conference. We felt that
the platform had somewhat widened, and that we could talk more
authentically to a group which was reasonably representative in the
sense of a random sampling of students from several universities. So
we shared this idea with the students. We did allow for situations
where students met alone—Black students met alone to discuss this
particular idea—and I think a decision . . . I do not think it is certain,
but a decision was taken at that particular conference, to press upon
our various SRC's to meet at a conference in order to look specifically
at this question.

   *I think there might be some uncertainty here. This decision was
taken by whom?* ——— As I said, we created a situation for Black
students to meet alone.

   How did you do that, or how did that come about? ——— Well, we
were faced with a legal problem at Stutterheim. It is an urban area,
and there exists what they call the 72-hour clause in the Group Areas
Act—I am not sure what it is, but a provision which allows a Black
man, an African, to be in an urban area, to be in town only for 72
hours without permit; thereafter he requires a permit to remain there.
So this problem confronted the conference and it was thrown at the
students by the leadership of UCM. There was a huge debate, a very
intense debate on this point, with some students saying that we should
as a means of protest not observe this rule, and others saying we
should in fact observe it by just walking symbolically across the
border of that particular town and coming back for a fresh period of
72 hours. Now, I was amongst those students who felt that this would
be a bit hypocritical. I thought that we should take the stance that this
portion of our law is objectionable and that if we come to be arrested,
we Black students will allow ourselves to be arrested, but the White
students who were there who were not arrested must protest against
our arrest. Now, of course there was a debate about this strategy, and
eventually we froze the situation where Blacks had to decide upon it

on their own because they were the ones who were affected. And the conference eventually accepted this, and the Blacks met on their own to look at this. And when we met on our own it was noted that in fact the 72-hour clause was being used as a tactic to get this meeting [stopped]. We have got no problems, we can walk across the border and come back for a further period, but the real thing that we should begin to talk about are problems affecting us as Black students, which we feel are not given full treatment in organizations of that nature. This point of view was canvassed by a number of students, and eventually a formal decision was taken by that group to work towards a conference which would be in December. Now, the group which was there was not representative of the various SRC's, so that it was still necessary for the students from each individual campus to canvass their SRC to accept the idea first, but all the same some kind of ad hoc coordinating committee was set up, in fact really we just appointed a convener from a particular campus to write to the various SRC's and to convey the ideas taken and formed at that particular meeting.

Would you say that that ad hoc committee was the first organizational germ of SASO? —— Yes. . . .

COURT ADJOURNS

COURT RESUMES

STEPHEN BANTU BIKO, STILL UNDER OATH

EXAMINATION BY MR. SOGGOT, CONTINUED: *Mr. Biko, I think we have got to the stage of dealing with the first conference at Marian Hill. Would you tell His Lordship in brief the essentials of what was decided there?* —— I think basically the conference went over the same points that were discussed at the UCM Black Caucus, which were essentially to look at whether the interests of Black students were being fully served within the given multiracial student organizations, and the finding was that of course these organizations were inadequate to fully satisfy the interests of the Black students—both interests in the educational sphere and the life of the Black student on the Black campus, and also in a sense in the political expression that comes from student organizations. We felt that what came out of organizations like NUSAS and like UCM was not in fact an authentic expression of Black thinking on political issues.

Was anything else decided? —— We then looked at a draft working paper which had been worked by the U.N.B. campus for the purpose of the conference. It was in the form of a constitution outlining a possible structure for a Black student organization, and the conference made what we regarded then as a final draft to be looked at by a properly constituted conference of the new organization, to which we gave the name South African Students Organisation.

Was the name born at that conference at the end of 1968? —— It was born at that conference, yes.

And when was the first conference of that organization as such, can you recall? —— It was called in early July 1970—sorry, 1969—at the University of the North, commonly called Turfloop.

And was a steering committee appointed? —— Yes, there was a steering committee. . . .

—— *Were you on that steering committee?* —— I was not on that committee.

Who was the leader of the steering committee? —— It was a man called Pat Matshaka.

Where is he today, do you know? —— I think he is a magistrate or a prosecutor somewhere. I am not quite sure.

Now, the question of Black Consciousness—did that figure at all at your 1968 conference? —— I think not in the final form as defined, but I think there were traces of it which were beginning to creep into the thinking of the student leaders.

And then would you now deal with the conference at Turfloop in July 1969? —— Yes. I think this was mainly a structural conference. We looked at the final draft which had come from the previous meeting, the December meeting, and adopted it as the Constitution of SASO. We then considered very basic policy questions, the one pressing one being what would be our relationship to existing student organizations. Now, there was lots of debate about this; some people were for a complete break, others were for some kind of retention of links. As a result we decided that we would not in fact not affiliate with NUSAS but we would recognize NUSAS as the national student organization. I must explain that the dichotomy here arose out of the differences in attitudes of the various students because of their university situa-

tions. Some of the Black campuses were actually debarred from participation in NUSAS by their various authorities. This tended to make
NUSAS some kind of romantic attraction to them, and they felt that
it would be a complete letdown to actually also join the bandwagon
with their administration in criticizing NUSAS, so they preferred to
leave it loose like that.

Now, were elections held? —— Yes, elections were held, and a new
executive was put up.

Were you elected to any position? —— Yes, I was elected as the
first president of the organization.

Who else was on the executive at that stage? —— Well, I had Pat
Matshaka as vice president, I had a Miss Manana Kgware—I beg
your pardon, I am not quite sure about her—I had Wuila Mashalaba
as Natal regional secretary, I had a man called Denamile as treasurer
—those I remember, I cannot remember the others.

Were any of the accused involved at that stage? —— No, none of
them were involved then.

*If I may interpolate, of the nine accused before court, which of them
did you know before their arrest?* —— Before their arrest I knew Mr.
Cooper, I knew Mr. Myeza, I knew Mr. Lekota, I knew Dr. Mokoape
and I knew Mr. Moodley.

All right. Then you became the first president? —— That is correct.

*Now, at that stage were any policy decisions taken? Had any policy
decision been taken other than the approach to NUSAS? How was
SASO viewed at that stage? Was it merely viewed as a trade union or
what?* —— Yes, it was mainly a trade union of Black students, and
the first conference as I said was structural, and the first task was for
us to build up a membership. It must be remembered that at that time
we did not have a single affiliate campus, we could not really take any
serious policy because this needs to involve students from the various
campuses. We were merely forming an organization there with the
consent of the various SRC's, and each SRC that was represented was
instructed to go back to their campuses and to get students well
acquainted with the reasoning behind SASO. And the task of the
executive therefore was to assist the SRC's in their campaign on their
various campuses.

Yes, and when did affiliation eventually take place? ——— It was either late 1969 and/or beginning of 1970, but between that conference and the next one several campuses began to affiliate. I think Turfloop was the first, then there were some of the seminaries. There was also my campus, U.N.B., and very late there was Ngoya and eventually Fort Hare.

Did you yourself qua president go around addressing the campuses? ——— Yes, I did.

And what sort of response did you find from Black students to the idea of SASO as conceived at that stage? ——— I got the impression from the response to the various meetings that I addressed that what had been expressed was in fact some kind of latent feeling on the part of the majority of Black students. There certainly never was a hostile reaction. On the contrary there was encouragement wherever I went.

Now, did U.N.B. itself affiliate eventually to SASO? ——— Yes, they did.

Now, I wonder whether at this stage it might not be appropriate for you to tell His Lordship, was there amongst the Black students themselves opposition . . . against the formation of SASO? ——— Yes, I would say perhaps the best experience has come from my own campus, which was U.N.B., where I had a day-to-day interest in the students. I think there was some kind of ambiguity in the attitude of some of the students in the first instance. Even though at that stage we had not completely canceled our recognition of NUSAS, students could see a foreshadowing of this. There were those students on the campus who were essentially pro-NUSAS, who felt that what was happening now was in fact against the whole spirit of nonracialism that NUSAS advocated. On the other hand there were again other students who felt that the position SASO was taking was very much in the middle and was not going the whole hog, the whole hog implying especially on the political questions. Some students felt that involvement of Africans with Indians and Coloreds is going to lead essentially to the same amorphousness that the nonracial organizations found themselves in.

They wanted a purely African organization? ——— Yes, some students wanted a purely African organization.

Now, just to get this point straight now, when did you break off with

NUSAS? ——— I think the formal decision was taken in 1970, but I think even in between the two conferences there was a drastic shift of attitudes. On the one hand NUSAS felt very threatened by the emergence of SASO, and thought that they should try and block its growth on the various campuses, and they did this in all sorts of ways, including smear tactics against the leadership of the organization. And also of course we became more critical—even before the final decision to cancel our allegiance was taken—we became more critical of NUSAS. It became quite clear that we were competing for attention on campuses, and therefore in order to survive we had to say what in fact was latently at the back of our minds about NUSAS, to make the students see exactly why they should fall in with us.

And was this accepted? ——— This was accepted, and then in 1970 a decision was taken to withdraw our recognition of NUSAS. . . .

At that first GSC was the question of the term Non-White raised at all, do you know? ——— I am trying to think about it. I know it was raised at one GSC or the other but I am not sure which one. I think it was that one.

Well, what was raised and what was said? ——— I think students in fact took a decision to the effect that they would no longer use the term Non-Whites, nor allow it to be used as a description of them, because they saw it as a negation of their being. They were being stated as "non something," which implied that the standard was something and they were not that particular standard. They felt that a positive view to life, which is commensurate with the build-up of one's dignity and confidence, should be contained in a description which you accept, and they sought to replace the term Non-White with the term Black.

Now, Mr. Biko, in 1970 in Port Elizabeth you people had an executive meeting of SASO? ——— Correct.

Would you tell His Lordship what significant decisions if any were taken there? ——— There were a number of decisions taken . . . [Pause]

THE COURT: *Show him so that he can refresh his memory.*

MR. SOGGOT: *M'lord, they do not exist, at least not in our possession. We had in fact made specific enquiries and have not been able to lay our hands on the Port Elizabeth Minutes.* ——— Yes, there were a number of decisions. I remember two specifically: We looked at our program for the year, as SASO—that is, the forthcoming year which would be 1971—and we recognized in the program certain days that we thought we should incorporate as days to be remembered by the various campuses for their significance. In the first instance there was what we called the Suffer Day, I think it was on May 10th, and secondly there had been already on various campuses a celebration or commemoration of the Sharpeville event.* At that meeting we decided to incorporate this as a formal day within the SASO calendar.

Now, that sort of commemoration—had it taken place previously prior to the birth of SASO, or only after the birth of SASO? —— Yes, I think it had antedated, you know, the SASO decisions, but sporadically—only on certain campuses on their own.

Any other decisions? —— We then decided also to organize what we called Compassion Day, which was sometime in August. I am not sure what the date was—it could be the 19th or the 24th, I am not sure.

August 17th perhaps? —— Yes. And of course there was our annual conference, which we fixed to be held in the first week in July, which is normally a common holiday to all students, and of course besides this there was the usual fresher reception period at the beginning of the year, which we took for granted . . .

Now, I know that this is not a BPC context, but was any other decision taken in relation to Black organizations? —— Yes, this is the second thing I was coming to . . . We felt at that stage that we were perhaps exponents of a particular philosophy that was important not only for students but for the entire Black community, and we felt that we needed to share this with existing Black organizations within the country.

Would you pause there. What philosophy was this? —— I think we had already begun to realize and accept that our attitude, which constitutes Black Consciousness, was a unique approach in the country, and that this is what we wanted to share with other organizations.

*On March 21, 1960, in the town of Sharpeville, police armed with machine guns and rifles fired into an unarmed crowd of Africans protesting the requirement that all Africans carry "reference books." Sixty-nine people died and nearly 200 were wounded, including many women and children.

You wanted to share with other organizations? ——— That is correct.

Yes, well, do carry on. ——— The focal point was that of coordination of efforts. We felt that there are a number of organizations which are in fact doing important work amongst Blacks in the country, and that they could achieve better results if they shared their efforts and delineated fields of activity so that they do not overlap in their activities. We mentioned a few organizations like IDAMASA.

What is that? ——— IDAMASA is the Interdenominational African Ministers Association of South Africa, and then you get AICA, which is the African Independent Churches Association, then we had AFECA, which is the Association for the Educational and Cultural Advancement of the People of South Africa. Then we also noted teacher organizations, both regional and national. These are the ones I can remember.

And what decision was taken in relation to this? ——— We decided that we would set up a series of meetings, bilateral meetings, with these organizations individually. We would send a delegation in the course of the ensuing year to share our view of, you know . . . coordinated efforts to uplift the situation and position of the Black man in the country. . . .

May I bring you back to the question of the holding of Heroes' Day and the Sharpeville Day. What was the logic or thinking behind that? I wonder if you would deal with that with a little bit of precision? ——— Well, if I can remember well from the debate there were two main reasons behind the holding of these events. Firstly, in our view we have people who were killed not for their own selfish ends, but in pursuit of what they believed was the struggle of the Black man within this country, so to speak. In other words this was a selfless death. We felt that it is only proper for us as Black students to remember these occasions in honor of these people who died, so to speak, for our cause. The second reason was that in our view we were in a particularly weak position as Black people in the country. We were faced with an all-powerful institutionalized machinery; that is, looking at the government structure, we felt that there was not adequate reason why periodically in our history Black people were being killed in this sort of way, and that perhaps if we show our abhorrence of this through constant services to remember occasions like this, White society might perhaps feel persuaded to be very strict with their police force especially, because this was the force that was most to blame in most of the instances. These are the two reasons, the first one being factual and the other one being psychological.

Yes, I have got that. May I ask you this: Before the establishment of SASO or even the germ of SASO, had you gone to Sharpeville commemoration services? —— I had gone once at Natal University.

Would that have been simply as a student or in any official capacity? —— No, no, it was as a student.

What was your understanding then as a student of what this was about and why it was called? —— Well, the theme which came out was mainly the first one: that of commemorating the lives of people who had died not in pursuit of their own selfish means but in pursuit of the struggle. This is the theme which came out. I do not know what the logic here was behind calling it.

And as a result of what was said there did you find that your feelings . . . that any racial hostility against the White race was encouraged or inflamed? —— I would say no. I would say on the contrary these services tend to give a certain amount of serenity, you know, they give a certain amount of content and identification with those people.

And looking into the future . . . Did you attend subsequently SASO commemoration Heroes' Day? —— Yes, I did.

And at those services or commemoration services, was racial hostility encouraged or inflamed? —— Definitely no.

What would you say was the prevailing theme, if there was a prevailing theme in these services? —— I think a sense of achievement, a sense of security in being united over a particular aspect of our history. Certainly the way SASO conducted the various services in our campus it was mainly a sermon, and we called various distinguished ministers to conduct a service. And I have no doubt that the majority of people there were moved by the way the whole thing was handled. In a way they tended to relate it to a Biblical sacrifice, you know, to say that these people died for us, to recognize the fact that we have got to dedicate ourselves to our struggle, so to speak.

Yes. Mr. Biko, Compassion Day—would you briefly tell us what that was about? —— Compassion Day was meant to remember specific situations of affliction that the Black man was subjected to from time

to time—things like starvation in places like Dimbasa, things like
. . . disasters like the floods in Port Elizabeth.

Where is Dimbasa? —— Dimbasa is a resettlement area outside
King William's Town where I stay.

Have you had direct experience with that? —— Yes, I have.

*And when you say starvation there, can you tell us what you mean
by that?* —— Well, one gets there a peculiar situation of families
who have been moved in most instances from the Northern Cape,
North Western Cape and Western Cape, who are settled in Dimbasa.
And in most instances the man is not in a state to work; the woman
of the family does not immediately get work when she arrives there.
They are given by the government rations, and of course they are
given a house. Their rations in most instances last for sometimes two
weeks, three weeks, but they are supposedly monthly rations. The
church has had to move in. I went there once with the minister of the
Anglican Church, visited about three, four houses. I could not take
it anymore. In all the houses there was no furniture except perhaps
a chair or a "bank" or some old bedstead, some a stove, and some
pots, and there was clear evidence of utmost suffering on the part of
kids there. That is what I mean by starvation. . . .

*What was the purpose of holding Compassion Day, apart from the
mere fact of recalling these disasters?* —— In a sense the main theme
in Compassion Day was to get students to develop a social conscience,
to see themselves as part of the community, and to direct their ener-
gies at solving problems of the nature we were thinking about on
Compassion Day. . . .

Now, I think that that brings us to the 1971 second GSC? —— Yes.

*Now, I do not propose to take you through the whole of that in any
way; I merely want to refer you to certain aspects of the resolutions
passed at that GSC—M'lord, I refer to SASO A.1. Would you please
have a look at SASO Resolution 42 of 1971, on page 249?* —— Yes,
I have got it.

*If you look at paragraph 1: "SASO is a Black Student organization"
—have you got that?* —— Yes.

Would you just read that, please, paragraph 1?
—— "SASO is a Black Student Organization working for the
liberation of the Black man, first from psychological oppression
by themselves through inferiority complex and secondly from the

physical one accruing out of living in a White racist society."

Now, the concept of Black Consciousness—does that link up in any way with what you have just read? —— Yes, it does.

Would you explain briefly to His Lordship that link-up? —— I think basically Black Consciousness refers itself to the Black man and to his situation, and I think the Black man is subjected to two forces in this country. He is first of all oppressed by an external world through institutionalized machinery, through laws that restrict him from doing certain things, through heavy work conditions, through poor pay, through very difficult living conditions, through poor education—these are all external to him—and secondly, and this we regard as the most important, the Black man in himself has developed a certain state of alienation. He rejects himself, precisely because he attaches the meaning White to all that is good; in other words he associates good—and he equates good—with White. This arises out of his living and it arises out of his development from childhood. When you go to school, for instance, your school is not the same as the White school, and ipso facto the conclusion you reach is that the education you get there cannot be the same as what the White kids get at school. The Black kids normally have got shabby uniforms if any or no uniform at school; the White kids always have uniforms. You find for instance even the organization of sport—these are things you notice as a kid—at White schools to be absolutely so thorough and indicative of good training, good upbringing, you could get in a school 15 rugby teams, we could get from our school three rugby teams. Each of those 15 White teams has got uniforms for each particular kid who plays; we have got to share the uniforms amongst our three teams. Now, this is part of the roots of self-negation which our kids get even as they grow up. The homes are different, the streets are different, the lighting is different, so you tend to begin to feel that there is something incomplete in your humanity, and that completeness goes with whiteness. This is carried through to adulthood when the Black man has got to live and work.

How do you see it carried through to adulthood? Can you give us examples there? —— From adulthood?

Yes? —— I would remember specifically one example that touched me, talking to an Indian worker in Durban who was driving a van for a dry-cleaning firm. He was describing to me his average day, how he lives, and the way he put it to me was that: I no more work in order to live, I live in order to work. And when he went on to elaborate I could see the truth of the statement. He describes how he has to wake up at four o'clock, half-past four in order to walk a long distance to be in time for a bus to town. He works there for a whole day, so many calls are thrown his way by his boss, at the end of the day he has to travel the same route, arrive at home half past eight, nine o'clock, too tired to do anything but sleep in order to be in time for work again the next day.

To what extent would you say that this example is typical or atypical of a Black worker living in an urban area? —— With I think some variance in terms of the times and so on and the work situation, this is a pretty typical example, precisely because townships are placed a long distance away from the working areas where Black people work, and the transport conditions are appalling. Trains are overcrowded all the time, taxis that they use are overcrowded—the whole traveling situation is dangerous. And by the time a guy gets to work he has really been through a mill. He gets to work, there is no peace either at work. His boss sits on him to eke out of him even the last effort in order to boost up production. This is the common experience of the Black man. When he gets back from work through the same process of traveling conditions, he can only take out his anger on his family, which is the last defense that he has.

Are there any other factors which you would name in order to suggest that . . . to explain why there is this sense of inferiority, as perceived by you people? —— I would speak . . . I think I have spoken a bit on education, but I think I must elaborate a little bit on that. As a Black student, again, you are exposed to competition with White students in fields in which you are completely inadequate. We come from a background which is essentially peasant and worker. We do not have any form of daily contact with a highly technological society; we are foreigners in that field. When you have got to write an essay as a Black child, the topics that are given there tally very well with White experience, but you as a Black student writing the same essay have got to grapple with something which is foreign to you—not only foreign but superior in a sense. Because of the ability of the White culture to solve so many problems in the sphere of medicine, various spheres, you tend to look at it as a more superior culture than yours. You tend to despise the peasant culture, and of course you despise the worker culture. And this inculcates in the Black man a sense of self-hatred which I think is an important determining factor in his dealings with himself and his like.

And of course to accommodate the existing problems, the Black man develops a two-faced attitude. I can quote a typical example. I had a man working in one of our projects in the Eastern Cape on electricity—he was installing electricity, a White man with a Black assistant. He had to be above the ceiling, and the Black man was under the ceiling and they were working together pushing up wires and sending the rods in which the wires are and so on, and all the time there was insult, insult, insult from the White man: Push this, you fool —that sort of talk, and of course this touched me. I know the White man very well, he speaks very well to me, so at teatime we invite them to tea, I ask him: Why do you speak like this to this man? And he says to me in front of the guy: This is the only language he under-stands, he is a lazy bugger. And the Black man smiled. I asked him if it was true and he says: No, I am used to him. Then I was sick. I thought for a moment I do not understand Black society.

After some two hours I come back to this guy, I said to him: Do you really mean it? The man changed, he became very bitter, he was telling me how he wants to leave any moment, but what can he do? He does not have any skills. He has got no assurance of another job —his job is to him some form of security. He has got no reserves; if he does not work today he cannot live tomorrow. He has got to work, he has got to take it. And if he has got to take it he dare not show any form of what is called cheek to his boss. Now, this I think epitomizes the two-faced attitude of the Black man to this whole question of existence in this country. . . .

When you have phrases such as "Black is Beautiful," now, would that sort of phrase fit in with the Black Consciousness approach? —— Yes, it does.

What is the idea of such a slogan? —— I think that slogan has been meant to serve and I think is serving a very important aspect of our attempt to get at humanity. You are challenging the very deep roots of the Black man's belief about himself. When you say, "Black is Beautiful" what in fact you are saying to him is: Man, you are okay as you are; begin to look upon yourself as a human being. Now, in African life especially it also has certain connotations, it is the connotation of the way women prepare themselves for viewing by society. In other words the way they dress, the way they make up and so on, which tends to be a negation of their true state and in a sense a running away from their color. They use lightening creams, they use straightening devices for their hair and so on. They sort of believed, I think, that their natural state, which is a Black state, is not synonymous with beauty. And beauty can only be approximated by them if the skin is made as light as possible and the lips are made as red as possible, and their nails are made as pink as possible and so on. So in a sense the term "Black is Beautiful" challenges exactly that belief which makes someone negate himself.

THE COURT: *Mr. Biko, why do you people then pick on the word black? I mean, black is really an innocent reference which has been arrived at over the years the same as white. Snow is regarded as white, and snow is regarded as the purest form of water and so it symbolizes purity, so white there has got nothing to do with the White man?* —— Right.

But now why do you refer to you people as Blacks? Why not brown people? I mean, you people are more brown than black. —— In the same way as I think White people are more pink and yellow and pale than white.

Quite. [Laughter] But now, why do you not use the word brown, then? —— No, I think really, historically, we have been defined as Black people, and when we reject the term Non-White and take upon ourselves the right to call ourselves what we think we are, we have got available in front of us a whole number of alternatives—starting from natives to Africans to Kaffirs to Bantu to Non-Whites and so on —and we choose this one precisely because we feel it is most accommodating. . . .

MR. SOGGOT: *Is your concern so much the restructure of the word "black" in the world of linguistics . . . as to alter the response of Black people to their own Blackness?* —— It is certainly directed at man, at the Black man.

And I think you were talking about your understanding of the Black man's own sense of inferiority and self-hatred and all that? —— Yes.

In the world of language, how does the Black man figure, how does he feel? ——— Yes, I think this is another area where experiences of ... Well, let me say difficulties that I have experienced. ... We have a society here in South Africa which recognizes in the main two languages, English and Afrikaans as official languages. These are languages that you have to use at school—at university, I mean—or in pursuit of any discipline when you are studying as a Black man. Unfortunately the books you read are in English. English is a second language to you. You have probably been taught in a vernacular, especially during these days of Bantu education up to Standard 6. You grapple with the language to J.C. and matric, and before you conquer it you must apply it now to learn disciplines at university. As a result you never quite catch everything that is in a book, you certainly understand the paragraph ... I mean, I am talking about the average man now, I am not talking about exceptional cases ... You understand the paragraph but you are not quite adept at reproducing an argument that was in a particular book, precisely because of your failure to understand certain words in the book. This makes you less articulate as a Black man generally, and this makes you more inward looking. You feel things rather than say them. And this applies to Afrikaans as well—much more to English than to Afrikaans. Afrikaans is essentially a language that has developed here, and I think in many instances it is idiom, it relates much better to African languages, but English is completely foreign, and therefore people find it difficult to move beyond a certain point in their comprehension of the language.

And how does this relate to the Black man or in particular to the Black students as inferiority? ——— An example of this for instance was again during the old days of NUSAS where [White] students would be something that you as a Black man experienced in your day-to-day life, but your powers of articulation are not as good as theirs. Also you have amongst the White students a number of students doing M.A., doing Honours—you know, in particular quarters —highly articulate, very intelligent. You may be intelligent but not as articulate. You are forced into a subservient role of having to say yes to what they are saying, talking about what you have experienced, which they have not experienced, because you cannot express it so well. This in a sense inculcates also in numerous students a sense of inadequacy. You tend to think that it is not just a matter of language. You tend to tie it up also with intelligence in a sense. You tend to feel that that guy is better equipped than you mentally.

THE COURT: *But why do you say that? Isn't English the official language of SASO?* ——— Yes, it is.

Well, now. Your complaint is against the language, but it is just the very language that you are using? ——— No, no, I am not complaining against the language. I am merely explaining how language can help in the development of an inferiority complex. I am not complaining against the language. The point in issue is that we have something like ten languages. We cannot speak all ten languages at one meeting; we have got to choose a common language. But unfortunately in the learning process this is really what happens. You do not grasp enough and therefore you cannot be articulate enough, and when you play side by side with people who are more articulate than you, you tend to think that it is because they are more intelligent than you, that they can say these things better than you.

But your language is very idiomatic. Well, is it not easier for you people to speak Afrikaans because Afrikaans is like your language— it is very idiomatic? ——— This is true, actually, unfortunately again Afrikaans has got certain connotations historically that do provoke a rejection from the Black man, and these are political connotations. I am not arguing for or against, but they are there.

MR. SOGGOT: *But your point as I understand it is that the Black man feels a little bit of a foreigner in the linguistic field?* ——— Right. . . .

Mr. Biko, still talking about the question of inferiority, you . . . If I may introduce this point in a certain way—an article "I Write What I Like by Frank Talk," Annexure 8 to the Indictment: "Fear—An Important Determinant in South African Politics"* . . . Who wrote that? ——— I wrote that.

THE COURT: *You say you wrote it?* ——— I wrote it.

Is it Annexure 8? Is this by Frank Talk? ——— That is right.

Isn't number 9 Frank Talk? ——— No, no, he was never Frank Talk, I was Frank Talk. [Laughter]

---

*The full text of this article is set forth in the Appendix.

MR. SOGGOT: *M'lord, the indictment alleged that he compiled and/or wrote it, but in fact it was never ever suggested that number 9 wrote this. Annexure 9, "Focus—Ugandan Asians and the Lesson for Us"?* —— Yes.

Who wrote that? —— I wrote that.

THE COURT: *Just let me get that again. Which is that?*

MR. SOGGOT: *M'lord, Annexure 9. On page 11 of "I Write What I Like," you say:*

> *"Township life alone makes it a miracle for anyone to live up to adulthood."*

What do you mean by that? —— This refers to the degree of violence that one gets in townships, which tends to introduce a certain measure of uncertainty about what tomorrow will bring. If I am in a different type of life and I spend a night at your place, somehow I feel unexposed to what I would call the elements—you know, I am not exposed to bad elements of society. When you are in a township it is dangerous to cross often from one street to the next, and yet as you grow up it is essential that kids must be sent on errands in and around the township. They meet up with these problems; rape and murder are very, very common aspects of our life in the townships.

And at nighttime what is the position? —— It is especially at nighttime. I mean, in the few days I have spent in Mabopane, near Pretoria, I have seen two cases of grievous assault—one landed on our door— and there is no relationship between the persons assaulted and the person assaulting. You see an old man being assaulted by a number of young men for apparently no reason whatsoever except that of course possibly it is the end of the month and possibly he might have some money around him. This does not surprise me. It is a common experience, but I have never learned to accept it all the same, because it is a bitter reminder of the kind of violence that is there in our society. Now, when I use that term there that it is a miracle to live to an adult age or whatever I said, the precise meaning of it is exactly that—that one escapes all these possible areas of pitfalls where one might die without any explanation. It is not because you are well kept, it is not because you are well protected, it is just a miracle, it happens. . . .

Whatever the causes, what you are saying is there is an insecurity in one's physical life in the townships. Does this have an effect on the Black man in relation to his sense of confidence or inferiority or whatever it is? —— You mean, the insecurity in the townships?

The physical insecurity. —— Yes, I think it has. I think it contributes to a feeling of . . . Well, it helps to build up the sense of insecurity which is part of a feeling of incompleteness. You are not a complete human being. You cannot walk out when you like, you know, that sort of feeling. It is an imprisoning concept itself.

Now, Mr. Biko, I am coming back to the theme of this questioning, namely conscientization, but I just want to divert slightly. Were you ever involved in actually monitoring people, ordinary people's conversations? —— Yes . . . [Mr. Soggot intervenes]

Whether it was in the street, or . . . —— You mean some form of research?

That is correct? —— Yes.

Would you tell His Lordship briefly what that was? —— M'lord, this was a research carried out, I think it was 1971. The purpose was literacy—I beg your pardon, it was 1972 . . . Now, the particular method we were using places a lot of emphasis on syllabic teaching of people. You do not just teach people the alphabet in isolation, you have to teach them syllables, and you have to start with words that have got a particular meaning to them—what we called generative terms. Now, the preamble to it was some kind of research in a specific area where you are going to work, which carried you to several segments of the community, to particular places where the community congregates and talks freely. Your role there was particularly passive. You are there just to listen to the things that they are talking about, and also to the words that are being used, the themes being important there. We also used pictures to depict the themes that they were talking about. Now, I was involved in this with a man called Jerry Modisane and Barney Pityana . . . [Mr. Soggot intervenes]

Was this in Durban? —— In Durban.

Who were you doing this research for? —— We were doing it for ourselves. I had been asked to participate in a literary program that was drawn up by SASO.

Well whatever this was, you listened to people? ——— That is right.
In what circumstances? ——— Well, we chose available circumstances. Now, in this particular instance we listened to women in
queues waiting to see a doctor or nurse at a clinic. Some of them had
babies on their arms or on their backs. We listened to people congre-
gated in sports fields watching sport. We listened to people in shebeens
—I did go around buying beer in a lot of shebeens—and we listened
to people in buses as well, and trains.
*What was it that people were saying if anything at all about their
condition of life? And the White man, if the White man or the White
government came up at all?* ——— The first thing to notice when
observing such situations is the constant recurrence of what I would
call protest talk about the situation of oppression that the Black man
is exposed to. Sometimes it is general, sometimes it is specific, but
always contained what I would call a round condemnation of White
society. Often in very, very tough language, some of which is not
admissible in court. I remember for instance a specific bus in which
I was traveling, and in most instances the topic was dictated by the
position of the bus on the way to town. As you are coming out of
Malazi you pass through a particular area, which is a hostel . . . for
adult male Blacks. Now, there are certain restrictions in hostels, like
they may not bring in women and so on. But each time we pass there
in the morning of course there is a stream of women coming out of
the hostel and people start talking about this, you know . . . [Mr. Biko
quotes in an African dialect] implying that these bachelors have got
lots of women, and from there onwards the theme builds up almost
automatically—why are they disallowed? Where does the White man
think these guys are going to get their sex from? That sort of thing,
and from there it blows up. And then again the bus goes through to
the industrial area called Jacobs. You pass through the southern part
of Jacobs, and there there is a constant stream of people getting in and
out of factories, and the talk centers around problems of labor and so
on. I cannot quite remember specifically what was said, but they start
from there again, and always central to this theme is the condemnation of White society in general. You know, when people speak in the
townships they do not talk about the government, they do not talk
about the Provincial Council or City Councils, they talk about

Whites, and of course the connotation there is with reference to obvious structures, but to them it is just Whites. And, as I say, the language is often hard, you know, sometimes to the point of not being admissible in court because it is swear words really.

And you yourself have lived for example in Ginsberg Location in King William's Town, is that right? —— Yes, I have.

And is that a rather poor rural location? —— Yes, it is a small township of about a thousand houses—very poor.

So you are familiar with life there? —— That is correct.

Now, the echoing of this sort of sentiment, did that take place there while you lived there? —— Oh yes, very common.

And you people talk of psychological and physical oppression—is there reference to oppression at all in any shape or form by people in their ordinary thinking? —— Yes, often.

Now, Mr. Biko, when you set out to conscientize people, is that then to bring to them the ideas of Black Consciousness? —— That is correct, yes.

Can you tell us when you conscientize people do you refer at all . . . Do you relate what you say to their condition and the various aspects which you have told His Lordship about, the question of starvation and labor and so on? —— This is correct. We do make reference to the conditions of the Black man and the conditions in which the Black man lives. We try to get Blacks in conscientization to grapple realistically with their problems, to attempt to find solutions to their problems, to develop what one might call an awareness, a physical awareness of their situation to be able to analyze it, and to provide answers for themselves. The purpose behind it really being to provide some kind of hope. I think the central theme about Black society is that it has got elements of a defeated society. People often look like they have given up the struggle. Like the man who was telling me that he now lives to work—he has given himself to the idea. Now, this sense of defeat is basically what we are fighting against; people must not just give in to the hardship of life. People must develop a hope. People must develop some form of security to be together to look at their problems, and people must in this way build up their humanity. This is the point about conscientization and Black Consciousness.

The question I want to put to you is this: Haven't these people got used to and come to accept their what you call existential conditions —their grievances, insecurity, the absence of food or inadequate food and so on? —— That is, I think, understating the position. I think it is possible to adapt to a given hard situation precisely because you have got to live it, and you have got to live with it every day. But adapting does not mean that you forget. You go to the mill every day —it is always unacceptable to you, it has always been unacceptable to you, and it remains so for life—but you adapt in the sense that you cannot continue to live in a state of conflict with yourself. You sort of accept, like the man who was working with the electrician was saying to me, you know, Oh, he talks in this way. This is his explanation of it, this is his sort of glib adaptation to it, but deep inside him he feels it. He cannot keep on answering back to him every day: Don't call me boy, don't shout at me, don't swear at me, because there is also the element of the job that he has got to keep. He has adapted but he does not forget it, and he does not accept it, which I think is important.

The other question which is related is when in a document of BPC or SASO—we will come to BPC later, but take it as an example—you refer to the Whites or the White government as oppressors, does this not alter people's feelings or their attitudes in relation to the White government or the Whites? —— No, I think it only serves to establish a common basis for discussion. What is contained in that expression is usually what the Black man himself normally says about the whole problem in even stronger terms. But when we talk about common problems or the problems that the Black man faces, what you are merely doing is to establish a point of departure for what you are talking about. And the goal for BPC or SASO usually is that of a build-up of membership, especially for BPC.

Now, Mr. Biko, perhaps I could take you to a completely different theme. On the question of your political struggle, I will return to this resolution after you have dealt with BPC, but I would like you to turn to . . . I think it is Resolution 50 of 1971, SASO A.1, page 255. Now, are you familiar with that resolution? —— Yes. . . .

Were you—let me put it this way—was there a commission which preceded the debate on that resolution? —— There was a commission on external affairs, I think, external relations.

And was that the commission which dealt with foreign investments?
—— Yes, this featured as a topic in their discussions. . . .

*And does this resolution express the SASO attitude on foreign invest-
ment?* —— Yes, I think it does.

*Now, before we go into details there, would you tell His Lordship
what is the SASO desire in relation to foreign investment—forget for
a moment what they wanted to do, what if they were given a wish would
they wish for . . . Would they want foreign investment to be there or
not to be there?* —— I think the desire as expressed at the time was
a rejection of the type of foreign investment which was there; in other
words, it was looked at as nothing but an exploitation of the Blacks
in this country by companies who belonged to governments which are
critical of apartheid in this country. In other words, on the one hand
Harold Wilson stands up to criticize the system here, and several of
his firms come to invest in this country amongst other reasons precisely because there exists in the country provisions for cheap labor
from the Black ranks. Now, we felt that this was unacceptable coming
from a foreign company—that kind of exploitation of cheap labor,
which devolves from the whole system of apartheid which is being
criticized at the same time by that government.

*And what would your desires have been as far as that investment
goes?* —— Our desire was that an ideal form of operation in this
country by foreign investors is one which negates the given concepts
within White society about the Black man, which reduced them to the
position of completely nonskilled workers who are merely an extension of the machine. We wanted foreign investors to help in the
build-up of the humanity of the Blacks, to give them opportunity for
training in technical spheres, to recognize to some extent trade union
work within the firms, to give the Blacks positions of responsibility
within the firms, in a sense to encourage humanity amongst Blacks
who are employed by them, negating the whole effect of apartheid on
Blacks in this country.

Yes, and if they did not do that, what would you then like to have?
—— Well, we just felt that they are in a sense selling out on us, and
they might as well get out.

Then they might as well get out? —— That is right.

Were there any other themes or thoughts behind the rejection of foreign investment, the one being that they participate in exploitation in hypocritical circumstances, that you have described? —— Right.

Any other features? —— Yes, there was another one: in a sense the relationship between a foreign government and its companies which invest in this country—and we believe South Africa is particularly sensitive like any normal country to criticism by the world of its policies. We believe that part of our political campaign is to make sure that as many people as possible criticize South Africa for its policies. Now, putting pressure on foreign companies about their participation in this kind of what we would regard as an immoral set-up was also calculated to make sure that the foreign governments also equally begin to feel unhappy about the fact of the participation of their firms in this country, and assist generally in building up pressure to make South Africa shift its attitudes gradually to a more acceptable stance. It was a political stance which was calculated to bring about political pressure to bear on South Africa to shift policies to make them more flexible, more acceptable to the world and to us as Blacks. . . .

THE COURT: *Well, we can take the adjournment now.*

COURT ADJOURNS

The Afternoon of May 3, 1976

The discussion of foreign investments is continued and explored in great detail. Biko introduces the concept of a nonracial society; he then says that the existing situation, with Blacks dominated by White racist attitudes and institutions, necessitates Black Solidarity. This, however, is part of a political process leading to the achievement of a South African society without racial distinctions. In this context, Biko examines and interprets African Socialism and the subsequent redistribution of wealth. The court's response is to press the issue of one-man, one-vote, thus underlining the fears of most White South Africans. The court closes the afternoon session by suggesting that the failure to achieve SASO and Black Consciousness objectives would result in hostility and violence.

COURT RESUMES AT 2 P.M.

STEPHEN BANTU BIKO, STILL UNDER OATH

EXAMINATION BY MR. SOGGOT, CONTINUED:

... Now, to get back to the SASO resolution, Resolution Number 50, you have already mentioned to His Lordship some of the reasons why you people rejected foreign investment. Are there any other themes which are connected with it? To your recollection? —— Well, I thought I detected another theme, which was basically that of a creeping sense of nationalism into economic considerations, the point here being that the wealth of the country must eventually be enjoyed by the people of the country. The idea here was that foreign investors will come and exploit the wealth of the country to their more advanced technological means than those we have for instance in South Africa, siphon off profits which rightfully in a sense belong here, and these go to profit societies other than our own societies, and this is a theme which has found a bit of airing in recent years.

People like, you know, De Gaulle and after him even the present President of France have constantly said this, especially about the growing investments of America into Europe. The point they are making here being that if they are not careful they are going to find that Europe will cease to be a power and that the situation will be that of America first, Russia second and thirdly American investments in Europe, and they will boost this line seriously to try and limit the extent of investments in France. I think it has been said also about Australia—I am not sure who is pushing it there. Now, this did creep into part of the thinking at the conference. One must understand here that this is a very sort of contentious topic, you know, people have various attitudes to it and people oppose it for several reasons. I will just highlight the . . . [Intervention]

What is of interest . . . Were there any pushers, so to speak, of the antiforeign-investment line whose aim was to achieve a weakening of the South African economy? —— No, this was not considered as an end of what you are talking about there.

Or the creation of wide-scale unemployment? —— Certainly not.

Now, I think we have been talking in the abstract as to what your stance was, your attitudes. . . . Mr. Biko, just for the moment I want to ask you—leave aside those details—what was SASO's aim, what did they want to achieve with their stance? Let me phrase it that way. —— Yes, I think our understanding of the position was that we were particularly weak in this area, there was nothing we could do. We took up discussion of this particular motion which was adopted, the resolution, amongst other things because foreign investment at that time was a topical question. There were several people talking about it. There were church groups from America and England specifically coming to investigate the position of their firms inside this country, to see how they were dealing with the whole question of Black labor and how they are fighting apartheid. So SASO took this decision purely as a policy matter just to have a view and to use it, you know, as a political stance.

In order to achieve what? —— In order to be able generally speaking to achieve the three points we have been talking about here, in other words to focus criticism on the foreign firms such that the foreign firms may themselves generate pressure on their governments to see the sort of untenable position they were in here. . . .

Yes, now as a matter of fact, what did you people believe could be accomplished as far as the withdrawal—the actual withdrawal of foreign investments was concerned? —— We never for a moment thought that foreign firms would as a result of this kind of stance withdraw.

What was your belief as to their ability to withdraw, even if they wanted to? —— Well, our understanding at the time—and I think it still appertains at this moment—is that certainly after Sharpeville the whole question of investment or participation in the economy of the country by foreign firms was tightened. In the first instance, to make it impossible for anybody who was intimately involved with the South African economy to withdraw at will. Certain regulations were put in besides—I am not quite sure as to their specific details, but I seem to remember for instance that there are several ways in which checks were placed on the wary investor, such that he could not pull out his money, in the first instance.

Yes? —— And of course if you are investing in machinery, in factories and so on, you won't take this to England with you, you will leave them here, so if any particular investor feels uncomfortable, all he can do is to sell it to the next investor, or to a South African concern. And in this sense, you know, it was impossible to foresee—even if one wanted to anyway—disruption of the economy system.

Yes, and would you have a look in this context at Resolution 51—that is the next one. —— Yes, all right.

Was this move, was this GSC noting that:
    "This council is not composed of people who are capable of keeping the foreign investments out by merely rejecting them, therefore substitute 'reject' with the phrase 'and discourage' "? —— Right.

Can you tell us how that came about and how it came to be . . . [inaudible]? —— Well, the mover of this particular amendment was Jerry Modisane. According to the Minutes, [he] was suggesting that this stance we were taking of rejecting is a colorless stance—it serves nothing, it does not commit us to anything. His view was that we should in fact adopt a program of discouraging foreign investment, which I think he foresaw as discouraging further capital, so to speak. Now, the argument against it was that we were not interested in mounting a program of de-investment, in mounting a campaign of de-investment, precisely because in the first instance we don't believe for a moment that those who invest here do so without being aware of the situation. They are quite aware of the situation, and it is up to them to decide, you know, to take action. We are not on our own going to mount a program in that direction.

Yes, and so it was defeated? ——— It was defeated, yes.

Now, would you please just turn to Resolution 50? Perhaps... I think that (i) to (v) speak for themselves. Could you deal with the resolution from there on, (vi), please? Would you just read each Roman subparagraph and very briefly explain what was intended and in what context the proposition fell? [*The court intervenes*]

THE COURT: *That is now . . . ?*

MR. SOGGOT: *My Lord, it is page 255, Resolution 50.* ——— Yes.

"Noting further that foreign investors seek profit from such exploitation and end up with a vested interest in its maintenance . . . [Indistinct]"

Now, I think this is looking at the relationship between government and the companies which invest in South Africa. In other words, if there is a large proportion of American investors in this country, it does imply that there were very close tie-ups between America and this country economically. Further:

"Foreign investors through this relationship are being closely tied up with the direction of affairs in the South African political attitude. America therefore is likely to be on the side which is likely to retain their investments in good hands, in other words to keep them profitable. Point number (vii): Make it possible for South Africa to [indistinct] world opinion to maintain her racist regime."

If South Africa has got some powerful countries backing it, whether tacitly or openly as a result of this economic relationship, therefore they are able not to care for instance about the attitudes of the Third World like Africa, Latin America or any other country which is critical but which does not have any major relationship with South Africa economically. As long as they win, the major countries will invest here.

"(viii) Boost South Africa's international image and make South
Africa an ideal land for investment whilst the social evils practiced by the regime are lost sight of."
I think it is now repeating really the same sort of theme in the above
two points.

Yes? ——— "Gives South Africa an economic stability that enables her to gain diplomatic and economic acceptance in the international scene."
I think it also says precisely the same thing.

"With perhaps one modification, that I think here the term economic stability was understood much more in terms of economic
involvement, an economic involvement that enables her to gain
diplomatic and economic acceptance in the international scene."
(x) Are forced to take a compromising stand on apartheid on
[inaudible] boycotts and embargoes."
I think this emphasizes the same point again.

*Now, if I can just interrupt you there. You people talk about foreign
investments. Have you ever taken an attitude towards trade with South
Africa?*
——— No.

Have you ever taken an attitude towards arms for South Africa?
——— No.

*Can you explain to us why foreign investment concerns you people
but the boycott of trade or of arms has not come into your horizon?*
——— I think foreign investment is an area of interrelationship between South Africa and other governments. We are of the belief that
if we are to move towards a peaceful solution our efforts must be
coupled with support from other people, from other governments, and
we see this whole foreign investment question as a possible vehicle for
generating pressure to sympathize with our point of view so that
South Africa can listen, not only to us but also to other people talking
about the same thing, so inevitably this whole change boost-up begins
to take root in the minds of those who are ruling us. Now, this whole
question of arms and trade . . . We don't see how arms affect us. I
mean, we are not in any way interested in making South Africa less
armed or more armed. I mean, as I state, we are interested in the
internal policies, and we are looking for a vehicle, and we picked this

one as a convenient one. It has never occurred to us in fact to pick
out the arms issue or the trade issue, the trade boycott issue . . .
precisely because it was not as topical and certainly not as applicable
to our particular situation as this one was.

Yes. Thank you. Would you please go on to the . . . [inaudible]
resolutions. "(a) Rejects foreign investment"? ——— Therefore

"(a) Rejects foreign investment as being in nature and having a
[inaudible] effect on the Blacks' creativity and initiative."

I think it refers to the argument that was often put up by some foreign
investors to the effect that foreign investment offers job opportunities
and therefore it helps the Black man in that way. And it also refers
to the attitude taken by people like Polaroid to say that they are going
to be involved in the future problems of the Black man by donating
part of their profits to welfare programs, and in this instance I remember eventually they gave money to AFECA. Now, we felt that this is
patern[al]istic, we felt that the point of application of foreign investors
must be the humanity of the men they employ rather than pandering
to considerations of materialism, like giving him a token increment
here, or giving him token assistance at social-welfare level. We felt
that the area of open [inaudible] is with the worker himself and his
humanity. If they can accept this as their responsibility to train Black
workers and to allow them all the opportunities, this was the real
thing. Anything else is patern[al]istic.

"(b) Rejects foreign investments because in no way do they alleviate the lot of Black people, for even if foreign investments are
withdrawn, the Blacks will be least [likely] to be affected."

Now, this point again refers to what is mentioned earlier on: that there
is no way in which established industry which has been set up with
foreign capital in this country is going to be killed, just because one
proprietor pulls out, because there is always going to be another one
who takes up, so from the point of view of jobs and job situations,
those Blacks who are employed in firms directed by foreign investment are going to continue in employment. What we attack is precisely the fact that when these people have got a point of leverage—
because they are not South Africans, because they are subject back at
home probably to more liberal attitudes—they don't make use of this.
They go out of their way in fact to destroy the system. This is what

we attack. And this is what you are referring to here as saying, "They don't alleviate the lot of Black people," and certainly even if they withdraw themselves we are not going to suffer, because there is no difference whether it is a South African proprietor or a foreign proprietor. The conditions apparently as the situation goes now are going to be the same.

"Paragraph (c) Rejects foreign investments with the belief that South Africa is economically viable to alleviate property if she wanted to."

Now again, this refers to the claim by foreign investors of again offering job opportunities. Our argument here is that South Africa is at a stage in its economic development where it can provide in fact most of the capital it requires to maintain . . . you know, the present growth rate economically. We believe that the so-called token gestures by Polaroid, giving money to AFECA, giving money to some other welfare organizations, you know, can be adequately fulfilled from within the country, so that it is not a risk—this is a primary reason for their existence here. We have got our own wealth, we have got a country that is viable economically, we can do all those things, and that they may not quote them as reasons for staying in the country.

And then (d)? ———

"(d) Further condemns the Black puppets who go overseas under the cloak of leadership and persuade foreign investors to stay in South Africa with the belief that it is for the betterment of the Black man."

I think this is an attack essentially on Bantustan* leaders—I think of Gatsha Buthelezi† especially, he did this—there may have been others, I know also that Cebe of the Ciskei Government did this—who

---

*In furtherance of their policy of separate development, the South African government has divided the country into White areas and African reserves or Bantustans. Although Africans outnumber Whites by more than four to one, the Bantustans constitute only 13 percent of the land. Each African tribe has been allocated its own "homeland" or Bantustan. The Bantustans are not integral land areas. The nine "nations" are scattered in 81 separate and noncontiguous parcels of land. The Zulu "homeland," largest of the Bantustans, consists of 29 different areas. In many ways, the Bantustans are quite similar to Indian reservations in the United States.

†Chief of the Zulu "nation" and designated Prime Minister of the KwaZulu Bantustan. He and Biko were bitter political rivals, despite the fact that Buthelezi is by far the most radical of the homeland leaders. The two men differed because it was Biko's belief that the artificial division of Blacks into ethnic groups was designed to fragment the Black struggle for emancipation.

go out into the world to specifically invite foreign investment without any understanding of what we as . . . Black people . . . think. Now, we believe that they are puppets in a sense—puppets not to us but to those who work against our interests, with generally White society. And when I say White society I mean White society's government power structures, so to speak. So we are taking them for speaking as if they are speaking for Black people, because they are not. . . . These are their own views; they have never debated it. They merely say, as we believe they do often, what they are expected to say by those whom they serve. . . .

Mr. Biko, would you please turn to Resolution 42? That is on page 249. [The court intervenes]

THE COURT: *Before you read this, now, point (c)—if you accept that South Africa is economically viable to alleviate property if it wanted to, are you only concerned with poverty there? If South Africa is economically as strong as you suggest, well, does it then really matter whether you discourage foreign investment or not?* —— In fact we believe South Africa is moving in that direction. The rate of investment in this country, or the rate of necessary investment, has dropped tremendously. As far as I understand, it is about 6.4 percent. So that in fact we believe that our nationalist philosophy in economy is shared even by the White government. They are gradually decreasing the level of foreign investment in the country.

But isn't it because of the economic positions throughout the world? There is inflation and there is a bit of a recession? —— Yes, I think the major question is dependent on a foreign power, or on foreign powers . . . they are trends, you can never predict . . . I think the tenet to draw the world now is for nations to depend mainly on what they can provide from within their societies, from their own economics, and I think South Africa has progressively encouraged, you know, a downgrading of the level of foreign investment in our economy.

MR. SOGGOT: *What is your—I am sorry, My Lord, am I interrupting?*

THE COURT: *I think you mean seeking capital more from local sources?* —— Yes.

MR. SOGGOT: *Well, what is your belief on that point as to South Africa's ability to generate sufficient capital for development?* —— Well, in some reports—I think it was an economic development report drawn up by one of the government departments that I came across at some stage—the figure I mentioned just now was stated: that South Africa is at a stage now where they require only about 6.4 percent of total investment from outside. The rest, which is about 93.6 percent, they can produce internally. So the level of importance of foreign investment has dropped in this country justifiably.

Mr. Biko, would you refer to Resolution 42 on page 249? In paragraph (2) there, you have referred to the definition of Black people which I will not trouble you with, but paragraph (3) I should like you to deal with. "SASO believes"—if you will read (a) please? —— Yes.

"SASO believes that (a) South Africa is a country in which both Black and White live and shall continue to live together."

Now, what does that mean? —— Well, this means that we accept the fact that the present South African society is a plural society with contributions having been made to its development by all segments of the community, in other words we speak of the groupings both Black and White. We have no intention of . . . of course we regard ourselves as people who stay here and shall stay here. And we made the point that we've got no intention whatsoever of seeing White people leave this country, when I say leave, I mean leave this country.

Leave? —— Yes.

L-e-a-v-e? —— That is right. We intend to see them staying here side by side with us, maintaining a society in which everybody shall contribute proportionally.

I wonder, in this context, would you please have a look at SASO G.1, Resolution 45? On page 206. —— Right.

Would you read from "This country belongs . . ."?

—— "Therefore we wish explicitly to state that this country belongs to Black people and to them alone. Whites who live in our . . . who live in this country on terms laid down by Blacks and on condition that they respect the Black people. This should not be construed as anti-Whitism. It only means that inasmuch as Black people live in Europe on terms laid down by Europeans, Whites shall be subjected to the same conditions. We further wish to state that in our operation it shall always be . . ."

Can you explain what SASO meant by that resolution? —— Well, I must explain I was not at this particular meeting, but from reading this document, what I understand it to mean is that this country is essentially a country in Africa, a continent which is inhabited always naturally by Black people, and that Whites . . . It is conceived that Whites are here and that they may live in the country, or they may leave the country, depending on their relationship with Blacks, and their acceptance of whatever conditions Blacks in this country shall lay [down] at a certain time. I don't know what time the resolution is referring to.

You yourself as you understand the position on the accession to an open society . . . How will people be able to vote? What rights for example will the White man have to vote? ——— Well, we view the voting as strictly being on a one-man, one-vote basis. That is the current theme in our talking.

Was this the current thing at that time? ——— It was a current thing at the time. We took the policy manifesto. I am not aware that it has changed.

Yes, then 3(b), please. That is on SASO A.1, page 249: Back to the second . . . ——— Oh, I see.

"That the White man must be made aware that one is either part of the solution or part of the problem."

I think this statement is self-explanatory. In a situation where you have a halving of privileges within society for the sole enjoyment or for the major enjoyment by one section of society, you do get a certain form of alienation of members who are on opposite sides of the line, and that the White man specifically has got to decide whether he is part of the problem—in other words whether he is part of the total White power structure that we regard as a problem, or he accedes and becomes part of the Black man—that is, the target of the problem. I think this is what that particular statement is saying.

Then 3(c)?

——— "3(c) That in this context because of the privileges accorded to them by legislation and because of their continual maintenance of an oppressive regime Whites have defined themselves as part of the problem."

Again, this I think speaks for itself. Generally speaking it is White society who vote at election time, it is they who return a government into power—be it Nationalists . . . the United Party, the Progressive Party. And it is that government which maintains legal provisions that creates problems for Black people—problems of oppression, problems of poverty, problems of deprivation, and problems of self-alienation, as I said earlier on. It is White society on the whole. Some may vote one way, some may vote another, but all of them belong to an electoral college, if one may speak in those terms, of the whole society, which is jointly responsible for the government that does all these things, or that makes all these provisions applying to Black people. And in this sense therefore they lose the natural right to speak as co-planners with us in our way of determining our future. This is what that resolution is saying. They define themselves in other words as the enemy.

3(d)?

—— "That therefore we believe that in all matters relating to the struggle towards realizing our aspirations, Whites must be excluded."

I think that speaks for itself.

Once the struggle is over, what is the attitude of SASO? —— The attitude is a simple one: an open society, one man, one vote, no reference to color.

And what do you mean by the phrase the "open society"? —— We regard an open society as one which fulfills all the three points I have mentioned just now. Where there can be free participation in the economic, social and all three of the societies by anybody—you know, equal opportunity and so on.

Then 3(e), have you any comment on that?

—— "That this attitude must not be interpreted by Blacks to imply anti-Whitism, but merely a more positive way of attaining a normal situation in South Africa."

Now again, this is a warning to the membership . . . that it is not our intention to generate a feeling of anti-Whitism amongst our members. We are merely forced by historic considerations to recognize the fact that we cannot plan side by side with people who participate in their exclusive pool of privileges, to make sure that both privileges are shared. We don't believe . . . We don't have faith in them anymore, that they are willing to share with us without any form of—

What sort of Whites were you thinking of at that stage? —— When we spoke of . . .?

Of this attitude to Whites, and in the struggle and . . .? —— Whites in general.

What sort of Whites had participated in the struggle with you as did the Blacks? —— Mainly the Liberals, mainly students, left-wingers if one may call it that, and to some extent the Progressives.

Yes, now 3 (f), Mr. Biko?

—— "That in pursuit of this direction therefore, personal contact with Whites, though it should not be legislated against, must be discouraged especially where it tends to militate against the beliefs we hold dear."

Now, we did not intend making ourselves a policeman organization over the formation of friendships between one individual and another. We did not intend discouraging any particular Black student, or a member of SASO at that time, from forming a friendly relationship with either his mother's employer or his father's employer or another fellow student or any White person within society, but we felt that where there was a possibility—and this was strictly within the political arena—of such a friendship militating against the beliefs that we hold dear, we must warn those who are involved.

Now Mr. Biko, I will return to this document in the context of dealing with some of the more overriding features of BPC as well. My Lord, with Your Lordship's permission, may I then leave this document for the moment? I think it might be more convenient to deal collectively with certain of the themes. It might save time.

THE COURT: *Just before you leave that document . . . Now, you say you people stand for one man, one vote?* —— Yes.

Now, is it a practical concept in the African setup? Do you find it anywhere in Africa? —— Yes, we find it, even within this country.

Now, apart from this country—I mean, now let us take any other country in Africa. Do you have one man, one vote in any other country? —— Yes.

Which country? —— Here in Botswana, not to go far.

Yes, those are under the influence of the South African background and traditions. Now take it away from the South African traditions. —— Where to, My Lord, for instance?

Well, not anywhere outside South Africa. —— You have it in Ghana. The one man . . .

What parties are there in Ghana? ———— I would not know what
parties are there now.

Well, why do you say there is one man, one vote there? ———— There
was at the time . . .

*Oh yes, that is so, there was. Didn't that disappear in Nkrumah's day
already?* ———— It didn't disappear. What has happened is that in
Ghana now there is a military regime, but the concept of elections—
be it for city council, be it for provincial council, or any of the
governmental structures that they have—is on a basis of one man, one
vote.

*Well, that may be the subordinate bodies, but now when it comes to
the important vote, affecting the country, is there any country in Africa
where you have one man, one vote?* ———— Well, I cannot refer to
specific instances but I know in Kenya for instance . . .

*Just recently I read that they say I think there are 46 countries in
Africa, and of the 46 I think only 5 countries have a democratic form
of government and they are just around South Africa?* ———— I saw the
same thing. I think what they said is that there are 46 countries in
Africa, there are 29 with nonmilitary government, but of that 29 a lot
of them are one-party states. Now, a one-party state is not necessarily
undemocratic, if it is selected by the people. . . .

Yes, but now just to test that—Russia also operates on that basis?
———— Yes.

*And of the 200, I think, and 45 million, only 14 million are Commu-
nists, and they are the people who really govern and decide who the
people should vote for?* ———— I have not gone into the Russian society.
I won't be able to dispute that.

*Yes, but you see, there again it is a one-party state and they also argue
like you. Everybody has the vote, but now what is it worth?* ———— Yes,
My Lord, let us take the Kenya situation for instance, where there has
been a [recent development] of the opposition.

*But I thought that disappeared when Oginga Odinga was assas-
sinated?* ———— No, Oginga Odinga has not been assassinated. He is
still alive.

Tom Mboya? ———— Tom Mboya was with the governing party,
and the governing party is still governing up until now.

Yes, but then they found out that he had a certain adherence amongst the people and . . . ——— I think, My Lord, you are mistaking Tom Mboya with Kariuke. It was Kariuke who was murdered, and it was Kariuke who had generated amongst the people a certain thought, but Kariuke was also operating from inside the governing party. You see, in Kenya there is a very good demonstration of what a one-party state can achieve by way of differing thought within the party. Kariuke was the advocate on the one hand of the common man, the worker, the servant in Kenya, against this whole development in Kenya, of a bourgeoisie within the ruling party. You had Kenyatta, on the other hand, who felt constantly attacked by Kariuke. Okay, Kariuke was allowed to air his views in Parliament; he was allowed to hold meetings throughout the length and breadth of the country, but still operating from within KANU, which is the ruling party. This is the essence of a one-party state: that there is no need to divide your men and let them lead other parties to . . .

Yes, but Kariuke didn't survive all this? ——— Oh well, My Lord, several politicians don't survive, it seems like Verwoerd didn't survive.* [Laughter]

But now you see, it is not his own people who killed him, it is not his own party people who killed Verwoerd? ——— We don't know who killed Kariuke. It has not been established.

Well, who did they accuse of having killed Kariuke? ——— Well, there are [rumors] there that it is probably Kenyatta, it is probably so-and-so. It has not been established, My Lord. But we know that in politics this sort of thing happens. Like, I mean, I could make an allegation here which would be preposterous. Amongst the Black society there is a very strong belief that Mr. Verwoerd's murder was generated from within the Nationalist Party and that a particular politician is named. This is the kind of belief which can sometimes go out and is believed by the outside world. The same thing applies to Kariuke.

Yes, but now you have only been able to mention the one country, Kenya of '46. ——— Well, I happened to discuss that with two Ken-

*Fifth Prime Minister of South Africa, who was stabbed to death on the floor of the House of Assembly on September 6, 1966. He was succeeded by current Prime Minister John B. Vorster. His assassin, Dimitri Tsafendas, a parliamentary messenger, was found mentally incompetent to stand trial and was confined to a mental institution.

yan Quakers who visited this country recently, that is why I know—
it came to me. I have also discussed Botswana with people from
Botswana who visited this country. The point in issue is that there
isn't much interchange of ideas between Africa and South Africa,
because it is not so easy from Africa to visit South Africa and vice
versa, as they have not been allowed to move around the country, so
I cannot from our own experience and dialogue with people quote
other instances in Africa.

*Well, are you prepared to say that there is one man, one vote in the
other countries?* —— Yes, I am. I want to say quite frankly that the
military in Africa tends to play a very important part in politics. The
military in Africa tends to often decide to declare the election, and the
election is some kind of coup. Okay, but then you get situations
throughout the world where there is chaos. You get in Italy a government resigning virtually every two months. You can't help it.

*Yes, because there you have one man, one vote? You see, that is the
trouble.* —— Now, I think we share the belief of one man, one vote,
with the government, because when they set up the Bantustans they
gave one man, one vote to the Transkei. To Zululand, to Bophu-
tswana and so on. They don't say to people only those who can
[inaudible] may vote. It is a one man, one vote. Suddenly they are
mature enough to . . . [Intervention]

*I am interested in whether it is going to work, that is why I am asking
you. Do you think it is going to work?* —— It seems to be working.
It seems to be working in the Transkei.

*Well, the Transkei is just starting. It has just started. But do you
think it will work in the Transkei?* —— I think one man, one vote
could work. I doubt if the Transkei itself will work. [Laughter]

Yes, but now why do you say that? —— I think that . . .

*Why do you say one man, one vote will work, and that the Transkei
won't work? I mean, it is inconsistent ideas?* —— No. You may find
that, My Lord, if Matanzima* decides to take the issue of the Transkei
independence to a referendum, there will be a beautiful vote, well-

*Kaiser Matanzima, currently the Prime Minister of the Republic of the Transkei, one
of several homelands granted independence by the South African government under
their policy of self-development.

controlled vote, people voting earnestly without force, but they may reject the concept of an independent Transkei.

They may reject it? —— They may reject it, yes.

Yes, well, that is another matter, and you will say that is . . . Will you blame one man, one vote for that? —— I will blame—no, I will blame apartheid. I will say the Transkei has not worked; one man, one vote has worked.

Democracy—doesn't it presuppose a developed community, democracy where you have one man, one vote? —— Yes, it does, it does, and I think it is part of the process of developing the community. . . . I think you may devise . . . the means of ensuring a proper exercise of that vote, but certainly you give them the vote.

Yes, but democracy is really only a success if the people who have the right to vote can intelligently and honestly apply a vote? —— Yes, My Lord, this is why in Swaziland for instance where they have people sometimes who may not read the names of the candidates, they use signs.

Yes, but do they know enough of the affairs of government to be able to influence it by a vote? I mean, surely you must know what you are voting for, what you are voting about? Assuming now they vote on a particular policy, such as foreign investment—now, what does a peasant know about foreign investment? —— I think, My Lord, in a government where democracy is allowed to work, one of the principles that is normally entrenched is a feedback system, a discussion in other words between those who formulate policy and those who must perceive, accept or reject policy. In other words there must be a system of education, political education, and this does not necessarily go with literacy. I mean, Africa has always governed its peoples in the form of the various chiefs, Chaka* and so on, who couldn't write.

Yes, but the government is much more sophisticated and specialized now than in those days? —— And there are ways of explaining it to the people. People can hear—they may not be able to read and write —but they can hear and they can understand the issues when they are put to them. . . .

Well, take the gold standard. If we have to debate whether this

---

*Military genius and ruler of the Zulu nation in the early 1800's.

government should go on the gold standard or go off the gold standard, will you feel that you know enough about it to be able to cast an intelligent vote about that? —— Myself?

Yes. —— I think probably much better than the average Afrikaner in the street, My Lord.

Yes, well, that may be so. Now, do you think you know enough about it to be able to cast such an intelligent vote that the government should be based on that vote? —— Yes, I think if . . . I have a right to be consulted by my government on any issue. If I don't understand it, I may give over to someone else that I have faith in to explain to me.

Well, how can you? I mean, that is your vote, and what about the ten other people who have votes? —— The same applies to everybody else, and this is why we have the political process whereby things are explained. I mean, the average man in Britain does not understand on his own accord the advantages or disadvantages of Britain becoming involved in the whole economic market, but when it becomes an issue for referendum, political organizers go out to explain and canvass their points of view, and the man in the middle listens to several people and decides to use what he has, the vote. But in the meantime he has got no particular equipment to understand these technicalities of the whole of society.

But isn't that one of the reasons why Britain is probably one of the most bankrupt countries in the world? —— I think I prefer to look at it more positively and say it is one country which is most democratic.

Yes, but now it is bankrupt? —— I think it is a phase, My Lord. Britain has been rich before; it may still get, you know, up on the ladder. I think it is a phase in history.

Yes, but something went wrong somewhere along the line, and is it because of its different democracy probably? —— I don't think so, I don't think so personally. I think it has been partly the whole decolonization process which has robbed Britain of a very fixed life, of what they used to get before. Now they are forced back on their resources, and they don't have much. It is a small country, smaller than Natal. What can you get? It has got 56 million people, no land to cultivate, very few factories . . .

Yes, but now capitalism really develops, and wasn't Britain powerful, and because she was powerful she developed. She became an empire and then that is how capitalism . . . It is like a snowball, it just grows and grows? —— Yes.

But she must have had good government at one stage? —— I think she could have had good resources at one stage, and she could have tightened the belt such that the distribution of wealth did not touch the lower man at some stage, like during the time of Adam Smith, even the time of the laissez-faire policy when you know, the few people who controlled industry in Britain went rampant throughout the country, manufacturing [inaudible], making themselves rich, and of course the government got rich, but the people didn't get rich. The people got poorer, and this is why in Britain now more than in any other country . . . [Intervention]

They had a vote? —— They had a vote then, and they have been gradually returning a more socialist government which is against exploitation of people. People are you know restoring the whole process—the wealth must come back to the people.

But doesn't that all go to show that one man, one vote is not the "clear all"? —— I think this is a debate which is going on in the world now, the debate between democracy and communism, between capitalism and . . .

Yes, they all have disadvantages? —— Yes, they all have. And I think we are also free to make up our own minds about it.

MR. SOGGOT: *I suppose that leads to a discussion on anarchy, My Lord. Mr. Biko, if I may just perhaps explore some of the questions further which His Lordship has put to you. As far as this country is concerned, do you visualize any particular impediment to the adoption and functioning of the one-man, one-vote system? And perhaps in your reply if you can give us any useful contrasts or comparisons with the political debacle . . . of many African countries?* —— And European countries? Yes, I would say basically that the South African Black in many ways is different . . . at the present moment from the stage at which several African countries took up independence. I think he is a highly Westernized man in the first instance, and his accommodation of the whole Western system becomes that much greater. I can say only the degree of literacy, functional literacy, and beyond that education, is that much higher, and thirdly I think he is faced with a different

problem—unlike any other country in Africa which has been inhabited by a colonialist. We have a situation here where we have Whites
who are part of this country; they have got nowhere to go to. They
are not hiding passports in their back pockets. You might get a few
Liberals doing this . . . [Laughter] But on the whole the basic governing force in this country, which is the Afrikaner, is a man of here. He
is in fact spurned by the countries where he came from, which are
mainly the Netherlands. He can't run there anymore. So that he has
got to devise a system whereby he can live forever with abundant life
right here, and Blacks recognize this. So I think, My Lord, the whole
process of political development in this country is going to accommodate the various factors, you know, that make up our society. . . . We
have got a stance and we know what is the stance. Our stance is we
want a one man, one vote. Whites say *ja,* we have got some suspicions
about that. Now, in the process of bargaining, surely some middle
situation must be achieved amongst the two forces. You can't bargain
without a stance, you know, but our stance is not exclusive of the
white man. When I say one Black man, one vote, you know—he is
saying one man, one vote. He is saying one White man, one vote. So
we reach somewhere in the middle.

   *Mr. Biko, I am going to change my direction and keep this theme.
If one goes back to SASO A.1 you have the phrase in paragraph 4:*
       *"The basic tenet of Black Consciousness is that the Black man
       must reject all value systems that seek to make him a foreigner
       in the country of his birth and reduce his basic human dig-
       nity. . . ."*
   *Now, I wonder if you would indicate to His Lordship how this relates
to the concept of Black values and "Ujama" which is referred to in a
BPC document—I am dealing with this now because this seems to be
an appropriate stage. Can you briefly tell us what all that is about and
what this involves in terms of the future society—in particular, economic society—which the Blacks—you people—want to bring about?*
   ——— All right. From the economic point of view I think the starting
point is that we as Blacks, and certainly as Africans in this country,
have had a form of economy, even in our rudimentary culture—I use
the term "rudimentary" now because the whole scope of knowledge
has so widened, you know, in latter years—we had an economy which

was mainly an agrarian economy centering around crops and centering around oxen, cattle and sheep and so on, small stock and big stock.
Now, the whole operation of that society had certain basic tenets, the
first one being: We did not believe in apportioning land for private
ownership by individuals. The land belonged to the tribe, and land
was held for the tribe in trust by the chief. The chief could say, Over
there we are going to have our grazing area, and you, Mr. Rees, are
going to sit over here, and have your farmstead here, and you are
going to live here. Now, when he does that he is not giving you what
is commonly held very dear by Western society, a title deed over
something that you have bought [or] something that you have been
given. . . . He is merely giving you a right to stay there. If the tribe
for one reason or the other may require to use that portion, he gives
you another place, and there is no question about it. But of course he
does not do this in a rude way. You know, he consults with the people
and everybody is free to consult in the various meetings that are called
by the chief, but the center point of what I am saying is that the
economic system has certain basic tenets. Now we are advocating
Black Communalism, which is in many ways similar to African Socialism. We are expropriating an essential tribal background to accommodate what is in fact an expounded economic concept now. We
have got to accommodate industry; we have got to accommodate the
whole relationship between industry and politics. But there is a certain plasticity in this interpretation precisely because no one has as yet
said this is it, and believed by all. You get Kenya, for instance, saying
they believe in African Socialism, but Kenya is almost a carbon copy
of the old British society, terribly capitalistic in approach, but they say
they believe in African Socialism. . . .

THE COURT: *Well then, of course, that is not African Socialism in
Kenya. I mean, even if they say so it is not African Socialism?* ———
This is the point I am trying to make, My Lord. That in the end it
is a very flexible concept—everybody says this is it. You know, we are
not quite sure, and even amongst us there is a constant debate about
this particular topic, Black Communalism. As far as I understand,
BPC right at this moment is still examining that concept to try to
come to a precise understanding that is common to everybody else.
Today I believe what is going on in Zambia, which is a 51 percent

[inaudible] nationalization, in certain spheres like the copper industry, or . . . what is happening in Tanzania, where government expropriates with compensation and government forces a system to be adopted by the whole community because they believe this is the best to do for this particular community. So there is a wide range of claims that are made on African Socialism by countries which in fact differ fundamentally in their economic concepts and operations.

Now, as far as you people were concerned, have the extent and ambit of governmental interference or nationalization or expropriation ever been settled? ——— No, it has not. I think the point we make here is the family accepts the fact that government must take a lead in the planning, but no one knows, or rather no one has as yet expressed in concrete terms, what type of lead, what type of control the government must have on private industry. No one knows whether there is going to be a private plot or not. You know, we talk of land in terms of being a people's thing, this is borrowed straight from [Inaudible] . . . Whether or not this is strictly applicable to an economic system that has so developed has not been fully debated. For instance, certainly what has been accepted now is a need to focus thought on this particular direction, but no one can tell me in very precise terms what the BPC/SASO policy on Black Communalism is and say . . . [The court intervenes]

THE COURT: *Anyway, it is a starting point?* ——— That is right.

MR. SOGGOT: *It is a starting point which leads in what direction? In what way does Communalism or these concepts of African Socialism inspire you people or direct you people? In other words how do you use it? . . . or foreshadow its use?* ——— What we have accepted is the introduction of the concept of sharing in the present society, right? Now, we have sort of given a rudimentary explanation for what we believe. We know that we . . . are dealing with a society which is basically capitalism orientated, although they do embrace a lot of socialistic attitudes. I mean, in South Africa for instance there is nationalization of—to a great extent—of several things like the radio, the railways, like Iscor for instance . . . Now again, we are talking of bargaining, we are talking of dialogue, you know, from two different standpoints between two people who are both interested in the future of the country. We would be developing our standpoint from this side, which is the platform from which we are going to talk to a people who hold dear a free enterprise system, and out of these two clearly you know the synthesis will come.

THE COURT: *But am I not correct in saying—I get that impression from your literature—that first of all you want to break down capitalism because capitalism sort of eulogizes the individual, and you don't want individuality to play such a role in your idea, in your community, because of your traditions?* ——— That is also correct, and of course there is a second point, My Lord, that capitalism tends to lock up wealth of a country in a few hands at the top. . . .

MR. SOGGOT: *You say that there are going to be two groups and you are going to bargain?* ——— That is right.

Do you visualize a bargaining in connection with the economic adjustment of the country? In the sharing of wealth? ——— Yes, we are bargaining here—I am implying an attempt at synthesizing two different viewpoints. You know, you've got two strong points in the society: The one is strongly capitalist, the other says, We are Black Communalist in approach or we are African Socialists or we believe in sharing. Now, you have got to synthesize that, you know. This is all part of the values, the beliefs, the policies that have got to be synthesized in the bargaining process between Black and White in this country.

. . .Is there any part of your program which suggests that all private property must be expropriated, full stop? ——— I am not aware of this.

Not that you are aware of? ——— No.

Then again . . . [The court intervenes]

THE COURT: *I think your counsel is probably afraid to mention it. Isn't it part of the policy to have a redistribution of wealth?* ——— That is correct.

Now, how can you have a redistribution of wealth without taking it from somebody? ——— My Lord, you can take from somebody without necessarily abolishing the principle of private ownership. I mean, even in our society, in our tribal society—you know as I said which is the starting point—you do have the concept of so-and-so owns so many cattle. The important thing here is what you personally mentioned—the individuality society. I own this cattle all right, but if someone is starting a house next door, it is custom for me to . . . have empathy with him, it is part of my cultural heritage to set him up, so that my relationship with my property is not so highly individualistic that it seeks to destroy others. I use it to build others.

That is your property. What about the White man's property? —— Now, this is precisely the point. Now, we may get a situation, and I certainly think it is a possibility, where certain people in the country according to whatever values are adopted at the time, own things that they should not have, which historically they have immorally got, to a point which cannot be forgiven. I am sure I mean we are just like any society, you know, you have got to create what you call some retribution. There has been an abuse or something, and someone has collected. . . .

That I can understand, but how do you deal with him? —— It does not mean that every White man or every rich Black man will be subjected to this, but I can just foresee—and this is my own viewpoint —I can foresee a situation where there will be people who own so much that they have got to be told, Give it back; we will give you what we think it is worth, you know. If you want to buy the land, because he may be in the position of owning the land, you pay him what you think the land is worth, not the sum he may fix perhaps.

Yes, but who is going to pay it? And where are you going to get the money from? —— Well, I am talking about the government. I am talking about a situation where . . .

You mean the government that . . . —— Yes, there has been a synthesis and we are now as joint Black and White settling discourse of this thing with those people of society whom we jointly feel we cannot accept in terms of their monopolistic property. You pay him a price. I mean the government does, anyway. They sometimes tell the owner, Sell us your property. They buy the property and they fix a price. Never mind what the man says. Well, if he says half a million and the government says it is worth 2 million he gets 2 million. If the man says R200 and the government says R150 he gets R150. This is the whole principle of expropriation.

Just to continue finishing off this theme of the synthesis of your new society, the values of this society, in the document here there are suggestions that existing values are no good and you have got to have new values? —— Yes.

Can you tell us what is foreshadowed, and the thinking behind it—

whether you are considering going back to the sixth century, or . . .
———— No, I think we reject the return to the bush concept, which is
what Bernard Potter suggests we want to do in the book . . . What
is the title of that book now?

Just indicate who? ———— Bernard Potter. I think he says, "Your
fault, Black man," and he is saying that the fault of the Black
man . . .

It is Potter? ———— Yes, now he says the fault of the Black man is
in his genes, and he suggests in the book somewhere that, you know,
what he wants is a return to the bush and that sort of thing. Now, this
is not really what he wants, you know. I think what we need in our
society is the power by us Blacks to innovate. We have got the very
system from which we can expand, from which we can innovate to
say this is what we believe, accept or not accept, things that are
thrown at us, and it is society that is a constant physical . . . [inaudible]
You know, cultures affect each other, you know, like fashions and you
cannot escape rubbing against someone else's culture.

But you must have the right to reject or not anything that is given
to you. At the moment we exist sort of as a limb of the White culture.
You know, we form what we must call a subculture, precisely because
of a situation that forces us to behave in a certain way. For instance
if you look at the subculture of drinking at a shebeen, now this is very
common in Black society, you know, everybody drinks at a shebeen
—I drink at a shebeen. Now, it cannot be traced back per se to our
tribal life because we didn't have shebeens in our tribal life. But it is
a subculture arising out of the fact that we don't have bars, we don't
have hotels where we can drink, so what do we do? We are either a
genius to invent a shebeen and to drink at the shebeen, and out of this
a subculture develops, you know. . . .

MR. SOGGOT: *The question I think which is of greater interest to us is
on the first day of the open society—on the following day—is there going
to be general destruction—any destruction or proscription of existing
culture and cultural values?* ———— I think a modification all round.

Now, what sort of modifications are envisaged? ———— I think again
it would depend very much on the bargaining processes and the result
thereof. I think SASO in its documents, and certainly in the many
speeches delivered by its [inaudible] all that they insist on is primarily

a culture that accepts the humanity of the Black man, a culture that is basically sufficiently accommodative of African concepts to pass as an African culture. What we are saying now is that at the present moment we have a culture here which is a European culture. This country looks, My Lord, like a province of Europe. You know, to anybody who perceives the behavior pattern it looks like a province of Europe. It has got no relationship rootwise to the fact that it happens to exist in Africa. And when Mr. Pik Botha* says at the United Nations, "We are Africans," he just doesn't know what he is talking about. We don't behave like Africans, we behave like Europeans who are staying in Africa. So we don't want to be just mere political Africans, we want to be people living in Africa. We want to be called complete Africans, we want . . . social Africans. [Inaudible] . . . said I must understand Africa and what Africa is about. And we don't have to go far. We just have to live with the man here, the Black man here, whose proportionate contribution in the joint culture is going to sufficiently change our joint culture to accommodate the African experience. Sure, it will have European experience, because we have Whites here who are descended from Europe. We don't dispute that. But for God's sake it must have African experience as well.

And is that the synthesis you foreshadow? —— This is the synthesis we talk about.

Now, Mr. Biko, still while we are dealing with overall themes, can we now get on to the question of the achievement of your freedom? I would like you to—I know this is shortcircuiting your evidence—but I would like you in this context to deal with BPC as well. We will look at the BPC documents tomorrow. —— Right.

But I think they can usefully be dealt with in the same breath as the SASO documents. Would you have a look on the same page at paragraph 4(c)? —— Yes.

Would you read that, please? ——

"SASO accepts the premise that before the Black people should join the open society they should first close their ranks to form themselves into a solid group, to oppose the definite racism that

*South Africa's foreign minister.

is meted out by the White society, to work out their direction clearly and bargain from a position of strength. SASO believes that a truly open society can only be achieved by Blacks . . ."
Yes, now I wonder if you would pause there. Now, I think—without troubling you with actual documents—in BPC A.1 there is in a resolution the following phrase—it is on page 2—and that is:
> *"A political movement be formed that shall consolidate the different sections of Black community with an aim towards forming a power bloc."*

Have you got that, and you know what I am talking about? Paragraph 5—"The primary objective the total liberation of all Blacks." Now, would you indicate to His Lordship your conception—SASO's conception—of the forming of . . . here it is referred to as "a solid group" and in BPC as a "power bloc." And how you visualize the generation of this so-called bloc as leading towards your liberation? ———— First of all, I accept that in our analysis the cardinal point is the existence in our society of White racism which has been institutionalized, and also cushioned with a backing of the majority of Whites. In other words a White child does not have to choose whether or not he wants to live with the White, he is born into it. He is brought up within White schools, institutions, and the whole process of racism somehow greets . . . him at various levels, and he attempts to have an attitude against Blacks. So Whites are together around the privileges that they hold, and they monopolize this away from Black society.

Yes? ———— Now, then comes the analysis. Can we in fact crack this cocoon, you know, to get Whites away from the concept of racism, away from the concept of monopolizing the privileges and the wealth of the country onto themselves without necessarily being together. Can you preach to them in other words as individuals? Now, our belief is that White society will not in fact listen to preaching. They will not listen to their Liberals. The Liberal Party has not grown within White society, and certainly we as Black people are unable to stand idle watching the situation.

Yes? ———— Now, we can only generate a response from White society when we as Blacks speak with a definite voice and say what we want. The age of the Liberal was such that the Black voice was not very much heard except in echoing what was said by Liberals.

Now has come the time when we as Blacks must articulate what we
want, and put it across to the White man, and from a position of
strength begin to say, "Gentlemen, this is what we want. This is where
you are, this is where we are, this is what we want. . . ." All that BPC
wants is to gain a majority of Black support so that it can authentically sound a . . . [inaudible] on behalf of the Black people. You know,
we must be able to say tomorrow that we don't want a Transkei as
Black South Africans, and know also that it is known by the White
society that we are speaking for the majority of Blacks in this country.
Now, the bargaining process again is not anything which will clear
that particular point in history. It starts now when we take a resolution at a conference and we say we are going to communicate the
contents of this resolution to the people concerned—whether it is a
university, in the case of SASO; or whether it is a sporting body
. . . a governing body, in the case of BPC. All of this is bargaining.
We are beginning to say this is what we are thinking.

Yes? ——— Now, at this given moment our strength is such that we
have got to deal with issues that are very, very low-key. Now, as you
develop strength you begin to pick up issue after issue, and it is all
over a course of time, and it is all not as clear-cut as perhaps it might
be suggested by this term here which says, "Form yourself into a solid
bloc and then begin to bargain." It is not as clear-cut as all that. This
is a frivolity. This is a way of putting the process into one paragraph.
The process in fact may take well over twenty years of dialogue
between Blacks and Whites. We certainly don't envisage failure. We
certainly don't have an alternative. We have analyzed history. We
believe that history moves in a particular logical direction, and in this
particular instance the logical direction is that eventually any White
society in this country is going to have to accommodate Black thinking.

Yes? ——— Now, we believe that we are mere agents in that history. There are alternatives. On the one hand we have groups that are
known in this country who have opted for another way of operation,
who have opted for violence. We know that ANC and PAC have done
this in the past; they have taken this step. Now, we don't believe it
is the only alternative. We believe that there is a way of getting across
to where we want to go through peaceful means. And the very fact

that we decided to actually form an aboveboard movement implies that we accepted certain legal limitations to our operations. We accepted that we are going to take this particular course. We know that the road to that particular truth is fraught with danger. Some of us get banned, like I am. Others get arrested, like these men who are here. But inevitably the process drives towards what we believe history also drives to: an attainment of a situation where Whites first have to listen. I don't believe that Whites will be deaf all the time. We believe that this is, you know, a last ditch stand, so to speak. There are signs right now of Mr. Vorster going to Smith to face issues. Inevitably he must know in his own mind that at some stage I must speak to everybody. Okay, but for the moment it is only a plan dismissed. Even the whole idea of Bantustans being given freedom— this is a way of accommodating political aspirations of the people, which is an inevitable accommodation of what the Blacks want eventually. But we reject this. What we want is a total accommodation of our interests in the total country, not in some portion of it. So we don't have a side program, we don't have any alternative. We believe ultimately in the righteousness of our strength—that we are going to get to the eventual accommodation of our interests within the country.

MR. SOGGOT: *Your rejection of the Bantustan solution . . . Do you consider that it has any political significance? At the moment?* ——— Yes, it has.

Is BPC a strong organization at the moment? ——— Well, I would not say it is strong. I mean, I don't know what strength you are using. For instance, I would not compare it to the Nationalist Party. It certainly has a following. It probably has got much more following than it has got members in the country. But part of what you are trying to kill has not quite died—the whole concept of fear . . . and Black people are steeped in fear. We want to get them away from this.

Black people are steeped in fear? ——— In fear, yes, they are afraid of existing structures and reactions, you know, from the System, so that they may not come forth. You do get in fact within Bantustans people coming from—coming to you to tell you that they agree with you, you guys, we know we must work for our bread. One man who

advocates propaganda in Radio Bantu here at home every day—it is
some sort of current affairs program—he came to me one time and
said, "You know, I don't believe in what I am saying, but I am paid
to say it." And I quite believe him.

Mr. Biko, you say that your present rejection has a political meaning.
—— Yes.

*Would this have a greater or a lesser meaning if your organization
were taken as in fact representative of the Black people?* —— It
would have much greater meaning.

Could you just tell us how you see that? —— At present the
. . . Let us refer to the whole Transkeian institution. I believe that if
BPC were an established organization that is known to represent the
majority interest of Black people, and if BPC were to say, We are not
going to accept the kind of independence which is being given to the
Transkei, there would be resulting action in the Transkei, in the form
of people saying to their Matanzima, We don't want this. But right
now Black people are operating under a veil of silence, and their
operational views are not known. And because BPC has not quite got
to that position where it can be regarded by everybody, all and sundry,
speaking for the majority of Black people, even when they speak about
the Transkei independence it is not sufficient for the people to come
and say they don't want this independence, because BPC hasn't developed this kind of complexion of speaking for the majority of Black
people.

*Now, assuming that it had developed that, what effect do you visual-
ize it would have on the government?* —— In . . .?

In the bargaining process? —— I believe it would have a soft-
ening process. I believe that inevitably this government will listen
to Black opinion. In my view this government is not necessarily
set on a Hitlerized [course]. I think it is biding time. From their
interpretation of the situation at the moment, the situation is such
that they can continue. Mr. Vorster can postpone some problems
and say, Well, the Colored issue will be solved by the next generation. Because he can see his way clear, even given the time of ti-
midity to which Black people have been pushed. But I believe that
as the voice which says "no" grows, he is going to listen, he is

going to begin to accommodate the feelings of Black people, and
this is where the bargaining starts. You know, any issue that you
win because of your "no" implies that you are being listened to by
those in power.

*I think the suggestion which may be made is that you are building
up a power bloc, and when you have got every man and woman in
your power bloc you will then confront Mr. Vorster? And force on him
the decision of war or peace?* ——— Yes, I said to you we don't have
an alternative. We believe that. In fact, the whole process of bargaining is then damaged in our operation. We are not interested in
armed struggle. We have stated clearly in our own documents that
we are not interested either in confrontation methods—by that
meaning demonstrations which lead to definite breaking of existing
laws, such that there is reaction from the System, what you call the
System.

Yes? ——— Now, our operation is basically that of bargaining, and
there is no alternative to it. It is based as I say mainly on the fact that
we believe we have interpreted history correctly, that the White man
anyway is going to eventually accept the inevitable.

*My Lord, I think that I would not start on the theme of the BPC.
Perhaps Your Lordship might find this a convenient stage . . .*

THE COURT: *I just want to ask him one question and then we can
take the adjournment. I think what Mr. Soggot is trying to say to you
is this, assuming now that one doesn't find any fault with your aims and
politics as such . . . But can it not be said that you are trying to achieve
your end in such a way that you are building up a hostile power bloc,
which is sort of oriented for action, and if you don't get your—if you
are not satisfied when it comes to, well, bargaining, that your power bloc
will then react and then you will have no control over the power bloc?*
——— My Lord, I don't . . .

*Perhaps I should put it in a different way. When I say that you
are preparing it in such a way, it means I am trying to convey that
the means that you adopt in order to build up the power bloc and
to conscientize people have the effect of antagonizing the Black people, and eventually you have a situation where you will not be able
to control this bloc if they don't get their claims met by the White
group?* ——— If I [may] contest the first point, My Lord, I don't

think the means [that] are used for conscientization have that effect at all of making—of antagonizing Black people, or of creating antagonism within Black people. On the contrary, what I would say is that our methods do in fact give hope. I think it must be taken in the context of a situation where Black people don't have any hope, don't see any way ahead. They are just defeated persons. They live with their misery and they drink a hell of a lot because of the kind of misery . . .

Well, that is why I say . . . ——— Now, when you speak to them, conscientizing them, what you are in fact doing is to rekindle their hope.

Yes, but the objection is not against conscientization as such. It is the manner of conscientization—pointing out to them what enemies they have in the White people. ——— Again as I said earlier on, this is just a common starting point. You are speaking about what that man knows, you are moving from there to talk about ways you go from here. You are giving him some kind of home within a group called the Black People's Convention; if you are in trouble go to the Black People's Convention. [Indistinct] You are saying this is what BPC is all about. You stand squarely on the side of the Black man, we understand the problems to be these. And they know the problem. No matter what you say to them they know the problem. As I say, they can express their problem stronger than you can. But now you move from there to create some kind of hope, some kind of opportunity. And in fact I think you are giving them some kind of psychotherapy to move away from being a defeated society to being a hopeful society, and you are not dealing out some kind of juggernaut that is going to get out of hand. When you are speaking of Black Solidarity all you are talking about really is just that feeling that you are speaking for the majority of Blacks. You are not going to have every individual placed in a room and taught point 1 to 20 which he can decide and . . . [Inaudible] No, he is just going to believe that BPC speaks for me; BPC is my movement. Right, and now my leaders are bargaining, and this is what they are saying, you know, and when we consult him he . . . says we want this or we don't want this. This is all . . . in a sense, in the same way that one is a member of the Nationalist Party. There is nothing sinister in it. You are just a member, you just support the party that to you gives you the best hope in a given society. This is what Black Solidarity is all about. It is not an army as such like some of my . . . [Voice fades]

The court will adjourn until tomorrow morning.

COURT ADJOURNS

Day Two

The Morning of May 4, 1976

Biko provides an extraordinary insight into the formation of BPC. His detailed account of various meetings has a near-visual impact and is a rare look at the dynamics of an organization—its origins, purpose and development. Biko also addresses the issues of Black trade unions, confrontation with authority, Black education, Black community programs, Black theology and South African Black Consciousness as distinct from Black Power in America.

COURT RESUMES

STEPHEN BANTU BIKO, STILL UNDER OATH

EXAMINATION BY MR. SOGGOT, CONTINUED: *Mr. Biko, I wonder whether you could not turn to the origin and formation of BPC. We covered the starting point yesterday when you told His Lordship about a SASO executive meeting at Port Elizabeth which took a certain resolution?* ——— That is right.

Would you tell us what that resolution was? ——— Well, it was mainly a resolution mandating the executive to send a team to consult with several Black organizations throughout the country, with a view to increasing the level of coordination amongst the various organizations that existed within the Black society. I think yesterday I named some of the organizations. . . .

All right, now subsequent . . . Perhaps before I take you to subsequent events, what was the thinking underlying the moving of that resolution, if you would just pause and give us your reply on the position please? ——— I think it stems from what we regard as totality of involvement with the Black community. By this we mean that Blacks must be able to offer for themselves the kind of services they need in various areas affecting them—be it in the field of culture, education, student leadership, religion and if you like even politics. Now, we felt that we had as students a valuable contribution to make to stimulate this kind of positive thinking within the Black community. And we also felt that there needed to be a certain level of coordination, consultation and sharing of views amongst the various Black organizations. Our view is that if you are in a voluntary organization as the Black man, you are there really not for yourself but on behalf of a number of people within the Black community, and that if we make this a shared effort it has the result of planned growth of the Black community in a prescribed direction.

Can you just indicate whether at this stage already the thinking was in the direction of forming some sort of organization, whatever its structure might be? —— Right. I think SASO foresaw the possibility, without wanting to ram it down the throats of the various organizations, of some kind of consultative organization in which all the organizations representing various aspects of the Black community could be represented, and in which they could share their views. And we should act also as some kind of guardian of standards of performance for each particular organization.

What do you mean by guardian of standards of performance? —— Precisely what I said earlier on—that when people do get into an organization, they are performing on behalf of the Black community, so to speak. If you are an organization of ministers, for instance, you are there on behalf of many, many people who are Christians within the Black community. So that what you want now to do in the consultative community is to make sure that you challenge anything which you feel is not in the interests of Black community, and let them defend it.

Yes, bearing in mind that later on we know that the proposal was to form what was described as a supercultural organization? —— Yes.

Had that idea crystallized yet? —— I think only the rudimentary idea of that.

Only the rudiments. Thank you. Would you carry on? Was anything done then in pursuance and in execution of that resolution? —— Yes, in the first few months of 1971 a delegation was formed by the SASO executive comprising people like Barney Pityana, myself, Mabandla, and as I said yesterday I think Aubrey was also . . . Yes, he in fact definitely was put into that organization.

Accused number 4? —— That is correct.

Is that Aubrey? —— Yes. Now, this delegation then went to see

several organizations. We made one trip to Johannesburg for SASO
because a number of little organizations are based here, namely
IDAMASA, AICA, AFECA.

Yes? —— We also had on the program then a side issue to tackle
with NUSAS. We wanted to settle some basic student problems that
were there between NUSAS and SASO.

Whatever it is, you then had a bilateral discussion? —— That is
right.

And what was the subsequent development? —— Well, I think out
of these several bilateral meetings it was decided in principle that
SASO would leave further handling of the negotiations to IDAMASA
. . . [Intervention]

That is the Ministers' Association? —— The Ministers' Association, yes. And IDAMASA was supposed to call a consultation
amongst the same organizations and others that it saw fit to call, to
a conference, you know, wherever the venue would be.

*Now, I would just like clarity on that. Was the idea at that stage that
SASO would then fall out of the picture?* —— SASO would feature
as an organization.

As an organization? —— But they would not do the calling of
other organizations to the meeting.

The initiative being left to . . .? —— To IDAMASA.

Good. Then did IDAMASA do anything about this? —— Yes, we
received an invitation to attend a consultation at Bloemfontein. I
think this was sometime in April of the same year, 1971. We sent along
Barney Pityana and Vuyelwa Nashalaba.

Is he a doctor, the latter person? —— She is a doctor.

And they went along and what was reported? —— Well, they reported that at least they had reached consensus on the idea of a
consultative organization, and they had also set up some kind of ad
hoc committee to call a further meeting of the same organizations, to
explore possible lines of consultation, in other words to look at the
issues a little bit deeper to get people to motivate and speak on the
various aspects affecting black people, at a subsequent conference.

*Would this then be the first ad hoc committee which eventually
[inaudible] after various metamorphoses in BPC? I just want to get
the . . .* —— In a sense, genetically, yes.

And was a name given to the proposed conference? —— They

decided to adopt the name National Organizations Conference.

And when was that to meet? —— The first meeting they envisaged
was to be sometime in August at Edendale, Pietermaritzburg, My
Lord.

*Now, what happened at the August meeting? First of all, were you
there?* —— Well, I was no more in SASO then but I had been invited
to this meeting to speak on some topic relating to African cultural
concepts.

Was that your topic? —— That was my topic, yes.

Yes, and would you tell us what was decided at that meeting?
—— I would have to see, you know, the Minutes to remind me
really.

I think, My Lord, it is [exhibit] LL. Was this at Edendale? ——
Edendale, yes—August.

*I wonder if he can be shown LL, please. Now, those purport to be the
Minutes of a meeting. Are those the Minutes of the meeting you are
referring to?* —— That is correct.

Have you seen this document? —— I can't remember if I have
seen it before.

Well, there is a reference to you on page 1. —— Yes, I can see that.

"Conflicts of African Society"? —— Yes.

Is that in fact what you spoke about? —— Well, the topic was
some aspects of African culture. It was the correct topic, yes.

*May I ask you to turn to page 5, please, of that document, about the
last quarter of the page, where it says, "In the discussion that followed
it was pointed out by the conference that . . ."*

—— "It was pointed out by the conference that (a) Violence
was not the answer to our political struggle. (b) Demand for
more land should be intensified. (c) Our attitude to the policy
of separate development should be made clear. (d) It is difficult
to see how one can reject the policy and yet operate within its
framework without confusing and misleading the masses that
look upon you as their leaders. They will tend to think that it
is a good policy because their leaders have accepted it in practice. The masses are normally not concerned with the ideological analysis and minute fineries. (e) Those working outside the
System do not necessarily constitute an opposition to those

working within the framework of the System. They may become a [inaudible] to those working within. (f) The process of
Black Consciousness and Solidarity does not exclude but includes all Blacks, those within and outside the government
structure of separate development. (g) We cannot regard the
System as an answer to our political future as long as it is based
on ethnic grouping and the principle of divide and rule. (h) The
African political future lies in Black Solidarity and unity of
purpose."

*Now, the first question I want to ask you, Does this reflect as far as
you remember what was said at that conference?* ——— Yes, this reflects the series of conclusions arrived at after the presentation by
Chief Gatsha Buthelezi of his paper.

*What was the main thrust, if I might use that expression, of Chief
Buthelezi's speech?* ——— Well, he spoke on the political future of
Blacks, as far as I can remember. He certainly spoke on the political
future of Blacks.

THE COURT: *He is number 6 on the agenda. Now, I see your name
appeared just below his? In brackets. Now, what is the name in brackets?* ——— The procedure at the conference was that to each speaker
there would be a main respondent who would highlight the points
made by the speaker and focus discussion around important issues in
the speech to avoid a loose discussion. So I was appointed to respond
to Chief Gatsha Buthelezi's speech. And of course the essence of his
speech was in essence an attempt to say to the meeting there is no need
for any operation except a considered support for what he regarded
as well-motivated people within the separate development policy, and
I think he mentioned specifically himself and the late Mr. C. M.
Sidamse . . .?

MR. SOGGOT: *Well, have a look at page 5, where it starts off saying
"Today."* ——— Yes.

"Chief Buthelezi stated that some Africans and some African
leaders of various African ethnic groups accept the policy of
separate development. They believe that it was a solution to the
problems of coexistence of all race groups in South Africa. He
was the odd man out because he did not accept the policy yet he
operates within its framework with clear conscience because 'My

people were compelled to comply with it.' He does not see what else could be done."

Now, does that correctly reflect part of what he said? —— That is correct, yes.

And did the house go along with that expression of opinion? —— No, not at all.

Mr. Biko, what I wanted to deal with is this: Bearing in mind the eventual outcome of . . . at the Donaldson Centre, you indicated to His Lordship that the idea was to have a—as it were, a liaison or a sort of supercultural organization? —— That is correct.

How did it come about that these political themes figured so largely at this Edendale conference in 1971? —— Yes, I think this was per mandate from the Bloemfontein meeting. The ad hoc committee was asked to examine the areas of concern in which the various organizations were working, and it had to be I think that any fear affecting Black people had to reflect a strong political complaint precisely because a lot of the problems have got essentially a political root.

If I may put the question bluntly: Was SASO or were SASO members responsible for in any way the introduction of the political thinking or political contents of this meeting? —— No, SASO was represented certainly on the ad hoc, but the main planning was between IDAMASA and AFECA, who were based here in Johannesburg and who did all the invitations and the decisions on what areas were to be covered and who should speak. I was the only SASO speaker at that meeting, and certainly all the speeches that were given reflected essentially a political grumble within the Black community.

Yes. —— And I think the most overtly political speech came from Chief Gatsha Buthelezi, who also realized the problem and pointed to it as being essentially political. And he was not invited by SASO—at that time anyway could not be invited by SASO.

Yes, then . . . [*The court intervenes*]

THE COURT: *In fact were these movements, if I may call them that, were they not primarily involved with culture, weren't they cultural organizations?* —— Some were educational, some were cultural, some were religious and there was . . . Some were, of course, a number of quasireligious like YWCA, YMCA, and then there was a senior organizations platform.

MR. SOGGOT: *Can you perhaps try and recollect what other organizations were there? You have mentioned AICA, IDAMASA, AFECA, YMCA.* —— YWCA. I would not remember the others.

You won't be able to remember the others? —— No. . . .

Mr. Koka—did he figure at all? —— Yes, Mr. Koka was there.

What was he . . . what organization? —— Mr. Koka. I am just trying to think. I don't know what he was working for at that time. I think it was some educational project which had something to do with trade unionism.

And what task was this committee given? —— The task was to draw up a working paper which would have to reflect very strongly on the kind of organization we wanted, to answer to the various needs spelled out at the Maritzburg conference.

When you say to reflect the organization, would this be in respect of its principles or its machinery or its constitution or what? —— Essentially structurally, that is, constitutionally, but also entailing the kind of thinking which was there. You know, which was spelled out at the Maritzburg meeting.

And was this committee given any particular mandate to draw a constitution along any particular lines? —— Well, I think it was given what one might call a blank check on the assumption that this would be looked at, you know, on review, at the subsequent conference.

A blank check? —— Yes, in other words there was no suggestion from the Maritzburg conference, no explicit suggestion, that this is what we want. You know, people spoke, people discussed, the people reflected their views and the ad hoc was allowed to glean material from all this in order to be able to draw up the working paper that was required for the subsequent conference.

Yes, then what was the next step? Was a working paper in fact drawn up? —— Yes. The ad hoc met immediately after the conference, where we analyzed what had been going on there, and we met once in between the two conferences in Maritzburg at Mr. Moleko's place, and I think we also met shortly before the conference . . .

And what did you draw up? —— Well, again the ad hoc felt that they were in a pretty untenable position, because some people were in Johannesburg, some people were in Durban. So they allowed a still smaller section of the ad hoc to work on a draft paper. So they asked Nkoapa mainly, with my assistance, to draw up a document. They did reduce it to some kind of thought. Now, their interpretation was a little bit varied, in that some people felt we should stick to the coordination idea and some other people on the committee felt that they had in fact amassed at the meeting a much more explicitly political orientation, and that without necessarily saying it in so many words, what the people were now looking for was some kind of vanguard movement, if I may borrow that term, to lead the entire Black Consciousness thinking. And this vanguard movement had essentially to be a political movement to be able to fulfill all the requirements of a vanguard movement.

Yes? ——— However, this thought was in the minority within the ad hoc. It was defeated in favor of drawing up a paper that reflected what people called a coordination idea, or the coordination theme of the conference.

And did they draw that up? ——— They drew it up.

What was that called? ——— Well, it was called Central Bureau for African Development, which was called CENBAD.

As a matter of interest, have you been able to lay your hands on a copy of that document? ——— No, unfortunately.

And as a further matter of interest, what was your attitude in that dispute? ——— Well, I was with the minority view.

With the minority view? ——— That is right.

And in favor of political organization? ——— That is right.

And did you persist in that view or did you give in, or what? ——— Well, I think there was a fair debate, and I think I was convinced, and I think I thereafter paid allegiance to the ad hoc's view.

To the ad hoc's view? ——— That is right.

Which was in favor of CENBAD? ——— In favor of CENBAD, yes.

Can you just tell us briefly what CENBAD projected? ——— Well, CENBAD projected an organization which would have as a basic working structure some kind of secretariat, a secretariat which would be consisting of experts in the various fields—economics, culture, education, religion—and these people would continually be doing research work and feeding their results into the various organizations that were involved with the Black world. They would certainly also act as some kind of coordinating council where reports from the various organizations would be continually . . . [Inaudible] They would draw up fund-raising papers for the various organizations. They would centralize all fund-raising for the various Black organizations. And they would also insist on maintenance of certain basic standards of performance. They actually did draw up some standards for the various spheres. They were supposedly full-time secretariat functioning to fulfill the organizations.

Now, was the next step then the meeting at the Donaldson Centre? —— That is correct.

Which took place in . . . ? —— That took place as I said between the 16th and the 19th, I think it actually started on the following day after the 16th.

Now, did you attend that conference? —— Yes, I did.

And can you . . . Perhaps I should refer you to the Minutes of that conference. My Lord, if the witness may be referred to BPC A.1. Now, Mr. Biko, could you in brief outline—and if you want to, if the Minutes confirm any aspects, refer to them—indicate to His Lordship what happened at the Orlando meeting? —— Well, in the first place those Minutes are hardly legible . . .

THE COURT: *They are hardly legible.* —— But I could . . . Unless there is a point of dispute?

MR. SOGGOT: *No, no, you can just tell us what you remember.* —— Right. Well, we started off by reading the Minutes of the Maritzburg meeting and then we were asked to present the working paper that had been drawn up by the ad hoc. It was presented, and I think there was a dispute very early in the reading of this document about the preamble of the document. I have forgotten now essentially what was wrong with it, but some members of the house felt that it was an apologetic preamble and was not focusing attention on what had been the underlying idea at the Maritzburg meeting.

Yes? —— The chairman I think . . . [inaudible] this, and I think subsequently the SASO delegation I think then walked out. It came back . . . [The court intervenes]

THE COURT: *Well, just check up on the Minutes. I think the SASO delegation wanted to move a . . . well, gave notice of a motion?* —— Yes?

Well, just speaking from memory I got the impression that that gave rise to the withdrawal of the SASO delegation? —— I think it had to do with an attempt to refuse the amendment, at least the preamble, to the document.

MR. SOGGOT: *Mr. Biko, would you just have a look at . . . On the first page of this document . . . I imagine it is your first page as well . . .?* —— Right.

The second last paragraph. I think that is what His Lordship is referring to. —— Right.

Will you just have a look at that? —— I think what I am referring to is the last paragraph where it says,

> "The SASO delegation returned and moved a motion calling on the conference to discuss the rationale in the working document."

Their target was always the rationale, which is the same as preamble.

Yes, would you carry on? —— Right. I think people had started talking about this document. They had begun to change the name, for instance, as the Minutes say, from CENBAD to Organisation for African Development, when the SASO delegation came back and re-raised the whole discussion on the rationale.

Now, can I just ask you to pause there? [The court intervenes]
THE COURT: *The working document—that was really to be in the nature of a draft constitution?* —— That is correct.

MR. SOGGOT: *But the rationale of that draft you say was opposed by the SASO crowd?* —— That is correct.

Who were the SASO people? —— The leader of the delegation was Mr. Nengwekulu . . .

Harry Nengwekulu? —— Harry Nengwekulu. Mr. Mokoape was . . . Whether he was an official of the delegation I am not quite sure now.

Is that accused number 4? —— That is correct. There were others. I just can't lay my hands now on the names.

Yes, well, let me put this to you: The one resolution is signed by Nengwekulu, Mokoape—that would be accused number 4. D. Madiba? —— That is correct—D. Madiba.

And . . . Shezi? —— Yes. I think that would constitute the full delegation.

Now, Mr. Biko, at that stage were you in SASO? —— Now, this was when?

The end of 1971? —— Oh yes, I was in SASO but I was not on the executive.

Now, do you have any personal knowledge of the appointment of those SASO men as delegates? —— No.

Have you any knowledge whether they went there with a mandate to push any particular line? —— I would not personally know.

You would not personally know? —— Yes.

And let me just ask you this: When the SASO members put their line across, what at that stage was your attitude? —— Well, it was an ambivalent attitude, as I say, because in essence I agreed with their interpretation of what was the underlying idea, the Maritzburg conference, but I was bound in honor by my agreement with the ad hoc, so in actual fact I opposed that at this meeting.

You opposed SASO? —— That is correct.

I am sorry I interrupted you, but just carry on. What happened then?
[*The court intervenes*]

THE COURT: *You were saying there was a disagreement between SASO and the rest on the question of the rationale, that is, of the preamble?* —— That is correct.

Yes, and then? They withdrew, you say? —— They withdrew and then they came back and they still pushed the same line at the meeting. I think what they did this time was to put across the idea that a political organization ought to be formed, and Mr. Morani put a countermotion to that idea. He moved that we should not accept the resolution to form a political organization because . . . [inaudible] we are not in a position to do that. Now, there was a long debate over that countermotion of Mr. Morani, which was reflecting in essence the whole—I mean, the feeling of the entire house; people were divided on it. I remember people like Mrs. Kgwari speaking very strongly in favor of a political organization. I remember that at some stage there was some adjournment, you know, for people to do counter caucusing. They got back to the debate and eventually a vote was taken, and the view of Mr. Morani was rejected by the house. The house agreed in effect that what had been foreshadowed by the Maritzburg meeting was a political organization, and that time was over for this supercultural organization which scratched at the top. What we needed was a real political organization to focus attention on real issues and to evolve a method of response from the people to political problems.

Would you say that any particular person or persons persuaded the house in favor of that resolution? Or rather against that resolution? ———— The viewpoint was widespread within the house, you know. People are not endowed with the same powers of articulation—certainly the students are much more articulate than the rest of the crowd. But I think Mrs. Kgwari too is quite articulate . . . but there are many other people who held the same viewpoint.

And what was the eventual outcome? ———— Well, after this the whole tenor of the conference changed. There was a bit of confusion because the one constitution which had been considered up to then was, you know, diametrically opposed in structure and function to the idea which was then accepted. So I think there was some other group . . . [Inaudible] There was some other smaller group set up now to specifically look at what was regarded as the cardinal point of a political movement—you know, aims, structure and so on—to present them back to the meeting. And of course the notable thing is that despite the change in emphasis people like Mr. Morani—they were opposed to a political movement at the time—still felt that . . . well, they are going to continue chairing the meeting up to the end.

And did he in fact remain in the organization, in BPC? ———— Yes, being a member of BPC, I know this; I don't know whether he has withdrawn his membership now.

THE COURT: *So is it correct to say that his attitude was that the draft constitution did not contemplate a political organization; it contemplated a cultural organization which would sort of then embrace all the other national organizations?* ———— That is correct. I think the whole house will agree that the draft constitution contemplated a cultural organization, but what he was . . . What was in focus was not so much the draft constitution but the underlying spirit of the Maritzburg meeting; that is what the people were debating about. . . . On the interpretation of the spirit—whether it was for a cultural organization or for a political organization. So in effect this resolution favoring the establishment of a political party was a censure of the interpretation by the ad hoc of the Maritzburg meeting.

Was that the type of difficulty that you people had on the ad hoc committee where you decided to join the . . . ———— That is correct. It was the same difficulty, yes. . . .

MR. SOGGOT: *Were there any people there who on the merits of the debate—namely, whether there should be a cultural organization or a political organization—opted for the cultural organization?* ———— Well, I think the starting point was that there were quite a number of people who felt like the ad hoc as a whole, you know . . . felt that we should form a cultural organization. But once debate was opened, obviously the whole idea of the ad hoc was not being questioned, and people were being thrown from one side to the other. I myself opposed the initial idea, but finally voted with the resolution to form a political organization. . . .

And did they have power to co-opt, do you know that? ———— They had power to co-opt, and this was in response to a point that I had made. When I had objected initially to the formation of a political organization embracing the whole concept of Black Consciousness, part of my line was that the platform which we had taken was not the right one, in the sense that we envisage forming a comprehensive Black organization that involved everybody, and . . . there had been no attempt by the organizers of that meeting to invite people from the Indian and Colored communities within the Black world, so that if we want to concede forming a political organization, we should go out of our way to first of all get a venue where people can all come and make sure that invitations had been sent properly, to Indian and Colored folk. But then the line was, that, well, this was just adopting this resolution in principle; we are going to put up an ad hoc, and this ad hoc will have all the powers to co-opt from the other groups, you know, people who are then going to plan a proper conference for a political organization.

Yes, and did any of the accused then come on the stage? As far as that ad hoc committee was concerned? ———— I know for a fact that Mr. Mokoape was in the original group, and I know also that several detachments . . . not so much in conference now, but amongst ourselves as people who have accepted this idea, of what kind of criteria we are going to use. I think specifically with reference to the Durban situation, we knew that there was an NIC at the time in existence, a very strong group which was pro–Black Consciousness, and I remember specifically that the names of people like Mr. Cooper and Mr. Moodley were mentioned.

That is accused number 1 and number 9? —— That is correct, yes.

Were they co-opted, do you know? —— I think . . . Yes, eventually they were co-opted because I subsequently heard of them being at meetings, at least I saw them at meetings of this group.

Now can you tell us when this ad hoc committee met again? —— I cannot remember the order, but I do remember that they had a meeting in Johannesburg early in January. They also had another meeting at Allan Taylor Residence—I cannot vow that there were no other meetings in between. . . .

Yes. Now, Mr. Biko, if you look at the second paragraph [of the Report of the Urban, Rural and Politics Commission] which refers to rural Blacks who are under various systems of control and so on, it goes on to say:

"Community service approach could be the only workable approach."

—— That is right.

And then the next paragraph goes on to say that

"No conclusion could be arrived at concerning this Black population group."

Could you tell us what that was about and what the conference had to say about it? —— I think the underlying thinking here was that rural folk are essentially the kind of people you cannot politicize through the introduction of political debate because of their hand-to-mouth existence. In this country a lot of the rural areas reflect a standard of living which is very low and an existence which is highly precarious from the point of continuity of life. A lot of kids died at an early age because of the lack of proper health facilities and so on. So that people tend to be overconcerned with matters of existence. And also another important observation is that people in such areas are in need of services which are glaringly absent in their total lives. Now, we felt that it was perhaps best for us to focus on the development of humanity and to couple that with the development of dignity and self-confidence by such Blacks, through the introduction in rural areas of community development services in whatever form. You know, subsequently this took the form of clinics and conceived agricultural schemes which were never put into implementation. . . .

Well, I will deal with that under a different heading. On the next page, page 3, the first paragraph—if you would read that please?

———— "A factor that seriously militates against an effective implementation of the ideology of BPC, Black Consciousness and Solidarity is the fragmentation of the Black population residentially. The commission decided on a strategy involving the urban residents in their local affairs by forming residents' action committees which would work against the daily oppressive activities of the System. These committees would make residents aware of the injustice of the System."

Now, can you give us the thinking behind that? ———— Yes, I think first of all the first paragraph merely points out that it is very difficult for BPC to have branches that involve all members of the Black population in a branch—in other words Colored, Indian, African, you know, who must learn to be together in the implementation of their ideas.

Is that the significance of the word "fragmentation"? ———— This is the significance of the term "fragmentation" eventually.

Yes. Carry on, please? ———— Then the second one suggests that again bread-and-butter issues are important for people in townships, and that perhaps what should be formed is what we eventually call some kind of vigilante committees of people looking after bread-and-butter issues, which is the conditions of lighting, the availability of schools and so on; and that these bread-and-butter issues should be talked about with an intention to, you know, to apply pressure to have improvement.

Now, this phrase, "These committees would make residents aware of the injustices of the System"—have you got any comment on that? ———— Yes, I think the main emphasis there would be on a common understanding which ties up with the whole idea of conscientization. People must be aware of their problems in a realistic way. They must be able to analyze their problems and to work out common solutions. In other words a community is easily divided when their perception of the same things is different. But if they all speak with one voice [such as] this is our problem here in the roads and the schools and so on, and this is our solution here, and they project this voice to whatever local authority, for instance, has to take care. The result is normally achieved that much easier.

Yes. —— So it was the usage of their common knowledge of common problems, you know, to arrive at a common solution.

COURT ADJOURNS

COURT RESUMES AFTER TEA BREAK
STEPHEN BANTU BIKO, STILL UNDER OATH
EXAMINATION BY MR. SOGGOT, CONTINUED: *Mr. Biko, will you have a look at page 4?* —— Yes.

As far as page 4 is concerned, would you have a look at the . . . It is about a third of the way down the page. "The BPC therefore resolves that . . . " —— Yes.

Would you read it, please?
—— "The BPC therefore resolves that: (1) It shall not encourage any organizations which are not representative of Blacks by BPC members. It shall in no way cooperate with Whites in mapping out a political direction. It totally rejects participation in or cooperation with System-created movements. The BPC further resolves to concern itself with the black people as such and ignore all irrelevant organizations or the ardent leadership of such organizations."

Now, does that represent BPC policy? —— Yes, I think it does, My Lord.

Now, you have already given us yesterday the benefit of your views on SASO policy in that direction. I don't want to duplicate evidence. Is there any difference in the thinking? —— There is a strong similarity.

A strong similarity? —— Yes.

And on the assumption that you people were in power, what would your attitude be towards cooperation with Whites? —— Well, . . . if we were in power and if we assume that by in power you mean we are participating in the government structures of the land, there would be no existence of Whites as a separate community as such. We would be dealing with "our community," meaning the community of our country.

And the phrase "it," meaning the BPC, ". . . totally rejects participation in or cooperation with System-created movements." Would you tell us whether the BPC concedes its policy as having nothing to do with any government organization or department or individual? —— Well, I think the stance, the political stance that we take is one of stating categorically that we shall not recognize institutions like Bantustans, like CRC, like SAIC, which are created to solve or to accommodate Blacks politically in this country. And this will go over to local institutions like Urban Bantu Councils or Local Affairs Committees. Now, this in no way implies of course that in an operational sense where such a particular institution has jurisdiction over certain areas of the communities' interests, it shall not be dealt with accordingly. For instance, if we want to get into a particular area and we have to apply through—well, through the Kwa-Zulu government,—there is no other way out, we apply to the Kwa-Zulu Government. It is a de facto situation that we are forced to accept. But we reject the central points in the creation of such bodies, which is not a solution to the Black man's problems.

Yes, now on labor and the Black man's role, I don't propose to take you through the tedium of dealing with the whole of this. But would you have a look please at page 5 paragraph (vii)? —— Right.

I wonder if you would read paragraph (a)? —— All of it?

No, just (a) please. (a) and (b) if you would? —— Yes.

"The commission recommends (a) The foundation or the founding of Black trade unions all over the country. (b) That these unions should belong to one umbrella union or council, e.g., The Black Allied Workers Union."

Now, what are the attitudes of BPC towards the establishment of trade unions and such a thing as the umbrella unions? —— Well, firstly we saw the need for the existence of a trade union, and we disputed the current fiction that Black trade unions are banned in this country. We recognize in fact that the government attaches no logic to their existence. They may be there but they have got no power to negotiate with existing government bodies on behalf of the workers. So in a sense what we were saying here was that in spite of this—in spite of the fact that there may be no sequence from the government's point of view to establishing Black trade unions—we should nevertheless establish them and we should nevertheless see or promote their coming together under an umbrella union, which would then be an independent thing controlling Black trade union work. Certainly not under BPC.

Not under BPC? —— No, just something we are just promoting.

Now, the question is whether your desire for a strong Black trade union movement was associated with any desire to cripple industry or weaken the country? —— No, I think the logic was essentially that even though they are not recognized now, the topic is so currently spoken about, it is so typical, that the mere organization of Blacks into a trade union movement which is coordinated facilitates the coming to the moment where the government will have to recognize Black trade unions.

Yes, now, let me put it squarely to you: It was suggested in this court that what was said in this conference was that BPC aimed at a general strike? —— No, what was said at this conference I think was—is— it should be contained in resolutions subsequent to this report. This is a decision of the conference about this particular report from the commission, and there is nothing in it suggesting any strikes or any strategy for a general strike.

As a matter of pure recollection, have you any recollection, or can you say whether there was any discussion about general strikes at all at this meeting? —— Certainly not.

Perhaps if I may link this particular theme up with something different, and that is . . . I don't know what page number it is, I think it is the penultimate page. The trouble is my numbers of my documents have been knocked off. It is page 44, your second last page.

THE COURT: *The beginning of the phases?*

MR. SOGGOT: *That is correct, My Lord. I want you in this context of your evidence to deal with phase (2) here, where it says, "No confrontation shall be sought with the oppressive party."* —— No, I am afraid I don't have that page here.

Mr. Biko, the problem is the numbering. Have a look at this. Have you got that, Mr. Biko? —— Yes, I have got it now.

And have you looked at phase (2)(c): "No confrontation shall be sought with the oppressive party"? —— All right, I have got it.

Now, I know I am taking you out of the chronological sequence, but would you tell His Lordship the thinking and discussion behind that proposition? —— Well, this phrase originates from the Commission on General Planning which led to the report.

You were in that commission? —— I was in the commission, yes. We had a long debate about this, not even a debate but a look at our history, you know, at the other movements which have existed and we had a look at . . . [Intervention]

Which movements? —— African National Congress, Pan African[ist] Congress and other political movements, you know, which have existed in our country, and we looked at methods of operation which seek to register a particular point. Sometimes even at the expense of breaking certain laws. An example I have in mind here is the Defiance Campaign.

What was that, just for the record? —— Well, the Defiance Campaign as I understand it was an attempt at cracking what is called petty apartheid. You know, all those notes on park benches and in Post Offices and, you know, shops, in some shops, saying Blacks this side, Whites that side. And it involved a mass demonstration by the African National Congress which implied that the membership would deliberately go and break this particular law in order to register their nonacceptance of apartheid, so to speak.

Were they arrested, do you know? —— Oh yes, there were mass arrests.

Yes? —— Now, there derived also from the PAC standpoint another campaign which involved a demonstration against passes. There were public demonstrations where passes were made up as bonfires throughout the country. Now, this is basically what we were looking at. Now, the term "confrontation" of course can be interpreted in lots of ways, you know. It can be interpreted loosely to mean what goes on between a prosecutor and a witness. It can also mean war. But specifically what they are referring to therein was directly seeking to confront the government or the Department of Police with an option of having to arrest people because they are breaking the law. This is what we were looking at. Now, we said we are not going to adopt this type of program. We don't seek confrontation in that sense.

And why not, if you don't mind such a blunt question? —— Sorry?

Why not? —— Well, I think there were several reasons which could be advanced for this, but basically confrontation has got a self-destructive content in it, in that side issues become main issues. Although your main thrust was a protest, let us say against apartheid, and you go and sit on benches and you get arrested, then a whole lot of trials will come up now, and you are to argue your way out of sitting on benches, and then sitting on benches becomes the main issue now. Whereas in fact your protest was against the very existence of apartheid. This is what we rejected basically.

What did you consider would happen if you people were to adopt similar campaigns? —— Oh, our understanding of the South African police logic is that they simply love confrontation, and also our . . . There is a basic fear in the Black community which tends to regard police as being trigger-happy.

Well, let me ask, what I really meant was, what did you think would happen to your organizations if you adopted such policies? —— We foresaw the logic again of bannings.

Of bannings? —— Yes.

THE COURT: *I think I missed that first piece of the evidence. You say they laugh at confrontation?* —— You know, police love confrontation because then they can . . .

They like it? —— Yes, because then they can . . . [Inaudible]

That is the police, now? —— Yes. The police within the . . . That is a belief within the Black community, you know, when Mr. Vorster says, "I will call my boys"—you know, Blacks understand exactly what he means.

When he says what? —— "I will call my boys."

Oh, I see. —— I think he said this against the English students who were protesting somewhere in Cape Town. You know, when they were threatening with more protests he said he would call his boys.

Now, what significance do you attach to that? —— I am saying Blacks understand this to mean he will unleash the police.

Oh, I see—boys, yes.

MR. SOGGOT: *Mr. Biko, you have now given us two aspects relating to confrontation. The one is it was opposed because of the political reasons given, and another, you feared your organizations would be banned?* —— Yes.

Any others that you can think of that were taken into consideration? —— I can't think of any specifically right now.

Now, it is common cause that the PAC and the ANC indulged in violence subsequent to their bannings? —— Yes.

Now, did the issue of violence come into your debate at all in this context? —— Never, not in the least.

Not in the least? —— No.

What was the approach of the BPC in its policy . . . How were you going to conduct yourself? —— Basically BPC accepted a third idiom: The very fact that we established ourselves in this time in history as a movement that was going to operate aboveboard implies an acceptance of the ambit of the law. In other words, we knew that we were constrained by law. There are certain things you may not do, sometimes there are certain things you may not even freely discuss, even for pure information's sake. And I think BPC has always conducted itself, certainly through my time, within the ambit of the law.

Now, in that context, what would you say about a general strike? How would the BPC, had someone proposed a general strike, have received such a proposal? —— If it . . . originated within the BPC floors I don't think it would succeed. I mean, if it is a strike which happens of its own, and in which BPC had to feature as an agent in society, you know, this is different.

Yes. Let me just put the question a little wider before I pass on from this point. The BPC as far as you know . . . At any stage after this meeting at Edendale, did it formally or informally consider strike action as one of the methods of political action? —— Certainly not, as far as I know.

Not as you know? —— No.

And still in this context, was anything kept secret in BPC? Was there as it were a nucleus or particular enclave or group which knew things but did not say? —— No, not at all. I think in any movement there are people who are more influential . . . than others, who discuss issues, but the operation of BPC is that anything has to go through

88   BLACK CONSCIOUSNESSBLACK CONSCIOUSNESS

either the conference or the executive before it can be regarded as policy.

And perhaps still in this context, although this involves a jump in time, did you ever know or hear of such a thing as a "supreme command" or some secret consultative or leadership body in BPC? ———— Not at all.

Now, Mr. Biko, if we may come back to page 5 on your document. On Black Business and Cooperative Schemes. ———— Yes?

Now, you will see there that the proposition is that Blacks should establish their own business houses? ———— Yes.

And I think that . . . there is also a suggestion that they should create their Black supermarkets? ———— That is right.

And also Black banks and floating of companies? ———— Yes.

Now, this would logically have fallen into your evidence, the context of the evidence yesterday, about African Socialism, "Ujama," and what it all amounted to in reality? ———— That is correct.

How do these proposals, which sound rather capitalist in appearance, fit in with the notions of African Socialism? ———— Yes, I think if you look carefully there, there is an operative word called "cooperative." Now, business ventures of this nature were supposed to be encouraged on a cooperative basis, in other words certainly we do want money within the Black group to circulate within the Black group. But not to the betterment of individuals who have got no relation with the whole development and growth of the Black population in this country. So that what we are encouraging is a setting up of cooperatives that can serve the Black community comprehensively, economically, in terms of in a supermarket, in terms of banks and so on. And that would have the interest of the development of Black community at heart, so that out of profits which for instance they do get they can plow back part of that profit into the development of the community.

Yes. Now, I wonder if you would then turn to page 8 of your documents . . . It is page 41 is it? I am sorry, 39.

THE COURT: *What page is it again?*

MR. SOGGOT: *Page 39, My Lord. I think on Your Lordship's copy it is the typed page 8. Have you got that, Mr. Biko?* ———— Yes.

This is dealing with the problem of Black education. ———— Yes.

*The resolution which is about two-thirds of the way down the page
is couched in . . . You will see it reads as follows:*
"*That education as it is has caused division of the Black commu-
nity, and this division militates against effective Solidarity, as
Solidarity is the vehicle towards the realization of Black Consciousness as a lifestyle. Therefore resolves: BPC should call a joint
meeting of all African, Colored and Indian teachers' associations,
that through this meeting BPC should strive to form a Black
Teachers' Association.*"
Do you remember that? ———— Yes.
Now, what was the idea of forming a Black Teachers' Organization?
———— I think it was to try and combat the existence within our
society of education which is based on a policy which is a fact, and
which has got the result anyway of dividing us Blacks. . . . We believe
generally that Bantu education, Indian education and Colored education are calculated to educate us for a role in society. Bantu education
has got a certain stultifying influence for instance on the development
of an African child. It does not train him for an independent existence.
In most instances it trains him for a subservient role and it emphasizes
all over again his Bantu-ness. If you look at the average history for
instance which is painfully taught to children I have to pay for at
school, it teaches them about Mangope and Matanzima and all that
sort of thing, and unfortunately it establishes in the minds of the kids
that themes we reject as Blacks are in fact a fact that cannot be
changed, so that it is a subtle form of propaganda, and beyond this
—teaching a kid about his Bantu-ness—it also teaches him to be a
Xhosa, a Xhosa, who is foreign from a Zulu, foreign from a Tswana
and so on, so that it entrenches in the mind of a kid the whole unholy
division of Blacks into virtual cocoons which can easily be repressed.
Now, we have got no way of changing that situation, precisely because
we do not control those who set up this system, but the least we can
do, at least at teacher level, is to let the teachers register in the minds
of the kids the germ of the ultimate truth: that though we have got
to learn this, the basic situation is a, b, c and d, you know. This is the
point of this kind of resolution.
*Yes, would you pass on to page 10, please, the "Report on Black
Communalism." That report—does it reflect the thinking on Black*

Communalism? —— Yes, I would say so. I think it was very difficult for instance to frame a resolution at the end of that report. I think
Mr. Morani was mainly responsible for this. He did a very good job
in touching on the various facets of Black Communalism.

*Was there discussion at the conferences as to whether a resolution
should be moved in regard to Black Communalism?* —— I can't
remember.

You can't remember? —— No.

*One or two points on this report. More or less in the middle of the
page, Mr. Biko, on page 10:*

> *Black Communalism, the philosophy of our fathers, is based on
> the basic respect of the Black man for the sacred value of the
> human individual as the basis for the existence of communities
> and governments."*

Does that reflect the thinking? —— That is correct, yes.

*And then would you turn to the next page, paragraph 4, if you would
read that please?* —— Do you want me to start at "Principally"?

Yes. ——

> "Principally the economic welfare of the community is basically
> the responsibility of the State itself. It shall be incumbent on the
> State to be the initiator of industry and to use the [inaudible] as
> a means of production provides . . . that individually or coopera-
> tively undertake such industry or production as they may profita-
> bly undertake, without recreating the common welfare basic mo-
> tive to the philosophy of Communalism."

Now, does that express the principle in your approach? —— Can
I just go over it quietly again? Yes, it does. I think it reflects basically
the belief that we have that the State cannot allow a complete free
enterprise system, that industry must be planned for by the State,
without necessarily curbing completely private enterprise, but certainly private enterprise must come under the fold of control by the
State.

*And how would you say the first paragraph on the next page . . .
whether that expresses your correct attitude?* —— Is that page 12?

"Business and Industry"? —— Yes.

> "Business and industry exist for the welfare of the community to
> supply service and goods to the best advantage of the community

and should subserve that purpose consciously and as legal and social obligations at ·pain of sanctions legal and social."

It is under pain of sanctions legal and social. ——— That is right. Now, I think that also expresses our basic thinking.

Your basic approach? ——— Yes.

You have no further comments, have you, on what is written here about Black Communalism? ——— No, not at this stage.

Good, and then finally to get back to the "Report of the General Planning and Organisation Commission"? ——— Yes.

Now, you will notice that it is couched in phases, so-called? ——— Yes.

Can you tell us what the word "phase" means there? Or how the word "phase" came to be adopted? ——— No, I think . . . in fact I don't think this phase 1, phase 2, phase 3, featured as such in the discussions. My understanding of it is that it is purely the sub-topicing devised by the writer of the report. We certainly discussed, you know, broadly. We never said this is now phase 1, this is now phase 2 and so on.

Now, there is as you will notice a [inaudible] Membership Drive Project foreshadowed by, to stick to the nomenclature, phase 1, paragraph (c)? ——— Yes.

"Three-Year Membership Drive Project for a membership target of one million?" ——— That is correct.

Now, can you remember who suggested that? ——— Is that in the commission?

Yes? Or in the plenary discussion where members were suggested? ——— I don't remember.

And as far as confrontation goes, was there any suggestion that there should be no confrontation in the initial period, by implication that confrontation was to come later? ——— No, there was no such implication.

Now then, we have it on the next page that . . . That is on page 45, My Lord, and it will be your page 14, I think, Mr. Biko. In the middle of the page, the convention noting that people present were not representative of the Black population? ——— Yes.

Can you tell us what that was about? ——— Oh yes. Well, I think what it said was based on the people who were at the conference at that time. They did not represent a cross-section of the population and certainly did not come from all the possible towns in the country. Now, our idea of a conference had been that it must be as widely represented as possible, so that we could be able to [inaudible] decisions binding the greater part of the Black community, so to speak. So I think this is a reference to the sample which was present at the meeting.

Yes, now after that meeting the next meeting I believe was your next conference—is that correct? I'm at the end of the year, which would have been your first conference? —— That is correct, yes.

And there certain resolutions were taken? —— That is correct, yes.

Would you say that they were in broad terms in conformity with the resolutions adopted at the Edendale meeting? —— Yes, from my study of the Minutes certainly. I was not at that meeting but . . .

You were not at that meeting? —— Yes.

I don't propose to go into any of the details of that meeting. I think that I have overlooked one thing, Mr. Biko, and that is phase 4 on page 13. —— Yes?

That says "Crisis Situational . . ." Can you very briefly tell us what that was about? —— That is the basic thought which occurred to the commission, that was that in any given situation of oppression there were momentary flashpoints during which a crisis manifested itself. To give an example, there might for instance be in a certain area in the country . . . strikes coming out. This in a sense is a crisis situation, in the sense that the Black community which is without leadership is faced with the need to respond to an issue, and as we said earlier on, often what happens in such situations is that our people become targets for sometimes brutal action, mainly from the police force of the country. That is the time of crisis we are referring to. Now, we are faced with having to decide what to do with such situations, as BPC, and certainly the commission could not come up with an overall blueprint of how to deal with such situations because often the situation is dictated by factors which are highly local, so we said it shall depend on whatever BPC branch is nearby that particular situation. I think that is the significance here of that term "situational."

How did it come about that you didn't go to the December conference? —— I had just been employed and I had been given a task, which was the production of a yearly book called *Black Review,* and the deadline for that publication is normally at the latest the 15th of January, if you start at the beginning of the year.

Now, Mr. Biko, we know that you were restricted. —— Yes.

And therefore you did not presumably participate in the activities of organizations, of SASO and BPC any further? —— Yes.

Did you receive documents put out by the organization? —— No, I think I got one document only.

Did you keep track of its literature? —— Well, there is a SASO branch at King William's Town, and in fact there is a regional office there. We do get also in the course of our office work a lot of SASO documents getting sent in, and BCP is one organization . . . [The witness speaks indistinctly] and from that point of view I do read some stuff and documents.

I just want to deal with this in an overall form. From your knowledge of the organizations after your restriction, would you say that there was any change in the ambit of their intentions? —— I have not formed that impression at all.

You have not? —— No.

Now, I want you to deal with the question of your community programs which would touch SASO and BPC. You yourself were involved in the BCP program, is that correct? —— That is correct, yes.

Now, I wonder if you would tell His Lordship what work you did, what work the BCP did and the extent to which conscientization as a process took place in these communal projects? —— Yes. The approach of BCP is three-pronged. First we engaged in the form of direct community development projects which are in the form of clinics, churches and so on. And then we engage in what we call home industries—these are economic projects in rural areas mainly, sometimes in urban areas as well, which are in the form of cottage industries, producing one article or the other. And the main purpose here is to give employment to people, and also to offer some kind of technical training in that particular skill, so that they can themselves go and live off that skill if they like. And thirdly we do leadership-training courses.

What is that? —— Now, we have specific categories, like we have women's courses which entail leadership training in specific women's skills, now, like sewing and knitting and crochet work, cookery and that sort of thing. We had for a long time, but no more now, training offered in the field of religion. And the particular topic we concentrated on then was participation by the Black leadership within the church in the decision-making processes of the various churches, with a view to airing the views of the Black man within the church structures. We also looked at Black Theology, and this was in fact where people like Dr. Manas Buthelezi became very useful. And of course we also had some youth programs in the beginning which went out to certain towns. We no more have them now.

Yes? —— Now, the logic here is a simple one, particularly with the community-development projects which form the bulk of the BCP work. It is essentially to answer to that problem which was diagnosed by—or rather mentioned by—us yesterday: that the Black man is a defeated being who finds it very difficult to lift himself up by his bootstrings. He is alienated—alienated from himself, from his friends, and from society in general. He is made to live all the time concerned with matters of existence, concerned with tomorrow, you know, What shall I eat tomorrow? Now, we felt that we must attempt to defeat and break this kind of attitude and to instill once more a sense of human dignity within the Black man. So what we did was to design various types of programs, present these to the Black community with an obvious illustration that these are done by Black people for the sole purpose of uplifting the Black community.

Yes? —— Now, where there is that we should not preach. We believe that we teach people by example. We believe that Black people as they rub shoulders with the particular project, as they benefit from that project, with their perception of its being conducted by Blacks, they begin to ask themselves questions and we surely believe that they are going to give themselves answers, and they understand, you know, that This kind of effort has been a lesson for me, I must have hope. In most of the projects we tend to pass over the maintenance of the project to the community. For instance, where I stay in King William's Town we revived a community creche, which was serving a basic need for the community in that a number of mothers could not go to work because they had to look after babies and toddlers. Or if they do go to work it implies that kids who are supposed to be school-going must stay behind looking after the toddlers. So that it became clear to us that this was a strong community need to provide a creche to that community. And we revived a creche which I attended actually when I was young . . . but it had gone defunct. And after a year . . .

What is it called? ——— We call it the Ginsberg Creche.

Yes? ——— After a year and a half of operating the creche we devised a system whereby we could pass over the running of the creche to the community. It has . . . It is now in fact being run by the community, and the community's appreciation of the significance of the effort is not lost to us. We are aware that they understand the precise intentions of having a creche like that. It is not only to provide the facilities, but it is also to encourage them to live on their own efforts. So that they have now to subsidize the creche more than we; they do.

THE COURT: *How does BCP link up with BPC?* ——— There is no structural link, My Lord, whatsoever.

MR. SOGGOT: *Right. Now, the community projects run for example by SASO, would you answer that now?* ——— Yes.

To what extent . . . Would you tell us what they were in brief outline, and the extent to which Black Consciousness was preached in these activities, and the extent to which BPC was sold or advertised or propagandized then? Would you deal with that? ——— Right. SASO as far as I remember had projects like what you call the New Farm Projects. I don't know if you have got an official . . . a description of this in one of your papers. But essentially the New Farm Project was a combination of two or three phases. The first one arose out of us being invited by a particular clinic to assist in this clinic. The clinic is outside Durban in an area called Inanda.

May I interrupt you? I want to show you a document called "SASO, the New Farm." Can you identify it? ——— Yes. This is the report that we wrote at the end of that project.

THE COURT: *Are you handing that in as an exhibit?*

MR. SOGGOT: *If we may do so, My Lord. I think that that would be Exhibit YY. I want you to carry on briefly on the basis of that document and tell us what that project was about and how it served your purposes.*

——— It was essentially a combination of preventive and curative medicine, and as I say it arose out of us being invited by a clinic in the Inanda area to assist on certain days to combat what the clinic found to be an unending queue over the days that they were functioning. We sent out a number of medical students in advanced years to assist the one doctor who was there. And of course we thought—or the medical students suspected from a rough study of the people they were treating—that there were essentially one or two or three major complaints amongst the people, which were in the form of an outbreak in that community, and they sort of interested us in doing a research in that area, which we did, to find out the living conditions of the people and the kind of food they eat, the kind of water they drink, where they get it from, and the living standards basically. Now, we found that some of the problems stem from a water complaint. People were getting water from a dam, and the dam was infected with bilharzia. This manifested itself in several complaints coming to the clinic on a weekly basis. So that we thought this heralded two things: firstly, a treatment of the root cause, which we interpreted as the preventive medicine, which implies provision to the people of an alternative water supply.

Yes? —— We had to lead taps from the Inanda/Phoenix settlement, for a start, with the ultimate aim of finding boreholes within the community for them to get an alternative water supply.

Well, Mr. Biko, whatever it is, you entered into this project in an attempt to deal with it in a scientific and as organized a way as possible? —— That is correct.

And are your methods and findings conveyed in this particular report? —— Certainly, yes.

Now, what is of interest is . . . First of all, were you involved in this yourself? —— I was involved myself, yes.

And you and fellow SASO men? —— Yes.

Did you talk Black Consciousness to people? —— Not in the context of this project. Certainly what we did was to encourage people, you know, to . . . Well, people could not understand in the first instance who we were, we got out there being a team of students, and we had to identify ourselves. We had to say to them where we came from, and of course the next question is, Oh, are you being paid by the government? They did not understand why a number of students just turn up to be of assistance. It did not happen before; it had always been White students. So we had to explain our role. Our role was a simple one: to assist in the upliftment of the Black community and to help Black people, like in squatter areas, like in that one, to diagnose their problems and to participate in the solution of those problems.

Did you yourself push Black Consciousness ideas of any kind expressly or implicitly with the people? —— No, certainly nothing beyond explaining why we were there, you know, and who we were.

And was there any propagandizing of any kind in favor of BPC? —— No, certainly not.

Now, what other projects were carried out in which you participated? I don't want you to go through the whole gambit of them ... belonging to SASO and BPC? —— Yes, I think as I have stated, in what you call a Home Education Scheme, which was undertaken in an area called Dadoodoo. This was outside Umkomaas, on the South Coast of Natal.

Yes? —— And there we were dealing with a community that had no very immediate educational institutions to further their studies. We were dealing with people who were corresponding matric, corresponding J.C., corresponding Standard 6 and so on. And the type of assistance we gave was to put out several students to deal with specific subjects. And of course the number of people who were doing that subject varied. I used to take history and English lessons and to some extent Latin, and again the number varied accordingly. It was a straight sort of tutor/student relationship. We encouraged the people to get on, but they were basically already corresponding with correspondence houses and ... [we] were just assisting them with the material.

And again the question is, Was there any propagandizing, and of Black Consciousness expressly? —— No.

Or of BPC or of SASO? —— No.

Any other project? May I say this is what you did? What was the policy of SASO in regard to these communal or community projects? —— There was in fact specific policy directive: that people must deal with the people in terms of what they have come to do there, which is that particular project, and no preaching must be engaged in. This was Mr. Pityana's policy. He was the general secretary who was coordinating all these projects.

Do you know whether that directive was reduced to a document? ——— I do not remember specifically this happening.

You don't remember? ——— No.

Is there any other project? ——— Those were the two that I was engaged in. I was partly engaged in literacy. As I indicated earlier on to His Lordship, yes. We planned for a literacy course, and I myself underwent some training in particular methods of literacy but I never really was involved in a broad program dealing directly with the community.

Yes, Mr. Biko, as far as Black Theology is concerned, I think it is common cause that this was something which was propounded and adopted by SASO and BPC, is that correct? ——— That is correct.

Can you in a very brief form, because there has been evidence on this, tell us the role which Black Theology played in the SASO and BPC organizations? ——— Yes, I think this is . . . Well, as far as my understanding of why it features so much . . . would stem from an understanding again of the Black experience. Essentially the Black community is a very religious community, which often reflects on beings, in other words, What is my purpose in life, why am I here, who am I? But I mean in this particular context in which we as oppressed people find ourselves in this country, inevitably you come to a block in your thinking, when you think about God, a God who is all loving, all knowing, but a God who allows me at the same time to be at the receiving end of suffering. So that it was beginning to create problems amongst youth especially. This whole religious question—what is God's intention with us, what does he want.

Are you yourself a believer? ——— I am myself an Anglican. . . . *Now, if we can go back to page 22, please. You will see there, just before paragraph 1, there is a phrase*

> *"The unexpected overseas press reaction to the formation of SASO, which interpreted the movement as [indistinct] of Black Power along the American . . ."*

It must mean American "lines," not American "lives." ——— Can you just tell me the page?

It is page 22, more or less over here. ——— All right, fine.

It is in the paragraph commencing "This portfolio . . ." —— All right.

What would you say about Black Consciousness and Black Power— are they the same thing? —— Well, they certainly are not. I think the end result or the goal of Black Power is fundamentally different from the goal of Black Consciousness in this country, that is, Black Power now in the United States where it was conceived . . .

Yes? —— Black Power is the preparation of a group for participation in already established society, a society which is essentially a majority society, and Black Power therefore in the States operates like a minority philosophy. Like, you have Jewish power, Italian power, Irish power and so on in the United States. The Black people are merely saying that it is high time that they are not used as pawns by other pressure groups operating in American society. They must themselves form themselves into a definite pressure group, because there were common problems with Black people in the United States, but essentially they accept that they are a minority group there, and when they speak of bargaining—you know, which word they use— they are talking within the American context of using the ballot box. They want to put up the kind of candidates they like and be able to support them using their block votes. So in that sense Black Power is a minority philosophy in the United States. . . . And the other thing which causes that: The American Black man is essentially, you know, he is accepted, he is truly American in many ways. You know, he has lived there for a long time. All he is saying is that "Man, I am American, but you are not allowing me to live like an American here in America." He has roots with Africa . . . but he does not reject his American-ness. . . .

Now, another odd point . . . Without referring to the documentation, the policy of SASO appears to have been against dialogue between the South African government and other countries. Is that correct? —— Yes, that is partly correct.

Can you give us the benefit of SASO's views on that particular theme? And why that was your policy? —— Yes. As I said yesterday, we saw international pressure on South Africa as important in the whole process of forces that were calculated to be able to change the viewpoint of the South African government concerning us Blacks.

Yes?—— Now, the whole dialogue approach to our—to Africa
—we thought and ·believed had been devised by Mr. Vorster and his
Foreign Affairs Department precisely to undermine Africa's solidarity and to begin to gain friends in Africa, so that South Africa could
afford to face the future with less of a combined criticism. We are of
the belief that if Africa loses its unity in criticizing South Africa, we
might get to a stage where Mr. Vorster can justifiably claim support
for his policy from countries outside South Africa. We never for a
moment thought that Mr. Vorster's intentions in Africa were anything but to promote South Africa as it exists, so that we felt therefore
we should discourage any country from entering into dialogue with
South Africa as of now.

*Was there any intention to weaken South Africa diplomatically in
order to weaken it as a regime?*—— Not really. The main intention
as I say was to make sure that the total pressure that Africa continually applies on South Africa through criticism remains intact.

*Yes, now Mr. Biko, you in fact are the author of many documents
inter alia under the title, shall I say nom de plume, of Frank
Talk. . . .*

THE COURT: *Before you deal with that, and before we leave this
[Exhibit] AAA document, now under the heading of "Organization
(b)" you say, "SASO is committed to liberation, therefore conscientization programs should be embarked upon." Now, what did you have in
mind by conscientization programs?*—— Well, conscientization, My
Lord, essentially . . . I don't know if I have dealt with it already
. . . is assisting Blacks in being able to grapple realistically with their
problems . . . not from a defeatist point of view, but from a point of
view which allows them to work out solutions, in other words to
elevate a certain level, I mean their level of critical awareness. Now,
conscientization programs are precisely the type of program we embark upon in communities . . . In other words, if we have got a
physical program like a clinic, we are helping the community to
remove from their mind the defeatist element that good comes only
from Whites. Here are Blacks working amongst us. Here are Blacks
achieving a particular end which [it] is thought could not be achieved
by us as Blacks. This helps in the building up process. This is conscientization. And liberation precisely implies that liberation from

present notions: We say that we as Blacks cannot achieve anything; anything good must come from White society.

Why didn't you deal with it under (a)—"SASO is committed to self-reliance"? —— Well, I think this is the point, breaking down at a convenient spot. I mean, I don't think there was any very profound thinking in breaking it down.

MR. SOGGOT: *Mr. Biko, I am going to refer you to two documents, the one is Annexure—I think it is 8—"What I Like by Frank Talk."* —— Yes.

Now, I am not going to take you through this document. Do you remember this document? I mean, do you remember the contents of this document? —— What I mean is what particular . . .

THE COURT: *Well, tell him what it is about.* —— Yes, what is the topic?

MR. SOGGOT: *Oh, I am sorry. "An Important Determinant to South African Politics". . . . You referred to it yesterday.* —— An important determinant to South African Politics?

Here—"an important determinant—" this is the one I referred to yesterday? —— Yes.

Do you remember this particular document? —— I remember.

Can you tell us in a nutshell what you were trying to convey in this document? —— Well, I was emphasizing in our minds the fact that on the face value Blacks are the fiend within Black politics, he cannot be taken to be reflecting the thinking that is going on within the minds of Black people? Because all too often fear tends to play a very important element . . . In other words, people are stopped from expressing their true thoughts because they fear what will happen to their jobs; they fear what will happen to their own personal freedom. I was referring to things like banning orders, and I think the article had been written at about the time Mr. Nemoramgoban was banned. Now, he was a particularly brave man. In the Durban situation he spoke forthright[ly], and all that had happened to him after he reestablished the NIC was to get another banning order. So that now it reflects generally the silence in many areas within the Black community, reflects not so much their nonthinking, but much more their fear about what will eventually happen to them if they stand up to be counted. I think that is what is meant. And of course it was also being

used as a rationale for accepting second-rate politics, namely Bantustans. I have heard Gatsha Buthelezi, for instance, saying something
like he is not going to willingly lay his neck to be chopped, you know,
he is going to use the apartheid institutions to achieve the same end
as you SASO blokes. He said this to me across the debating floor.

Yes, now Annexure 9, "Focus, Ugandan Asians and a Lesson for Us"
—can you again give us a concise idea of what it intended to convey?
———— Yes. I think at about the time that Amin decided to order an
exodus of Indians from Uganda, there arose in South Africa some
extensive debate about the significance of the pact between Africans,
Coloreds and Indians. Now, in Durban this was handled in a very
naughty manner I think by a gentleman called "Politikus" who used
to write in one of the Indian papers there—I think it is . . . I have
forgotten the name of the paper; but anyway, it was a man we knew,
and he was trying to exploit the Ugandan situation to create amongst
Indians a panic mentality about their pact with Africans and Coloreds
within the sphere of Black Consciousness.

Yes? ———— Now, the article was in fact written to place the logic
of the Ugandan situation in perspective, that where you enter a country with a passport in your back pocket and you refuse to identify with
the people of that country, you are laying the very field of a suspicion
which will later crystallize, that anybody who is of Africa must be
fully of Africa in terms of his citizenship, in terms of his complete
identification with Africa, and not have British citizenship, a passport
in his back pocket, his money somewhere in a bank in Europe—and
thus hope to exploit the riches of Africa. This is what we are criticizing there. And I was trying to point out that there are in fact differences between the Ugandan situation and here. I mean, our Indian
community is essentially rooted here—that figures: We are citizens—
but as long as a mentality which is similar to that one in Uganda is
to be found here there will be problems.

Yes, now, Mr. Biko, as far as SASO/BPC documentation as a whole
is concerned—I am talking about the material which you are aware of
—have you ever had occasion to believe that what was said or written
had or was likely to arouse feelings of hostility? ———— Not in the least.
As I said yesterday, the primary intention, and I think the result
achieved, has always been that we are giving hope and a way out to

the Black community who are faced with an apparently impossible problem right now. They do not know where to turn, they have lost hope, and we are trying to reinstill a sense of hope through their being together, and I think there has nothing been . . . I mean, there has been nothing in the SASO language which has been new to the people. It is merely starting from an examination of the problems that we experience as Black people—to have a point of departure to inviting people into BPC so that we can move towards a solution of our problems.

Yes? —— The language used by SASO is pretty, I think, commonly used in the Black community, and as I said yesterday often perhaps expressed in what I'll call vulgar terms. So there is nothing which would create any sense of hostility. And the response from various meetings called by BPC or SASO, that I can recall, is one of a sense of new identity. You know, I mean, I recall when I got home and when the first branch of BPC was lodged in King William's Town, a particular friend of mine who is a worker in King saying this to me, you know: I never knew that I would at this late stage discover myself; you guys have given me something to live for. There is a kind of hope that we are trying to instill in the Black community as BPC and SASO.

Have you any comment to make on the language used by Blacks and the same language used by Whites? For example on the word "kill"? Does that . . . Is that word used in any way differently? —— Yes, I think His Lordship did refer yesterday to this—that the African language is a very . . . What word did he use, now?

THE COURT: *Idiomatic?* —— Idiomatic. That is correct. Idiomatic —and this occurs both on the offenses and defenses. If the court can allow me just to give an example. You do find an expression in a shebeen, for instance, where a black man says . . . [The witness quotes in Xhosa] Now, that is a Xhosa expression. It will cause no headaches amongst Xhosas; it is properly understood. But when you interpret it into English—and this is . . . the problem sometimes in the SASO documents—you express in English and the idiom is different. Now, that expression in English implies—if the court can allow me the privilege to say, "Whites are shitting on us." Now, that is a very strong expression in English. I would never use it. But in Xhosa you

can easily say it. Now, simply because the language accommodates
that kind of idiom . . . it has been said all the time that Afrikaans and
the African languages are rougher than English. English claims to be
a fine language and so on. That is precisely because they don't accommodate a very honest expression sometimes of basic feelings, you
know.

But you use one word in a number of ways. . . . ——— That is right.
You see, so that often a document . . . because you are reading [it]
in English sounds very very strong. If you were just to put it in the
vernacular of the area you would find it so weak that it would be
absolutely of no significance to the people.

MR. SOGGOT: *Well, the phrase "The White man wants to kill us," for
example. Would that have different shades of meaning to different
people?* ——— No, if you say . . . [The witness quotes in Xhosa] for
instance, now that means that "They are making the lives difficult for
us." You can say it for instance if you are required to stand in a queue
for a long time. You can say it if you are supposed to do hard work.
You can say it in many situations, but precisely the same expression.
As My Lord was saying just now, it implies different things in different
situations. But it is the same word.

It sounds like an elastic Black metaphor, is that right? ——— That
would be correct.

THE COURT: *But I mean, you can do a lot of things if a man uses it,
sees him using it.*

MR. SOGGOT: *Mr. Biko, can I refer you to the Allan Taylor Residence
meeting on the 19th of March 1972, where a gentleman called Harry
Nengwekulu spoke?* ——— What was the occasion?

It was a Sharpeville Day I believe? ——— Oh yes.

You were there? ——— I was there, yes.

And do you remember that Harry Nengwekulu spoke? ——— Yes,
he spoke there.

*And can you tell us whether you and/or other people had discussions
with him about his speech afterwards?* ——— I think it was myself and
Mr. Pityana—I don't know if there were others—who had a talk with
him. I think he had overused in his speech some words which could
be subject to lots of misinterpretation. He was just busy saying, well,
you know, with reference to the White population . . . if I remember

. . . as a violent population, referring to the various things they do to Blacks which he called violent. Now, we were quite happy with his explanation, but we felt that at that time, you know, the press was in the habit of deliberately picking up negative things in what was said by SASO or was done by SASO people, so that we felt that this was the kind of thing which would lend itself to misinterpretation, and we spoke to him strongly about it, precisely because he was in fact inebriated.

COURT ADJOURNS

The Afternoon of May 4, 1976

This cross-examination begins the bitter duel between Biko and the State prosecutor, Advocate Attwell, which will mark virtually all further testimony; the exchanges are often laced with sarcasm and viciousness. Attwell almost immediately attempts to link SASO with the banned African National Congress (ANC) and the Pan-Africanist Congress (PAC), both allegedly Communist organizations. Attwell also scrutinizes the clandestine nature of SASO's movement and ideas. When asked what area of South African life might be most receptive to change, Biko replies "sports." Attwell takes Biko through a series of questions, seeking an explanation of "conscientization." Biko also points out that Blacks perceive Whites, government and the System as being virtually interchangeable. Biko explains what is meant by "Black" as opposed to "Non-White," and the need to avoid creating a "leadership cult." Biko also discusses whether or not BPC is a political organization or a political entity.

COURT RESUMES

STEPHEN BANTU BIKO, STILL UNDER OATH

MR. SOGGOT: M'lord, I have no further questions.

CROSS-EXAMINATION BY MR. ATTWELL: *Mr. Biko, would it be correct to say that you are in fact one of the founding lights of both SASO and BPC?* ——— That would be more correct about SASO and less correct about BPC.

And one of the foremost protagonists of the Black Consciousness idea? ——— That would be correct.

And that in no small measure were you responsible for the constitutional framework of these organizations and many of their basic policies, as we have come to know them through the documents? ——— To a great extent, yes.

Now, certain tendencies had exhibited themselves to you and certain of the other founding members at a stage which pressed you into the idea of forming a body like SASO, is that correct? —— Correct.

And this was in fact at that time something of a unique organization to found, was it not? —— Correct.

In fact, it had no parallel in our history before? In fact, I think one can say in history there has been no parallel to the SASO organization? —— Outside the country I do not know, but inside the country certainly not.

And that it was a venture which must have been fraught with numerous dangers and one which you approached I should imagine with great caution? —— Correct.

In the past, organizations which had worked primarily for the Black people had had a somewhat difficult path and history in this country? —— This is correct.

And there are references in the documents to the past organizations described in terms such as "which stood high in the defense of Black dignity and righteousness which were banned during the sixties"—I gather that is a reference to the banned African National Congress and the Pan-Africanist Congress? —— Well, it may be.

Well, how did you understand those references in documents? —— I would have to pinpoint a specific reference.

I will come back to specific references. Just now, if we may, it is true, is it not, that at the formation of . . . If we can start with SASO being the earlier organization . . . the work which had been done in the past on the part of Blacks by other organizations was closely scrutinized? —— From the student front, yes.

Had there previously been a Black student organization? —— There had been groups like ASA, which is the Association of South African Students—I am not quite sure now what the full names were —and ASUSA which was the African Students Union of South Africa.

Now, these organizations apparently failed, is that correct? —— Yes they faded, I would say, in history.

Now, their efforts must have been analyzed by you people when you formed SASO? —— To some extent, yes.

Now, what is the reason for the failure of those organizations? —— Well, they certainly were not molded in the same form that

SASO was. They were not a federation like SASO was. SASO was a
federation of SRC's from the various campuses. They were individual
member organizations, and I think they put forward policies to which
people had to subscribe, you know, as part of their affiliation to the
organizations. And certainly I think their interests were not mainly
on the campus. Their interests were in linking up the students with
the outside scene. In other words, they were more politically charged.

More politically charged? ——— Yes. So that they had in a sense to
relate to the historical survival of these various national movements
to which they had affiliation, like ANC and PAC.

*Were ANC and PAC specifically studied by yourself and the other
founder members of SASO to try and ascertain what these organizations had done and where they had gone wrong?* ——— Not seriously.

Not seriously? ——— No. I think reference could have been made
at one meeting or the other to failures of ANC and PAC or even in
more broad terms to failure of past movements, but no one ever was
charged with the responsibility of doing a study on PAC and ANC
and making known their findings to us about it.

In your view what was the failure of the ANC and the PAC? ———
Quite frankly I have not done a study on this myself.

So you are not in a position to comment on that? ——— Well, I can,
yes, I have some personal views which have not been [sufficiently] well
formulated to be aired in a court like this.

*I see there are references in the documents too to the banning in the
sixties of the previous organizations which had created a void in the
Black community?* ——— That is correct.

Which SASO and then later BPC were designed to fill? ——— As
part of that void, yes.

This vacuum that had been created? ——— Yes.

*Would you go along with those sentiments that the bannings of the
organizations in the sixties . . . I gather primarily the PAC and ANC
had created a void which SASO and BPC were designed to fill?* ———
I think what we SASO founders noticed as being most glaring was
absence of output from the Black universities of people who could give
some kind of lead to the Black community in a properly formulated
direction. What was happening now was that people were going to
universities to acquire degrees, and to so to speak melt and join the

rest of the professional elite that was not well motivated within our society. So we felt it was the duty of a student group to contribute in a properly formulated manner to the community, because again in the Black community it is only a tiny minority of people who ever reach university, and we feel that it is wrong for people [who] have opportunity not to think of others who do not have. So that part of what you learn at university must be plowed back into the community, and this can only happen if there is a guiding student organization which operates on Black campuses.

To revert for a moment to the previous Black student organizations which you did refer to, did they have, in the same way that SASO has, a goal of general liberation of the Blacks? —— I think in a sense, yes. I mean, I must point out that ASA and ASUSA were very sick and more or less dying by the time I got to university so that I cannot form a very good judgment of what they had to offer, but I do know historically that they were more associated, they were more or less student wings of the national movements that were there. ASA was more in line with ANC thinking, and ASUSA was more in line with PAC thinking.

And what was ANC thinking and what was PAC thinking at the time? —— As I said to you, I cannot analyze very intelligently before this court, I just know that historically it was said at the time.

You see, there is also I think in one of the reports, or some of the reports at GSC's and things, an indication that branches found when they went round trying to sell SASO and build up membership, that there was a reluctance on the part of many Blacks to commit themselves or identify themselves with SASO because they were afraid that SASO was something like ANC or PAC? —— I think I pointed out in my evidence-in-chief the main debate around SASO, I think it was not fear as such. I think once SASO was launched, the main debate was whether to go along with the new line which some people accused of being a pro-apartheid line, and these are mainly NUSAS-orientated people, and others attack for being all inclusive, you know, in the sense of Indians, Africans and Coloreds having a common identity. These were the two main streams of thought.

Did you never come across any complaints on the part of any SASO or BPC officials that they found a reluctance on the part of members

of the public to identify with either of the organizations because of a
fear that somehow these organizations were in a way like or related to
the ANC or PAC, which had been banned? ———— Yes, I think that
debate occurred right within the founding group. That was before
SASO was actually launched, and the main emphasis even there was
that precisely because it is an organization to take care of the interests
of the Blacks, it is going to meet with lots of attacks from [a] society
like ours, which essentially looks after the interests of Whites, and
therefore gets scared of anything which speaks of Blacks alone and
their interests. This was the trend right in the founding stages of
SASO.

In other words that some people would identify it as akin to PAC and
ANC? ———— This was not necessarily the emphasis; the emphasis was
merely the fact that it speaks for Blacks, and the interpretation if you
like was that the powers that be are against Black interests, so to
speak, and anything which therefore protects Black interests is likely
to suffer.

And you also gave evidence that at the inaugural BPC convention
during the general planning and administration commission, the ANC
was considered in the context of the methods [they] had adopted [and]
which BPC would consider at that stage [but] then opted for some other
... [The witness intervenes] ———— This was not at the plenary session,
really; this was at the commission discussions.

During the formation of BPC? ———— Yes. The commission, which
was about three members, looked at those methods and decided that
they are going to discard that line and offer a different line.

Now, it must then have been the object of the founder members of
these organizations, both SASO and BPC, to make it very clear to people
that these two organizations were not like ANC or PAC? ———— Well,
not in that sense. I think you must understand one thing about the
Black community again: that ANC and PAC are important movements in the history of the Black community in the sense that they
affected people's lives and they created allegiances. When you are a
new movement and you want to be in favor with everybody, any
untoward reference to past organizations to which people may have
some rudimentary allegiance may harm you, so that BPC and SASO
certainly never made any untoward movement towards this allegation

to any particular movement at any stage. We spoke positively about ourselves and as little as possible about anybody else except existing groups, you know, like White society and its power structures.

A previous defense witness, accused number 1, told the court that BPC was keen not to make the mistakes which the ANC and PAC had made? —— This is very well possible.

Now, what mistakes would they have been? —— Well, as I said in the first instance during my evidence-in-chief, the choice of most of these organizations which put you foursquare against the powers that be in the form of demonstrations, civil disobedience and so on. You know, one can make an inference from that. I mean, it is clear that we said previously, No confrontation. It implies obviously that someone else somewhere in the past chose the confrontation method. What I am saying is that we did not go out of our way to criticize what ANC and PAC did. We merely stated what we are going to do, which is no confrontation. . . .

Now, SASO, I should imagine, at its inception and during its first conference or two, must have advanced very cautiously—would I be correct? —— Well, depending on . . . cautiously on what basis, but I mean on some basis, yes, we did advance cautiously.

In the sense that it was a unique experiment? —— That is correct.

It was attempting to do something in a field where previous organizations had failed and met a harsh end, if I can use that phrase? —— That was not our main concern.

And it would probably be under close scrutinization of the authorities? —— We thought about that, but we did not over-bother about that, and we were quite convinced of what we were doing.

Now, would you agree with me that SASO could hardly openly preach violent revolution or anything like that? —— Well, SASO would not do so if it did not intend doing so, but if after founding itself as an organization aboveboard it had that intention, I think it would have proceeded in a different direction.

It nevertheless could hardly openly advocate a violent revolution or violence against the authorities? —— Precisely. Because this was not the purpose.

Even if it was, it could hardly have openly advocated it in documents and its constitution et cetera? —— Well, I have not experimented with that kind of organization, so I would not know what [I] would think if that was our intention.

Could an organization do that? If an organization's ultimate aim was a violent confrontation . . . [The witness intervenes] —— Yes, it could.

It could openly preach that in its constitution? —— It could, not in its constitution—in its paper works. I mean, many of us still do receive documents, for instance, written by ANC and posted surreptitiously directing us in a certain way. I mean, I am sure Security Police will tell you that so many people have handed over such documents to them. This is open through the post, it arrives at your doorstep and you read it. If you are scared you take it to the police and you say; This is what I received yesterday. I mean, if SASO intended working that way, I am sure there are ways and means of working, not necessarily confining it to absolute silence.

But then it is driven underground, is it not? That organization is an underground organization? —— Yes. What I am trying to suggest is that an underground organization can still openly pursue a course through the post.

But an aboveboard organization—or on the face of it an aboveboard organization—which intends to work in the public arena can hardly openly advocate violence in documents with any hope that it will have a continued existence? —— Well, I mean, I find that a very difficult question to answer, because it is too hypothetical. I mean, I do not see why anybody would exist aboveboard if his intentions are underground.

I would like to refer you to one document at this stage if I may, Mr. Biko—SASO P.1. I refer Your Lordship here to page 290 of the document. Mr. Biko, I think it will be the second last page of this document which is a report on the proceedings of the National Formation School held at Fedsem, 11th to the 13th May 1973. Did you perhaps attend this formation school at all? —— I am sure I could not have attended it.

No, I ask this because if you look on the second page, which will be page 278 of Your Lordship's papers, under delegates which did attend in the Fort Hare delegation, if you like . . . Can you see the Fort Hare delegation on the left, the third group of delegates, the last name looks to me like S. Biko? —— I think it is Diko.

It is Diko? It is not yourself? —— No.

I see. Anyway, if we can then look at page 290. Do you see a heading there: "Development of Political Thoughts"—the typed page 13? —— That is correct.

Would you just read the first paragraph of that?
       —— "Because of political starvation Blacks were becoming dissatisfied. Whites realized this and introduced a number of bills, e.g., the Native Land Bill, Native Representative Bill and Native Trust Bill etcetera. These laws were completely contrary to what they purported to do; they left the Black people dispos-[sess]ed and landless. Dissatisfaction resulted in the formation of trade and industrial workers' unions, which [were] geared to a type of physical and not psychological liberation. The lack of political insight rendered them ineffective. Other people began looking at their situation more analytically. This resulted in organizations like ANC and PAC, but because of multiracial overtones of a totally African image these groups could not bring about total liberation to the people."

Now, just stop there for a moment. Do you agree with that analysis?
—— Well, I think it is a superficial analysis, if you like.

Now, the group then dealt with this particular analysis—and I would like you to just have a look at the conclusion (e)—it would be the conclusion at the bottom of the page 1953 to 1964, and read that to the court if you would?
       —— "A reactionary group amongst Blacks became prevalent. PAC was formed and banned during this period. Most of the groups were concentrating in one form or the other on physical liberation, and it looked like they were ignoring psychological oppression. Another thing: There was no definite philosophy to which people could look . . . Many organizations were banned during this period, and there ensued a period of temporary lull."

Now, pause there for a moment. Do you agree that the authors of this document seem to have analyzed the failure of the previous organizations, specifically the PAC here, as having concentrated on physical liberation and having ignored psychological oppression? —— This is what they seem to be attempting to do, yes.

Do you agree with that? —— With their analysis?

With that statement? ——— No.

Would you agree with me that SASO and BPC did in fact concentrate to a large extent on psychological oppression in their approach?
——— Yes, but I think as I said in my evidence-in-chief the whole community development program is in fact directed also at alleviating suffering, which is a form of physical oppression, and by physical liberation we also imply liberation from those actual conditions of living which oppress you.

What I really want here is that the writers of this document seem to have analyzed the position and stated that the previous organizations concentrated purely on the physical liberation aspect and ignored the psychological liberation? ——— Yes, this is what this man is saying here, yes.

Right. Now, do you agree with me that SASO and BPC concentrated on both the psychological and physical liberation, that the psychological liberation of the Blacks and psychological oppression was highlighted by SASO and BPC? ——— It seems to have done that.

Because if you read the next page, paragraph (f), it then in fact concludes their statement. If you could perhaps just read that to the court?
——— ". . .disillusionment with multiracial organizations who to ranging degrees wanted White leadership and domination. People fell into a deep lull until in 1968 when moved towards formation of SASO. In 1969 SASO was formally launched and Black Consciousness finally adopted as a philosophy. After SASO has grown numerous other organizations on various places . . .
I am sorry. It is an incomplete sentence.

Yes, it is probably "have grown." This is also in line with the previous statement that previous organizations had no definite philosophy to which the people could look? ——— Well, from the way this man is writing he is looking at several periods in history. As you can see under (d) he is relating what happened between 1948 and 1953, under (e) what happened between 1953 and 1964, and under (f) what happened from 1964 onwards. I do not necessarily get the impression that it is a continuous logic. I think it is continuous years, if you like— merely noting what happened from 1964 onwards—so I would not necessarily say what he is saying here springs necessarily from what he said before that.

Yes, but do you agree with me that there is a criticism there firstly about the lack of—[The witness intervenes] —— Yes, I have agreed on that.

Psychological oppression and the fact that there was no policy to which the people could look? —— Yes, he says that they were more concerned with physical oppression.

Physical oppression, and another thing, in the next sentence—that there was no definite philosophy to which the people could look? —— Yes, I have said of course I do not necessarily agree with this statement. I think in fact before this there were probably much more explicit philosophies in some other spheres.

And then in the next paragraph the writer seems to suggest that SASO does provide such a philosophy, and you have agreed that SASO does concentrate on psychological oppression as well? —— Right.

You said you did not attend this. Did you come across this type of reasoning in SASO at all or not? —— Certainly not this type of reasoning. I think we have done before a survey of activities within the Black community in the past. We have looked at several phases, especially like ICU of olden days—you know, the Industrial Commercial Workers' Union—but we have never sort of extrapolated this type of logic. I mean, I should imagine this was someone's contribution to the conference, or to this particular formation school or whatever it was called. . . .

In your own view at the moment, do you consider that the Blacks are in a position to overthrow the State by violence? —— I do not think so.

One of the defense expert witnesses expressed the view that South Africa was militarily at the moment and for the foreseeable future anyway too strong, and that they would repulse any such attack by the inhabitants. Do you go along with that? —— Well, I have not studied the strength of the White army, so to speak. I have not done that.

But you did express the view that you did not think it was feasible? —— I do not think it is feasible.

The defense expert also suggested that the most productive sphere in which the Blacks in this country could work towards change was the

Black worker sphere. Do you agree with that statement? —— If you are talking about fundamental change perhaps it is a possibility, but I think there are other spheres which lend themselves to easier use. Take the field of sport, for instance, which I think is in the vital interest of society also in that it foreshadows attitudes in other areas. I think the country now is at a stage where considerable pressure can be applied fruitfully in the sphere of sport to have fundamental changes—because you know the whole world is activated, and people have got attitudes, and South Africa is feeling the pinch in one way or the other.

But in what sphere in your opinion can the Blacks exert the most pressure and be most effective? —— I am telling you now: sport.

Sport? —— Yes.

How do Blacks exercise great pressure in sport? —— Well, I think the importance of groups like the South African Rugby Union, the South African Cricket Board of Control, and you know, various sporting groups within the Black spheres that control sport administration—their influence has grown tremendously over the years to a point where they do command a very extensive audience in the external world. And I notice that even people who are regular politicians like Gatsha Buthelezi are now joining, and I think it is simply because this is one sphere where the end is imminent. Springboks will not remain all White for a very long time unless they are going to play inside the country amongst themselves.

And do you foresee that sport can bring about a fundamental change? —— I think it is a foreshadowing of attitudes. I think unless White people in this country are illogical, if you are going to mix on the sports fields and mix fully like it is eventually going to happen, then you have got to think about other areas of your activity, of your life. You have got to think about cinemas and bioscopes, you know. You have to think about your shows and dancing and so on. You have to think about political rights. It is a snowball effect. And I think the outside world is merely tackling this to bring to the mind of White South Africa that we have got to think about change, and change is an irreversible process, because, as I say, I believe in history moving in a direction which is logical to a logical end.

So you would not agree that the Black worker sphere is in fact the

*main sphere in which Blacks can be most effective? ——— Not now
certainly.*

*I think at this stage, Mr. Biko, I would just like to get clear certain
terminology which is used by the Black organizations, if we may, and
what you understand by such terms. Firstly you have this word conscientize? ——— Yes.*

*Now, I have here a definition of conscientization which I would like
you to read if you would and then comment on it.*

——— "Conscientization is a process whereby individuals or
groups living within a given social and political setting are made
aware of their situation. The operative attitude here is not so
much awareness of the physical sense of their situation, but much
more their ability to assess and improve their own influence over
themselves and their environment. Thus in the South African
setting, for instance, it is not enough to be aware that one is living
in a situation of oppression or residing in a segregated and probably inferior educational institution. One must if conscious be
committed to the idea of getting himself out of the morass. One
must be aware of the factors involved and dangers imminent in
such an undertaking, but must always operate from the basic
belief that he is in a struggle that must be seen through in spite
of the dangers and difficulties. Thus then conscientization implies
a desire to engage people in an emancipatory process, in an
attempt to free one from a situation of bondage. The framework
within which we are working is that of Black Consciousness."

*Now, what is your comment on that exposition, if you like, on con-
scientization? ——— I think it is fairly correct.*

*Is that how you understand it and is that how SASO and BPC
understood conscientization? ——— Yes,* generally so, yes.

*And if one comes across the term that it is used for conscientization
purposes et cetera, is that the sense in which it was used? ——— Yes,*
certainly.

*I do not envisage handing that in as an exhibit, M'lord. It was merely
for the witness' comments. Then there is talk of the System? ———*
Yes.

*And an attack on the System, and the System is responsible for this
or that. What do you understand by the term System? ——— Well, I*

think it has got a fundamental meaning, but I do not suppose that this is generally how it is understood by everybody. The fundamental meaning of the term System is those operative forces in society—those institutionalized and uninstitutionalized operative forces in society—that control your being, guide your behavior, and generally are an authority over you. This is implying government certainly. This is implying the agents of the government, the police especially. Now, there is a tendency for instance in our ranks to regard the police as the System. This is only because really people tend to come all too often against police, but the System is the entire process, the governmental process that operates in a particular given area.

That is the branch of the System which they have most to do with? —— Yes.

Or come into contact most with? —— Yes.

Now, I get the impression from SASO and BPC documents that whether one refers to the System or the government or the Whites, these three terms seem to be used to mean the same thing? —— Yes. There is a fair argument for the interchangeability of the terms, but I think it is the understanding . . . Yes, as I say, it is the System—that is the understanding of it as I have described it.

And if one finds an attack by any particular author in a document, and he refers to "The Whites have done this" or "The government have done this" or "The System has done this," it all means basically the same thing? —— Sometimes the term Whites, for instance, is used interchangeably with another term, which is White racism, but again the term White racism has got to be understood also to be closely tied up with the System. In other words you get institutionalized racism, which expresses itself through agencies of the government, and you get noninstitutionalized racism, which expresses itself in the open street, for instance, outside in the square. The whole relationship between Black and White shows a certain form of racism. There is no toilet outside here, and just now I went into the toilet which is marked "White" and everybody around was looking at me almost wanting to stop me. And I was just waiting for them to stop me, and I would have asked where is the "Black" toilet. Fortunately they did not stop me. But what they were showing me is racism. It is not institutionalized; it is there all the same in our society.

And that to SASO and BPC the System is White, and the government

is a White government? —— Not true absolutely. There are extensions of the System in the Black ranks which are organized as part
of the System.

Those are the Non-Whites, is that right? —— Like Gatsha Buthelezi . . . No, I think there has been a tendency to drop that name
altogether. I think we do see them as essentially Black people nowadays, I mean [inaudible] was Non-White sometime back, but people
are sort of dropping it off now. But you do get parts of the system
which exist within the Black ranks—Gatsha Buthelezi is certainly as
black as I am in color, and possibly aspirations, but operates within
a system which is created for him by the White government, and in
that sense he is an extension of the System.

But you yourself have used the term Non-White? —— I have used
it in the past certainly.

*I think if I am not mistaken, the document BPC T.1 according to
the evidence was compiled by you, the document entitled "The Definition of Black Consciousness"?* —— Yes.

Is this document one which was compiled by you? —— Yes, certainly.

*This I think was widely distributed throughout SASO and BPC
offices and was in fact one of the foundation documents?* —— This
document was used for a formation school during December, I think,
1971 or early January, I am not quite sure now. But anyway it was
distributed to those people at the conference; it was meant for them.
It could have been subsequently used by the organization; I do not
know.

*I think you will find if you go through the document that numerous
of the things expressed here have found expression in other documents
and resolutions?* —— It could be—yes.

*Now, you set out at the top of this document to define what you mean
by Black Consciousness, and you define Blacks?* —— Yes.

*Then if you would have a look at the paragraph which starts after
(2): "From the above observations therefore"?* —— Yes.

You say:

> *"We can see that the term Black is not necessarily all inclusive,
> i.e., the fact that we are all not White does not necessarily mean
> that we are all Black."*

—— That is correct.

"Non-Whites do exist . . ." —— That is correct.

"And continue to exist and will exist for quite a long time. If one's aspiration is Whiteness but his pigmentation makes attainment of this impossible then that person is a Non-White. Any man who calls a White man 'Baas,' any man who serves in the police force or Security Branch is ipso facto a Non-White." —— That is correct.

"Black people—real Black people—are those who can manage to hold their heads high in defiance rather than willingly surrender their souls to the White man." —— That is correct—yes.

So you yourself are a proponent of this term "Non-White"? —— That is correct.

You say you find that it is now falling into disuse? —— Yes. I think what has happened is that instead of it being understood as an intellectual concept, it has been used as an insult by many people within the movement, which has made the leadership wish to see it off its records completely. But I think as an intellectual concept it is a valid term. You know, anybody who does not identify with the struggle called the Black struggle towards attainment of our total goals as Black people, that is Black, any color, does not qualify to be called Black.

I think you have expressed the same sentiment in your "I Write What I Like" article "Fear—an Important Determinant . . ." —— I remember that.

Where you stated that:

"One can of course say that Blacks too are to blame for allowing the situation to exist. Or to drive the point even further, one may point out that there are Black policemen and Black special branch agents. To take the last point first, I must state categorically that there is no such thing as a Black policeman. Any Black man who props the System up actively has lost the right to be considered part of the Black world. He has sold his soul for 30 pieces of silver and finds that he is not in fact acceptable to the White society he sought to join. They are extensions of the enemy into our ranks." —— That is correct. I think what you must see here as being juxtaposed in that paragraph is the political concept Black with the descriptive concept Black. Now, in our definition of a Black man, if

you refer to the SASO policy manifesto, you will find that we not only refer to people who are psychologically, socially and so on oppressed, but also identify as a unit in the struggle towards realization of their aspirations. Now, that is a political definition. Now, there is a descriptive term Black, you know, which implies purely an observation of the external factors. For instance, I could look at you and because of your short hair think that you are a Colored and therefore call you Black [laughter]—that is purely descriptive. I haven't gone into your political thinking. I haven't gone into your aspirations. But if we are talking politically and we differ in political interpretation, you know, I might get to a point where I feel that you do not qualify politically to be referred to as a Black.

Perhaps in this context you could have a look at the BPC constitution, the interpretation clause where you people define what you mean by Black under the main point. This is BPC B.2, M'lord. In point number 1 you define what you mean by Black? —— Yes.

Perhaps you could just read that?
—— "Unless inconsistent with the context, Blacks are to be interpreted as those who are by law or tradition politically, economically and socially discriminated against as a group in the South African society, and identifying themselves as a unit in the struggle towards a realization of their aspirations."

And is that in fact what you believe? —— That is the political definition of the term.

Now, I should imagine that being what you are, you have had a lot of contact with Blacks? —— Yes.

And Black thinking? —— Yes.

And Blacks from all walks of life—both intellectuals and rural Blacks, if we can call them that? —— Right.

Now, how have you found Blacks interpret terms like "liberation movement"? What do they understand by "liberation movement"?
—— Well, I think that there certainly is a varied interpretation to that term. I think this is occasioned by certain confusing factors in society. In the past few years there has been an increased reference to liberation movements in newspapers, by which was meant forces operating in Mozambique, Frelimo, for instance, and over the past few months MPLA, FNLA and so on. This is the one view. Then you

get another view which has crept up in our society also of late of a group called "Ingratagazulu," which calls itself a liberation movement. Now, Ingratagazulu is Gatsha's baby. It is an organization which is supposed to back what he says. It is a Zulu cultural organization. He calls it a liberation movement, and it is a mass movement. It has got lots of people who subscribe to it, and they call themselves the members of a liberation movement. So that it is a very sort of elastic term also. I think the term liberation movement in general is understood to mean a movement working towards liberation, and the whole method which was implicit in the name before has tended to fall off.

What did you find was implicit before? —— You know, before as I say it was forces operating outside and making incursions into the country, in the form of guerrilla attacks, for instance, but now this has dropped off because I don't think Gatsha Buthelezi is making guerrilla attacks.

Do you find there are still lots of people who understand liberation movement in that old sense? —— This certainly would be, and certainly mainly in Natal for instance they would see it in the new sense.

Amongst the Zulus especially? —— Yes.

Freedom fighter? —— Freedom fighter is again . . . There is an intellectual interpretation of the term, and the historical interpretation of the term. The intellectual interpretation of the term means anybody who fights for freedom. Now, I would describe and I have described myself to people who ask as a freedom fighter, but at the same time I do know that there is this historical interpretation of the term which relates to the movements that have been operating on the borders as well.

When you used the term to describe yourself, to whom have you been addressing yourself? —— Oh, other folk.

Not other intellectuals? —— Certainly with intellectuals but with ordinary folk as well.

And when you describe yourself as a freedom fighter to people who are not intellectuals do you define the term? —— In some instances I have defined it. I am trying to think historically now who I spoke to. In some instances I defined it, but in some instances it has been taken for granted.

By people who know you? —— Yes.

And if somebody did not know you, and you met them for the first time, or you met a group of people for the first time, and they were not intellectuals, would you describe yourself as a freedom fighter? —— No, I did not define it but I did use it once with the Special Branch, who were being introduced to me, who wanted to know what my profession was, and I said I was a freedom fighter.

I think that was tongue-in-the-cheek, not so? —— He laughed.

It was a bit of tongue-in-the-cheek, not so? —— Well, it was making conversation, and if you have got to live with the Security Police on your neck all the time you have got to devise a way of talking to them, you know, and this is one of the ways.

They understand only one language. [Laughter] The point I want to make is that . . . Would you describe yourself as a freedom fighter to people you did not know and who were not intellectuals without defining the term? —— No, I do not think so. It depends of course how it crops up in conversation.

Why would you not? —— It depends, I say, how it crops up in conversation. I mean, if my intention is to perhaps deal with what I am doing fully, then I would go straight into the hub of the matter and talk about what I am doing, but if a person—and this depends on how it crops up—wants to know what you do, right? Now, I am not working right now, for instance. I am not working. I am persecuted for my political beliefs or mental beliefs. I have not done anything which is against the law, and I have got no profession as such. So if a guy in a round table is asking, What is your profession, and someone says, I am a doctor. What is your profession? I am a lawyer. They come to me, I always say, freedom fighter—precisely because this is what the State wants me to do, to sit at home and think about my freedom rather than be involved in creative work.

But there you were talking to other people who were a doctor and a lawyer—they were intellectuals? —— Right. Common people do not normally ask you for a profession.

The word confrontation as used in many of the documents here and by numerous of the SASO and BPC members in speeches and bandied about—how does SASO and BPC understand confrontation? What does it imply? —— Well, I think mainly as I spoke about in my evidence-in-chief. Confrontation in the South African context we understand as causing a reaction to breaking a law, no matter in pursuit of what—just breaking a law deliberately.

Any law? —— I am talking about breaking a law in group form.

Any law? —— Any law. It may be for instance a municipality by-law which says you may not walk on a particular pavement. You walk on it. This is in a sense provoking reaction; in other words, it is confrontation with the System.

You say then that provoking or courting arrest is confrontation as you people understand it? —— Yes.

Is this what you people were doing when you attended your UCM conference and you decided that if 72 hours was up you should not apply for a permit but you should sit around? —— No. I explained this to the court. I think what we wanted then was to create an opportunity for us Blacks to decide on this, with an intention to have time to talk about the issue, you know. In other words, we used it as some kind of strategy to get Blacks to meet. Certainly there was no intention of not obeying that law. But we used that argument precisely to get an opportunity to talk amongst ourselves.

But would that have been confronting—[The witness intervenes] —— It would certainly, if we did not go out of the area and the police came—that would be confrontation, yes.

So you do not understand there to be an inherent quality of violence? —— Not necessarily, no.

That conference—while we are busy with that conference—how long was it scheduled to last? —— UCM conferences lasted basically about four days, five days. I do not know how long this one was to last.

Was this one due to last longer than 72 hours? —— Oh yes, certainly.

So that possibility did arise? —— It did arise.

That you would require the permit? —— Well, we were discussing it on the night before we completed the 72 hours, and the conference would certainly have gone beyond that.

Did you people eventually get permits? —— Well, we did not ask for permits. We got into cars and some walked outside the area and reentered the area for another 72 hours.

And the others? —— Which others?

The others who did not go out and come back? —— Well, there was a symbolic participation in the march by everybody, Whites as well as Blacks, as far as I remember.

So in fact you technically complied with the law? —— That is correct.

So you did not confront the System then? —— No.

Is confrontation—as you people understand it—is it wide enough to cover bargaining? —— I said earlier on when I was speaking that the term confrontation itself really can be used very loosely. When two opposing viewpoints are put against each other and backed by their exponents, this could be called confrontation.

But would it include bargaining? —— In the terms in which we used this particular word, certainly confrontation would not include bargaining; bargaining in fact is running away from confrontation as understood. I think I have explained what we meant by confrontation.

Because there is talk in all the documents of an eventual situation where you have a collective bargaining with the Whites? —— Yes, that is correct.

I am trying to find out whether one could substitute the word confrontation for bargaining in that context? —— No, I say no.

Have you noticed that South Africa's regime has been criticized for its involvement in South West Africa, as the illegal regime in South West Africa? —— Well, it has been criticized, and I am sure I have also been party to this.

You have also been party to it? —— Yes.

In that sense is South West Africa considered a foreign country to South Africa? —— Actually, SASO does not include any technical college or institution of higher learning in South West Africa precisely because we regard Namibia as another country, which has been colonized.

All right, we will talk about it as Namibia, then. Do you consider Namibia to be a foreign country? —— As another country—when you use the word foreign—yes, foreign in the sense of being another country.

Is that how SASO understands it? —— That is correct.

And BPC? —— We do not include Namibia, and certainly BPC does not include Namibia.

I see. Now, SWAPO, for instance, would that be a foreign organization? —— It is a foreign organization.

Is that how you people view it? —— That is correct.

How would you describe SWAPO as regards its attitude towards South Africa? —— [Pause]

Perhaps I can help you there? —— Yes, please.

If I describe SWAPO as hostile to the Republic, what would you say? —— Oh yes, I think it is hostile.

Now, if we can turn for a moment to your own knowledge, Mr. Biko, when did your association with SASO end? —— Effectively when I got banned.

I think you are going to have to be a little bit more definite than that with "effectively" . . . [The court intervenes]

THE COURT: *Was that in March 1973?* —— That is right.

When last did you serve on the Executive of SASO? When did your last Executive portfolio end? —— Oh I see, 1971.

Would that be in July 1971? —— July 1971.

The conferences are normally in July, is that correct? —— That is correct.

Now, when you concluded your Executive association with SASO, how many Executive portfolios of SASO had you yourself held? —— Only two actually.

And they were? —— First was presidency for one year, then it was director of publications for one year.

Now, if I may ask, you were obviously one of the leading lights in SASO? —— That is correct.

Why did you stand down in the July of 1971 and not continue on the Executive of SASO? —— There were two reasons for it; in fact, you can also ask me why did I not stand again for presidency in 1970. Our belief was essentially that we must attempt to get people to identify with the central core of what you are saying rather than individuals. We must not create a leadership cult, we must centralize the people's attention onto the real message that we carried. This is the reason why, if you notice, more or less all the first presidents of SASO served one year and changed. It was also the reason why that particular column which I was assigned to write, which is "I Write What I Like by Frank Talk," was written under a pseudonym, because if you tend to deal with issues all the time people tend to relate to the person in terms of their personal affiliation or disaffiliation to him as a person. Now, we wanted them to focus on the message. This is the reason. Now, in fact I was asked in 1972 July to come back onto the Executive by a particular caucus group and I refused, because I thought I had served my purpose. I had made my contribution and it was time for new leadership to start out. So I had already stayed too long by being in the Executive for two years.

You were also director of publications? ——— Yes.

What was the readership of the SASO newsletter? ——— Numbers? Well, we used to send out up to 3000 to 4000 sometimes. I think the limitation of the SASO publication was money rather than readership. We never had problems with the returns, but we could only print a certain number because of money considerations. . . .

Do you consider yourself to be qualified to give evidence about SASO and BPC policy? ——— I think so, yes.

Would you tell the court why you consider yourself qualified to do that? ——— I think it is primarily for the reasons you put forward yourself: that I was there at the beginning of both movements; I was one of the main protagonists of the Black Consciousness philosophy, which I think has broadly been the guiding light to BPC and SASO policy, certainly in SASO on the political question. . . .

[In your newsletter] did you ever include articles which were critical of SASO? ——— I must think hard.

I think you would have to think very hard because I have not come across any. ——— Well, you would have to give me actually all the SASO newsletters.

Well, you would remember them if there were such things? ——— No, no, not necessarily, because I think we could for instance reprint something which appeared somewhere on some campus against us, and put up a reply to it, you know, something like that.

Well, then it would be an attack on that particular critic, would it not? ——— No, what I am saying is that you do include it anyway in the newsletter. I do not know honestly. You would have to ask Strini about this.

I will ask Strini, don't worry! But you were director of publications and I want to know . . . —— Yes, yes, as I say even when I was director he acted as editor for me most of the time, so he has a longer association with the newsletter than myself.

You cannot offhand think of anything? —— I cannot offhand. I know that they accepted all my Frank Talk writings, that is all I know.

Do you think Frank Talk reflects SASO opinions? —— Not necessarily—I mean, mainly my opinions. One could say to a great extent also that I was of influence in SASO, and therefore the very fact that they allowed that column implies that they had confidence that I would be throwing the right sort of line. But I cannot say hundred percent all the time this is what SASO thought. Sometimes it was an important issue that I wrote on.

Looking at the other accused here, those that you know, I think you have intimated you know accused number 1, Saths Cooper; number 2, Muntu Myeza; number 3, Patrick Lekota; number 4, Dr. Mokoape; and I think you said number 9, Strini Moodley. Do you know the other accused at all? —— Yes, I know them now. I met them, yes.

Apart from here, did you know them before their arrest? —— No.

Those that you do know you knew before their arrest? —— I only knew three—that is, Strini, Saths and Aubrey—before I was banned. Since I was banned and before their arrest I then met Lekota and Muntu. But that is not quite true—Lekota, I knew him politically then, but he was at the same school where I was actually. I knew him then as a soccer star on our team. [Laughter]

Yes, he has the nickname "Terror," is that right? —— Something like that. I think it was Terror.

Or Lek—is he also known as Lek, or don't you know? —— I do not remember that one—that probably came in jail.

Well, maybe the Terror came in jail too.

THE COURT: *Did he earn his name?* —— Terror? As a striker, yes.

MR. ATTWELL: *Now, you have told the court that coming from you one naturally assumed that the thing was going to be the official viewpoint?* —— I am saying I cannot vouch for this.

No, obviously—don't be too modest, Mr. Biko. Coming from Saths Cooper, would you expect that to be the official viewpoint of BPC, for

instance? —— I think his position was relatively senior in the organization and he was generally held in high esteem, so that one can
roughly say that about him.

*What would you say about accused number 2, Muntu Myeza, com-
ing from him?* —— Well, I have never watched him in operation. I
have never been able to watch how people respond to him, so I cannot
make any estimate.

*It is a pity you were not at the Durban rally. Number 3, Lekota—
is that another man that if he says something one can accept this is
likely to be . . . [The witness intervenes]* —— I would not be able
to say this about him either. As I say, I have only known him politically since I was banned, so I never really watched him in operation.

Dr. Mokoape, number 4? —— Dr. Mokoape—I think he had lots
of influence in the context of BPC and also in SASO, but you see,
Aubrey has never really taken up senior executive positions in SASO;
he has always been a man who operates somewhere on the fringes of
the organization.

*Now, while you have mentioned that fact—he was obviously one of
the leading people in the foundation of SASO, is that right?* —— Not
of SASO.

Not of SASO? —— No.

*Well, from a very early stage he was in SASO, is that right? From
the time of the second GSC?* —— No, quite late. I think he got
involved minimally in 1970 in one or two community development
projects, like Dudu [indistinct] I think he talked there. Then in 1971,
as I said, he was on a delegation that came to see several organizations
here in Johannesburg. Aubrey as far as I remember has never attended
a single conference of SASO, or at least up to the time I was there he
had never attended one.

Of SASO? —— Yes, as far as I remember. Within SASO Aubrey
could have been said to be an influence, you know, to some extent on
the leadership that he met. Certainly he never had a broad consultation with students, except of course those on his campus.

Was he influential on the U.N.B. campus? —— Yes, he was.

Did he serve on the SRC there? —— Yes, he did—some years. I
cannot remember specifically which years now.

*But he certainly was one of the leading lights in BPC from the very
word go?* —— Certainly, yes.

He was in fact one of the conveners of the inaugural convention?
—— That is correct.

Why was it that he never served on the Executive of BPC? ——
I would not know. It depends, I think, for a medical student who has
got to a stage where you must finish you are going to accept the
demands of your profession, you are either a good doctor or you are
no doctor. I think he probably decided towards the end that he had
to fulfill certain requirements within the course. You will have to ask
him, I am just . . . [Pause; laughter]

*Accused number 9, Strini Moodley—would he be a man from whom
you would expect the official policy in all likelihood?* —— Yes, very
well distinguished SASO person, but I think he always played subservient to the main people who were in an organization. He was in a
very ticklish position. He was in contact with the day-to-day work of
SASO—no more; and as a result of course he had to actively play
subservient to the elected leaders like Barney Pityana and like Temba
Sono and Jerry Modisane, because if you tend to push yourself too
much, then there is conflict in the office.

He was in fact a very effective director of publications? —— Very,
very.

*I notice at one of the GSC's he was congratulated for elevating the
SASO newsletter into such an authoritative organ?* —— Well, he
could have been.

*What do you understand by a political organization? What would the
ultimate aims be of a political organization?* —— Well, I think the
term political organization is a pretty loose one. In fact, it does not
exist as far as I remember in political science. A political organization
in political science would be equated to what we call a pressure group.
Now, a pressure group is a group which has interest in one or more
aspects of the people's political life—when I say political life I am
talking about those aspects of people's lives which are affected by
political decisions or decisions made by political groups, Parliament
and so on. You may apply yourself, for instance, if you are in the
Institute of Race Relations to the one field which is the right of
individuals. If you are a national association of agriculturalists you
may apply yourself to the price of maize, the price of agricultural

products, and insofar as you push that program you are a pressure group.

Would they be political organizations? —— I am saying that in political science, you know, the term political organization does not exist.

All right, perhaps I can be a little bit more definite. BPC considered itself in juxtaposition to SASO to be a political organization? —— Right.

Now, what do you understand by political organization? —— Now, political organization—in that context I think BPC foreshadowed a political party. In other words, they are a political party in the making. They had a viewpoint to put across, but they have got no structure to fit in, right? So they operate like a typical pressure group. This is the difference.

Why did not BPC call itself a political party? —— Well, a political party incidentally is a group that normally operates within a particular platform, whether that platform is the South African Parliament, or it is the Coloured Representative Council or it is Matanzima's Transkei; ordinarily the term party implies a participation in the electoral process, this is how I understand it. Now, BPC did not call itself a political organization or a political party; it just became describable as a political organization because it is operating outside any particular electoral process.

Did you say BPC never described itself as a political organization? —— Never called . . . I mean, if you look at the name Black People's Convention—that in fact is not a party or an organization, like the Labour Party of South Africa—they call themselves a party; or the National Party of South Africa—they call themselves a party.

Did legislation that existed at the stage BPC was formed . . . Did that consider at all as a factor whether to call yourself a party or not? —— No, it was not considered. I think perhaps if one may jump your statement, there were one or two statements by some people who said, you know, you might be infringing the Improper Interference Act or something like that, and we said, Nonsense. We have the right to operate as we are—that is, as an all-inclusive group of Black folk. All it means is that if we as BPC, as we are presently constituted, decide to take part in the Transkei elections, right, we are then chargeable, or certain members of the group are chargeable under the Improper Interference Act. But nothing prevents us from existing. The law limits our actions. If by choice we want to participate, for instance, in the all-White Parliament, we would be infringing [on] the Improper Interference Act, but that is theoretical.

Were any other infringements of that Act considered? ——— As far as I know this was the main one. I do not know if there were any others.

Did you people study that Act when you were faced with this argument that you might be . . . [The witness intervenes] ——— I certainly was one of the people who interpreted this. I never studied it, you know, but I knew it as part of our country's laws. I mean, one gets to know laws without studying the actual legislation.

Are there any rules there about the funds of a political party? ——— Oh yes, yes. There is also provision that a political party operating here should not be funded from outside—something like that, I am not quite sure.

Have BPC complied with that—could BPC have complied with that requirement? ——— Oh yes. I think BPC, for instance, as it exists now, as far as I know, has never existed mainly on external funds.

Never? ——— Well, I do not say they do not get it. I say they do not exist mainly on external funds, as far as I know.

Do you know the sources of BPC's funds? ——— Not now. I have been out of contact with BPC for a long time really. . . .

Does BCP push a Black Consciousness line? ——— I think one can extrapolate a consciousness line certainly from their programs, in a sense that they are founded on that idea, that we have got to do something as Blacks. But they do not preach, they just work—if you see what I mean—and they see any form of consciousness arising out of mere example, as I was indicating in my evidence-in-chief.

There is lots of talk in SASO and BPC documents about being associated and working in cooperation with relevant organizations? ——— Yes.

Would you consider BCP to be a relevant organization? ——— Certainly. That is why I worked there.

And did SASO and BPC consider it to be a relevant organization? ——— Yes, I think so.

And did they in fact work in close collaboration with BCP? ——— In some programs, yes. But, I mean, again BCP has been subjected to some criticism by SASO, you know, at the same time BCP has been approached by SASO on one or two projects, like the Black workers' project that they had and like the youth programs that they had.

I am coming to the youth programs. What interest did BCP have in the Black workers' project? —— Our interest was to provide basically a facility in and around Johannesburg in the form of what is now commonly called a worker-advice office, and SASO had another view, but . . . you know, close to what we are talking about. All of us were hoping eventually that [these] kind[s] of functions were going to be taken up by an umbrella Black trade union organization, so that BCP saw itself as promoting that sort of concern, and SASO on the other hand saw herself as promoting that sort of concern, so we merged and worked together for a time on the project.

When was BCP founded? —— BCP as BCP? Well, let me say it was founded in 1972.

After BPC or before BPC? —— Let us see, now, yes, it could be slightly after, but I think the logics of BCP were worked out in the course of 1971, because the man who founded BCP was invited to join that group, which was SPRO-CAS, in the course of 1971, and he worked out some logic which he presented to the sponsors, and they said go ahead and found what you want, which he did.

But would I be correct in saying that BCP answered those people's requirements who at the December 1971 conference had expressed the need for an organization other than a political organization, which SASO pushed for and which eventually became BPC? —— Well, if you look at the proposed structure in the December documents you would realize that you are wrong.

In what way would I be wrong? —— In the sense that CENBAD was an interorganizational operation which required organizational affiliation to it by all the Black organizations existing in the country; BCP, on the other hand, could not care two hoots about other organizations affiliating to it. They are a service organization; they exist and depend on existence for the desirability of their services. They do share notes—like, anybody is free to comment on what the BCP does —but essentially they do not have to please SASO or BPC or ASA or IDAMASA or be answerable to them. They are just another organization, like IDAMASA in effect.

Was Mr. Morani in BCP? —— Never, no.

THE COURT: *Why was there a need for BCP? Couldn't BPC have done all the work which they are doing in BCP?* —— Well, M'lord, all I can say is that BPC was not quite doing it, and secondly the BCP logic was that for that kind of community service you did require an organization with full-time staff with a little bit of expertise and whose total concern is community development.

Specialized staff? —— That is right, yes.

MR. ATTWELL: *Did BPC consider itself to in fact be the chief Black organization in the country under which all the other Black organizations ultimately fell?* —— No, I think they saw themselves as the leading organization in the political sphere, and I think they could rightly or wrongly consider themselves as the most important organization in that sense, because they were dealing with political questions.

Perhaps I could just refer you then to BPC R.2. I will just read to you what it says here, which is a background paper to BPC, it says:

> *"Presently BPC is the only political movement of Blacks by Blacks for Blacks in this country. It acts as a mother body of all Black organizations—the South African Students Organisation, National Youth Organisation, South African Students Movement (High and Junior Secondary School movements), Black Allied Workers Union, etcetera."*

Would you agree with that statement? —— From the political point of view, certainly. I think most of those organizations referred to there would look for leadership, political leadership, to the BPC.

And BCP as well? —— Well, BCP is a mixed bag, and this is one of the criticisms—it is a mixed bag. But I think their craft, which is community development, is certainly not mixed; the staff that works there knows what they are doing. The directors, you know, they come from all walks of life, and they offer probably some kind of important dimension in that sense to the organization.

COURT ADJOURNS

Day Three

The Morning of May 5, 1976

With passion and anger, Biko outlines the South African government's terrorist campaign against Blacks. Attwell attempts once more to link SASO with the banned ANC and PAC. The significance of the student movement to the development of Black Consciousness and the political nature of the BPC are also discussed. Just prior to the tea adjournment, Attwell manages a seething indictment of SASO.

After the tea break, Attwell directs his argument at the language and statements used by Black Consciousness leaders, maintaining that SASO does indeed promote racial hostility. In this remarkable sequence of questions, Biko—by sheer force of personality—reverses roles and actually cross-examines his interrogator. Attwell quickly returns to a matter discussed the previous day, the notion that the economic sector was particularly vulnerable to change. Biko neatly avoids the trap.

COURT RESUMES

STEPHEN BANTU BIKO, STILL UNDER OATH

CROSS-EXAMINATION BY MR. ATTWELL, CONTINUED: . . . *Have you got Resolution 46 of 1974?* —— Yes, I have got that.

The one "noting with grave concern and disgust the display of naked terrorism"? —— Right.

Would you just have a quick look at that and tell me whether you ever came across language like that in the GSC's which you attended yourself? —— Well, I just find this a usual expression of indignation which you would get from SASO, I think. You would get it in 1971, in fact. You would get it in the discussions over particular resolutions. I do not think there is anything particularly new to me in this resolution.

It may be that Black thinking did not change, but do you find a difference in the expression and the language used in the 6th GSC and the ones you attended? —— Would you like, for instance, to point out one word which could not have been used in 1970 which was used in 1974 here?

Not about one word, Mr. Biko, the general tenor—for instance, that particular resolution? —— Well, I think it is an expression of indignation.

Did you find such expressions of indignation in your GSC's? —— I am sure if you look thoroughly through the 1971 conferences, for instance—or, if you like, even 1970—you might pick up things of this nature.

Unfortunately I do not think we would be able to look at the 1970 one. I think that is the one that is missing. Perhaps you would have a look in the tea adjournment at the 1971 one, and tell us if you can see any language like this? —— Okay.

The same type of language is used in other of the resolutions. Here I do not confine you to 46 of 1974. You can have a look at any one of them—57 of 1974? —— Let me just get it clear. Which 46 are you referring to? There are two 46's.

I told you, yes. It is the one which starts "With grave concern and disgust at the display of naked terrorism"? —— Oh yes, okay, fine. THE COURT: *While we are busy with 46, now will you look at page 15, there is a resolution, paragraph 3 of the resolution—now what does that paragraph mean?* —— I think, M'lord, the statement "the day of reckoning is nigh and that time and truth are on our side" is in fact an expression of what I constantly referred to yesterday: that we have a particular perception of history, that history is going to move in a particular logical direction which is eventually going to . . . manifest itself in the White population recognizing the need to accommodate Black aspirations within the political structures of this country. I think this kind of prediction has been made by many a person— Labour Party, Buthelezi, SASO, BPC. It is made by Black people; it is an example of how people live on hope, and we are saying there, "Truth and time are on our side."

Yes, but now in what context do you use the day of reckoning? —— The day of reckoning, as I say, is that stage at which this recognition of the fact that you cannot stay anymore . . . You cannot live anymore with people without giving them a stake in what you have. It is not as if the day of reckoning is us standing in judgment of White society. It is just a historical day of reckoning; history will eventually prevail over humankind. I mean, I was not at this particular meeting. You would have to ask the people who were there—I am just interpreting.

THE COURT: *Yes, well, that is all we are wanting.*

MR. ATTWELL: *It also [says], for instance, there in point 3 that the Blacks are being subjected by the Whites and the White government to "direct terrorism"?* —— Yes.

Do you think that is a valid statement? —— I think it is much more valid for instance than the charge against these men. I think that what we have to experience . . . certainly is much more definite, much more physically depressing than the charge you are placing against these men for the few things they have said.

Which men are you talking about? —— The nine accused.

Well, perhaps you could expand on that then, Mr. Biko? —— Sorry?

What do you mean by that? —— I am talking about definite violence for instance. . . . Actual forms of violence—people being baton-charged by police, beaten up, like the people who were striking in March at Henneman. I am talking about the situations of police charging on people in places like Sharpeville without arms, and I am talking about the indirect violence that you get through starvation in townships. I am talking about the squalor that you meet at Winterveld as you go there now. I am talking about the kind of situation you get at Dimbasa if you go there now, where there is no food, there is hardly any furniture for people. I think that is all put together much more terrorism than what these guys have been saying. Now they stand charged. White society is not charged. This is what I mean.

What do you understand the charges are against the accused? —— Well, I have been made to understand they are supposed to have conspired at some point in history—I do not know when—to overthrow the State through unconstitutional means. They are supposed to have fanned the feelings of Blacks to result in a state of racial hostility, something like that. This is what I understand. And I have been interested in this case all along, when I first heard about it I thought there could be something my men have done. After a long,

long time the State closed its case. What have they done? They have
produced a mass of documents, and this so-called, you know, conspiracy as far as I am concerned exists only in the minds of the Security
Police and probably you, Mr. Attwell.

You refer to them as your men? —— Yes, sure, these are my men.

Do they work for you? —— Not specifically; they work with me.

With you? —— Yes.

In close contact with you? —— Actually I do not know some of
them, but we share a belief about our society—that is what I mean
by saying they work with me.

Some of them you do not know? —— Yes.

*But you are ready to defend them because . . . although you do not
know what they have done?* —— I defend them because I believe in
our organizations. If they are being charged for being in SASO and
for being in BPC, I have got faith in the validity of SASO and BPC.
I have not yet been disappointed to a point where I castigate them.

*You, of course, together with the rest of SASO and BPC members,
have been engaged in a liberatory struggle against the White System?*
—— Oh yes.

And your sympathies I gather lie with the accused in this case?
—— Well, I have been called here actually to come to court per
subpoena, and my understanding of that significance is that I must
speak the truth in court. Sure, I have sympathies with my men, but
I will not stand between my men and the truth.

*While we are talking about evidence in this trial, when were you
approached to give evidence in this case, Mr. Biko?* —— Well, I got
what one might call a questionnaire from Mr. Chetty sometime in the
latter end of last year. This questionnaire contained various questions
about the formation of SASO, about the trends that led to SASO
within NUSAS before that, and within UCM before that, and about
various conferences that I attended up to 1970. I answered all the
questions as truthfully as I could, and I indicated voluntarily to Mr.
Chetty that should I be required to come and defend any of the
assertions I made there. I was available, precisely because I realized
on looking around that there were in fact very few people who had
been there at the beginning of SASO—certainly not amongst these
guys here, and certainly very few amongst people who are generally

available to give evidence, so I indicated I was available. I subsequently got a subpoena in November—it must have been about the middle of November—to come up. So I came up believing I was going to appear. I did not appear. I went back home, and I got another subpoena about two weeks back and that is why I am here.

So in effect you volunteered to give evidence? ——— I did volunteer to give evidence, yes.

Because as you say there is a misconception about SASO and BPC, and this would be an opportunity to clear the air as it were? ——— Because I recognize myself as one of the few guys who was there, and who are available at this moment to assist the court on the historical questions.

Can you assist the court on what has been happening very recently in SASO and BPC? ——— No, I am talking about historical questions; that is, the formation of SASO and so on. I can talk about SASO up to a certain point, and certainly I am sure you have got men who can talk about SASO beyond my point, which is about effectively speaking [the] 1972 conference, and a little bit beyond that because I still had a bit of knowledge of what was going on. But 1973, 1974, 1975—you would have to get other people, and I am sure you have got plenty amongst the accused.

Don't you consider yourself capable of giving any idea of what the organizations were doing in those years 1972 onwards? ——— These would be my thoughts and my interpretations, but they cannot relate strictly point for point to facts.

In that period after your banning . . . [The witness intervenes] ——— Yes, that is what I am talking about.

Did you have any contact at all with any of the accused? Either by telephone or correspondence? ——— As I said, after my banning I met Mr. Lekota and Mr. Myeza in their context.

In the context of SASO? ——— Right.

Did they come down to King William's Town? ——— Well, they were on business, you see, and my home is in King William's Town, and I am interested in SASO, so they c[a]me to chat to me about developments in the organization.

And BPC officials? ——— Well, Mr. Mangena came—he is no more here now. None of the accused in fact ever came.

Who was Mr. Mangena? —— Mr. Mangena is a gentleman who got convicted of terrorism in Grahamstown sometime back.

Do you know what the charges were against him? —— The charges were that he recruited two people to join a BPC program which involved violence—in other words, training somewhere in Africa and the violent overthrow of the government. Eventually of course the judge in that case found that BPC had no such program, because evidence was led by BPC officials . . . [The court intervenes]

THE COURT: *Where was that case?* —— It was in Grahamstown, and Mr. Mangena was convicted so to speak on his own absences.

MR. ATTWELL: *He was convicted of the charge?* —— Yes.

Were you approached to give evidence in that case? —— No.

Are you sure? —— I must be sure, because I assisted Mangena to get money for the defense.

Where did you get money for the defense? —— I think we must have got it from the South African Council of Churches eventually.

But you were never approached as a possible witness in that case? —— No, it was a case of two men meeting in a train with him, and two men saying he said A, B, C and D, you know, and this A, B, C and D was supposed to be a BPC program, so BPC came and said, We have got no such program, and the judge accepted it.

Yes, but that was at the end of the case, was it not? —— Yes. . . .

. . . if I may revert to something we were touching on yesterday, Mr. Biko: to the ANC and the PAC being banned in the past, and SASO and BPC then filling the void which was created. What is your understanding, limited as it may be—what are the reasons for the banning of those two organizations? What were they doing that led to their banning? —— Well, I think you are asking for my opinion. My opinion is actually that much as they did engage in some programs at a certain point in history which constituted what we called yesterday or defined yesterday [as] confrontation, the real reason for their banning, if you go to the root cause, is basically the fear that White society and institutions have for the Black man. I think this was the real reason.

But then wouldn't SASO and BPC result in that same fear? —— I do not know. I cannot vouch for instance that SASO and BPC will

remain unbanned forever,* but at the same time one must understand
that there is a progressive change in attitudes which constitute[s] what
I called a historical process yesterday. I think White society now is
not at the same point as it was in 1960. In 1960 you could never get
Dr. Verwoerd—it was Dr. Verwoerd then—going to Rhodesia and
persuading them to listen to Nationalists, to form a joint government
with Nationalists, but nowadays you do get Mr. Vorster doing this,
so there is a progressive change. So that whereas perhaps at that time
White society was against change, nowadays you know they may be
considering listening to what the Black man is saying.

But you say their methods were rejected by BPC? ——— Yes.

At the formation of BPC? ——— Well, let me put it . . . We did not
pass judgment on their methods as such. All we did was to say; We
will not use the same methods.

What methods would you not use? ——— I did define this yesterday
as confrontation, and I did define confrontation as implying going
against existing laws in order to register a protest over a particular
issue.

*What did you do to allay the fears of any people that SASO and BPC
dissociated themselves with the methods of ANC or PAC?* ——— The
point is that no such fears were ever expressed within the context of
SASO and BPC. I think it was quite apparent to everybody what
SASO and BPC [were] all about, and certainly we spoke of the whole
development of the human being—in other words, the Black man
discarding his own psychological oppression. Every day in our meetings they saw this as being the thing that BPC and SASO were
promoting . . . [Mr. Attwell intervenes]

*Do I understand you correctly: Nothing specific was done to allay any
fears if they did exist?* ——— To understand me correctly you have to
say that there were no fears expressed.

But apparently the Whites were scared? ——— Well, we did not
have White membership, so if you are talking about within the context
of BPC . . . certainly there were no Whites within BPC.

There were no Whites in BPC but surely you were addressing yourself

*SASO, BPC and the other organizations espousing the Black Consciousness philoso-
phy were banned on October 19, 1977, a little more than a month after Biko's death.

to the Whites indirectly anyway? ———— I have spoken to White audiences incidentally about Black Consciousness in the past, and not so much about BPC and SASO specifically, and I found no such fear. When I addressed a group in Cape Town, for instance—where there was NUSAS, there was ASB, there was a group called NEFSAS, and of course SASO—I spoke about our viewpoint, and incidentally this was found most acceptable by the Afrikaner students. They said to me in no uncertain terms: This is the way Afrikaner nationalism developed, right; we wish you guys well. I have made personal friendships with the president of the ASB in those days as I said yesterday, Mr. Johan Fick. I have met him recently in Johannesburg. He was telling me then that he was chairman of the Jeugbond, and he was inviting me to his room at RAU—Rand Afrikaanse University. He never got frightened. He recognized what I was saying as what has been said in his history, so as far as I could detect in that gathering the Whites who were there had no fears for themselves personally, it was just a question of realizing that you cannot maintain a false standard of living for a long time at the expense of people, that you have to accommodate, and it implies everybody coming down a little bit, one or two steps.

Mr. Biko, one of the themes advocated or expressed by you in one of the documents before court was the fear which the Black man has, is that right? ———— That is right.

Do you consider that the White man in South Africa is scared? ———— I think the general White population may very well be under the influence of propaganda to a point where they do not realize just how inevitable change is, but I think the White leadership, especially the leadership of the three main parties in this country, is aware of the inevitability of change, and I think there is a certain fear which is gnawing at them about which direction this change should take. Okay, they certainly do not want to find themselves overtaken by events. They want to be moving with the events. So there is an element of fear certainly in leadership, but I do want to say that the average White man often is not aware—the way he treats Black people at this given moment in shops and post offices and so on, indicates that he just is not aware of the inevitability of change.

Can you point to any document of SASO or BPC, press releases or anything else, where there is a clear dissociation by those organizations

from the methods of ANC or PAC to allay any fears there may be?
———Yes, sure. I said to you we did not pass judgment on the methods of ANC or PAC, neither did we discuss them, at plenary sessions certainly. We have always operated on the basis of our own approach. There was no need at any given stage to dissociate ourselves from anything, from the past.

You see, I am trying to find out whether you people were genuine when you say that you rejected the methods of PAC and ANC?
———I said this was considered at a very small commission, right. That is where the words "no confrontation" originated, because at that commission it was discussed, and these were the people who looked at previous history and the methods used. Certainly we did not canvass that point in the plenary as such. We just spoke about the significance of no confrontation without reference to ANC or PAC.

I put it to you that in fact quite distinct from disassociating yourself from ANC and PAC there was a subtle association with them? ———You would have to tell me specifically how.

Well, I could point to one document [pause] I refer Your Lordship to BPC K.1. This for instance you will notice is a letter written and signed by Zithulele Cindi, accused number 8, in his capacity as secretary-general of the Black People's Convention, and it is headed a box number, Johannesburg, South Africa, which seems to suggest it may have been sent overseas. If you would have a look at the second paragraph, where it starts "Black people in this country"? ———Yes.

Would you just read that to the court?
———"Black people in this country have endured this oppressive system for over 300 years, and needless to say, because of their pride in themselves (Blacks) they struggle to deliver themselves from this social, economic, political, physical and psychological bondage. They have done this through their two political organizations, viz. the African Nationalist Congress and the Pan-Africanist Congress. Up to and until 1960 these were the legitimate political bodies that could express the views, feelings and aspirations of the Black people and offer representation wherever possible. It was not their fault that they [were] outlawed by the racists. [They were outlawed] because they stood high in the defense of Black truth and the preservation of Black dignity."

Now, what image is BPC giving out of those two organizations, ANC and PAC, in this particular document? ——— Well, I think this is just reference to two organizations which exist in the history of Black people.

With approval or disapproval or merely a statement of fact? ——— I think, Mr. Attwell, one thing you must realize is that the concept [of] struggle—which is struggle from liberation of yourself, from anything threatening you—is continuous through history. At different times it is picked up by different people in different methods, okay? But the struggle is what we attach ourselves to. We must recognize that the ANC and the PAC were involved in the struggle, and were not involved in the struggle for selfish purposes; it was certainly on behalf of Blacks and for the liberation of Blacks. We may or may not necessarily approve of their methods, but the fact is they exist in history as protagonists of our struggle. Without agreeing with them, we give them their due for existing in our history and for pushing the struggle forward. I think this is the context in which reference to ANC and PAC has been made in this document, and I am sure I have made the same reference myself in a sense in some of the articles I have written.

I have no doubt, Mr. Biko. I am merely stating do you agree with me that this is an approval? ——— It is not an approval. It is not a passing of judgment. It is a recognition of what has happened in history. An approval implies subjecting whatever has happened to systematic analysis so that you can arrive at a judgment whether approving or not approving. In this case it is just mere reference to a particular phase in our history as Black people.

And when BPC talks or SASO talks in its documents of "our true leaders who have been banned and imprisoned on Robben Island"? ——— That is correct.

Who are they referring to specifically? ——— We refer to people like Mandela, we refer to people like Sobukwe, we refer to people like Goban Beke, Casadra. You know, it is a whole mixed bag of people belonging to any of those movements, for instance.

And what is the common factor in those people? ——— The common factor is that they are people who have been pushing forward the struggle for the Black man in a selfless sense.

They include the leaders of the ANC? —— They do.

Do you know any of these banned persons personally? —— Like?

I am asking you, you have named a lot of people—Do you know any of them? —— Which banned people? There are three banned people here.

Banned and restricted and people who have been on Robben Island? —— Oh yes.

Could you name them? —— I have met Mr. Sobukwe, for instance.

In what connection? —— Because I wanted to meet him.

When was this, Mr. Biko? —— It was in 1972.

Was there anything specific that you wanted to know from him? —— Well, no. I was on a tour of the country for Black community purposes which took me to collect some information from Mr. Stanley Ntwasa in connection with some cases that he had had that year, and because we were in Kimberley of course we took the opportunity of seeing Mr. Sobukwe.

When in 1972 would this have been? —— This was about September, late August—September.

Do you know if any of the other accused know any of these people, particularly Sobukwe? —— No one here has mentioned meeting him.

Accused number 4? —— Aubrey could have talked about him, but I do not know if he has met him.

Sobukwe is a particularly relevant person in the history of the Black struggle in this country, is he not? —— He is an important figure.

Is he a constitutional expert, would you say? —— Sobukwe?

Sobukwe. —— I definitely do not know, I do not know his training.

There was evidence before this court that there . . . It was rumored that BPC people had seen Sobukwe about the drawing up of the BPC constitution? —— Well, I would certainly deny this. I do not think so.

You did not? —— Sure, as far as I know no one did. No one reported to me going to Sobukwe.

But you cannot speak for other people, you can only speak for your-

self? ——— Well, you would have to ask the people who were in charge of drawing up the constitution.

Who were they? ——— Probably Aubrey would know better. Saths would know better. I would not know much in that line.

THE COURT: Was he not still in Robben Island in 1971?

MR. ATTWELL: *The BPC was formed, M'lord, in July 1972—yes. Do you know when Sobukwe came off Robben Island?* ——— I cannot remember specifically. I think it was June of some year, whether it was 1970 or 1971 I do not know, but I think it was the middle of the year.

Can you point to any document of SASO or BPC which specifically and unambiguously rejects violence? ——— I would have to think about that. You would have to give me a whole lot of documents to look through.

You know these documents as well if not better than I do, Mr. Biko? ——— Actually I do not. I do remember coming across something useful in that sphere in the past two days but I cannot remember where I saw it.

You were director for publications for SASO at one stage? ——— That is correct.

In which capacity you gave out, I am quite sure, numerous documents . . . [The witness intervenes] ——— Well, I mean I would have to refer here specifically to BPC because I think SASO is irrelevant in that context. SASO was a student organization and they had a very defined field of activity, which was students. If you are talking about the possibility of violence, you know, surely you must be referring to BPC and not SASO, okay?

I am referring to both, Mr. Biko. ——— Well, you will not find it in SASO, because SASO operates within the students, and they certainly push forward a philosophy of Black Consciousness, but their field of activity, their membership, is confined to students. I do not see how students can form an army.

It is also open to scholars, is it not, according to the constitution? ——— It could be, but I do not remember any scholar group affiliating to SASO.

Are scholars allowed to become members . . . [The witness intervenes] ——— At some point in our history we allowed groups of scholars to affiliate en bloc certainly.

And it is in the constitution, is it not? —— Yes. I do not remember one group affiliating as such.

But SASO eventually transferred its complete youth program and scholar affiliations to BCP, did it not? And left the whole youth and scholar side of it to BCP? —— No, I think it was youth leadership training programs that were transferred to BCP.

Did it not transfer its whole youth program to BCP? —— Youth leadership, I am saying.

Is that all? —— That is all. They have all disappeared in fact.

And have you worked in BCP in connection with SASSAM? —— Only insofar as they were involved in the youth leadership program.

NYO, TRYO and the other regional youth organizations? —— That is correct.

And Black high schools? —— No, not individual Black high schools.

Did you in BCP assist in the formation of any of these regional youth groups? —— Yes, I think, you know, without necessarily working for it as an end, we assisted in that we brought together various organizations, youth organizations from several regions, spoke to them about the whole concept of problem solving and youth work, and I think the question was put to them of whether they did not foresee the possibility of solving their problems better as a unified force, and I think eventually they did hold a conference, you know, of their own and amalgamated into the formation of NYO, for instance.

Offhand you cannot point to anything, any document, where a specific and categorical rejection of violence by SASO or BPC was made? —— I am not talking in negative terms like that. I think I am talking in more specific terms of what we intend doing, you know. In other words the whole line of thinking, the whole process of bargaining, which is what we are talking about, and violence has never been considered in BPC as far as I know.

It is not in the constitution is it, a rejection of violence? —— No, it is not there.

Do you agree with me that both constitutions are wide enough to cover a violent confrontation? —— Well, as far as I am concerned I think the term violent is not in the constitution of the P.R.P. of the

U.P. I doubt if it is there in the Nats. constitution either.

Yes, but I am interested in your specific constitution. —— What I am saying is that when people draw up a constitution they talk positively, they talk in terms of what they are going to do, not in terms of what they are not going to do.

Yes, but you people had a peculiar background—you had prejudice you had to meet? —— Yes.

A suspicious bunch of authorities that were keeping an eye on you? —— Mmmm.

A difficult time was forecast for both organizations from the start? —— That is correct.

And a lot of rejection was expected? —— That is correct.

And a lot of resistance was expected? —— That is correct. So?

And there is no specific rejection of violence in either constitution? —— Why must it be there?

I just want an answer yes or no. —— It is not there . . . [Mr. Attwell intervenes]

That is all I want to know. —— Precisely because we never thought of it.

Fine. Do you see any significance in the fact that the Black Consciousness movement originated in a student movement rather than some other sort of movement? —— Yes, I think there is a lot of significance.

Yes, could you expand on that? —— I think it is similar in many instances to development of many philosophies. They either start with the so-called intellectual class within a society, or alternatively where this is not a strong section of a society they start within the student world. I think liberalism for instance as a concrete philosophy started within the intellectual class in Britain especially. I think the doctrine of Marxism, if you look it, started within an intellectual class in the German universities, and so it goes with most philosophies. Now in our given society we do not have an unlimited number of so-called intellectuals within the Black situation, and certainly those who are there often are embroiled in the whole problem of existence. So we do not have researchers. We do not have people with free time to look at problems of the Black people and to evolve ways and means of cutting out our problems. But on the campus you do get a little bit of free thinking and experimentation, and this is why Black Consciousness evolved from there.

Would you agree with me that students generally speaking are the most easily and effectively mobilized group in a society? ———— I think in most self-sufficient societies students can be, you know, a pretty wishy-washy group, but I think students in this kind of context see themselves as playing a very serious role in the evolution of a way out of the morass in which we are right now.

I am not sure that that is an answer to the question I am looking for. I am putting to you a proposition: Students generally speaking would be the most easily and effectively mobilized group in a society. Would you agree or disagree with that statement? ———— I would not necessarily make it as categorical as all that.

THE COURT: *But are they not volatile reformers?* ———— Well, I have seen students who did the exact opposite. I mean, the Afrikaner students are forming a brake on the Nationalist Party which is against all rules.

No, but a student is like that? ———— Ordinarily, M'lord, students are in the forefront of change, but I am saying the Afrikaner students are depicting a very strange situation where they are forming a brake on the Nationalists. When the Nationalists want to lessen the stringent situation that is there now, you get some of them saying, Aha, we cannot have equality of opportunities of this, we cannot have this, we cannot have that. So they are in fact a strange phenomenon.

But you will get an equal number of students that will say, No, you are not going far enough; you must give them more? ———— If you look right through the world, ordinarily students are much more liberal than their governments. As I am saying, you know, the specific rebel, the Afrikaner student is a strange one which I have not quite been able to analyze myself, and I think in the same way we cannot make the kind of rationalization or generalization like you are making right now about students. We have in our own country three student groups, you know—the English liberal students, the Afrikaner very conservative students and the Black student ranks which are concerned with liberation.

Well, a student has greater opportunities to make contact with new development and new occurrence of thought and new ideas and new ideologies? —— That is correct.

They are always experimenting; they think they have the solution? —— That is correct. In most cases this is correct.

MR. ATTWELL: *So you find some of the White students a strange phenomenon?* —— Afrikaner students.

Or some of them? —— Yes.

Yes. Mr. Nengwekulu also in one speech talked about these strange people with their strange logic? —— Oh, yes he does that, he does that, yes.

There are also references in the SASO documents to the campuses being "latent wells of power." Have you come across that type of expression? —— I have not seen that expression myself.

Would you agree with that type of statement? —— Well, in the sense of giving leadership to the community, it is a statement that can be made, certainly.

And generally students are going to be the future leaders of society, are they not? —— Yes, of course. When you talk about students being leaders, you do not really talk about every individual student. I think there are duds at university as well.

The leadership potential is there, and leaders will inevitably be drawn from that class? —— This is correct. This is correct.

Would you consider SASO to have been the nursery of BPC? —— I think only in terms of giving a skeleton a bit of flesh to a philosophy that was later to be adopted by BPC, in that sense, yes.

And BCP again going lower down to scholars and busy with the leadership potential and this sort of thing... [*The witness intervenes*] —— This is not the main thing in BCP incidentally, and I think, if you care to know, the youth leadership program in BCP died off some one and a half years back; it is not the main thing.

Well, let us talk about the theory behind it, then? —— No, no, no, I think it does not fit it. It is [illogic], I must point it out.

Yes, but you are trying to apply the practice. I gather that SASO and BPC were at certain stages of their history in drastic straits and not getting much done anywhere? —— Who is this?

Both SASO and BPC? —— You mean in their development?

There were difficulties left, right and center, and they were not getting much done, and lots of projects failing and lots of things not being done? —— This is correct.

I am talking about the intention. —— This is correct, yes.

And BCP working with the youth at schools and busy with leadership potential? —— Yes.

Leadership for what? These people would go to university and ultimately into the open society . . . [The witness intervenes] —— No, I am saying your logic is faulty, at that point, precisely because BCP decided to discontinue that program in favor of other programs, which are much more in line with the nature of the organization.

THE COURT: *Well, I think what counsel is trying to put to you is this: In this particular setup didn't the students find that they were really a lot of students, and they had to involve the Black people as such, and they as students could not do it because the Black man in the street is suspicious about a student with his wild ideas, so they felt that in order to reach the grass roots it was . . . and to involve the Black masses, if I may put it that way, they had to assist in the formation of a body such as the BPC in order to reach the masses. So they were a body in order to organize the students—the BPC was there then to organize the nonstudents—and then, well, in order to get the young people involved you required a further body, and it is possible then that they sponsored a body like the South African Students Movement?* —— As I say, M'lord, the logic was not so much that SASO feared rejection from the community if they did it themselves, but I think the correct logic is that whereas SASO saw the need for a totality of involvement, in other words several organizations dealing with several aspects of the Black community including leadership, they were quite clear about the ambit of their own operation being within the student sphere, so they merely sought to encourage a correct perspective amongst the existing organizations, and in the process of doing this, a political organization also became a possibility, and they pushed that as well. You know, this is what they did.

But didn't the students in some way operate through the BPC? Well, were they not automatic card-bearers of BPC? —— Not automatic, you had to join. I had to take a card of BPC.

But there was no difficulty in becoming a member? —— You had to be over a certain age.

Well, apart from certain qualifications? —— That is right, he had to be over a certain age and if he wants to, well, he joins. It was not automatic that because he was in SASO therefore you qualify for BPC. Most students at university incidentally are under age.

MR. ATTWELL: *What was the age limit for BPC?* —— I cannot remember it specifically now.

Is it not seventeen years? —— I really do not know now. I could just look at the constitution.

Would it be in the constitution? —— It should be somewhere in the constitution.

THE COURT: *It does not say. The constitution merely says membership shall be open to—oh, no that is SASO?* —— That is SASO, M'lord.

MR. ATTWELL: *M'lord, if I can refer Your Lordship for instance to Annexure 4, which is "Inkululeko Yesizwe" which says: "Membership of BPC is open to all Black South Africans over the age of seventeen. Each member is required to declare . . ." and then there are eight or nine things that they have to state on acquiring membership. Doesn't that mean that in fact at the age of seventeen you would cover virtually every Black student at a university?* —— There are quite a few students at sixteen to seventeen at Black universities.

Then the Bantu education is not so bad? —— They just show intelligence, they tend to skip certain stages. Most of the people who get to university are the cream of the Black students.

I think some of them skip the logic classes, Mr. Biko? —— I do not know.

THE COURT: *Why do you say that, Mr. Attwell?*

MR. ATTWELL: *I do not think their policy is very logical, M'lord. I trust that we will prove that to Your Lordship during the course of this case.*

COURT ADJOURNS
———————

COURT RESUMES

STEPHEN BANTU BIKO, STILL UNDER OATH

CROSS-EXAMINATION BY MR. ATTWELL, CONTINUED: *M'lord, I asked Mr. Biko whether he would have a look during the tea adjournment at the Minutes of those congresses that he had been to, and*

compare them with the language used in resolutions I did refer the
witness to. Mr. Biko, did you avail yourself during the tea adjournment
of an opportunity to have a look at these two sets of Minutes which are
before court? —— Yes, I attempted that.

Can you help the court at all now in relation to the questions I asked
earlier? —— Yes, this is an attempt. I did not quite go through the
1972 Minutes, but I do not think it is necessary, and of course as you
said the 1970 Minutes are not there. First of all I might just point out
that this particular resolution you are referring to here refers to
apparently a situation of removal of people from an area.

You are referring now to Resolution 46 of 1974? —— Yes.

And in that sense I did not quite get a parallel in the other Minutes,
but the language certainly I think is contained to some extent in
Resolution 35 of 1971.

That will be in SASO A.1, M'lord—perhaps you could read to the
court what you have in mind there? —— This is a resolution arising
out of . . . [The court intervenes]

THE COURT: *On what page is that?* —— This is page 10 of the original document, 248. It arises out of a visit by the SRC's of Wits and
Stellenbosch to several Black campuses. I am not going to read the
whole resolution. I just want to read the concluding part which says,
"We therefore strongly condemn this gross arrogance on their part
and accordingly advise Black campuses to shun and refuse to meet
these misdirected adolescent White students who are out to destroy
our Black Solidarity." I regard this as strong language. Of course, the
point of application of the language is not now the South African
government; it is just students. Then in Resolution 95 of the same
document we get a reasonably similar situation in that there was a
train accident somewhere, and SASO took a resolution. Now again,
the situation is not quite the same in that there could be no direct link
with the government, but in point 3 of that resolution SASO says:

> ". . . further regards these 'accidents' as one of the subtle ways
> of violence representative of White South Africans to which the
> Blacks are constantly exposed."

Now, I think in a sense the language that is used has become stronger
in that the incident is more direct. There is a mass removal of a whole
population at Doornkop, and the level of disgust that it arouses in the

minds of Black students who are opposed to this is that much higher
because it is a direct action by government. Now, unfortunately as I
say in these Minutes there is no quite similar incident, but if you go
again to Resolution 13 and 19 of the 1972 Minutes, you do find phrases
like "violent White racist regime" and so on. I do not quite propose
to go through all of them.

MR. ATTWELL: *If you will just read the specific words you have in mind
there?* —— Resolution 13.

You are now referring to SASO C.3 are you? —— C.1. Yes. This
is a reference to Bantustans. That this GSC noting . . .

> "1. the strides and progress achieved by the government in
> further destroying the Black man's work for emancipation as
> represented by the creation of Bantustans, CRC, SAIC and
> UBL;
> 2. aware that these institutions are extensions of the oppressive
> System which are meant to appear as if for us whilst working
> against our interests;
> 3. realizing that Black people are thereby beginning to be sys-
> tematically divided in terms of aspirations;
> 4. noting that constant usage of these foreign platforms by some
> dissident government-appointed leaders with the cooperation of
> the press has led some Black people to believe that something can
> be achieved out of exploitation of the System;
> Therefore resolve to commit ourselves to the task of explaining
> to the Black people the fraudulence and barrenness of the prom-
> ise falsely suggested by these White racist institutions; to instruct
> the Executive to have nothing to do with the so-called leadership
> of the White racist institutions."

Now, I think again the term "White racist regime," "White racist
institutions" begins to occur in these resolutions, but again the topic
of Bantustans is not as emotive as the removal of mass populations,
but I am just trying to illustrate the similarity of language. Then we
go to Resolution 19:

> "That this GSC noting that South Africa is being isolated from
> the world and barred from membership of various international
> agencies because of her racial policies;
> 2. that several of these platforms have indicated that because

South Africa is not a member, no recognition can be accorded
to SASO

Therefore resolves to inform all these international organizations:

(i) that SASO is a Black students' organization committed to the
liberation of the Black man and asserting his human dignity;

(ii) that it is committed to fighting all aspects of racial discrimina-
tion;

(iii) that the White racist regime of South Africa usurped political power and implements it against the will of the Black people;

(iv) that SASO and the Black people cannot be held responsible
for any of its actions;

And we affirm the right of the voice of the Black people to be
heard on as many international platforms as possible."

Again, I think this is a condemnation of the government in similar
tones to this present resolution that we are looking at, but again the
particular issue at stake is not as emotive as the Doornkop removal.
Now, I have not been able, M'lord, to go through all the Minutes. The
time just did not allow this. I do remember that in the 1970 Minutes
which are not before court, when we expressed our withdrawal of
recognition from NUSAS as a national students' organization, we did
express it in pretty tough language. So that the usage of tough language by SASO is quite usual, quite common. It is an expression of
the way Blacks feel about issues of this nature. And when you focus
it on a particularly emotive issue like removal of people, and not only
removal of the population from one place to the other, the way it is
often done, I think it gives a pretty good background to why there was
an elevated sense of disgust amongst the students as shown in this
motion. As I was saying earlier on, there are various forms of terrorism by the government and its institutions, and this was seen by SASO
as also a form of terrorism against the population of Doornkop.

*Mr. Biko, I do not want to labor the point, but will you have a look
... I really meant the language in the 6th GSC and 5th GSC in general.
I mean, I am not confining myself to that one resolution about the
removal. If you will perhaps just look at the 6th GSC Minutes, SASO
N.1, I mean take a look at Resolution 31 of 1974, it is on page 7, page
103 of Your Lordship's papers?* ———— Right.

Do you see there under point 3 "an indication of the determination by the forces of imperialism to systematically eliminate Black people who are etcetera" and then in "Resolves—2. to re-affirm our dedication to the ultimate destruction of the forces of imperialism in Africa"? —— Yes.

Now, that sort of language . . . [The witness intervenes] —— Could we just deal with that resolution? Again, I think, you know, you have got to look at it in the context in which it came.

Yes, well, I am merely interested in the language, but if you feel that you want to make any specific point there? —— Yes, what I am saying here is again wherever you have a particular incident, you have got to take it in context to look at the particular resolution that accompanies it. I mean, South Africa has always condemned terrorism, but when three folk are killed on the Beit Bridge, all you people start churning public reaction against terrorism in very, very strong terms. Now, in a similar manner although SASO has always spoken about the fact that Black people are periodically killed, you know, through various forms of accidents by the South African Whites, when their own men Tiro and Shezi die, obviously you must express this condemnation in much stronger terms just to show the government, to show the System that you just cannot accept this going on anymore. I think this is the theme that is in this resolution. You have got to look at it in the context.

Would you agree with me that the Whites are described in various documents of SASO and BPC as imperialists? —— Well, I do not think this occurs all that much.

But you have seen it? —— I have seen it certainly in some documents. I do not think SASO goes around saying that Whites are devils, Whites are imperialists, Whites are the enemy. You know, you do find this in some documents certainly.

Well, to whom would they be referring when they talk about the forces of imperialism? —— Well, no one knows who killed Tiro. Tiro was killed by a bomb purported to be sent from some country somewhere in Europe, you know; it is a postulation. Obviously it was someone with an evil intention.

Is he necessarily an imperialist? —— It is someone with a European sort of background. I mean, the whole connection of Geneva and the finding also of the Botswana government, or their statement anyway, indicated that Tiro was killed by people with certain powerful influence, and this is I think from where SASO got this whole idea of an imperialist plot, so to speak, which may not necessarily be correct. And of course when you express an emotion like that one, you do not seek to be particularly correct— you make a guess.

You blame the Whites for it? —— Sorry?

You blame the Whites for it? —— It may very well be the Whites, I am sure.

Did you ever hear any suspicion that it was not a man overseas, a European overseas, or a person overseas responsible for Tiro's death? —— I received various theories personally. Someone suggested to me that it was a BOSS* network operating from abroad, you know; when I say BOSS I mean South African BOSS. Someone said to me, No, it could be South African originated, you know. I got many, many theories, none of them proved.

Do you know anything about the allegation contained in one BPC document that the perpetrator of this dastardly deed was somewhere in South or Southern Africa? —— Well, I did not get that particular document.

Did you ever come across that sentiment? —— No, I did not get that document.

THE COURT: *It does not say somewhere in Southern Africa; it says not far from.*

MR. ATTWELL: *M'lord, if I have to refer to it specifically?* —— Well, far in Southern Africa might mean not far from South Africa.

I refer Your Lordship to Annexure 4, page 48 of the indictment, M'lord, where it states the following, under the heading "Tribute to Tiro" it reads:

> *"O.A.R. Tiro was murdered by a parcel bomb in Botswana. John Dube was similarly murdered in Zambia. Brother Tiro was permanent organizer of SASO. Brother Dube was in charge of the ANC offices in Lusaka. Both these freedom fighters were in exile from the land of their birth at the time of their assassinations. Somewhere in S. Africa are the perpetrators of these dastardly deeds, going unpunished."*

*South Africa's special intelligence force, the Bureau of State Security.

You say you never came across that sentiment? —— I never heard
that.

*You do not think it ties up at all with this particular resolution we
have referred to here?* —— It could very well. I do not know. I do
not know which came first.

*I think this one was—no, no, that would purely be speculation. If one
has a look for instance at Resolution 44 of 1974, talking about the
homelands?* —— Yes.

> *"This GSC noting the growing false feeling of relevance of home-
> land, CRC and SAIC leaders in Black politics manifested in their
> convention of the summit conference resulting in the rape of Black
> Solidarity in their concept of Federation, Resolves—*
> *2. to condemn these atrocious opportunists who pose as leaders of
> the Black people."*

. . . that sort of language? —— This is not strong.

You do not think that is strong? —— No.

*And if you look at Resolution 46 of 1974, he talks about "naked
terrorism, inhumanness, brutality, White South African system which
perpetrates its malicious acts of injustice, an outrageous capitalist regime in the decadent South African society, that it accords certain
officials of the system ecstasy to witness the rape of Black humanity
and go out of their way to express smoothness for this callous removal; the fascist nonrepresentative regime of South Africa perpetrates these monstrous acts indiscriminately on the Black community
recurringly, as in the unpardonable instances . . ." And it goes on in
those terms. It says "to mention a few in very light terms"?* ——
Yes, but I think a lot of those particular words used there are, you
know, descriptive terms. You know, you might say that the government is unrepresentative, but this is true. It might be that the removals are atrocious, this is true. You might say that the society is
decadent—many people have said that we have got a sick society.
Here they just put them together particularly because this situation
of Doornkop is emotive.

Yes. Language is merely putting words together, is it not? ——
This is correct.

Look over the page:

> *"To condemn in no uncertain terms the savage atrocities the*

*moribund organization called the South African government
perpetrates . . ."*
—— What is the meaning of the term moribund organization?
I would like to know—perhaps you could help us? —— I do not
know. I did not draw up this resolution. I mean, you say that it is
strong language. What does it convey to you?
I say it is derogatory. —— What does it say?
. . . And calculated to incite hostility. —— What does it say in
precise terms?
Well, we will come to that in a minute: [Laughter]
     *"3. To impress on the Black community especially those under-
     going this direct terrorism that the day of reckoning is nigh and
     that time and truth are on our side . . ."*
*And then of course it says that they are going to communicate the
contents of this motion to the Bantustan mass media—including the
papers, I should imagine—international organizations and other relevant bodies. Black bodies?* —— Yes.
*Now, this type of description—what effect do you think it will have
on anybody?* —— Well, I think you have got to direct me to a
specific somebody.
All right, to the ordinary Black man in the street? —— He would
not understand the language.
He would not understand the language? —— No.
*Does he understand words like terrorist, decadent, outrageous, atro-
cious?* —— In various forms they do—words like terrorist certainly
—but atrocious and so on they would not understand.
Have a look at Resolution 48 of 1974 . . . [The court intervenes]
THE COURT: *You asked what moribund meant. Does it not mean that
it is a dying organization; it is near to its end?* —— This is what I
understand it to mean, M'lord. I mean, I do not think it can be said
to be derogatory. I think it is used in the same way as decadent; it is
a sick society; it has got to give in at some stage to the forces of history.
MR. ATTWELL: *Then if you would have a look at page 16—actually on
page 17 of that document—it is a Resolution 48 of 1974 concerning the
Van Wyk Commission of Inquiry into matters relating to the University
of the Western Cape. It talks about the "power structure" in point 1
there "with its ramifications to terrorize and repress Black students,"*

and then on page 17 it talks about "part and parcel of a grandiose diabolic scheme by the South African White racist government." —— Mmmm.

That is Mr. Nefolovhodwe, number 6? —— Page what?

That would be page 17 of your document at the top, point number 3, "grandiose diabolic scheme." —— Yes, that is correct. I think what can be made of this document is specifically that in the first few conferences SASO had a lot of internal issues to set up, so that a lot of their time was taken by elaborating on their structure and so on, and they paid only passing attention to issues that were affecting them. Surely by 1974 their structure had settled down. They were looking at issues affecting them in the universities and in the broad society in which we live, and it would appear to me from looking at these Minutes and the particular issues they focus on, that at this particular GSC there were a number of emotive issues that did arise —like the removals, like the death of Tiro and Shezi and so on . . . [Mr. Attwell intervenes]

Have one last look at . . . [The witness intervenes] —— So I mean the trend of the Minutes cannot certainly be the same as 1971, 1970 and 1972.

Fifty-seven of 1974, specifically on page 22 of your document, page 118 of Your Lordship's papers—it seems to concern education. He talks about "This basic tenet, it is the educational prostitution and treacherous violation of human rights," and in point 4 there:

> *". . . that in this country education offered to Blacks has been designed by the racist minority White regime to subject Black people to perpetual servitude,*
>
> *in pursuance of their sinister goal the Whites have nefariously so framed . . ."*

That type of language is what I had in mind. —— Sure. I mean, that has been used for decades now. I am sure even stronger by people before us.

Yes. Well, we will be submitting to His Lordship at the end of the case that the language did get progressively more militant? —— Mmmm.

You, I gather, do not agree with me? —— I think you know SASO had more opportunity to express itself on more issues as time went on. This is all I am prepared to say.

Did it not feel more secure . . . [The witness intervenes] ——— But
I want to suggest that here the basic language, you know, White racist
regime. This is endemic to SASO expressions because 1) this is what
we feel, and 2) it is true, and anyway I think you cannot possibly fault
that. It is a racist regime and it is a minority regime.

*And while we are busy on this particular point about what the Blacks
generally and genuinely feel, you did express in your evidence-in-chief
that you found during discussions with Blacks, in the beer halls and this
sort of thing, that they use language, some of them, far worse, you said,
than SASO did?* ——— This is correct.

And certain people I suppose far less than SASO did? ——— Yes,
yes.

*And SASO and BPC were there to articulate the feelings of Blacks.
Do you agree with me?* ——— Yes, to articulate their feelings on issues.

*Now, which sentiments would SASO and BPC be articulating—the
sentiments of those that are very militant and use very harsh language,
or those that use the lesser language?* ——— Mr. Attwell, I think if you
conducted a survey you are very unlikely to find more than a fraction
of a percent of Black people who are pleased with the situation that
exists. Now, BPC sees it so as a political pressure group, right? They
seek to represent the interests of the majority of Black people, and the
majority of Black people are displeased with what is going on, so BPC
therefore seeks to articulate that displeasure with the System. And it
takes various forms. I cannot say which sentiments—a whole lot of
complaints. It would take us a whole three weeks to put them one by
one.

Yes, I merely want to know which group of Blacks. ——— The majority who are displeased about what is going on right now.

*And if it articulates these feelings, would it be the feelings of those
people who are viciously anti-White and militant, or the others?*
——— They represent all Blacks. I think they synthesize all the complaints. Some people complain about squatter conditions because they
stay in squatter conditions; others complain that they have got small
yards—you have got to synthesize all this and come up with what they
call the Black viewpoint.

Now, you said the vast majority of Blacks would have these feelings?
——— Yes, sure.

Some would not, is that right? ——— Well, I am just being scientific actually. I have never come across a single Black man who does not complain. But to be scientific I have got to say a fraction of a percent might agree with you.

Now, you know the accused are charged with causing or encouraging or furthering these feelings of hostility? ——— I have heard this, yes.

And do you consider there is a difference between causing something, encouraging something or furthering something? ——— Oh well, I am sure there is a difference because they are words with different meanings.

What do you understand the difference to be? The difference between . . . Let us start with cause and then encourage and then further—what is the difference? ——— To cause racial feeling, racial hostility, I would understand it to be exactly what, for instance, the System does to us. You know, they constantly knock against your head so that you can respond. I mean, you can adopt an attitude to them.

Is it to create something which does not already exist, to cause? ——— That is right.

To encourage? ——— To encourage would be to further it.

So encourage and further you see sort of synonymous? ——— Right.

They would be something which already exists in some form or other which you carry further? ——— That is correct.

Now, would this type of—call it propaganda, language, call it what you like—would it not encourage or further feelings of hostility . . . ? [*The witness intervenes*] ——— Well, I said in my evidence-in-chief that it does the exact opposite. I think it gives people a new humanity that they did not have. I think Black people are subject to daily experiences which do all the things that you are talking about—cause, encourage and further, you know. Each time they are insulted by a White man, for God's sake, you must feel like reacting. Now, what BPC does is to seek to give Black people a hope—some kind of inner sanctity, some kind of hope in togetherness, right? So that they have a way out—they can see the future. As it is now . . . people are just feeling daily insulted, daily moved to reaction and not knowing what is going to happen. You have got a beautiful situation for a potential explosion, and I think this is what led to the strikes in 1972 and 1973 in Durban. It is precisely this problem of not having a hope. The moment you have some kind of organization which speaks for you like a trade union, like a BPC, then you develop a hope, you develop a view of history, you begin to know where you are going. And I think that cannot be called furthering racial hostility.

Right. Now, if I can carry your argument a little bit further; if one does this . . . one assumes that this is a relief valve, call it what you like? —— Right.

And it would then mean that this is an escape from inner frustration by expressing it, and that you then have some inner calm. How does this then tie up with BPC's idea to get a mass of members all involved and active and united—would it not have the opposite effect? —— I think again you have got a wrong interpretation of Black Solidarity. We are not envisaging getting a committed membership, a number of people who constitute almost what you might call a standing army, no. We are looking forward to—as I said yesterday—getting a majority of Black people behind us, behind what we say, in the same way that the Nationalist Party has a majority of people behind them right at this moment. They do not constitute a homogeneous mass that can be called to action any day. There are wide differences even amongst them. But at least there is a central feeling. They constitute what you call—*die volk*—and the Nationalist Party, the Broederbond—these are their spokesmen. At least they have got a home; they have got a leadership. You cannot call them tomorrow to action because they are all scattered throughout the country, but they have got an identity and they have got a vanguard in the form of the Nationalist Party, the Broederbond and all the other Afrikaner cultural organizations which speak for them. Now, the same thing applies to Black people. We are trying to create a situation where BPC speaks for the people, gives them a home, gives them dignity, so that they can feel that they are human once more, which is not what they are feeling right now at this moment.

You want to involve all the Blacks, do you not? —— Certainly not necessarily all. I am sure not all the Afrikaners are in the Nationalist Party, for instance.

All right. How many Blacks are in South Africa? —— I do not know. Various figures have been given, some people say 18 million, others say 21 million, others say 24 million. I honestly do not know.

What do you believe? How many? —— I would say roughly about 20 million Blacks arȩ in this country.

You see there are references in the documents to 30 million? —— Could be.

And this seems to be a fairly constant figure in the documents? —— Could be.

Which appears to be somewhat higher, about a third higher than most people estimate? —— Okay.

Do you see any significance in this inflated figure? —— No, I think the only thing significant is BPC's belief to know from Black experience that a lot of Black people are in fact not registered. For instance, in Soweto; the current official figure for Soweto is about 800,000. Black thinking points to about 1.5 million in Soweto, because for every, say, 6 people who are registered, there are 2 who are not registered or something like that. Now, I think those figures come from that kind of thinking; there is no other significance beyond that.

THE COURT: *It is because the population figures are taken from a census?* —— That is correct.

So they do not necessarily go by the number of people who are registered? People are really counted in households? —— Well, of course, M'lord, when the census official comes around to my home as a Black man, he never really says to me, We are counting the people who are here in the country. It is a typical White situation again; he comes in and he says, How many people live here? Now, the first thing you think about is registration. If I have got people squatting in my house I am going to be arrested. So if there are 10 people but 6 registered you say, Six, Baas [laughter], so he writes 6 and he goes next door. So you see this is how it is relevant. If it was explained to people nicely that we are only counting, we will not prosecute, people would give the correct figures. But they never know, they are never told.

MR. ATTWELL: *And do you consider that might make up the leeway between 20 million, which is the accepted figure . . . [The witness intervenes]* —— I am saying that this might explain the logic of the inflated figure.

It is not reference perhaps to a broader mass of Blacks than exist in South Africa alone? —— No, I do not think so. I think that is imagination.

Have you found expressions in SASO and BPC documents that your struggle is part of the Black struggle, the Third World struggle against the forces of imperialism in the world? ——— I have used that expression myself.

Yes, now how does that tie up with this? ——— Well, if you look at our adherence to the Komasi Declaration, and if you look at the history of the Commonwealth Students Association, the central point that we were accepting then is that what is happening in this country, which is what primarily concerns us, is but a microcosm of the global problem between Black and White throughout the world. If you look at history, by a strange accident—and this is what we seek to find out in Black Theology—it appears that all the Black nations have not fared well and all the White nations have fared reasonably well, and all the White nations have exploited at one time or the other the Black nations, but not vice versa. Okay? So that much as we recognize the problem right here in our country as between Black and White, there is a broader problem throughout the world of Black and White, which has got to be corrected in the course of history.

I am merely trying to decide whether the 30-million figure does not perhaps tie up with this vision that your struggle is part of a struggle on the part of Blacks in Africa against the Whites in Africa? ——— No, no, no.

In other words it would tie up with movements where Blacks have not yet assumed power in other countries in Southern Africa? ——— No, no, I think that is imagination.

That is imagination? ——— That is correct.

THE COURT: *Before you step off the previous point—now, you say that because of the conduct of the White man you have an explosive position which led to the strikes in 1922?* ——— No, no, I was referring to 1972 and 1973.

Oh, 1972? The strikes in 1972? ——— Yes.

Now, isn't there a danger that if this extravagant language is used it can have an agitatory effect on the Black man and worsen that explosive situation? ——— No, M'lord. As I have submitted before, I think this language . . . is indeed quite mild and quite within his experience of White society and the way he himself ordinarily expresses it. If it was the intention of SASO or BPC to arouse people into reactions, they have got many, many individual situations that they could paint in very, very colorful language to achieve their result. They could talk of starvation in highly emotional language which could achieve the result. They could talk of the many, many murders that one gets in townships, and tie it up somehow with the sociopolitical order in order to achieve their results, but they never do this. All they do is to look broadly at issues, and certainly it is not the preoccupation of SASO and BPC, as I know them, to go around saying, Whites are this, Whites are that; Whites are enemies, Whites are racists. We use these terms in the course of language to articulate existing thoughts amongst Blacks, because it is a starting point in the building up of our membership, in our building up of our humanity within our ranks. And I do not think Black people truly speaking are affected at all by this. They look at the central thing—that is, we have got a common grievance, we have got common experiences. Let us start from there building our society. I think if you look at it again historically—if you look at the Afrikaner documents describing the whole Afrikaner/English problem—you will find that language was used to express the common problems of the Afrikaner as distinct, in terms of their relationship with the English. This is what you do when you want to define a starting point, to say what your problem is.

Don't you emphasize it in this particular way? And can it not have the effect of making the people more hostile than they are? ——— M'lord, I can refer you to typical examples of how Blacks react to this sort of thing. There is a document here for instance which you have referred to—Harry Nengwekulu, I think the defense also referred to it, you know, talking about violent White society. Now, I was at that meeting. My estimate of that crowd was certainly above a thousand —it could have been much more. But for God's sake when he was talking about this violent White society and in a sense ridiculing White society, the people just laughed. Not one of them stood up to say, Down with White society. You know, they just felt an inner peace to feel somehow that they have got a psychological ascendancy over White society, in that they can be able to articulate their problems together, and to talk about it and to laugh over it. I think this is the conduct at many a SASO meeting or BPC meeting. I have never seen a single meeting where people were aroused into action. Personally I have never seen one such meeting.

What would you have to do, then, to arouse them into action?
—— As I say, M'lord, you can in fact pinpoint events and use very colorful language, you know, designed to make people think along with you step for step as things are happening to Black people. As I see it, you can pick up a simple issue of a starving child, describe how the ribs are pouring out of the chest, describe how the legs are swollen, you know—describe a whole lot of things about the child. This can touch the mothers in that society. Then you can pick up something else which can touch the men. You can arouse people in that sort of way. But if you talk grossly and you are looking at it microcosmically, you are not going to arouse their emotions as such, but certainly you are going to get across to them that you are speaking about something they know.

Well, just to give you an example of what I have in mind . . . Now, it often happens in the experience of the courts that a European might accidentally run a Black man over with his motor car in a Bantu area or a Black man's area, and then the Black people are immediately hostile to the White man because he has been involved in that sort of accident with the Black man. Now, isn't that because a feeling has been built up and whenever anything like that happens it triggers off their emotions? Now, can't this type of language have the same effect?
—— Well, I can use the same example, M'lord, and say that if you take a White man to walk along with me into a township without any apparent connection between the two of us, I shout to a mass of people: Here is a White racist pig, they just look at him. If you just utter one word: Kaffir,* they will go for you. In other words it is what comes from White society that provokes reaction from Blacks. Blacks are used to experience from White society . . . They are used to this kind of experience, and this is the thing that they get angry at—not so much the description of it—because the experience makes a much greater impression in their minds.

But does that logic apply in these things? Now, we also find that often a Black man will have an accident and collide with the White man, and the Black man will run away. He immediately thinks that the White people or the White man will assault him? —— That is correct

---

*A term of degradation used by Afrikaners when referring to Blacks. Similar in emotive terms to the word "nigger."

also, M'lord. He is running away from what he believes about White
society.

Yes, because there is a suspicion against each other? —— That is
correct.

*And now, isn't the danger that if one is not careful about the lan-
guage employed that you build up that suspicion and you really create an explosive situation that can be triggered off with the most insignificant event?* —— Yes. All I am saying, M'lord, is that it is
nothing new—these whole incidents that we count as part of our
experience—they are nothing new to the Black man; they do not
add to his experience at all. He has had it before; he probably has
experienced it. All that we are directing ourselves to is a creation of
the belief that this is a common problem and we must act together,
and I think this is in fact the effect it has on Black people when you
speak in this kind of way. I have spoken myself to lots of meetings,
and I really mean it when I say I have never detected a single state
of aroused emotions against White society. On the contrary often
the result at the end of it all when anybody comes to say: I am
joining BPC, I am joining SASO, or I identify with what you are
saying—it is a feeling that for once I have got a home in this kind
of movement.

*Does it not really depend on the reason why you say it? If you say
it because you want to move them into action and they know it, well,
then they are allowed to be swept along. If they know that you are
merely recounting events to them, then they sit and they listen to the
events that you are recounting?* —— Ordinarily when BPC addresses
meetings, gatherings or sends out pamphlets, the purpose is to advertise itself, and in order to advertise themselves they have got to define
who they are, who they stand for, what they represent. And the tail
end of BPC documents, SASO documents directed to the mass of
people is often either by tacit or by overt statements: that the person
must join BPC, the crowd must identify with BPC. And this is the
operative thing at the end of each meeting: people joining or not
joining, depending on whether they are convinced that this is what
represents them or not. You know, the purpose is never to arouse
people to do something against White society. At the end the only
action they take is to join or not join BPC.

MR. ATTWELL: *Well, BPC can take that action on their behalf later on?* —— What action is this?

The action eventually, the bargaining, call it what you like—they will be taking the steps? —— Correct—bargaining.

You had no control over the readership of these things, did you? —— Well, I did . . . [Mr. Attwell intervenes]

You never knew exactly who was going to receive these things? —— I did say yesterday that you send them . . . If you are SASO you send them to your constituents, the students. If you are BPC . . . I mean, Minutes like this for instance, of BPC or of SASO, go to the membership.

And when Nengwekulu speaks at a public meeting? —— Well, that is spoken. It goes to the people who are sitting right there, at the moment.

Now, assuming for a moment that it is not going to affect the Blacks or create any hostility in the Blacks, don't you think it will create hostility in the Whites? —— As far as I am concerned, the Whites have been exposed to SASO thinking, to BPC thinking, and there are quite a few reporters and so on who go to our meetings, and we would talk openly with them about this, and all that it does is to awaken them to the realization that we are in fact running out of time for conciliation, right?

I understood you earlier to say that lots of Whites are not aware of this, is that right? —— Well, I am talking about those Whites who do get to these meetings, reporters and so on.

But lots of Whites are not aware of these things? —— Lots of Whites are just simply not aware.

Now, what effect is this going to have on them? —— Well, how can it have an effect if they are not aware?

If they get in possession of these things? —— But, I mean, you have just agreed with me that they are not aware. They do not know that there is a need for change precisely because they are not exposed to the Black man's views. It is the politicians who are exposed to the Black man's views, and those are the people who are aware, who are attempting to remedy the situation. The average Afrikaner man in the Free State who farms who does not bother to read the Rand *Daily Mail* and all these funny papers [that] report on Blacks—he is not aware of what the thinking is. All right, he is aware of what *Current Affairs* says, and what the folk say in the party, and his belief is that, you know, "We are okay" sort of thing. So the whole prospect of change has not presented itself to him in an urgent manner. It is precisely because he is not aware of this that he is not going to be aware that change is necessary.

So do you think this will have a good effect on him if he becomes aware . . . [The witness intervenes] —— Ordinarily people who get exposed to Black thinking begin to be aware of the need for change.

Basically I think you people accept the fact that the Whites are scared of the Blacks, is that right? —— Sorry?

The Whites in South Africa are scared of the Blacks—there is a basic fear? —— Yes, I think there is a basis of *"Swart gevaar"** mentality which is traceable to the actions of the System.

Now, that type of White man who is afraid—what effect will this have on him? —— Well . . . [Mr. Attwell intervenes]

"Black man, the time now is to rise, liberation is inevitable, break the chains, seize the time, the day of reckoning is nigh"? —— Right.

[The White man in] the racist moribund organization—what is he going to think? —— He does two things if he is in government. On the one hand he carries out repressive measures against spokesmen of the Black people; this is why, for instance, we call it a struggle. We know that if you speak on behalf of Black people things happen to you, not because you are legally wrong, but just because you represent proper aspirations of people. You get banned, okay, you get arrested, you get detained for two years before you appear in a court like this one. On the other hand he also begins to open up, he tells Koornhof to "hamba gashli"† on the question of multiracial sport. All right, you begin to see two Blacks in the rugby Springbok team. He also tells somebody else to open up Nico Nalan theater. In a sense it is a two-way thing: He is aware of this call, he is afraid of these guys— he certainly is worried of the move of people like Strini Moodley, Saths Cooper and Dr. Mokoape—he puts them in jail; but at the same

*An emotive phrase in Afrikaans meaning "Black Peril."
†"Go carefully" in the Xhosa language.

time he begins to release certain areas for entertainment . . . [Mr. Attwell intervenes]

Putting them in jail and that sort of thing is going to lead to a situation where more hostility is caused, not so? —————— Unfortunately it does. This is what we criticize in the logic of the System—that whatever good they do they undo by using force, okay, which force results again in an offsetting of whatever Blacks are beginning to think about the good they are doing.

What good do you people say they are doing in your documents? —————— Who is that?

The Whites? —————— It is so little that it is not worth commenting on. [Laughter]

So you did not comment on it? —————— No, it is not worth commenting on.

I agree with you there—the Whites are described in these documents as people who have done no good. I would agree with you. Getting back to this 30 million Blacks, you say you never envisaged—or 20 million —you never envisaged a solid mass of 20 million people with which you would eventually bargain, or who would be behind you when you go and bargain? —————— We did not foresee a situation where we stand in front and there are 20 million behind us and we say: Do this or else. No, we never envisaged that situation.

Now, the Whites have been portrayed in the documents as people who will not listen, is that right? I think you even expressed in your own evidence-in-chief that they do not even listen to their own White liberals, and that the government is not here to please us, and why should we think it will please us now? Now, the point is unless you have a mass of Blacks behind you, what is there in your bloc which is going to make the Whites listen? —————— I said to you that the whole bargaining process is not supposed to start at a particular point in history; it has started right now. You know, when we speak in these strong terms, we accept the trend of thinking of White people. When the international world condemns South Africa they accept the trend of thinking. At some point South Africa itself will begin to want to bargain in a realistic fashion other than through Bantustans. We want to be ready for this sort of thing. We want to continue mounting criticisms and pressure as a people on South Africa, so that when a period of negotiation, which is inevitable in terms of our looking at history, comes, we are there to be talked to.

I find that an interesting observation. Why do you say that a time will come when the Whites will be prepared to negotiate? —— The point is . . . [Mr. Attwell intervenes]

What is going to make them reach that stage? —— It is probably the same kind of thinking which made Mr. Vorster tell Smith to talk to his Black nationalists. I am sure that he sees the two situations as completely analogous: You have got a White minority ruling over a Black majority in Rhodesia, you have got a White minority ruling over a Black majority [in South Africa]. At some point in history Mr. Vorster went along to Smith to say: Don't bother dilly-dallying with the chiefs—talk to the nationalists. He actually made it possible, and in doing so he spoke with the guy who is supposed to be South Africa's archenemy, Kaunda, and they made it possible for Smith to meet with Muzorewa and Nkomo. Now, I do not think Mr. Vorster is completely logical. I think he understands that this will eventually happen here. When I talk of Mr. Vorster, I talk of leadership. I am not talking specifically of the person.

Now, when he talks to people like Mr. Muzorewa, etcetera . . . you consider [them] to be the true Black leaders, for instance, in Rhodesia? —— Yes.

How does this tie up with your attitude that he must not talk with Mr. Hofwebanye, or he must not talk to Mr. Banda or he must not talk to the other African leaders under any guise of dialogue? —— Precisely because in this plan that he had for Rhodesia, there was 1) African participation in the person of Kaunda with the backing of Nyerere, Machel and the Botswana president. It was based on an acceptance of part of the Lusaka Manifesto which is an essentially African document. When we reject the ["leaders"] coming out here to talk to Vorster, it is because we see this as participation in a program drawn up by Vorster, which program implies acceptance of South Africa in Africa, and South Africa giving very little back.

Do you consider those talks to have been a failure? —— I think so.
Do you think this is inevitable? —— I think so.
Because the Whites in Rhodesia will not listen? —— Well, I think

they were a failure because of the particular intransigence of Mr. Smith, who just does not seem to realize that the clock is ticking on.

Because he is a White man? —— Not necessarily that, but I think he is a stubborn man more than anything else. He could have been a minority Japanese governing in Rhodesia, but all the same he is a very stubborn man. . . .

I do not see how you are going to achieve what you want. —— Because you anticipate that Whites are going to refuse.

That is a possibility? —— Well, let us take a situation of, you know, five soccer teams playing for a particular cup—take the Currie Cup if you like. You can get for five consecutive years team number C constantly being at the bottom of the log but they continue to play the next year, because the whole idea is they believe eventually they have got a chance to win. This is our logic: We have got no alternative; we have just got to play the same game because we believe eventually we will win. We have got that same kind of hope that is inherent in a sportsman who enters the league and loses on many, many years, but eventually he may win.

You mean the wheels turn and eventually it will change? —— I have said it constantly: History moves in a logical direction.

Now, why do you not just sit back then and let the wheels turn—it will come? —— History works through people and we have availed ourselves to history to work through us.

Are you trying to hasten the process? —— No, we are trying to logicalize the process, make it more logical.

What, at the BPC inaugural convention, was the significance in choosing a membership or working hard for a membership of one million Blacks in 3 years? —— Well, I think it was just a target quite frankly. It was just a target. When you embark on any program, for you to move with any sense of logic and direction, you have got to set yourself a target. We could have said 800,000 people, but that is a more awkward figure [than] one million in 3 years.

Is not 30 million better? Is that not what you aimed at? —— No, no, I think the figure one million which is put there is for the immediate membership for BPC. Now, you do not get everybody being involved in an organization—you get people who approve of what you

are doing. But we set out for that target precisely because we wanted
to appear as what we wanted to be, which is a people's movement, and
a million seemed a convenient number to us.

So there is no significance in that figure at all? ——— I do not think
Your Lordship should attach any particular significance to that particular figure of one million.

*It is not to be a sort of central core of dedicated . . . [The witness
intervenes]* ——— What I mean is the number itself is incidental. We
could have said 500,000; we could have said 2 million; we just said
1 million.

One million is a substantial number, is it not? ——— That is correct.

*And I think one million dedicated Blacks set out on a certain course
could certainly affect the events of history, if you like, in South Africa?*
——— They would certainly entrench BPC within the Black community.

*And effect vast changes if they wanted to, if you acted unitedly as one
million solid Black people?* ——— Mmmm—affect the rest of the millions. There are still the other millions you have not counted. They
are important too in backing up whatever the actual membership is
doing and suggesting.

*All right. Now, let us assume for a moment that you people, or that
an organization, wants to weaken the existing system. How would you
go about it?* ——— Weakening it in what sense?

To bring about its eventual downfall, to overthrow it? ——— No, I
will tell you what we want to weaken, what we want to weaken
. . . [Mr. Attwell intervenes]

No, I am talking theoretically now, Mr. Biko. ——— Yes, what we
want to weaken is the resolve to hold on to power in the present way.

*I would like you to look at this thing then as a hypothesis. You are
in an organization which is wanting to take over, to overthrow the
existing system?* ——— Mmmm.

How are you going to go about it? ——— Again, that is a theoretical
question.

Yes, it is a theoretical question. ——— I find it very difficult to
respond to that, M'lord.

*How would you weaken a society, an existing society? What will you
attack?* ——— I have not given any serious thought to that.

Well, perhaps I can prod you in a certain way. We have had evidence from experts that a system depends basically on internal support for the existing system, and especially in the modern sense, external support for the continuation of any system? —— Yes.

So I put it to you that one would have to attack the internal support for that system and the external support for that system. Would you go along with that? —— That is now directing yourself at weakening the resolve to hold on. When you weaken the System you can weaken aspects of the System, physical aspects, right? You can weaken the economic order. You can weaken the whole social order by creating panic amongst people, for instance, and throwing bombs like the IRA are doing in London and so on. That is now weakening the System physically. But if you are applying yourself to change the minds of the internal support, the only result and effect can be a weakening in the resolve of the governing power to continue governing as they are. Now, certainly this we are interested in doing. We are interested in changing this almost stoic stance of the government to continue ruling as things are going on now. But we are not interested in weakening the physical aspects of the country, if you see what I mean.

In other words, harming it to such an extent that if you were eventually able to take it over it would be worth nothing? —— Correct.

Well, the System I think you defined yesterday? —— Yes.

As being the government in power, the machinery that the government uses, etcetera. I am talking of System in that sense, the rulers if you like—that is the sense in which I am using it. How would you overthrow it, what would you do? —— Well, we just hope eventually to get to a stage where they too will find it necessary to give in, through a whole process of bargaining.

Once you make out that they are illegally in power, to destroy any support they may have? —— I do not think they have got support from the majority, quite frankly, because they have no support from the Blacks.

You make out that they are illegally there? —— They are.

They are foreigners for a start who do not belong here? —— In terms of what we regard as natural law, which is an arguable point which I do not want to argue now, from our point of view we regard them as being illegally there.

And provide an alternative? —— Right.

You then set about creating situations or exploiting situations where you can make capital? —— Like what?

And advance your cause, if there is disturbance, if there is disorder, if there is anything which does threaten it, get in on the bandwagon and exploit it if you can? —— Perhaps you might give an example.

Well, let us take a strike. Take anything you like—something which threatens the existing balance? —— That could very well depend on your particular chosen method.

Yes, and then externally of course you could try and cut its sporting ties, its cultural ties, dialogue ties, political ties, etcetera, so that you isolate it from any friends it may have overseas? —— Yes, you might very well do that.

And do you agree that internationally today, international support and diplomacy etcetera is very important for the continued existence of any state? —— Yes. You are much more comfortable when you have got support.

They talk about no country is an island today? —— That is correct.

What do you think in the end result is the basic strength of South Africa? What is its real strength? What enables it at the moment to defy world opinion, as you say? What enables it to defy the rest of Africa? Where does its real strength lie? —— I think two reasons. In the first instance the country has got a hell of a lot of natural resources which through the technological culture brought in by White society have been successfully tapped; the second thing, the country has utilized the availability of Black labor in mounting up an industrial monster, in other words in creating a very well-organized industrial system within this country. Thirdly, the country has devised ways and means of oppressing the Black people and completely cutting them away from any access to power. And [fourthly] of course one can also say that the security system, the internal security system which is really no security system at all for the country but a security system for the White System, has been so devised as to make it virtually impossible for the Black man to do anything but be contained within that structure. Now, South Africa becomes rich as a result. They can afford to spend a hell of a lot of money on the army, and there are certainly no immediate dangers from neighboring African states in the sense of being attacked. They have accommodated within themselves inbred compromises for the Western countries through allowing participation within the System, thereby identifying themselves with Europe and America. They have got support from those countries in the United Nations. I think this is what gives them strength.

Well, if I can crystallize all those thoughts into one idea, it seems to me it boils down to South Africa's economy? —— And race policies.

Well, the Black workers—once again, they reinforce the economy, do they not? —— Indeed, sure.

There are indications in the documents, certain utterances for instance like "the Black workers are the cornerstone to liberation"? —— Some people could have said that, yes.

One of the accused has in fact said so specifically. Do you agree with that statement? —— Well, I did say yesterday that my own analysis points in a different direction. I mean, I do not think this is the point at which one can effectively start. I think there are other points, but it is a valid point to somebody who can support it.

And I think in your exposition at the moment you have given very good grounds for such a statement? —— Mmmm.

In other words, the economy and the Black workers' sphere would be a particularly effective sphere in which to work if you want to effect change? —— It is a possible area.

It is a dominant one, if I understand your argument now correctly? —— Precisely because you understand the argument you also realize that it is the area of greatest resistance.

Greatest resistance to . . . ? —— By the System.

But if you can get the workers on your side, and if you can hit at the economy, that would be one of the most effective ways . . . [The witness intervenes] —— I think yes, intellectually . . . [Mr. Attwell intervenes]

In which any organization could work? —— Intellectually one could submit this, yes.

And foreign investment—I think you mentioned now—through foreign investment South Africa has entrenched herself and got interests in the foreign world? —— Yes. I was talking about something much different. Foreign investment is of very little significance now. I was talking of bilateral trade between countries, which is not the same thing as foreign investment.

But if you get a withdrawal of foreign investment and you can discourage foreign trade, you hit them very heavily? —— If you can discourage foreign trade and get countries to do what has been done to Rhodesia, you can hit at the country.

And if you can get the Black workers, you can effect change very, very quickly? —— Intellectually, yes.

You can cripple the country in three or four days if you have a general strike or something? —— Well, I am not such an expert as to know how many days it would require.

Well, a very short time, I should imagine? —— Well, let us accept your . . . [Mr. Attwell intervenes]

Because it plays such a significant role. —— Mmmm.

You expressed in your evidence-in-chief that the Blacks in South Africa are according to you very religious people? —— Correct, yes.

Would you agree with me that they are also very fond of culture, art, etcetera, Black music? —— Music, yes. I think theater is only beginning to catch up of late. All these are innovations. I mean, the stage is an innovation in a sense in Black culture, it is something which has come of late. You know, in our culture back in the tribal eras, there was no stage, there was just complete involvement—what we call open theater.

Would you agree with me that one of the great advantages of Black theater, Black drama and poetry being recited etcetera, is that one does not require a literate audience? You do not require someone who is to be able to read, is that right? —— Well, you have got to understand the language.

Yes, but you do not have to be able to read, is that right? —— Sure. I mean, it is not like those foreign films where the words are projected onto the screen; it is said by word of mouth.

And lots of Blacks are, according to documents, still illiterate, is that right, in South Africa? —— About—what—55 percent are functional illiterates, I think. This was correct sometime back. I do not know now.

In fact there are literacy campaigns by both organizations, I think, to improve literacy? —— Right.

In other words they consider it a fairly serious problem? ———
Right.

*You have also said that a lot of the Blacks because of conditions as
they exist are very concerned with matters of existence, very down-to-
earth things—they haven't got time for high words and attending fancy
meetings etcetera. They are more concerned with the every day-to-day
continuing existence?* ——— Correct, yes.

*Would you agree with me then that very effective spheres for your
organization to work to effect change would then be in a religious sphere
in South Africa for Blacks?* ——— Yes.

If you could get the church on your side? ——— Mmmm.

You could exert a terrific influence on the Blacks? ——— Mmmm.

*If you could utilize this feeling for culture, and you could utilize
drama, poetry, music, literature—it would be another very effective
sphere to use?* ——— I think you have missed the point, you know, of
what is generally called Black theater. I think it is, as I said, it is
directed at development of the humanity, you know, the humanity
within Blacks. It gives some kind of sedating effect, especially after
any experiences at the receiving end. It is nice to see it being parodied
on the stage. It is nice to get someone reciting a poem to you like
groups like TECON usually did on what it means to be Black, you
know: "I thank you Oh Lord for having created me Black." It is nice
to get some people in a very dramatic way posing this question to you:
Do you castigate yourself for being Black, and going on to point out
to you just how human you are—blood runs in your veins like it runs
in the veins of the White man—making you think positively about
yourself for a long time. This as far as I have experienced is the way
in which theater has been used in confronting the Black man with
himself, to remove the element of alienation in the Black man.

*In other words, Black theater has had a purpose. It has not purely
been entertainment?* ——— Yes, it is entertainment with a purpose. It
is relevant entertainment.

*And that because Blacks are concerned with matters of existence, as
you state, that especially in the towns Black workers would once again
be a particularly effective group to work on?* ——— The term Black
worker is a bit misleading because I think 90 percent of Blacks are
workers. When you are talking about Blacks you are talking about

workers, you know, in a sense. I think you must remove this kind of distinction.

All right, workers generally. But then in the rural sphere with people living very close to nature . . . I think you will agree with me lots of the Blacks live very close to nature in the rural sphere? —— Yes.

Once again an effective way to work with these people would be community projects, things that affect them most closely? —— Yes.

Clinics, hospitals, dams, whatever you want to do? —— An effective way of assisting them and certainly of bringing them to this humanity we are talking about.

And through community projects once again one could influence these people very effectively? —— In a sense.

Because that is the thing they are concerned with every day? —— I think one can help them to build themselves up. This is correct.

Is this a postulation? We are just theorizing at the moment? —— Well, I am talking of reality.

Tell me, is it a pure coincidence that Black religious groups played such a significant part in, for instance, the formation of BPC? You were talking about IDAMASA and AICA—the organizations you did refer to—which have all been religious organizations, or a lot of them? —— IDAMASA and AICA. Well, I think the importance of it is in that they are made up of people whose daily work is pastoral care of large sections of society. So that when SASO worked a plan to see them, this certainly counted. But I must say they were unfortunately one of the very, very few Black organizations existing at the time, and they caught up with this whole idea of Black Consciousness and the development of Black Consciousness and so on, precisely because it is a persuasive philosophy which no Black man who listens to you seriously can resist. It speaks the truth, you know, this is the whole point about it. . . .

COURT ADJOURNS

The Afternoon of May 5, 1976

Biko discusses SASO and BPC as barometers of opinion in the Black community and as organizations designed to serve all sections of that community. Attwell loses a key exchange when he asks Biko whether a strike that SASO supported was in fact a confrontation. There follows a lengthy analysis of the bargaining or collaboration process envisioned by SASO and BPC. Attwell switches back to attack what he considers excessive language in SASO and BPC documents; Biko points out that such language serves the justifiable political purpose of registering Black feeling and is not necessarily inflammatory, as implied by Attwell.

COURT RESUMES AT 2 P.M.

STEPHEN BANTU BIKO, STILL UNDER OATH

CROSS-EXAMINATION BY MR. ATTWELL, CONTINUED: . . . *Now, if I may turn just broadly to SASO and BPC at this stage. Do they have the same broad and basic goals?* —— SASO and BPC? I think one could perhaps say SASO's approach is slightly more intellectual than BPC's; they have got the same broad approach. SASO is obviously a student organization; it has got lots of student issues that crop up in their normal day-to-day work. BPC is more of a political organization and therefore much more directly related with political issues.

But the feelings that they both expound and their objects—Black Consciousness, Black Solidarity, generating a feeling of community, etcetera—would be broadly the same? —— I would say they are guided by the same ideologies.

And it is true of course that SASO played a very significant role in the establishment of BPC, is that right? —— This is correct, yes.

Now, at the stage of the establishment of BPC you were still in SASO, still a member of SASO? —— That is correct, but no longer in the Executive.

But you still played a prominent role in SASO? —— Well, yes, I was a student leader still. . . .

The SASO leadership—are they all necessarily students? —— As far as I know, yes.

All of them? —— As far as I know.

Was Mr. Myeza, accused number 2, a student at the time he was on the SASO executive? —— I would not personally know that.

And Mr. Lekota? —— I would not know that.

You don't know, and the two organizations collaborated closely in many fields? —— They did work together, yes.

In fact I gathered from numerous reports that many of the Heroes' Days and Sharpeville commemorations were shared by the two, especially up on the Reef, etcetera? —— In fact, to be specific, I think this is the [one occasion] where they, you know, usually work together, because it had been a SASO day historically and BPC also cashed in on this particular day, so it was a significant day in the history of the Black people.

Sharpeville Commemoration Days—were they inaugurated by SASO? —— They were started I think by individual SRC's. What SASO did in the 1970 executive meeting in Port Elizabeth was to formally include them on the official SASO calender. . . .

Now, both SASO and BPC propagate this Black Consciousness, Black Solidarity, and they are both involved in this liberatory struggle? To free the Blacks from psychological and physical Black oppression? —— That is right.

Now, in a liberatory struggle, would you agree with me that one has to do three things? The one would be to identify one's grievances and formulate them, so that you people know what you are arguing about? Secondly, you would need to identify a person responsible for these grievances, someone against whom your actions will be directed or to whom you would address yourselves in the hope that you could achieve some sort of amelioration or a change? And thirdly an organization or rally around which the people could work to achieve their change? —— That is a fairly reasonable analysis.

Would the rallying point be Black Consciousness and Black Solidarity within a movement such as SASO and BPC? Who could organize this? —— Yes, a common identity. Let's put it that way.

*And when you identify enemy—I would just like your comment on
one specific little part in a SASO newsletter. I refer Your Lordship here
to K.4(a), which is a SASO newsletter; it is a General K.4(a). On page
93 of Your Lordship's papers, which would be page 16 of the newsletter.
If you could just read the particular passage marked there on the top
left. Would you agree with those sentiments?*

———— "It is a well-known fact when people are seeking to liberate themselves that the enemy must be located and defined. The
basic tenet of the government policy in this country is White
supremacy and White domination. This supremacy and domination makes oppression and enslavement of the Black man a
reality. Therefore by definition White man or White men become
adversaries. However, it is true that some White individuals and
organizations do make overtures to Black people regarding their
problems, and it is true that some Blacks are swayed by this
attitude."

*And in the next paragraph—I think if you just have a look at it—
the idea that Blacks should be swayed by White Liberals is discouraged?* ———— That is correct.

*Now, is that in fact SASO's viewpoint? That one identifies the enemy,
and the enemy is the White man?* ———— Yes, I think SASO does that,
but I think again I have said in my evidence-in-chief and elsewhere
that when we speak of Whites we speak of them as a totality of power
in the sense that they are responsible for the government that does all
the things that Blacks complain about. And when you complain or
you talk about Whites in general, you are talking in that context.

*I think both SASO and BPC aim to involve all the Blacks, if they
could, in this struggle, is that correct?* ———— They certainly seek to
represent the majority.

*BPC also permeating the entire life of the Black man? Every sphere
which could possibly lend itself to their approach?* ———— That is what
you call totality of involvement.

Yes, and . . . ———— That does not necessarily mean that BPC must
do this itself. It must promote within the Black community institutions which can be run on their own, like trade union work for
instance, like the relevant church organizations, like relevant cultural
organizations. You don't seek to control these. You don't seek to

operate these yourself . . . but you are merely promoting their coming into being, so that Blacks can have their own organizations looking after their interests.

And if you don't have some sort of control, then you are not necessarily going to have a united Black mass that can speak with one voice eventually, are you? —— Well, you don't need a control. I think you need a common identity and a common sort of orientation. Like, SASO doesn't have any control over BPC, and BPC doesn't have any control over SASO. In effect therefore BPC doesn't seem to have any direct control over Black students—this is SASO's field—but the two have a common ideology and they . . . owe allegiance to that common ideology.

Both BPC and SASO, then, involve themselves through projects in virtually every sphere which they felt they could? The educational sphere, the workers' sphere, Black religion, or Black Theology, as you call it. You want Black press, you wanted Black banks, you worked through literacy, community projects, to get to the people in the rural areas? —— No, SASO does. I have not had any evidence of BPC projects really.

But with SASO you would say yes? —— Yes.

Then you have symposiums, seminars, formation schools, rallies; you put out publications, which are all directed at publicizing and pushing these certain objects and goals of SASO and BPC? —— Mainly BPC, yes.

Mainly BPC there? —— Yes.

Now, is all this used for conscientization purposes? We defined yesterday what was meant by conscientization? —— No, I would say most of it is used precisely for what you said earlier on, which is to make the organization known and accepted, to explain the organization to the people who shall eventually form the membership, you know. This is the aim.

Have you come across any statements in documents that all the projects are geared for conscientization? —— It could very well be there somewhere.

Have you come across such a sentiment? —— I can't specifically remember.

Would they be wrong or would they be right? —— I think it would be correct in general, but I think again it must be said that both SASO and BPC conceivably for instance could be involved in a project purely for assistance where necessary.

But to build up the good will of the organization? —— Sorry?

To build up good will for the organization? —— I am saying for no other purpose except purely for assistance. And this is conceivable.

Did they according to your knowledge engage in any such activities purely for that type of purpose? —— Yes, I would say for instance when students in the various campuses in and around Durban went on strike [they] could not have their normal meals . . . SASO offices were phoned by students and asked to provide lunch. I remember running around in a Kombi with Mr. Moodley buying food for students, and this is some form of project which is not to conscientize anyone; it is just to assist naturally the students.

But the students, you say, were on strike? And that is why they weren't getting food? —— They were on strike on their own steam.

So in effect your action was helping to perpetuate that strike? —— That is not correct. We were helping to give food. We were asked to give food and we gave food.

Without that food they would have had either to go back or leave the university or something? —— Well, this is a postulation, you know, that you can make.

What other postulation is there? If you don't feed them and they have to get their food . . . ? —— They would have gone out to eat. They probably wanted to continue sitting where they were sitting.

And you aided the striking students? —— This is your conclusion.

Was that a situation of confrontation? —— Which one?

This one with the students striking? —— Well, one would have to go into the individual merits of the strike, and I don't have all the facts now. As I say, I don't know what was the background of the strike. All that happened was that Mr. Moodley and I were sitting around; they phoned and said to us they need food. Okay . . . They are at such and such a place; could we be of assistance? If we need to we can charge them. Is it all right to go and get the food? And we went to get the food and brought it to them.

So you assisted them without an investigation into the merits or demerits of their actions? —— When people need food they need food.

Is this the SASO attitude? —— Sorry?

Is that the SASO attitude? —— No, that is what I mean by help-ing people in a state of need at a particular moment, no matter what prevents them from getting the food.

So even if they were making the most unreasonable demands imagin-able? —— We had nothing to do with their demands or with their actions. We had to do with a request that they needed food, so we gave them food.

And if it had been White students who asked for food, would you have given them food then? —— They are not necessarily our elec-torate, but I mean, it would depend on the particular circumstances. I mean, if I meet White students somewhere on the beach in Durban and they are stranded and they need food, I am sure SASO would be compassionate enough to carry food to them.

Was the portrayal of Whites, the way they were portrayed, in the documents, and in speeches, and at rallies and seminars, etcetera, conducted by both these organizations part of the conscientization pro-cess? —— No, as I said, it was part of your first part, your analysis, defining your common problem.

There is talk, at especially the BPC inaugural convention, of no collaboration with the Whites or the government during the struggle? Are you familiar with that phrase or would you like me to refer you to this? —— Yes, I was referred to that thing earlier on.

You recall that? —— That is correct.

Now, speaking purely from the language point of view, a struggle, by definition—when does the struggle end? —— A struggle ends, I think, when a defined goal is achieved.

And what was SASO's goal and BPC's goal, in that sense? —— I think we have constantly said it: It is liberation.

Now, the point is it ends then when you achieve your victory, is that it? When you have achieved what you have wanted? —— Hmmm.

Now, if you have no collaboration with the Whites or the System or the government during the struggle, where does the period of bargaining come in? —— I have said it before. It has started actually. When SASO formulates the resolutions about the attitudes of Black students to Bantu education, to separate universities and so on, usually at the tail end there is a provision for communication of this to the authori-ties concerned. In other words, this whole phrase that you are quoting, "No collaboration with," does not necessarily imply you do not recognize the de facto power of an existing institution. You bargain at a low level of human rights. You bargain at a still higher level perhaps with Bantustan authorities. You may still need their permission when you want to get into their areas, and you usually apply for this, but the fact that you are referring to there is "We shall not work within or work on a policy as defined by the System." This is what we regard as collaboration.

Do you agree with me that to bargain with the government and the White System would mean to collaborate with them? —— No, I would not agree with that.

Not agree with that? —— No.

What is the difference between bargaining with someone and collaborating with someone? —— I will just define what I mean by collaboration. Working within a plan as drawn up by the System, for instance. Whether it is Bantustans . . . or Urban Bantu Councils, but you are collaborating in the sense that you are participating in a program which is meant to be for you, but drawn up by the very persons you are directing yourself to.

Then you have the same phrase, "There will be no collaboration with the Whites in mapping out the political direction"? —— That is correct.

How does that tie up with your . . . ? —— Now, that particular usage of the word "collaboration" implies a working with Whites, in drawing up your plans.

What political direction do you have in mind? —— Any.

Now then, isn't the bargaining process the mapping out of the political direction? —— No, it is a method of achieving a particular result. When you talk of mapping a political direction you are talking of drawing of plans, in other words, Where shall we first focus our attention? Do we direct ourselves to all the bishops of the country, or do we direct ourselves to all the, shall I say, cultural organizations amongst Whites? Or do we direct ourselves to the sporting world? This is all mapping of a political process. Now, what we are saying is that we don't want to sit down with Mr. Attwell and plan with him what steps we shall take. We are going to sit down on our own as Blacks and work it out.

But then how much give-and-take is there going to be at the bargaining stage? —— Well, this is a historical question. I think it depends entirely on history; it depends on the relevant strength of the various bargaining parties. It depends certainly on things like outside pressure. No one knows—we cannot prescribe a synthesis; a synthesis happens. What you can prescribe is a possibility of the thesis and antithesis coming together; the final result cannot be calculated in fine measurement.

Do you anticipate during the bargaining that there will be give-and-take from both sides? —— Sure. Yes, I do.

There are indications in the documents that Black Power portrays an all-or-nothing image?

MR. ATTWELL: *This is an in-the-air argument at the moment, My Lord.*

THE COURT: *There is such a passage in the . . . documents referred to yesterday . . . on Black Power.*

MR. SOGGOT: *Yes, My Lord, that is what I had in mind.*

THE COURT: *That is Magagula's . . . ?* —— Yes. I don't think we were talking about Black Power here. We were talking about the central ideology of SASO and BPC which is Black Consciousness basically, so if we are talking in the air at least let us remain in that realm of Black Consciousness.

MR. ATTWELL: *I want to refer you then to a letter which was written by accused number 1. I refer Your Lordship to General Exhibit G.5.*

THE COURT: *It is the same point?*

MR. ATTWELL: *It will be along the same lines, My Lord. Perhaps you would look at the second page of that document. If you have a look, I think you can start at the top of the page by . . . "Putting BAWU onto the map forever"—do you see that? The third line?* —— Yes.

He then addresses the people and says,

> *"That we have heard you are progressing on the worker field and cutting the grass from under the White feet of the Bolton Hall crowd who are intent only on getting Black workers' support only as far as their own White positions of power and privilege are preserved forever. That is the typical role of the White Liberals [one] they will never give up of their own accord. We have to make them give it up by getting Black workers to realize that we are on*

their side, that our future is bound together and our future lies in our hands, not in the hands of the few White Liberals who are bent only on saving their own positions of power with the Black worker, so that they can control and use Black workers when the time suits them. They are not fighting for our liberation; they are just maintaining the oppressor status quo. That is why it is so very important that we never give an inch in our fight, especially on the labor scene. We don't need to meet anyone halfway or anywhere. It is for them to make concessions, not us; we have got nothing to give. We want and we haven't got. The strong do not shift from the principles that are so dear to Black people, and the sure liberation of Azania from the White foreigners."

How does that tie up with the give-and-take which you people envisage?
——— I think it ties up beautifully.

Perhaps you could expand on that? ——— It is said here, as you know I have been saying all along, that it is for them to make concessions. It is for them to give; we have got nothing. We have got nothing but a paper policy for this thing. We may have, for instance, a view of the kind of state we want. We may have a view of the kind of relationship we want between workers and employers. That is all on paper . . . It is purely a system that we are maintaining and that we own as Blacks, so that when you bargain you contrast what you have drawn up on paper with what is in existence, and the process is an assimilation between the two different standpoints. One is on paper. It is nothing, as it says—we have got nothing. The other is the standpoint of the White System, which must make concession to accommodate to the demands of the Blacks. This fits in very beautifully with what we have been saying. I don't even know who this letter was directed to; I am just talking theoretically.

Apparently to friends in Durban. Presumably BAWU workers. So that is your explanation of that particular theme expressed there? ——— Yes.

THE COURT: *You see, the point that counsel is really trying to drive at is the following: If you bargain it is a matter of give-and-take, and then you are really getting concessions from the System?* ——— Yes.

Now, it is your express policy not to proceed on that basis . . . to work for a total change? ——— I think the change is total in the sense that it obviously implies a radical departure from presently accepted values, which values are a total negation of our existence. They seem to suggest we are not there. Now, we regard it as a radical change for Whites in the first instance to learn to accommodate within the total power structure within the country the very existence of Blacks, and to make them a party to the formulation of decisions and the election of institutions that govern people. Now, the relevance of this statement is simply in saying that we have got nothing to give. The direction of concession has got to be in terms of practical reality from one side. Theoretically we give only in that we may have our standpoint, which is our policy, which we may have to learn to delete certain items from in the process of the bargaining. We might get, for instance, if we take the Rhodesian situation [Joshua] Nkomo, who has got a paper policy saying, "This is my policy," as Smith is saying, "This is mine." When they meet at the table they are bargaining. Smith must make certain concessions; Nkomo must make certain concessions, in order that they arrive at the middle of the road. One might say, "We want a transition government for twenty years"; the other might say, "We want it for six months"; and Britain then comes up in the middle and says "All right, we will make it two years." This is in a sense assimilating both aspects in the bargaining process—but Nkomo has got nothing, and Smith has got all. They look at the reality of the situation.

But doesn't it suggest that you are really, then, if you bargain, you are really trying to alleviate your position? You are not getting the total change which you see as the only future that you have in this country?
—— I think, My Lord, there are certain limits to what you can expect from the person you are bargaining with, as the ultimate analysis. For instance, I mean, we will still reject the fact that you are on the roll, but on a separate roll, you know—you may want to be on a common roll. This may be very basic in the whole bargaining process, but there may be certain things where it does not really matter all that much if you give in. So now we are not talking about a concrete situation, so I cannot point out what is basically acceptable and from which you may not make any departure and something in which, you know . . . is give-and-take . . .

So you don't contemplate a complete surrender? —— No, certainly. I mean, we are working against an existing system which may insist on certain things . . . in a particular form. I mean, the ultimate result of the whole bargaining process is highly theoretical at the moment, you know, because in the first instance the very, very concrete demands have hardly been formulated even by, you know, BPC, but that bargaining is foreshadowed in the thinking is what we are trying to suggest here.

MR. ATTWELL: *Because I put it to you that in fact the image projected is one of an uncompromising "all or nothing" stand?* ——— Can you suggest that . . .

And that the bargaining process of give-and-take is not what BPC has in mind? ——— You suggest that this letter emphasizes the . . .

Not only this letter. It is representative of numerous other . . . ——— Well, why would they speak of concessions? If bargaining was not foreshadowed even in this letter?

What does it say about concessions? ——— "We don't need to meet anyone halfway or anywhere; it is for them to make concessions."

Not us? ——— Not us. Now, the word "concession" implies a voluntary concession—a voluntary agreement on the basis of pressure certainly, but voluntary on the part of the person who is presented with the pressure, so that White society here is going to make concessions. Now, if he wanted to express what you are suggesting, he would have said, "We shall take it over whether they like it or not," which is a different statement altogether.

Have you come across any statements that "We shall take the land"? That "It has been stolen from us, the willful owners"? ——— I can't say certainly. I can say to you this now is not SASO policy or BPC policy, but I can't say that every particular document that is there does not say this. . . .

Now, when you went through the documents, did you find that the Whites were referred to in one or more of the terms which I will now enumerate [to] you—forget about the frequency at this stage—but that the Whites were described in various documents as either robbers, thieves, thugs, murderers, killers, racists, Nazis, Fascists, people out to exterminate the entire Black nation from the surface of the earth, inhuman, brutal, flogging people to death, and that type of sentiment? ——— I think one does find some of the phrases in some of the documents.

And did you find the expression that these atrocities were committed every day as part of a predetermined plan, as I said, to wipe out the Black nation from the surface of the earth? —— That could have been there yes, I . . .

Did you find that when you looked through the documents? —— I don't remember it specifically, but I don't want to say it is not there.

Now, that sort of talk—what do you think that sort of description of the Whites is going to have on the Blacks who would read that? —— Well, I would say this certainly occurs in SASO and BPC literature. I would say that it is not the preponderant thing that is in SASO and BPC literature, and I would say that if you throw it out like that, it is always out of context perhaps. The possible effect is the same as if we are discussing idioms. I think the words do have meaning. I am not saying they have got no meaning, but I think they portray no new feeling, incidentally, about White institutions, White society, to Blacks. As I said earlier on, I think Blacks have used more direct swear words about White society than this. I think I must again mention the point we touched on with Your Lordship sometime back: that one has to look at the terminology in the context of the analytical value of language, the meaning of words in particular languages—that languages of African origin certainly tend to attach meaning not so much to the bare word but to the situation, to the emotion behind the word. What might sound very strong in English translated back, for instance into Zulu, or back into Xhosa, sounds pretty mundane, and I did make this concession again that Afrikaans has a, you know, a comparable quality in this respect with African languages, in that you assume the idiom of the languages . . . You take the expression of the language, you do accommodate what might seem to an English gentleman as a hard expression, which put into Xhosa, for instance, means very little. And I think I did quote to court some terms that are used in common talk without any show of emotion amongst Africans, which [when] we translate [them] into English, become even so strong as not to be admissible to this court.

I think you personally have a particularly fine command of English, and I don't want you to necessarily respond thereto, unless you feel you don't have. Would you agree with me that both you and accused number 1, for instance, and accused number 9 are very articulate people in the English language? ——— I would agree about the two of them.

You would be modest about yourself? ——— Well, I can speak the language to some extent certainly. I don't speak it as well as I speak Xhosa, let me tell you this.

Now, the descriptions for instance that the Whites are intransigent, insensitive people out to actually exterminate people from the face of the earth [as] a predetermined plan . . . [Mr. Soggot intervenes]

MR. SOGGOT: *My Lord, may I interrupt my learned friend? What my learned friend is putting in his question is in fact . . . It seems to be a collection or a skimming off of some adjectives from various documents. I wonder whether in all fairness to the witness if he is to be asked the significance of these words and their . . . [The court intervenes]*

THE COURT: *Well, that is what he said. He said it depends on the context of each word.*

MR. SOGGOT: *That is perfectly so, My Lord, and that is why I would suggest—although I can't tell my learned friend how to cross-examine—that in fairness perhaps the documents should be put to the witness.*

THE COURT: *Well, the reply would probably come back again in its context.*

MR. ATTWELL: *Right. Perhaps we can look at one document. Look at BPC E. 7. It is a document which purports to deal with Sharpeville, and it starts off with*

> "This document is set out to inform us about the events of a very tragic day in our history, the 21st of March, 1960. On this day scores of defenseless Blacks, men, women and children, were massacred because they wished to register their rejection of the notorious pass-laws."

Have you got that? ——— Yes.

> "The guns of the oppressor rang at Sharpeville, at Langa and at many other places in this country. The answer to the Black man's demand for a fair share in their land was bullets. The incidents at Sharpeville, Langa, Vanderbijlpark are merely part of a pattern, part of a well-planned coldly executed plan to muzzle down Blacks in this, their land. We remember with sadness the killing of our people by the White police . . . in the miner strike of 1920, the Ntabulenga incident of 1920. Now, even in a recent Namibian

strike. We are left with no alternative but to see this as a deliberate plan to annihilate us." —— Yes.

That type of sentiment. Now, before we comment on that, perhaps you would also have a look at BPC J.2, which is a Tribute to the Late Nthuli Shezi, vice president of the Black People's Convention, issued by the Black People's Convention. BPC J.2, My Lord. Will you have a look at the third paragraph of that document, for instance:

> *"The violent assassination was inflicted by an agent of protection of White racism, superiority and oppression on our Black brother. It should not be regarded as being directed towards him alone, but should be regarded as an . . . assault on the entire Black community. . . . Who can deny that the ravages of poverty, disease and violation of all forms in the Black lives are neither situational nor are they accidental. Who can deny that the thousands of Black children and Black mothers and fathers who die of starvation inculcate a deliberate attempt to extinguish from the surface of the earth the entire Black nation."*

Now, that type of sentiment—do you seriously in BPC and SASO believe that that is the intention of the government and the System: to systematically and premeditatively extinguish from the surface of the earth the entire Black nation? —— Well, I think you should know that in politics like in poetry there is license for what one might call justifiable exaggeration. I think you heard me this morning, for instance, talking about various situations in which the Black man finds himself at the receiving end of aspects of the System. I spoke about squatter areas, I spoke about Blacks now and then being shot by police, and I said this is terrorism. Fortunately we are . . . We don't mean the words in the analytical sense, as I was saying earlier on. This is a form of political talk. Okay. When you say that someone is a terrorist, you mean it. You bring him to court, but when we say you are terrorists—you know, you are killers and so on—we don't really mean you should go to court. We are merely registering a complaint, you know. I mean, this is a bit of political license. Now, I want to say also that you will find the kind of talk in BPC/SASO documents—I don't even know if these are BPC or SASO documents—but anyway, you will find this kind of talk, but I want to say it is not the kind of thing that BPC and SASO go around saying, you know, as everyday

people. It occurs in the documents certainly, but the central message
of SASO and BPC is internal within the Black community; it is
creative, okay. They will and they must, I think—whenever there are
incidents of this nature—they must register a complaint. They must
make it felt that the Black community is complaining about those
things. This is the only way they have to protect themselves against
society, like White society, because they have got no other means.

*The question was, Mr. Biko, do you people seriously believe what
stands here . . . * ——— I have explained . . . [Mr. Attwell and the
witness speak simultaneously]

. . . as emotive language? ——— I have explained that it is a bit of
political license that every politician uses.

Is this part of conscientization? ——— Again, this is not. This is just
registering what Blacks feel about certain situations. You have picked
on two issues, for instance, which I think are in themselves emotive,
which I think Blacks would want to prevent from happening. Blacks
don't want to see another Sharpeville, okay, but Blacks don't have a
way of protecting themselves from assault, which does come from
what we regard as trigger-happy police. Okay, we have got reason to
believe that police in many instances are trigger-happy. When I say
trigger-happy, now, I mean they are prone to want to exploit a situation like that, you know, to get at the Black man—like it was said by
eye-witnesses at the [inaudible] incident: When people were beginning
to go away, police went for them; they released dogs. Now, we want
to prevent this kind of thing from happening. We want to instill within
the police force through their superiors a certain level of discipline.
The members of the police must feel that people are complaining.
People cannot accept the fact that at Sharpeville people were shot,
people cannot accept the fact that Mushuli just died in jail like that.
You must protest each time this kind of thing happens so that it does
not happen some more. If we don't protest there will be more of it.
We have got no way of protecting ourselves from society.

*You raised an interesting point there when you say I have picked on
two issues here. What two issues do you have in mind?* ——— You have
picked on Sharpeville, you have picked on Nthuli Shezi's death, both
of which are emotive.

But these two documents don't confine them[selves] to Shezi's death or to Sharpeville? ——— Well, so far we have just read . . . about those two issues.

Don't they both generalize at this sort of thing? If you have a look at BPC J.2 again . . . ——— Yes, sure. They move from a specific incident, okay, they generalize. This is how you justify a complaint, and if you are a politician you do that sort of thing. It is done by both Whites and Blacks in this country.

Do they use emotive incidents to make generalizations? ——— Yes, but let us not confine to Blacks. It is used by Whites as well. There are more insults coming from White society to Blacks.

We are confined to Blacks here at the moment, Mr. Biko. ——— All I am saying to you is that it is a natural thing. It is not as if this is a peculiarity, you know, of SASO and BPC. You do find it in some documents of SASO and BPC. There is the usual business of SASO and BPC. Okay. But you do find this kind of language in some documents, like you would find it in any other political setup within the White world.

It says,

"*Poverty and disease and violations of all forms—they are all part of a deliberate attempt to extinguish from the surface of the earth the entire Black nation"?* ——— No one, for instance, even raises that kind of thing in a meeting. No one gets that impression. All that an ordinary Black listener who understands English gets is that we have been had, okay? Our situation is bad; that is all. If you ask him directly after the meeting what did Saths Cooper say, or what did Aubrey Mokoape say, about [inaudible] he will not remember. Because he is not geared to remember words. He is there to catch the meaning, and the meaning here is that we are in a bad way as a result of White society. This is what I meant when I referred to language as being important. You haven't got the Black experience, unfortunately, Mr. Attwell. I cannot explain this to you. You have got to be Black to understand what I am talking about.

Well, I got that impression the very first time I read this document. ——— That is because you are White.

But this document could have got into the hands of thousands of Whites? ——— That is not directed to Whites.

But it could have got into their hands? ——— Well, if you took it and distributed it, yes. But I don't think these people send the documents to Whites. They send it precisely to the people they meant it to go to, who are Blacks.

And if they leave it lying around or something, anybody could get hold of it? —— That is just theoretical.

This document, the evidence before court suggests, was distributed during the unveiling of the tombstone of this particular Shezi? —— That is correct. . . .

And this sort of language, do you consider this as racially inflamma-[tory]? —— No, I think if you put this again . . . If you put this into Zulu, you would find that this is what any old man . . . If you pick up an old man from the village and ask him to speak about Nthuli, at his funeral, and tell him the facts—that he died through being pushed onto the rails, as we believe, by a railway worker at some station—and you tell him that the quarrel started when Nthuli Shezi was protecting the rights of women at the station who had been molested by this man, as we believe; if you ask any old man to go and talk, with that kind of background, that is precisely the kind of things he would say. Not necessarily the same words, but words like "soldier" and so on are going to come in there, and condemnation of that kind of man, that kind of mentality—that is what is being condemned here, not necessarily the specific man who pushed him, but the kind of society which gives that kind of mentality to a man to make him feel that he can freely push someone onto the rails. You must condemn the entire society because that man is not alone in developing this feeling against Blacks. He is rooted in a society, a society which has got a particular history and a particular relationship with Blacks, so he feels somehow that it is right when he does this. He might even feel in his own small mind that he is representing his people correctly by pushing this person onto the rails. Now, when we talk about him, therefore, you have got to reflect on the society, and that society is a White society. And I think that even an old man would be able to make that assimilation even within Black society.

The point is these are not in Zulu or in any other language—they are in English. —— But they are understood by people who are rooted in that sort of culture, Zulu, Xhosa and so on. No matter what they are expressed in—in English or Afrikaans or what—they are understood by people who are rooted in a particular culture.

Would you say this . . . ——— They don't sit down to look at one word as such and say, What does it mean? No, they listen to the whole paragraph. And understand the combined meaning. They are not analytical with the English; they listen to block words when you are talking.

Is it only English which has this peculiarity of attaching a specific significance to the word? ——— I don't know other languages. I know a bit of Afrikaans, a bit of English, a bit of Xhosa . . . Zulu and all the other languages share one common factor—that of attaching not an analytical but some kind of emotional meaning to situations, whereas English tends to be analytical. You have got to use a precise word, you know, to convey a precise meaning. And I think this is the problem we are having—one of understanding when we look at these documents.

But isn't that one of the dangers that BPC was faced with? Portraying its precise meaning in this language? It shows out of its own free will that it adopted it as its official language? ——— I am saying both the drawers of this particular piece and the recipients will have no doubt about their communication. You in the middle who are an Englishman—who looks at words you know piecemeal—you may have problems. But the person who drew this up and the person who perceives it within a crowd has no problem. They are at one, they understand what they are talking about. You may not understand it because you are looking at the precise meaning of words.

Are you suggesting that if I were to translate this into Afrikaans, word for word, literally, . . . I would not get the same impression that I get from this document? ——— Literally?

Literally word-for-word identical to Afrikaans? ——— Well, I don't know, let us think about Zulu and think about Xhosa, then I will be an expert there, but certainly I have got a vague impression that even in Afrikaans you would not be able to convey the same meaning if you translate that word for word.

Why did BPC choose this language to convey its meaning? ——— It is communication with a lot of people who speak several languages, right, but at least they can commonly speak English. Not to any degree of sophistication but to some degree.

*Will they necessarily each interpret this back into their own language
to see whether this is . . .* ———— You don't have to interpret it back
into your language because your values as a person—whether you
speak English or not—your values are affected by your culture, so
. . . you perceive a document in terms of your general make-up, in
terms of your understanding. And what I am saying to you is that not
one Black person looks at this thing in terms of the precise meaning
of each word. After this has been read, for instance, if you ask a Black
person how were Whites described in that document, he will not
remember the precise words. He will just have a vague idea. This is
all I am trying to say to you about the meaning of language.

*All right. Now, he reads that document and all he is left with is a
vague or general impression?* ———— Of the precise words; the meaning
is there.

What is the meaning of this? ———— Well . . .

In BPC J.2? Look at J.1 and J.2. ———— It is a description of White
society, specifically of this man in terms of the role which he was
playing, right. He stands in the middle. On one hand he is portraying
the rights of women, on the other he is portraying them against a
particularly violent society, okay, which is White society. And what
happens is he dies. Now, symbolically he dies like a soldier; a soldier
dies fighting for a cause. His cause was to protect the rights of women;
this is basically what the document is saying. No matter what individuals are saying, that is what the man catches that they are talking
to.

*I would agree with you that he is made here a symbol of the Black
community, and that this White official, whoever he may have been, is
made a symbol of the White System?* ———— I have explained why.

*And what impression is the man who reads this going to have of the
White System? Whether he be a Zulu or a Xhosa or an Indian or
anything else?* ———— It is the same old thing, you know. It is again
what he knows, okay. Now, at the funeral the focus of course is on
the man who is being buried. Now, if you go to any Black funeral the
trend is the same. We attempt to bring to light the good facts about
the person who is dying. We are paying our last respects to him.
Secondly we talk about how he died. This is, you know, the average
conduct of any funeral amongst the Blacks. They are just held in that

context. The man—who is he? What does he believe in? and so on.
What does he stand for? And what caused him to die? We normally
say in Xhosa, for instance, there will be a speaker about the life of the
person . . . [The witness quotes in Xhosa] There will be a speaker
about the sickness of the person, okay, that is now . . . [The witness
again quotes in Xhosa] It is done in any funeral, so that as a speaker
you must find . . . If I am called upon to speak at somebody's funeral
I must go out of my way to trace his life and bring out what is good
in him. So this is quite logical—besides, it is an African funeral.

*I submit to you that they brought out all the good in Mr. Shezi,
whatever good there may have been, and neglected any weak points that
he may have had?* ——— This is done.

*And brought out all the evil nasty possible things they can about the
Whites, and ignored all the good that there may or may not be. Would
you agree with me?* ——— I think they have not finished all the evil.

They have not finished all the evil yet? ——— No, no.

Would you have gone further than this? ——— You could have gone
further if you wanted to.

Would you have gone further? ——— Who is that?

You? ——— Not necessarily me, but I am saying anybody could
have gone further if he wanted to. If the intention was to try and
portray White society as bad, and use that to make everybody who
was there angry, you could have produced a whole litany of evil if you
cared to. This just shows the selflessness of the death, in that someone
—in view of the mentality which he has got from a society, which has
got no respect for Black people—killed Shezi. It could have been
prevented; that is all that this thing is saying.

*If I understand you correctly, then . . . you consider that one of the
possible ways to [portray racial hostility] would be to list a whole lot
of all the things that the Whites do against you?* ——— I said that if
really the intention is to cause that kind of feeling to come out to the
fore amongst Blacks, you can again use their [conception] of language;
you have got to use very colorful language. Take a simple event, not
describe it now in concrete terms, but play around the nastiness of the
various aspects of the event—you can carry [the message] across to
the Blacks and they can become angry. It is thus necessarily enough
to make anybody angry in Black society. This is really regarded as a

description of the circumstances in which the man died. All right. We must blame that guy who pushed him, okay. We have got to, and we have got to explain that it is not as if he personally hated Shezi. He is portraying a mentality which he has borrowed from his society, but if one had to make society angry at that funeral, there would be a whole litany of things we can pick up, and we would describe them in precise language calculated to, you know, bring out the emotion of the Black man . . . It is not difficult to make people angry if you want to. Thus this was not the intention here. It was purely to describe the circumstances in which the man died. That is all.

You say it is not difficult to make the Black man angry? —— If you want to, you have just got to draw up whatever you say in very beautiful floral language—concentrate on the detail. You can, assuredly.

What more do you think the man who drew up this document should have done, if that had been his intention? —— This is all fair comment on the factual evidence, at least on the factual situation of what happened at that funeral. I mean, at that station, a fair comment.

You consider this fair comment? —— Completely fair comment.

And that it is part of a grander plan, a diabolic plan, to . . . —— I am talking about this document here. We are confining ourselves now to the graveside.

All right, we will confine ourselves to the graveside. The other one of course is related to this, isn't it? —— I don't know, I don't know where they are. . . .

COURT ADJOURNS

Day Four

The Morning of May 6, 1976

Attwell cross-examines Biko on foreign investment. Biko restates the role that foreign investment should play in South Africa and addresses the withdrawal of business interest from South Africa. Biko then notes that the goal of the Black worker should be change, not contentment. Following the tea adjournment, Attwell continues to assert that the policy of SASO and BPC is intended to incite racial hostility; he quotes extensively from various speeches given by SASO and BPC leaders at the Sharpeville Commemorative Day meeting.

COURT RESUMES

STEPHEN BANTU BIKO, STILL UNDER OATH

CROSS-EXAMINATION BY MR. ATTWELL, CONTINUED: *Mr. Biko, just to round off where we ended off yesterday—we were busy with the Shezi funeral, which you attended?* —— Correct.

Can you tell the court: Did any of the accused now before court attend that funeral? —— I am sure some did attend, but I cannot remember specifically now.

So you cannot point to anyone? —— I cannot specifically point to anyone.

Now, dealing with the accused shortly, you said that you knew certain of the accused before their arrest, and the others you have met subsequent to their detention during this trial? —— Correct.

Did you visit the accused? —— In jail, you mean?

Yes, after their detention? —— Yes, I did.

And you have seen them on occasion here in court? —— That is correct.

Did you attend any of the court hearings, court proceedings in this trial? —— Yes, I did. I came during the time of the evidence of Dr., or Professor, van der Merwe. During his evidence, I made an appearance.

Was that the only witness giving evidence that you heard? ———
[Pause]

Was this before or after you knew that you were a likely or possible defense witness? ——— Well, I knew I was a likely witness, but I did not understand it to mean that I may not come in until I was told by counsel that I should not come in.

And the final question is, Have you had access at all to any of the transcripts of evidence, the official transcripts? ——— No.

I have in mind what I am showing you now—this type of thing? ——— No.

Not at all? ——— Not at all.

Are you aware of the evidence given by specifically other accomplices for the State? ——— Like who, for instance?

Well, I can put it to you directly: There were witnesses—Ledwaba was one—there was a witness Ahmed Bawa, there was a witness Harry Singh. Are you aware of the testimony of any of these people? ——— Well, except for brief reports in the press, I am not aware.

Did you discuss the evidence of any of those people or anybody else with the accused at all? ——— Not with the accused. I am sure I talked about Harry Singh, for instance, at home with some of my folk down there, but not with the accused.

Did you know Harry Singh at all? ——— Yes, I know him.

Was he quite a senior member of BPC? ——— Not till I left Durban. I do not know if he became one afterwards. . . .

You will remember that Aubrey [Mokoape] did attend the DOCC conference in December of this year as a delegate of the SASO delegation? ——— That is correct.

That is accused number 4? ——— That is correct, yes.

This GSC in fact took the Resolution on foreign investments? ——— That is correct, yes.

Which set out the SASO viewpoint? ——— Yes.

Now, if we could perhaps just have a quick look at this—page 17 of your numbering, page 255 of Your Lordship's—Resolution 50/71. I do not intend dealing with the preamble, but it says here under "Noting further that foreign investors . . ." Do you see that at the bottom? ——— Mmmm.

> *"(vii) make it possible for S.A. to spurn world opinion to maintain her racist regime;*

(viii) boost S.A. international image and make S.A. an ideal land for investment whilst the social evils practiced by the regime are lost sight of;

(ix) give S.A. an economic stability that enables her to gain diplomatic and economic acceptance in the international scene."

Do you see that? —— That is correct.

Now, I think in your evidence-in-chief you stated that there was perhaps a mistake or a wrong impression created by certain words used in the ninth paragraph? —— Mmmm.

What was that again? Could you just point that out to the court? —— Well, I was referring to the term economic stability. I said it could have meant, as far as I understood it, economic involvement which results in diplomatic and economic acceptance, in other words involvement of other nations and countries in our economy results in them having to bat an eye, so to speak, to whatever South Africa does.

Do you think that one could then replace the word stability in fact with involvement here? —— This is my understanding of that particular clause.

Now, if you do that, would you then just read it, reading "involvement," and tell me if it makes sense? —— ". . . give S.A. an economic involvement that enables her to gain diplomatic and economic acceptance in the international scene."

Does that make sense to you? —— Yes. It is an incomplete sentence but certainly the understanding here is involvement with other groups, with other nations, other countries.

Should it not have read "gives overseas companies an economic involvement that enables S.A. to gain . . ."? —— No, I think the focal point is South Africa and her involvement with other nations economically.

Is it correct? I think you prefaced your evidence on foreign investment, as have previous witnesses, both for the State and the defense, in stating that foreign investments was a very contentious matter? —— It is contentious all right.

Now, contentious in what regard, Mr. Biko? What was inherent in this particular aspect that made it such a contentious matter? —— Well, it was contentious as far as I am concerned insofar as it was topical. It was an area where South Africa was being criticized by various people in countries which invest here. It was contentious in that there was a stage at which, for instance, companies involved in our economy here did not know how to respond to their situation of involvement here. It was contentious in that several companies abroad sent teams here to investigate the behavior and operations of their companies. It was contentious in that governments like Britain, for instance, began to give directives to their companies that were involved in our economy to behave in a certain manner. In other words, the term contentious here is being used only insofar as it was an issue being raised throughout the world, and it was an issue on which criticism was being focused onto participation by other nations in our economy at that level.

Was it contentious also in a sense that it evoked a wide diversity of opinion? ———— It was topical and there was lots of debate.

Did the Blacks differ amongst themselves also as to the advisability or nonadvisability of economic investment in this country? ———— Yes, they did.

I notice this resolution was adopted unanimously with acclaim? ———— No, *nem con* does not mean unanimously; *nem con* means without anyone opposing. There may be people who abstained.

But with acclaim? ———— With acclaim certainly, because some people felt very strongly about it—about certain things.

Now, the preamble in fact sets out the understanding, of SASO anyway, as to the extent of foreign investment in this country? ———— Yes, well, I would put it this way: This is the presentation by the particular commission, and it was accepted.

And in fact those figures suggest a fairly substantial investment by foreign investors in the economy, would you agree with me? ———— Well, if you really look at the total capital required for South African industries, they are not all that significant. They would constitute, I think, at this particular stage probably about . . . certainly not more than 12 percent, and I think the current foreign investment in our economy is about 7 percent now. . . . [Mr. Attwell intervenes]

Let us confine ourselves to when this was taken, in 1971? ———— Yes, I am looking at it in terms of total capital required. There is much, much more generated from within, you see. So although it looks like a hell of a lot of millions when you look at it on paper, percentage-

wise, as I say, it is certainly not more than 12 percent, even at that
stage.

*And 12 percent of the country's economy is a fairly substantial slice,
is that correct?* —— Not seriously, really.

Not really? —— No.

*You then went on to point out in your evidence-in-chief that in fact
SASO went no further than merely rejecting this foreign investment?*
—— Yes.

*It did not go so far as to include discouragement of foreign invest-
ment?* —— Mmmm.

*Could you perhaps just once again outline to the court the reason for
not going the whole hog and including discouragement as well?* ——
Well, I explained to the court that SASO took this resolution precisely because the issue was a topical one, and many people from
abroad and from within were asking what our point of view was. We
had not taken a decision on the issue, and we decided at this particular
conference merely to take a policy decision, just to indicate to our
membership what our attitude was. We did not seek to involve ourselves in a program, a campaign to discourage foreign investment. We
just sought to have an attitude, a policy attitude.

*Now, if I may ask, Why didn't SASO want to get involved in a
campaign to discourage foreign investment?* —— Well, there are a
number of reasons—I think some of them I pointed out in my evidence-in-chief—the main one being that even if you ardently believed
that foreign investments were bad, and that they should be got out of
the country, it was in fact impossible to do so, for two reasons: because
the companies involved in the South African economy have not come
here out of ignorance, they have come here out of knowledge, in fact;
they have come here particularly amongst other things to exploit the
existence of cheap labor in our labor law provisions, and secondly the
country itself anyway has tightened up its control over foreign investment since the days of Sharpeville, and it now is very difficult for a
firm to pull out their money. As you would know, of course, they
cannot pull out their factories. So it is difficult to pull out their money
from the country in the first instance. They have got to go through
a whole rigmarole, through government-controlled measures, some of
which I do not actually understand myself.

Do I understand you correctly, then, that SASO considered it not a feasible type of thing it could do? —— Not a desirable thing, for several reasons.

Did it consider it was possible to do so? —— Well, we had never looked . . . If you can look at this amendment, we took it out precisely because we did not want to involve ourselves in that program.

It says that "the council is not composed of people who are capable of keeping foreign investors out"? —— Mmmm.

Now, what then is the difference between SASO and BPC, because BPC went far further than merely rejecting foreign investment, it in fact discouraged it? —— I am not aware really. I think BPC as far as I know could have had bilateral meetings with particular firms or could have applied pressure on particular firms, but I think the understanding which was envisaged stemmed also from this type of stance. I think everybody was aware basically that there is nothing much you can do in this sphere. The little you can do is to use your political aptitude to bend things your way a bit, in other words to bring about some kind of influence on foreign firms which are in this country, to relate more closely to Blacks, and to relate certainly to the attitudes that Blacks have. We want to see our workers being trained. We want to see our workers being given positions of responsibility within the firms. In other words, we want to see the whole humanity of workers within firms like Heineman and all the foreign firms that are in this country developed by the firms to understanding our attitude.

Do you dispute the fact that BPC went further and in fact discouraged foreign investment? —— I am not hundred percent aware of all the programs taken by BPC. All I am saying is that the attitude towards foreign investment which was in BPC was very similar to the one that SASO took.

I would like to refer you then to the resolution taken by BPC at its first national congress in December of 1972, document BPC C.3, Resolution 20 of 1972 on page 7 of your paper.
THE COURT: *It seems that the policies are very similar; now, is that coincidence, or how do they manage to have similar policies?* —— I think, M'lord, there are certain very influential people of SASO, for instance, who were also members of BPC, and in a sense what stance SASO takes does often get more expression, you know, within BPC.

There is a relationship in that sense, you know, a structural relationship.

Is it correct then to say that the policy of BPC was very much under the direction of SASO? —— Not really. I think they were related. I mean, there is evidence where BPC takes policy where SASO took it up.

MR. ATTWELL: *BPC C.3, M'lord, Resolution 20 of 1972, on page 9 of Your Lordship's papers, page 7 of the typed document. Have you got that, Mr. Biko?* —— Mmmm.

You will notice that it says,

"*The congress noting:*

1. the vital role played by foreign investors in maintaining and supporting the economic system in South Africa;

The system is designed for maximum exploitation of Black people;

That the riches and resources of this country belong as their birthright;

Further noting:

that foreign investors claim that their presence in this country contributes towards the development of the Black community."

—— Right.

"*But this claim is disputed by the reality of the Blacks' experience in this country;*

Therefore resolves:

To reject the involvement of foreign investors in this exploitative economic system, and

To call upon foreign investors to disengage themselves from the White-controlled exploitative system, and mandates the National Executive to make known our stand on foreign investors, known both in this country and overseas through all available channels."

Do you agree with me that goes further than merely rejecting foreign investors? —— You might say the word "do," but I think it is just a political stance, again, from which to operate.

You notice there "a call on foreign investors to disengage themselves"? —— The point about it, Mr. Attwell— I know the BPC attitude to this, I know the people involved, and what I am saying here is that not one person I have met in BPC ever hoped or thought at any given stage that investors were going to pull out. But when you are going to operate a political program, like applying pressure on foreign companies, you take a stand and you operate from that stand in a certain direction.

Do you know who the mover and seconder of that motion were at the BPC congress? —— No, I do not know.

There appear to have been a Mr. Nengwekulu and a Mr. B. Mafuna —that would be Bokwe Mafuna. Are these people known to you? —— Yes, I know both of them.

They were both SASO members at one stage, were they not? —— Not Mafuna.

Nengwekulu was a SASO member? —— That is correct.

I refer, if Your Lordship does require reference here, to BPC C.4 on page 50, which does give the proposer and seconder of that particular motion. You notice in point 1 that the vital role played by foreign investors is stressed? —— Right.

Now, do you know any steps that BPC did in fact take in its resolution to discourage and call upon foreign investors to withdraw? —— I would not personally know.

I think you said yesterday or the day before in your evidence that the actual purpose of this call was to exert pressure? —— Yes.

On South Africa. Was it in any way to hurt or cripple the economy of the country? —— No, certainly.

Would it have that effect? —— As I said in my evidence-in-chief it could not have. We were quite aware that it could not have.

Now, there are other documents before court put out by other of the accused which seem to suggest that a total withdrawal of foreign investment would cripple this country and bring the racist government to its knees? —— I would have to see that in its context.

Well, I can refer you to those particular . . . [Pause] You said in your evidence now that "We were aware that it could not have this effect"? —— Yes.

When you say "we," who are you referring to there? —— I am talking about the general leadership within SASO and certain general leadership within BPC . . . [Pause] I am sorry—I am being disturbed by Mr. Rees here.

THE COURT: *Try and be inaudible, Mr. Rees.*

MR. ATTWELL: *I refer you to a document BPC C.9, a statement issued by the Black People's Convention, and purportedly given out—if you look at page 3 of the document—by Roy Chetty in his capacity as public relations officer, Sipho Buthelezi in his capacity as secretary general, Aubrey Mokoape, accused number 4, in his capacity as chairman of the Durban Central BPC branch, and Harry Singh in his capacity as chairman of the Overport BPC branch. These are influential people in BPC, correct?* —— Correct.

Now, if you will have a look at the second page of that document— page 21 of Your Lordship's papers—the middle paragraph which begins "Advocates of continued investment claim that if foreign investors withdrew, this would result in large-scale unemployment of Blacks." Have you got that paragraph? —— I am just trying to find it.

The sixth paragraph on that page. —— Right.

"Advocates of continued investment claim that if foreign investors withdrew, this would result in large-scale unemployment of Blacks. Withdrawal can only mean the downfall of the Vorster regime. Black people have pledged themselves to fight for freedom whatever the cost. Black people have endured much suffering and cannot suffer beyond this. Black people in general are prepared to suffer any consequences if this means ultimate Black freedom."
Now, how does that tie up with what you have just told the court? —— Yes, I do not think this implies necessarily that withdrawal will result in economic downfall. I think this refers to the whole area of criticism, that the Western countries tend to contain or get sustenance—that is, sustain a bit of their relationship with South Africa precisely because of their economic ties at investment level. Now, any form of complete disengagement will result in freedom by countries to be as critical as they wish. South Africa then loses the kind of defenders it has at United Nations. It cannot anymore spurn world opinion. I think this is [a] conclusion one can draw from this statement. As I said before, these men are quite aware that foreign investment is very low in this country in terms of the total capital required, and even if all foreign firms were to go out now really, South Africa will not even seriously limp economically. This we know. As I said again in my evidence-in-chief, ac-

cording to studies by the Department of Economics what we require is something like 6.4 investment from outside; the rest can be produced from inside the country.

Perhaps you would have a look at one other document, BPC C.8, a document entitled "foreign investment" by Nkwenkwe Nkomo, accused number 5. Will you have a look at the second page of that document, Mr. Biko? Have a look at the paragraph just under the middle of the page—"On the other hand . . ." Do you see a paragraph starting like that? —— Yes.

> *"On the other hand it would serve a purpose if foreign companies closed down completely and all employees lose work. This will be the time when Black people will realize that it is better to be idle than to be exploited. It will serve to redirect Black initiative and creativity."*

This ties up with what is said higher up in the document in the second paragraph, when he refers to incidents like Doornkop, Limehill, Rooigrond and other similar ones [that] "could only succeed through the use of commodities manufactured by foreign investors. The involvement of foreign investors in the Black banks should be discouraged, because it is aimed at curbing the creativity and militancy of the Black people." —— Right.

How does that tie up with . . . ? [Pause] —— Again, I think this is purely a speculation. The point about withdrawal of foreign investment is this: that when a man who invests here has got to withdraw, he has got to sell to somebody. He has to sell either to another foreigner or he has got to sell to a South African. Either way the factory goes on; either way the capital which was involved in that business continues to generate a kind of livelihood for the people employed by that firm. So that the fact that it is a foreigner or a South African who has the firm has got nothing to do with employment, for instance, of Black labor. Now, this I regard as pure speculation because it is not possible that anybody is just going to close down and leave his capital idle in this country. This is just pure speculation for this man. It serves the purpose of encouraging people in his particular thinking. Now, I have not read the whole document, so I do not understand what the whole thinking is. But it is certainly pure speculation.

I appreciate that the actual physical buildings, factories, cannot be removed. —— Yes.

But the investment is, I submit, shown in the document and appreciated by both SASO and BPC to be a very substantial one? —— The point at issue is that he cannot just take his money and go out. Any foreign investor cannot just take his money and go out. He has got to sell to somebody.

The question of immorality is stressed, is it not? —— This is the point. It does not mean that his actions are necessarily moral because he cannot take out his money.

No. He can close down his company if he is prepared to lose a couple of hundred thousand or a half a million, but it will have the effect of pushing Black workers out . . . [The witness intervenes] —— Where have you ever seen such a capitalist who is prepared to lose 200 million or 100 million just like that?

I did not say 100 million. Some of the foreign investors are fairly small. —— That is correct. They are small, but no capitalist wants to lose anything. In the first place he came here to make money. If it gets hot he has got to sell. Who does he sell to? Another foreigner —easier—or a South African?

So that is your interpretation of those documents? —— Yes. . . .

Mr. Biko, I see in Resolution 83 of 1971 apparently the constitution was amended to read under point (iv):

> *"Any member of the Executive Committee who acts against the interests of the organization shall be asked and/or forced to resign."*

Do you see that? —— Yes.

Was that section ever used by SASO to your knowledge? —— Yes, it was used.

When was that? —— Against Mr. Temba Sono.

Can you perhaps detail for us the circumstances of that particular Sono incident? —— Well, he issued what we regarded as a very important policy statement.

Where was this delivered? —— At a conference of SASO on the opening day during a time when all the press was there. He issued a very important policy statement which differed substantially with established SASO policy, and he did this without consulting the Executive. His paper was never seen by anybody up to the moment when it was delivered. We thought that he was attempting to get leverage, you know, to lever the whole position in the direction that he was thinking by using that moment of maximum publicity, so we thought that he was acting against the interests of the organization and SASO.

What was it that he said that you people objected to? —— Well, in a sense he was advocating collaboration with Bantustans to some extent. He was advocating coalition with liberal groups, and he was generally admonishing SASO on its stance, you know, with regard to the two groups. It was not so much that he could not say this—he could have said these things openly at a meeting. What we saw as being amiss was the whole conduct in saying those things—choosing a moment when there would be maximum publicity, and choosing a moment when there was no debate. He was just delivering an address in place of someone they had invited who did not come. So that the newspapers were going to give some kind of report to say SASO president says A, B, C and D, which gives a whole different slant to our policy, so because he did this we kicked him out.

Was there any policy resolution which he infringed in giving his address? —— Yes. I have just named two.

Had you at that stage adopted a firm stance on homelands and liberals? —— Yes. . . .

THE COURT: *If you look at the paragraph starting with "realizing," three lines from the top, in the third subparagraph [of the GSC Resolution 25 of 1972]:*

"*realizing that moves towards the 'trade unionism' as presently constituted are only in the nature of producing a contented worker*"

then, "therefore resolves"—5—

"*to run clinics for leadership in service training and imbue them with pride and self-confidence as people and about their potential as workers*";

Now, didn't SASO want a contented worker? —— No, not a contented worker in the context in which we understood it, to mean someone who sees himself as merely an extension of a machine. In other words, one who accepts completely the whole system of oppres-

sion in which he lives. You know, as far as we understand Blacks—
as I said yesterday virtually all Blacks are workers—Blacks should
not be contented; Blacks should not accept what is going on because
it is wrong. Now, the kind of trade union movements we were referring to then were movements which were under the direction of the
White taxer, movements that are played around with by taxers, like
the government workers' union, for instance, of Mr. Rubelo, which
we did not respect because we felt that there was no inherent Black
thinking in it. There they were told what to do. They were sent all
over the world to go and represent South African workers, so to
speak, but essentially the thinking was White thinking, and Mr.
Rubelo we saw as expressing White thinking. Now, what we wanted
was authentic Black thinking between trade union movements.

*Isn't it another way of trying to conscientize them, to create griev-
ances and let them work for a cause, and that is the only way to unite
them because then they try and pull together in order to relieve the
grievance, as the case may be?* ———— I think, M'lord, it is perhaps the
wrong word to use there. I do not think we create grievance, I think
we recognize existing grievances, and we subject them in conscientization to a system of analysis, such that we can come up with solutions
to the problems. Now, all we are saying is that within so-called
orthodox trade union movements, which are under the influence of
taxers, there is in fact very little Black thinking. It is an authoritarian
movement where the leadership states what should happen. It has
more like a club effect, where the man at the top merely says; This
is what we are doing today, and the people never think. The people
do not even know really and truly their rights as workers. They are
not educated to understand their participation in the whole economy
of the country. Now, we believe that a worker is entitled to know his
role in the economy, to know what happens to the kind of product
he produces, to know how profits come to be made, so that he can be
in a strong position to bargain with the employer with respect to the
distribution of profits within an economic undertaking. This is what
we understand a developed worker to be. Now, in this country this
seems to have even more significance, because also thrown in is the
color question. So all we are really talking about here is the kind of
trade union which does proper training of workers to understand their

role in society, to understand just how much of a pillar they are to
the whole economy of the country.

COURT ADJOURNS

COURT RESUMES

STEPHEN BANTU BIKO, STILL UNDER OATH

CROSS-EXAMINATION BY MR. ATTWELL, CONTINUED: *Mr. Biko,
we were busy with the Resolution 25 of 1972, and His Lordship
drew your attention to point 3 on page 17 of your papers—page 100
of Your Lordship's papers—that the present moves towards trade
unionism constituted are only in the nature of producing a contented worker. Now, in that context, do you know whether SASO
did anything about contented workers?* —— Well, I said they
started off this project called the Black Workers' project, which
was generally to operate along these lines—that is, to encourage
the formation of the Workers' Council—and eventually decided to
abandon it. I am not quite sure for what reason. I think there
were areas of practicability which posed problems; in other words,
it became a massive undertaking which could not be sufficiently
done by a student organization.

You say eventually they dropped it? —— Yes.

*Did they go any distance with this project at all before they dropped
it?* —— Well, I think they went some distance. They did a hell of
a lot of research in the area of investigating existing labor laws, and
trying to formulate out of this material which was later used by trade
unions, but as far as I know this is basically what they were doing
before they decided to abandon the project. . . .

*The theme of White violence against Blacks is in fact a pet theme
of SASO?* —— I think a pet theme of SASO is more correctly unity
of Black students.

*And in fact you yourself said that you consider the Whites here to
be more likely or more correctly to be terrorists than the accused before
court?* —— Yes. I said that.

Were you scared that anything he said was racially hostile? ——
No, I was at the meeting—I think Nengwekulu talked . . . For

instance, he evoked laughter from the crowd. In many, many parts of his talk he just evoked laughter, the way he was speaking. He was not demagogic, he was just speaking. And I think the crowd just laughed, you know. Now, if a man is evoking hostility amongst people, I do not expect that one of the manifestations of that hostility would be laughter.

It was BPC's policy, you said, not to inflame racial hostility? —— Sorry?

It was BPC's and SASO's policy not to inflame racial hostility? —— I have not said this.

Was it their policy? —— To do what?

To cause racial hostility? —— No, it was not.

Were any people ever remonstrated with or taken to task for doing this, either in SASO or BPC? —— I cannot remember specifically.

Are you aware of the fact that accused number 4 was convicted of inciting racial hostility at the meetings? —— I heard rumors to that effect.

Was he ever spoken to about that? —— No, I was already in King William's Town.

And that Harry Singh had also done so? —— I also heard rumors to that effect.

Do you know what they said? —— I haven't got a clue what they said.

I would like to read some of what they said to you and ask you if that was in fact BPC policy. I refer Your Lordship here to BPC E.4, M'lord. This is a transcript of a tape recording made at a meeting at which inter alia accused number 4 and Harry Singh spoke. Now, on page 1 of the document you will see it is headed Aubrey Mokoape. Now, he says:

"Ladies and gentlemen, I welcome you all in the name of Black people who have laid [down] their lives in defense of their country, in defense of their land, in defense of their dignity, and I say from those people—I bring you this message—'Power to the People.' We have gathered here today to commemorate our brothers and sisters who were murdered cowardly by the heavy fire-power of the White man, by the heavy [militancy] of the White people's structure. Black people who were unarmed who had come merely to register

their disagreement, who had come merely to cast their votes against oppression. These Black people were murdered, were killed callously without mercy, because they dared to say no to the White man's laws, because they dared to say no to the White man's will, because they dared to say; 'No, we won't be ruled in our country, in our country of birth, by people who have no right to rule us.' These Black people were murdered despite the fact that they were unarmed. Amongst these people were women, and there were children, and these too were murdered and killed by the White people's structure."

It carries on in the next paragraph, second last line:

"Brothers and sisters, White people in this country have displayed amply their willingness to at any time murder and kill Black people at each time when we register our vote of no. Every time we call out in protest, they run for their guns. Every time our leaders stand up to speak for us, they lock them in Robben Island. Every time our fathers and mothers call out and stand up and say; 'We want a living wage' they bring out their saracens, their camouflaged soldiers to come and intimidate them.

At no stage in the history of this country has the White man ever been prepared to talk to the Black man. The White man is always, always ready to show off his guns when the Black man talks. And I think this is for one reason and one reason only: that the White man is afraid. They are afraid, they are afraid. They shiver in their cowardice. Every time a Black man stands up and speaks the truth, they all go for their guns because they are afraid of the Black man. They are afraid of the widening powers of the Black people, and I think for these reasons we should take courage. Every time our Black people are mowed down, we take courage. There is no time for looking back, no— each one, we've crossed our Rubicon. We crossed it a long time ago. We crossed it at Bambata in 1906 when he declared that the first Black man . . . that he was going to fight for the liberation of his country and this land. And I think, ladies and gentlemen, I wish to welcome you all here, and I am very happy that you turned out in all these numbers, to come and commemorate your heroes. *Every family has its hero, and therefore we should regard these Black people who died in the struggle as heroes. They are people who died fighting, and I think that . . . we have many more heroes, and we should be prepared because the tree of liberation is watered by the blood of masses or martyrs.*

Without further ado, ladies and gentlemen, I am going to call upon the first speaker of this evening, Mr. George Sewpersadh."

Mr. Sewpersadh then delivered a speech, and on page 5 of the document Mr. Mokoape responded to that speech by saying:

"As Mr. Sewpersadh has pointed out very clearly to us, the violence against Black people is not limited only to Sharpeville, nor is it limited only to Langa in 1960, nor to Bulhoek in 1921, nor to Bondelswarts in 1922. The violence of the White people against Black people is manifest in various ways every day of our lives. Every day of our lives our children are dying from starvation, and . . . if this is not a manifestation of White violence, then what else is?"

It carries on a little bit lower down:

"The White man is violent against the Black people in every walk of life, and Mr. Sewpersadh pointed out this very aptly when he said, 'There are those amongst us who are banned. There are those amongst us who are languishing in Robben Island. There are those amongst us who . . . have been put in very remote places who can hardly eke out a living.' This is part of the master plan of the White man to keep us in perpetual servitude. Let us hear more—Ah! about this violence. And now we will be addressed by Miss Mamphela Ramphele, who is chairlady of the Black People's Convention . . ."

who then gives a speech which apparently was too indistinct to transcribe. Then Mr. Mokoape carries on:

"The greatest tribute that we can pay . . . those people who lost their lives at Sharpeville—at Langa and at all other places in this country—the greatest tribute that we can pay them is to carry on relentlessly with the work that they began, to carry on without fear, because we have only but one road, and that road is total unadulterated revolution."

Then lower down on the page, Mr. Harry Singh was introduced to the audience and he made a speech.

THE COURT: *I think perhaps this would be a convenient stage to take the adjournment.*

COURT ADJOURNS

The Afternoon of May 6, 1976

Attwell leads Biko through an analysis of an article written by Biko entitled, "Fear—an Important Determinant in South African Politics." Attwell seeks to show that this article, and others like it, incite racial hostility.

COURT RESUMES

STEPHEN BANTU BIKO, STILL UNDER OATH

CROSS-EXAMINATION BY MR. ATTWELL, CONTINUED: *Mr. Biko, before the adjournment we were referring to the transcript of the proceedings at a Sharpeville Commemoration Meeting and speeches by Dr. Aubrey Mokoape, accused number 4, and one Harry Singh. I think we got to Harry Singh's speech. Now, page 6 of your documents, Harry Singh started off:*

> *"Power and Solidarity—Black people, the 21st of March is a day the Black man will remember. It is the day when all of us here know that the massacre that happened at Sharpeville . . . that Sharpeville didn't start thirteen years ago. Sharpeville started way, way back when that longhaired paleface terrorist by the name of Jan Van Riebeeck landed here. It was then that the plundering, the massacre, the raping and the brutality against our Black people was carried on, and carried on up to this very moment. Any time, any one minute in a little corner of South Africa, you will get at least ten people, and that is a very conservative estimate, ten people being either raped, brutalized, terrorized or being flogged to death on the White farms, being flogged to death by a White. That is the bastard nation in South Africa because he has no right to live in South Africa. He came over and took the country by force of guns, by no marriage at all. The people who have a right to South Africa are we Black people, and we shall fight for our country back again. We must also remember that Sharpeville and*

Langa haven't stopped. They will continue happening. They will continue happening daily until the time that every Black man has won his freedom, even if it takes ten Black men to drop every minute. There are others who will fight on, who will fight relentlessly until we have our land back. For too long now the White man has had it very cushy. He has had his guns and his Law. And his Law says that the Black man cannot defend himself. He must be shot down. Women must be shot down, and if there are people who are protesting they must be shot down. They must be raped. The White man has got his cars. An eye for an eye and a tooth for a tooth. You have also learnt the little bit which that White fool has been teaching his children when our wives, when our mothers have been raped and kicked. We have now reached a point where we can also say an eye for an eye and a tooth for a tooth. We are entering the 322nd year of the limbo slavery which was forced upon us by the White pattern.

The time has come for all of us here to start thinking very seriously about our future and exactly what strategy we are to use."

And he goes on, on the next page, at about the White man becoming afraid. And the second paragraph:

"We have reached the crucial point in our struggle. We have to make important decisions about our survival or the suffering that we must carry on in these Gestapo-type attacks on our families and our homes. No property in the entire world even collectively would surpass the atrocities, the brutalities, that are being carried out on the Black people in South Africa. And these are being perpetrated by the "Baas," by the "Baas" protectors, I beg your pardon, of this Fascist State, this mad White state of ours. The people who rule by force, by guns, by saracens, will do anything. As lately in Mundini helicopters were flown out and the armed force for people who were defenseless, who were only asking for a—begging actually—for a decent living wage, and this White government's policy was to send out the army, the helicopters, the army in camouflage suits. And the excuse was that the helicopters were just flying around on a practice session. You should have realized by now that despite the politicians here, people are not isolated. This is one

*master plan by the White man to subjugate us, to keep us in an
entire subjugation and to keep us voiceless. Our answer for this
life-and-death problem must be a concerted action as Black people."*

*And he carries on in the same vein that the Black man should stop
sitting down and taking everything that the White man has given him.
Now, this type of thing—were these people acting within the mandate,
or within the ambit of BPC policy?* —— I would not be able to say
that with precision, because I have not really studied this document.
I have just sort of looked while you were reading. I would say that
certainly it would appear to me they are speaking as individuals. I
don't think they were there to represent BPC or to sell out BPC
policy. They were stating their feelings on issues, from the way the
speeches run. I mean, of course, you notice there is a bit of a difference
between the two speeches. I think the first one, at least the comments
by Mokoape, are more or less so far as I can see what one might call
fair comment. They are certainly hard words, but they are fair comment all the same. There are parts of Mr. Singh's speech which are
a little bit excessive. Again, I was not at this particular meeting. I
don't even know if the particular transcripts, for instance, have been
vouched for.

Let us assume for one moment that they are correct? —— Yes, but
certainly as I say in Mr. Singh's speech there are parts which are a
bit excessive.

*Would you have a look, for instance, at the second last page? You
will find Dr. Aubrey Mokoape winds up the meeting with:*

*"Brothers and sisters, I think these words have been spoken by no
less authority [than] Reverend Bartman, who felt that the White
man has become subhuman, that the White man is in the way, has
become a devil, that the White man has become a beast and that
he can only be helped by one thing, by quite quickly removing
him."*

—— Yes.

MR. SOGGOT: *My Lord, if I may interrupt, the words "quite quickly,"
as I understand it, was not common cause. The accused found that
indistinct and that was not admitted to.*

MR. ATTWELL: *Very well, My Lord, for the purposes of this particular*

witness' comments we can leave out the words "quite quickly" there.
―――― Did you pose me a question?

Yes. Now, I was saying that you could still consider that to be fair comment? ―――― Well, one would be able to know what Bartman said, but as far as I can see he was referring to a speech made by Bartman. Now, I know Reverend Bartman very well. He is a minister of the Methodist Church, a very reasonable man. If he made an assertion like this one that Whites have become subhuman, he would develop that logic, he would illustrate what he means. Now, it is very difficult now to take this without that context.

But generally speaking, Dr. Mokoape's statements you feel are fair comment? ―――― Most of them, yes.

And represent what BPC feels? ―――― Well, I mean, I don't necessarily know if BPC has commented on all the things he speaks about. But I would say he speaks like a BPC man.

Now, is it in fact true that at virtually all the conference gatherings, Sharpeville meetings, that you people in BPC and SASO organized, one finds ministers, Black ministers, who were present and normally addressed the gatherings, and one finds Black poetry and/or drama and/or music which is presented, Mr. Biko? ―――― I think the form varies from campus to campus. The usual form at U.N.B. was normally that of a service first, followed by a few speeches. The service would be an authentic service conducted by a respectable minister, and thereafter of course there would be the speeches from either SASO or BPC or the community at large.

And poetry? ―――― Now and then you would find poetry.

And at GSC's and/or conventions of BPC, dramas presented, Black music, poetry read and that sort of thing? ―――― In SASO meetings, yes; at BPC meetings, not the ones I attended.

Mr. Biko, you were restricted in March, 1973? ―――― That is correct.

What were the terms of your restriction? ―――― Well, the usual terms. Prohibiting me from attending gatherings which are described, official gatherings, and other types of gatherings, confining me to the King William's Town magisterial area, prohibiting me from entering any so-called Bantu area or Colored area or Indian area except the one where I stay. Prohibiting me from working within—at least from entering premises of factories, press and so on. Prohibiting me from

compiling, editing, disseminating any publication in which government policy is either defended or attacked.

Was your role in SASO and BPC affected thereby? —— Yes, there
was a prohibition also stopping me from associating or taking part in
the activities of SASO, BPC and lately BCP.

*And this effectively cut you off from the mainstream of SASO and
BPC?* —— Yes.

*Now, King William's Town as such—has it ever been a particularly
active or important area for SASO?* —— Not before I came to King
William's Town.

But since then it has? —— It has.

And that is responsible—is attributable—to whom? —— Well, I
don't think it is entirely coincidental. I think because I am there, there
tends to be a movement in and out of King William's Town of people
who are important to SASO and BPC who therefore find a way of
talking to the local community. I think this is how the BPC branch
in King William's Town became settled, because people in the first
place live and thereafter work in the context of the township.

Who were these people? —— I mentioned Mangena as one. There
were several others, people like Baqwa, before he got banned—several.

Is that Jeff Baqwa? —— Yes. There are many. I just can't recall
them now readily.

Any of the accused? —— I don't remember seeing any one of
them. Mr. Lekota passed once through there, either going to or from
a meeting at Alice.

Now, would this mean that you were in fact not totally au fait *with
current events and happenings in BPC and SASO?* —— I think I
kept pretty well informed of the main thinking. I might not know any
new actions. For instance, I might not know that there is a meeting
in Stanger or something like that, but I have kept myself informed of
the major policy developments within BPC.

Have there been any policy developments? —— Very important
ones, yes.

In which sphere or in what regard? —— I think, for instance, in
the last conference of BPC they did spell out in more precise terms
the kind of future society they were looking forward to.

Which convention do you have in mind now? —— This was the conference in December last year.

In December of last year? —— Yes.

Oh, after the accused were detained on . . .? —— That is correct.

Well, unfortunately that goes outside the ambit of what we are busy with at the moment. Would you have been aware of any necessary shift in emphasis or anything like that between the period of your banning and the arrest of the accused, for instance? —— Yes, if there would have been a major shift I would have been aware.

If it had been something really significant? —— That is correct.

If you were approached by someone and asked to refer them to very significant people, for instance, in BPC, who would you refer them to? —— Right now?

Well, let us assume that this had happened before the arrest of the accused? —— Before the arrest of the accused? I think it is conceivable I would have sent them—referred them—to some of the accused.

Such as? —— People like Mr. Cooper. I am not sure now about the others. I had heard of him. I did not know him then, but I could have referred people to him because he was respected.

Was he respected? —— Yes.

Accused number 4? —— Well, as I said earlier on, Aubrey had never really taken an executive position, so that if it was an organizational matter I would not necessarily refer to him. I would refer to him on other matters—like, if one wanted for instance an exposition —I regard him as a man who has a very good mind. I could have referred people to him for that sort of thing.

Accused number 9 as well, I should imagine? —— That is correct. He was more with SASO really.

More with SASO? —— Yes.

Now, where would you say the real power base of BPC is? —— Are you talking about places or people?

I am talking about places. —— I think to a great extent Durban and Johannesburg. But I think now also the Eastern Cape.

Yes, but now if I may then limit the ambit of the question to before September, or before the end of 1974? —— Durban and Johannesburg, yes.

Why is Durban so insignificant? —— Well, I think one has got to

look at it historically again—that from that area basically came people
who were very much ahead in the exposition of Black Consciousness
in the country. People like Pityana, myself, Moodley, Cooper—we
were all in Durban, and in that sense it was conceivable that BPC
would be strong in Durban. But again, this is not a strength so much
related to numbers as it is related to influence.

Influence? —— Yes.

*Yes. That is why I talked about in fact the real power base—forget
about where the head office is or so on.* —— Right.

*Who decided that Johannesburg should be the head office of BPC
and why was it chosen?* —— I haven't got a clue.

You don't know? —— No.

*Do you know of any moves at any stage during BPC's history to shift
that head office from Johannesburg anywhere else?* —— I think the
question has been debated. I cannot pinpoint now precisely where.
People have talked of it shifting, but I don't remember a decision
being taken.

To which place or places did they have in mind? —— Well, there
was a stage when Cape Town people wanted it there, and then there
was always this wrangling. Durban people wanted it in Durban. Cape
Town people wanted it in Cape Town. But it has remained in Johannesburg.

*Was any one center ever considered to be the possible alternate which
was previously considered, or don't you know?* —— I cannot say.

*Now, I am interested in your personal knowledge: Which country
. . . surrounding South Africa is the one through which most of the
people who have been leaving for guerrilla training . . . have gone
through?* —— That is a queer question. I don't know anything about
people who have left for guerrilla training.

According to the newspapers and things do you . . .? —— I have
heard of training camps in Zambia, for instance, but I have not heard
how people get there.

You have not heard how they get there? —— No.

Now, do you know Mr. Sipho Buthelezi? —— Yes, I know
him.

He was the previous Secretary-General of BPC? —— That is correct.

Where is he now, do you know? —— I know that he left the country, and I know that he went to Botswana.

Mr. Nengwekulu? —— Yes, I know him.

Where is he now? —— He is in Botswana.

And Mr. Bokwe Maphuna? —— He is also in Botswana.

Mr. Jeff Baqwa whom you referred the court to? —— He is also in Botswana.

Have you yourself had any contact with these people whilst they have been there? —— Yes.

In what connection? —— Well, when Tiro died I got a phone call. I am not sure now which gentleman spoke to me, but one of the gentlemen spoke to me about it. They had been apparently trying to get through to Johannesburg and failing, and they wanted to inform some people inside the country that this thing had just happened. I think it was a few hours after it had happened. So they asked me to phone somebody in Johannesburg—I have forgotten who now—to try and get the message through to the parents.

And in other connections apart from Tiro's death as such? —— I have also been phoned once in connection with some cultural event that was going on there sometime in May. I think there was a big cultural festival going on there. Somebody wanted to find out some names of bands—what you call jazz bands—in my area.

Any other? —— I can't remember anything else specifically.

When was Southern African Students Movement formed? —— I think this was formed during 1973—but I am not sure—either 1973 or 1974.

Before or after your restriction? —— It was . . . Well, moves were made during my time, but I think the actual culmination was after I had been banned.

You probably know of the pro-Frelimo rallies which were held at a certain stage here in September 1974? —— That is correct.

Was there ever going to be a rally in King William's Town? —— There was going to be one, as far as I heard, in East London.

Not in King William's Town? —— Not in King William's Town. . . .

How many Sharpeville Commemoration Meetings have you personally attended? —— I think I must have attended one every year since 1971.

Always in Durban until your restriction? —— That is correct.

Then you mentioned that one of the things behind the Day of Compassion was that you recall natural disasters. Do you recall having said that? —— Yes, that is right.

What would the purpose be in recalling natural disasters? —— Well, as I said, the significance of Compassion Day was precisely to let students inculcate some kind of social conscience and to prepare themselves for service within the community, when they get into the community after studying. So therefore anything that creates a state of need could be a good focal point for Compassion Day. That includes the natural disasters.

Did I understand you correctly in your evidence-in-chief to have said that Pityana or SASO had insisted or laid down a rule that there was to be no preaching or conscientizing of the people during community projects? —— Yes, I think there was such an understanding. It was not a written code, but there was such an understanding. Whether it originated from him or not, I am not quite certain. But he used to insist on this sort of thing. . . .

Do you know [Bokwe Maphuna]? —— Yes.

Did he ever assault a White policeman or anything? Was he involved in a case of assaulting a White policeman? —— Yes, I actually attended a court hearing where he was charged with assaulting a traffic cop, which according to him was the actual reverse of what had happened. He had been clapped by a White traffic cop and he went to lay a charge, and apparently the traffic cop on receiving notice of this decided to lay a countercharge, and his case came first. So Maphuna now was in a situation where he had to answer why he beat up the cop, and in actual fact the cop had beaten him up.

Was he convicted? —— Yes, something like R 20.00. I don't know what it was.

There is a reference in one of the poems [to] Maphuna having done something along these lines. I am merely trying to ascertain whether there was such a thing. Your literacy training program—was this based on the approach of any specific person? —— Yes.

Who was that person? —— Paul Lafrere.

Now, I think perhaps could you just elaborate to the court what he believed, what is his policy? —— Well, I think he advocates what he calls education for self-reliance, so to speak. He believes that the orthodox methods of education which have been standardized over history have got a certain inhibiting influence on the students and the pupils, and do not encourage creative thinking or reasonable thinking on the part of the students. I think the term "conscientization" in fact originates from his philosophy about education. He believes that education should direct itself at raising the level of critical awareness on the part of the receiver. He believes, for instance, that the old system of learning, where you start with vowels and then you couple the consonants with them, and then you go on to words, is not creative. He believes in what he calls syllabic learning. You have got to take words that mean something to the person you are talking to and you have got to create out of these particular words syllables, and as soon as the person can recognize the particular syllable and pronounce it, he can form other words from those basic syllables, and in this way his knowledge snowballs much faster. But of course this whole philosophy is directed at adult education rather than kids.

Is it, in other words, education with another purpose as well—not mere literacy? ——— I think it is education for education's sake, but it is a type of education, you know. I mean, any education is described . . . [The witness speaks indistinctly]

Now, you said in fact to your understanding he was the author of this phrase "conscientization"? ——— Yes, it appears within his philosophy of education.

And is this the sense in which you described conscientization to the court? ——— . . . Yes.

Where is this man stationed—Paul Lafrere? Do you know? ——— I don't know where he is now. I think he has held various positions at various universities, and he was in the States sometime back. I don't know where he is now.

Has his philosophy of literacy ever been applied in any other country or countries? ——— I think it is applied in Swaziland. It has been applied throughout Latin America.

Latin America? ——— Yes.

THE COURT: *Don't we have it in our schools too, Mr. Attwell?*

MR. ATTWELL: *The Paul Lafrere method?*

THE COURT: *Well, they teach you to recognize words? I remember when my sister was young she came home with a book, and she was in the grades, and there was a picture of a cheese in a plate and she said "K-a-a-s . . . hoed." She thought it was a hat.*

MR. ATTWELL: *Is the example which His Lordship quoted the sort of thing Paul Lafrere attempted to eradicate?* —— Well, I can't comment, you know.

You can't? —— No.

Do you agree with His Lordship that that is the sort of problem one finds? —— [The court intervenes].

THE COURT: *Well, that is criticism against the System, Mr. Attwell . . .*

MR. ATTWELL: *Does the Paul Lafrere method have a political bias?* —— Well, if you are holding on to power which depends on the lack of awareness by those you are holding in your power, you can feel that it is very biased against you, but for the man underneath it is a welcome philosophy.

Is it something that has been applied by oppressed people? —— Sorry?

Is it something that has been applied by oppressed people? —— I think you do get groups, in America usually, using this particular system without any intention of following it logically to its political end, if you like.

Which groups in America do you have in mind? —— Groups that he has been working with in America . . .

Minority groups? —— I would not particularly know who. But I know that he has been working in America.

I think at this stage we could turn to the annexures, to the charge sheet which we have now found out you were the author of? —— That is correct.

The article "I Write What I Like" by Frank Talk, My Lord—this will be in K.4(a), I think. Will you have a look at . . . It starts from page 77, that particular article. I may refer you to page 78, the second page in this indictment. You say in the top paragraph:

> *"To look for instances of cruelty directed at those who fall into disfavor with the security police is perhaps to look too far. One need not try to establish the truth of the claim that Black people in South Africa have to struggle for survival. It presents itself in ever so many facets of our lives. Township life alone makes it a miracle*

for anyone to live up to adulthood. There we see a situation of absolute want in which Black will kill Black to be able to survive. That is the basis of the vandalism, murders, rapes and plunder that goes on while the real source of the evil, White society, are suntanning on exclusive beaches or relaxing in their bourgeois homes. "

Are those your real sentiments? —— That is correct.

Then in the second last paragraph in the lefthand column.

"Clearly, Black people cannot respect White people, at least not in this country. There is such an obvious aura of immorality and naked cruelty in all that is done in the name of White people that no Black man, no matter how intimidated, can ever be made to respect White society. However, in spite of the obvious contempt for the values cherished by the Whites and the price at which White comfort and security is purchased, Blacks seem to me to have been successfuly cowed down by the type of brutality that emanates from this section of the community. " —— That is correct.

Are those also your sentiments? —— Yes.

Then . . . the second paragraph on the righthand column on page 11—

"This is a dangerous type of fear, for it only goes skin deep. It hides underneath it an immeasurable rage that often threatens to erupt. Beneath it lies naked hatred for a group that deserves absolutely no respect. Unlike in the rest of the French or Spanish former colonies, where chances of assimilation made it not impossible for Blacks to aspire towards being White, in South Africa whiteness has always been associated with police brutality and intimidation, early morning pass raids, general harassment in and out the townships, and hence no Black really aspires to be White. The claim by Whites of monopoly on comfort and security has always been so exclusive that Blacks see Whites as the major obstacles in their progress towards peace, prosperity and a sane society. Through its associations with all these negative aspects whiteness has thus become soiled beyond recognition. At best therefore Blacks see Whiteness as a concept that warrants being despised, hated, destroyed and replaced by an aspiration with more human content in it. At worst Blacks envy White society for the comfort it has

usurped, and at the center of this envy is the wish, nay, the secret determination in the innermost minds of most Blacks who think like this to kick Whites off those comfortable garden chairs that one sees as he rides in a bus out of town, and to claim them for himself.

Day by day one gets more convinced that Aimé Césaire could not have been right when he said: "No race possesses the monopoly on truth, intelligence, force, and there is room for all of us at the rendezvous of victory."

And in the very last paragraph of the article, once again you say,

"One will therefore not be surprised if it proves very difficult to accept that 'There is room for all of us at the rendezvous of victory.'"

Now, what did you have in mind? —— I think this article speaks very well for itself, if you read all of it really. It is a commentary on the decadence of our society. It points out the rising animosity between Black and White which has been brought about by history, and by three hundred years of oppression, as our guys normally say, and my warning here is that if this situation is not corrected, it can lead to a hardening of attitudes, especially on the Black side. Blacks may very well get to a position where they feel permanently that they cannot live side by side with Whites. And this is a warning in a sense to society to perceive this trend.

Where is the warning expressed in warning terms? —— Throughout the entire . . . You have got to read the whole thing in its context, you see, and if you look at the title, right, I am trying to eradicate the thinking that is prevalent in White society, so to speak, which makes them operate from fear as a basis. In other words, they do not necessarily look at things that are done by Blacks logically. They look at them in terms of to what extent do they threaten our position as White society? And this is the basis for police brutality, for instance. You know, the operation is such that one gets the impression that White society wants to continually remind us of our position, you know, the way police ride around townships, for instance. There is no need for them to speed at the kind of pace at which they speed normally, but somehow as a sign of authority, as a sign of saying, "We are there." Police vans just loom through townships and everybody has got to run away from the police van because it is authority. Now, this is sort of inculcated fear in Blacks, you know, a fear against authority, and I am saying this is an unhealthy fear because it is the kind of fear which, if it goes unchecked, generates an uncontrollable response, some kind of blowup. I am trying to say our society because of these things is becoming very sickly, and it may get to a point where we may not be able to live side by side. Now, if you want to pick up that theme you have got to read the entire article, not just pieces.

Where do you get a cause for a check on this system that you . . . ? —— I think it is endemic in the warning.

Can you refer us to any specific . . . ? —— I said to you you have got to read the whole article, you have got to study that article. I mean, this is a commentary on society, if you see what I mean.

This would have been circulated in the SASO newsletter in three, four thousand copies to Blacks all over the country? —— That is right.

Specifically in campuses? —— That is right.

And you say at the very end: "The stage is therefore set for a very interesting turn of events." —— Where is this?

Right at the end there, the closing words of the article that you wrote? —— Yes.

What interesting turn of events do you have in mind? —— I have got to read that paragraph first.

Yes, by all means. —— Yes, I am saying, if you read the paragraph that the White strategy so far has been to systematically break down the resistance of the Blacks to the point where the latter would accept crumbs from the White table. And on the other hand, Blacks have shown that they reject this unequivocally, okay, and I am saying then the stage, meaning what is to happen thereafter. All right, it will likely be interesting. As soon as Blacks demonstrate beyond any doubt that they don't want Bantustans, CRC's, and SAIC's, we would like to see what Mr. Vorster will have to offer.

Is there an indication that Blacks will respect Whites if they change? —— I think it is endemic in the warning. As I say, you have got to read the whole article. You have got to understand what it means, and you will see that there is no particular stance I am taking. I am just commenting on society, right? And I am saying in my commentary what is going on is unhealthy, okay, and I am warning that it may prove even more unhealthy if it goes unchecked. In that kind of statement obviously . . . you can extrapolate a statement that if things improve, things might be better again at relations level.

Now, if this was a warning, to whom is it directed? —— To both sides. I am against the kind of fear that is there in Blacks—this bottled-up fear. In a sense I am trying to get Blacks to look at issues more positively, and I am also against the kind of mentality that emanates from White society, which seeks to promote that fear in Black society.

THE COURT: *Well, isn't it more correct to say that where you paint the picture and you show the inherent dangers, and you say, Well now, there is the picture?* —— I don't think it ends quite there, My Lord. I think the slant of the article, you know, shows that it is a warning to society. Now, any warning normally implies, even if it is tacit, that there should be changes.

Well, that is what I am suggesting. There is no express warning; there is a picture, and from it appears inherent dangers, and you say, well now, there is the picture. Now, whoever looks at it must see for himself how this picture affects himself? —— That is correct.

MR. ATTWELL: *The paragraph on the lefthand side on page 12, the second last paragraph:*

"One can, of course, say that Blacks are to blame for allowing this situation to exist. Or to drive the point even further, one may point out that there are Black policemen and Black Special Branch agents." —— Yes.

"To take the last point first, I must state categorically that there is no such thing as a Black policeman. Any Black man who props the system up actively has lost the right to be considered part of the Black world. He has sold his soul for thirty pieces of silver to find he is not in fact acceptable to the White society he sought to join. These are colorless White lackeys who live in a marginal world of unhappiness; they are extensions of the enemy into our ranks. On the other hand, the rest of the Black world is kept in check purely because of powerlessness." —— Yes.

Now, what must the Blacks do? You condemn the fact that they allow the situation to exist? —— Yes.

What must they do? —— I think, for instance, if a man kicks you in the back when you are innocent . . . Or let us talk about the other guy we were talking about yesterday, the man who insulted his assistant who is under the ceiling. If the Black man had from the very beginning objected, that kind of relationship would not have developed, so that . . . the White man in that situation is to blame for insulting the Black man. The Black man is also to be blamed for allowing the situation to develop. This is what I am trying to suggest to you. If he had said, No, you can't refer to me like that, I am also a father of four like you, then I am sure the White man would have thought seriously about it. But because there is no response—because the Black man just keeps quiet and accepts everything, you know—prejudice tends to build up against him, and certain practices become entrenched.

And the beginning of the next paragraph seems to tie in with this: "Powerlessness breeds a race of beggars who smile at the enemy and swear at him in the sanctity of their toilets. Who shout "Baas" willingly through the day and call the White man a dog in their buses as they go home."

—— Yes, this is what I call the two-faced approach by the Black man to Whites. I think we have talked about it already.

So it is powerlessness that is basically the problem for the Black man?
—— Certainly, yes.

And is SASO and BPC going to remedy that powerlessness of the Blacks? —— Yes. . . .

THE COURT: *But you make the observation that the newspapers report the number of murders in a place like Soweto. Now what, do you say, what is the cause of the murders in Soweto?* —— My Lord, I submit that it is the squalid conditions under which we live. Whether it is a whole totality of factors . . .

Why do you say that? I mean, we hear those cases, and in fact the murders are not confined to Soweto. They are all over the country? —— Indeed they are.

But they always start at the beer drink? —— That is correct.

But now why do you say that? They are busy enjoying life when they commit these murders? —— Well, you have got to look beyond the beer. You have got to look at the mentality of the man and what forms that mentality. You know, all the factors in his life which lead to a situation where he finds it very easy to whip out a knife and stick it into another man. If you have been built up through society properly there must be something telling you in your mind that it is wrong to whip out a knife and stick it into another man, but somehow when you have been battered in your development, your mentality changes; you become somewhat a sick man, but a sick man who will live on and on, and go on to drink beer, and in that process stabs another man. Now, when he gets to court, of course, the court does not inquire into the sociological environment in which this man grew up. He just inquires where the knife came from, where it went to and who put it there. It is a very superficial way of looking at it.

MR. ATTWELL: *Who all knew that you were Frank Talk?* ——— It has been a very closely guarded secret.

Who knew? ——— I think it was the editor and the general secretary.

Who would they have been by any name? ——— Mr. Pityana and Mr. Moodley.

Nobody else? ——— I am aware that some people could guess from the style, you know, of writing, but generally . . .

Is there something in the style that is peculiar to your writing? ——— Anybody who writes regularly develops a style.

THE COURT: *Why did you keep it secret?* ——— I think I have explained this yesterday, My Lord. The main idea was to let people focus on the contents . . .

And not on the man. I see. ——— And not on the man.

MR. ATTWELL: *You are also the author of the article "The Definition of Black Consciousness," BPC T.1? While you are waiting for the document, speaking purely now in hypothetical terms, Mr. Biko, do you consider that it is feasible to teach people to hate one another and then expect that at some stage in the future these people will love one another and get along with one another?* ——— Well, I have never experimented in that sort of thing. I won't be able to give an answer.

Is it feasible or isn't it? ——— I really don't know.

Didn't you consider that? ——— No.

Have you never considered it? ——— No.

Has it never been discussed by SASO or BPC or anything else? ——— No.

Now, will you have a look at this article? Do you identify it as one which you drew up? ——— Yes.

Once again . . . The theme, about in the third paragraph—which we referred to previously in your evidence cross-examination—that any man who calls a White man "Baas," any man who serves in the Police Force or Security Branch, is ipso facto Non-White? —— Yes.

And thus not a . . . person who is part of the Black struggle? —— Yes.

Now, you then state in the middle paragraph on that page:
   "Blacks no longer seek to reform the System, because so doing implies acceptance of the major points around which the System revolves." —— Yes.
   "Blacks are out to completely transform the System and make of it what they wish."
Do you see that? —— Yes.
   "Such a major undertaking can only be realized in an atmosphere where people are convinced . . ." [An airplane drowns out the voice of Mr. Attwell]
Did you find those two paragraphs? —— Yes.

Now, if we can start with that second sentence which I quoted to you, "Blacks are out to completely transform the System and make of it what they wish," and read it in conjunction with the fact that they no longer seek to reform what exists, but a complete transformation of the entire System—where does one find in that a recognition that there will be some semblance of White values left in the future society which you people envisage? —— I think you would have to wait for a definition of that future society, and this is what I am saying BPC has finally given. You must examine that, and perhaps you can get an indication within that of what shall be retained.

What did you envisage when you wrote this? —— The point about any political philosophy is that it develops over time. Now, we are speaking here about various systems in the air, so to speak. We were going to get to a stage, and I think BPC has got to that stage now, of beginning to define in detail what they want, but a philosophy as I say is never complete over two or three months or two years. Some philosophies take twenty years to perfect, before it can be a fortified body of thought. . . .

Now, surely it was dangerous to give out this type of document without specifying, especially relating to the White fears [there] may be? —— What document are you talking about?

For instance, this definition of Black Consciousness and the future society? —— What is dangerous here?

In that you seek to transform a System and make of it what Blacks wish, and throw overboard virtually everything that is existing at the moment? —— I don't find that there at all. I just find it a statement, a policy statement, of where you stand.

And did you agree with me that the Whites basically are afraid of the Black Consciousness and Black Power movements? —— Not all Whites are afraid actually.

Well, if we can talk about Whites collectively, as you people generally do, would you say that they were afraid of the Black Power and Black Consciousness movements? —— I think you are talking collectively now about the majority of Whites.

Yes? —— I would say the majority of Whites are not even aware.

Not even aware of . . . ? —— Of Black Consciousness.

They are not aware of it? —— No.

Was this designed to remedy that situation? —— No, no, no. This was a working paper at a SASO formation school where I was living at seventeen. We used this; this is a working paper. All these documents were talks too. This is skeleton thinking. The main thing was the lecture. From each particular paragraph, you know, I could take certain points and talk at length. This was not meant for general distribution; it was meant only for those people who were there. But even if it was meant for general distribution, there is nothing dangerous in any of the assertions that are made here.

THE COURT: *Well, let us just follow the practice. I think they have referred to a formation school as a seminar already. If it is in the nature of a seminar, you come there and you deliver this paper and then you discuss the views expressed in this paper, and it is developed and cut down, as the case may be?* —— They change, My Lord. Some are like that, where people read papers, and [there are] group discussions around several points on the papers, and then they report back. Some are pure training sessions. Now, this one was a pure training session. In other words I was supposed to talk to a group of SASO students about Black Consciousness. There were three papers. The first one was "The Rationale for Black Consciousness," the second was "The Definition of Black Consciousness," and the third one was "Practical

Implications of Black Consciousness," all of which were written by me and all of which were spoken to by me. And they formed the whole core of that training seminar. They were meant, in other words, for the participants. Unless you were at the seminar, a lot of things for instance here would be in the air, because this is not a full development, although it is called a definition it is not a full development of what Black Consciousness is all about. There had to be explanations, and these were done as I was talking.

MR. ATTWELL: *I was speaking about the second paragraph on page 2 of this document, about the one major force in South Africa against which the Black Consciousness approach is pitted, namely White racism. Do you see the second paragraph?* —— Yes.

> *"Its greatest ally to date has been the refusal by us to club together as Blacks because we are told to do so would be [inaudible] so while we progressively lose ourselves in a world of colorlessness and amorphous common humanity, Whites are deriving pleasure and security, and entrenching White racism and further exploiting the minds and bodies of the unsuspecting Black masses."*

—— Yes.

> *"Their agents are ever present among us, telling us that it is immoral to withdraw into a cocoon, and that dialogue is the answer to our problem, but it is unfortunate that there is White racism in some quarters, but you must understand that things are changing. These, in fact, are the greatest racists because they refuse to credit us with intelligence to know what we want. Their intentions are obvious; they want to be barometers by which the rest of the White society can measure feelings in the Black world."*

Now, the dialogue that is referred to there—to which you have objected —do you see the dialogue there? They tell you that dialogue is the answer? —— Yes.

Now, what dialogue are you rejecting there? —— If you look at the total of that . . . You will see if you look closely at that that this refers to multiracial bodies.

Multiracial bodies? —— Yes.

How do you see that that is a reference to multiracial bodies there, can you just tell us? —— I am talking about agents, right, moving amongst us. They tell us that dialogue is the answer. In other words, we must not clothe ourselves in a cocoon—we must avail ourselves of a mixture with Whites in multiracial organizations.

Their agents, who is that a reference to? ———— I am talking about White society.

White society? ———— Yes.

"*. . . are ever present telling us that it is immoral to withdraw into a cocoon and that dialogue is the answer.*"

———— That is correct.

Now, dialogue—is that the same as bargaining? ———— No.

Not? ———— Not at all.

Here you are putting out that Whites are telling you that dialogue and talking is the answer? ———— I am just talking about Liberals who get in amongst us and criticize us for being on our own and who say that we must get back into multiracial organizations because this is the way ahead, and that we must encourage a mixture within our levels, so that we can understand each other and so on and so on— all the arguments that the Liberals put out.

Is there a reference to Liberals here in those words? ———— No, I have not put in those—I mean . . . I just chose to put it in this form, that is all. [Indistinct]

Why in this form? ———— This is what I was thinking while I was writing, Mr. Attwell.

To close that paragraph off, the last sentence:
"*Sure, there are a few good Whites, just as much as there are a few bad Blacks. But what we are concerned with here is group attitudes and group politics. The exception does not make the [rule a lie] it merely substantiates it.*"

In other words, there are a few good Whites? ———— There are a few good Whites.

There are a few good Whites? ———— The statement here suggests that there are a few good Whites.

If there are a few good Whites it means that most of them are bad? ———— In attitude, yes.

And you are going to change them with dialogue, with bargaining? ———— We shall change society, and people's attitudes will change.

How are you going to change this bad lot of Whites who see no good in the Blacks? And you don't want to talk and dialogue is a waste of time? How are you going to change that? —— If you change society you regulate people's habits. If you regulate people's habits in a particular way, you know, they are changing their habits. You begin to change their attitudes. This is our answer to it all. The only answer is to change society.

Look at the second last paragraph on that page:

"The future South Africa in the case where Blacks adopt Black Consciousness is the subject for concern especially among initiates. What do we do when we have attained our Consciousness? Do we propose to kick Whites out?"

Now, if I may stop there for a moment, why did you raise that consideration in this article? —— It is because of . . . Inasmuch as this is a . . . This question you are asking me now, it was asked at that time by a Liberal, a person who was arguing against our point of view.

By Blacks too? —— No.

Wasn't this a paper read at the formation school? —— That is correct.

Where Blacks attended? —— That is correct.

So was it in answer to any doubts or fears that . . . —— No, it was not directed at Blacks. It was answers—the people who were there with answers. When you have a philosophy you have to have answers to questions that may be put by anybody.

So we must assume that that is in fact for the Whites' benefit? This particular little piece? —— How do you mean the Whites' benefit?

This is for the Whites, especially the White Liberals? —— [Pause] *"What do we propose to do"?* —— Yes.

Is that right? —— I am talking to Blacks to be able to explain to any man, right, when he asks me, and I am saying that the people who were asking the questions at the time anyway were Liberals.

Now, obviously then it was a matter of concern to you people about what would happen to Whites? When you people came to your bargaining and the ultimate rendezvous of victory, or whatever you want to call it? —— I don't know what is the question which I have to answer?

It was a concern to SASO and BPC what was going to happen at that stage? —— We were worried about society.

And society is made up of members from all different sorts of people?
———— That is correct.

And it was obviously therefore a factor which you people considered because it was a matter of contention? Certainly amongst certain sections about what was going to happen to certain sections? ———— Yes.

Now, if I put it to you that the position of Whites in your contemplated society of the future is extremely vague at the best, what would you say to that? ———— I would refer you to BPC policy as I have been doing for the past hour.

This policy which was adopted at this last conference which you just spoke of? ———— That is correct, yes.

But Mr. Biko, is that good enough? ———— It must be good enough because as I said to you an organization develops over years, a philosophy develops over years. I cannot, when you are asking me now, confine myself to the pre-1973 era, okay; I have got to refer to developments within BPC. I must not sit here and postulate. It has happened; they have defined a bit, you know, clearer.

Now, is it purely fortuitous that a couple of months after the accused or a year after the accused were arrested, BPC got down to deciding what was going to happen to the Whites? ———— I would say that as far as I am concerned BPC is not guided by what happens here. They are not going to wait for these men to be released. They just continue. I think this is a time in their history where they are now in a position to make certain logical expositions of this aspect of their philosophy.

What has happened to make them now be able to do this? ———— It is . . . because of environmental factors, the whole sort of political system is . . . throughout Southern Africa is vibrant with change right now. BPC may want to declare what they are saying—I don't know what the reason is, I am just like you on the . . . [The witness drops his voice and speaks indistinctly]

But it was still obviously a matter of concern to you? It was a question that was raised? ———— Yes.

And now you have sought to answer it here, and I put it to you that that position was sketched very vaguely by BPC, certainly at the time you drew up this document, and I submit, until the time the accused were arrested? ———— This was not for BPC or for SASO. It was just in aid of understanding the philosophy of Black Consciousness.

I am submitting it to you that SASO and BPC were extremely vague up until the time that these accused were arrested about what the answer to that question was? At the very best? ———Yes.

At the very best? ———Yes.

Now, let us see what your answer to that question was which you saw fit to raise here. What was your answer to this question? Read it there after what you said there? What were you supposed to do? ——— I don't think I even attempted to answer it.

Now, why not? ——— I was just talking about attitudes to this question. I was not talking about the answer to that question.

What is the answer you give here? Will you read it to the court? ——— "Do you propose to kick out Whites? We have defined what we mean by true integration, and the very fact such a definition as this does illustrate what our standpoint is . . ." *Carry on?* ——— ". . . we are much more concerned about what is happening now than what will happen in future. The future will always be shaped by the sequence of present-day events."

Now, what sort of answer was that to allay anybody's fears? ——— Can't you read . . . This is defined in the SASO manifesto which defined integration at length. Now, all those people who were there are quite aware of what is said about integration in the SASO manifesto. I did not want to repeat it; I did not attempt to answer this.

I put it to you that the SASO policy manifesto is very vague about what is going to happen to the Whites? ——— In relation . . . ?

About what is going to happen to the Whites? ——— Let us talk about it; produce it.

Well; you seem to know it, tell us first . . . ——— If you produce it, then I will refer you to what I am talking about.

Right, we will have a look at the SASO policy manifesto.

THE COURT: *Are we getting anywhere, Mr. Attwell? He says here what will happen in the future. He says the future will always be shaped by the sequence of present-day events.*

MR. ATTWELL: *And that future is never defined, My Lord.*

THE COURT: *Well, he says it depends on the sequence of the present-day events. He does not know. There are a lot of variables—he does not know how it will develop. He is not a prophet.*

MR. ATTWELL: *No, My Lord, I submit that these people have worked
. . . that it will I hope appear from what I am driving at in a minute.
I have put certain propositions to the witness, but what I . . . The gist
of my argument is that these people have created a situation, one in
which they foresee difficulties and possibilities, such as they even raised
themselves, and then they provide no answers thereto. They created a
difficult and dangerous situation, and then they leave what is going to
happen just in the air.*

THE COURT: *What would you have done if you were in their position?
What would you have done?*

MR. ATTWELL: *Well, My Lord, I submit that they have in certain
circumstances illustrated . . . I said for the witness' benefit that at best
they made it vague. And that is what the witness has done here, I am
submitting.* —— Well, I referred to integration as defined there. Let
us get down to that definition—that integration definition.

*That is SASO P.2, My Lord, the SASO manifesto, the policy mani-
festo.* —— Yes. Now, if you look at point 5 there.

"SASO believes that the concept of integration can never be
realized in an atmosphere of suspicion and mistrust. Integration
has not been an assimilation of Blacks into an already established
[order] drawn up and motivated by White society. Integration
implies full participation by individuals in a given society and
proportionate contribution to the joint culture of the society by
all constituent groups."

And I think this lays out quite clearly SASO's outlook to the future
society. It also lays out the position of the White man in that society.
He is an individual free in society, who contributes like any other man
to the joint culture of the society. It answers that question whether
we kick out Whites or not.

*You said earlier on in the SASO policy manifesto under point 3:
"That the Whites have defined themselves as part of the problem and
that therefore the Whites must be excluded during your struggle." You
have also stated in BPC documents that your stance will always be
pro-Black? It also states here on page 2 that a truly open society can
only be achieved by Blacks. And that Black values would be para-
mount. That is your argument?* —— It is stated clearly here that
there will be proportionate contribution to the joint culture by all

those who form up the society. That means that White people will be included, Blacks will be included, and all of us will contribute proportionally to the joint culture of our society. And this exists in SASO's policy manifesto, which is the most important document of SASO. It is a categorical statement of what SASO believes the future society is going to be like. So you cannot say for a moment tthat we are ambivalent about it. We are quite clear about it.

Were the same sort of things expressed in BPC? —————— They express it now, I am telling you. It took SASO two years to come up with this policy manifesto, from 1969 up to 1971. It took BPC about the same sort of time to come up with their policy manifesto, which came up last year. It takes time for any organization to come up with a clear line, because you have got to work it through the thinking of the organization.

They have first got to see what their members feel? —————— And I don't think SASO was thinking about this trial when they drew this up.

I think they possibly were because I think they are being very vague? —————— I don't find it vague. I find it stark clear. It may be vague to you but that is because you just refuse to accept . . .

This was a very early document of SASO's, not so? —————— That is correct.

1971. Are you able to state that this forms still the basis of SASO's . . . —————— I have no reason to believe that it has been changed. I said so yesterday.

But since your banning you have not had an awful lot to do with SASO? —————— That is correct.

Now, if we can look at this bargaining process you people talk about. I gathered from your evidence-in-chief that you said it would not necessarily be at a specific point in time? —————— Yes.

That it may be a long process? —————— Yes.

Now, how does that tie up with statements like
> *"For too long have we been quiet. It is time we made our demands. Stand up, Black man, the time is now, break the chains, liberation is inevitable."*

—————— Well, you have to look at all those statements in their context if you are going to interpret them, but what I did say was . . .

"The day of reckoning is at hand . . ." —— I prefer to put it positively, as I put it yesterday—to say that the bargaining process has started. It may have started . . . [The witness drops his voice] "Pressure is being applied in some spheres." All right, in the whole sporting sphere, for instance, Black society is collectively applying pressure on White society and White society is giving in. This is part of the whole process of bargaining. You can't date it and say it shall start on the 1st of September 2003, you know, it starts right now, it just continually intensifies and takes a particular direction along with history.

THE COURT: *I think the point that counsel is really trying to make is this. That if you decide on a policy and you don't really stipulate how the policy is to be achieved eventually, don't you then by implication leave it to the people responsible to give effect to that policy, to adopt whatever means they wish to adopt? I mean, is there anything to prevent a supporter of BPC or a supporter of SASO to resort to the means referred to by counsel?* —— I think, My Lord, what I am trying to suggest here is that the logical development of BPC could not have been concluded within the time referred to by counsel. The point at issue being that any political organization or political party takes a long time to crystallize its philosophy. What BPC was concerned with right at the beginning was to collect for herself membership. Now, the whole inflections in politics which will ultimately result in a very well-defined statement of where they are going would take time inevitably. It would need to go through debate, so that what I am trying to change in the allegation from Mr. Attwell is the thinking that BPC policy has developed its final conclusion and [that] the vagueness that is there, as he suggests, is intentional. The point is that when these men were arrested, they were arrested during a development.

Assuming now it is not intentional, isn't it pointless in that if you have to find your objectives toward liberation, at least in total change, now you don't say how that is to be achieved apart from the conscientization? Now, assuming new collaborators in the process of conscientization adopt a means which really has the effect ultimately to create a hostile power bloc, now can you say it was excluded in the original plan in which you have formulated your objectives? —— I think any action which anyone takes on behalf of BPC would have to be traceable to decisions by BPC. I don't think there is anything in BPC documents which suggests that this type of action which . . . may lead, let us say, to an upheaval must be taken. But I think where it is silent, it is left to the Executive to interpret. But I think the processes have always been crystallizing, and the whole direction of BPC has been traceable to those who are very close to the movement.

Yes, assuming now you decided as a policy to make use of pamphlets to conscientize people, and then the people who are responsible for the pamphlets use extravagant language and perhaps . . . can create ultimately a hostile power bloc. Now, wouldn't that be within the contemplation of SASO or BPC, who decided merely on the objectives without saying what the people may say in the pamphlets? —— One could also make the other postulation, My Lord, that instead of . . . There are several methods a man would . . .

State the other point. I just want to see how it affects my point. —— Sorry?

Just make the other point. You say that may be the other . . . —— — Yes. You are quoting an example . . .

Yes. Now I want you to quote. I want to test my example against yours. —— Right. I am saying that one could also in the course of distributing pamphlets send out another message for instance which is quite contrary to the thinking of BPC, you know. He can say for instance that . . .

The one can rule the other one out? —— Yes. Here is a pamphlet: Be a good preacher and don't complain if Whites kick you.

Yes, but now if you don't have that sort of pamphlet—it was a very good point you were making—but now just assuming you don't have that sort of pamphlet . . . —— What type of pamphlet are we talking about, My Lord?

The one that you have in mind? I can see your point. The point that I am putting to you is that if you don't circumscribe the means by which you have to attain the objective, then by implication you can authorize your supporters to use whatever means they think would be suitable means? —— Yes, that is correct.

Now, I give you an illustration where they use extravagant language and can create a hostile majority; you give me the illustration where they just do the opposite, they use—well, soft language, and they try and keep the people quiet, in order to achieve that object? So you have two contradictory means. ———— That is correct.

Now, of course I can see then the one will eliminate the other and you can . . . Well, it destroys the point in a way which I put to you originally. ———— I see the hypothetical point, and one can make it either way.

Yes, but now to try and come back to my point again . . . But now if you don't have the type of pamphlet which you envisage, and you have the type of pamphlet which I envisage, now wouldn't that be an indication then that that is the type of thing which SASO and BPC implied? ———— Yes, well, you see . . .

If your circumstances intervene, then of course it will show that it wasn't within that contemplation and it wasn't implied, because the opposite also applies? ———— Yes.

But now if you don't have an example of the opposite, then there is no evidence to show that the intention was not to have the instance that I mentioned to you? ———— That is correct.

Well, do you follow the reasoning? ———— I follow your reasoning. But are there suggestions that there are in fact pamphlets from SASO which hold your line?

No, no. Well, you see, I am just trying to . . . You see, he is putting a point to you. Now, perhaps you can deal with his point because now I am making you aware of what the value of his point can be. ———— Yes. Now, could you direct me back to what you are asking?

MR. ATTWELL: *I wonder whether I still remember my point.*

THE COURT: *You see, he used a lot of words, and those words he could only explain . . . Oh yes, that is correct.*

And those words he could only have extracted from the pamphlets, because they don't appear on any policy documents? ———— That is correct. . . .

COURT ADJOURNS

Day Five

The Morning of May 7, 1976

Biko argues for the creation of a nonracial society without any particular minority protection. It is Biko's contention that minority rights are guaranteed when everyone is equal before the law.

Following Attwell's cross-examination, Soggot, in redirect examination, attempts to mitigate any damage done, and specifically, to deny that BPC is anything more than a political organization. He considers the language which so offended Attwell as the simple expression of Black reality in South Africa. Finally, the court seeks to clarify its understanding of Biko's concept of the bargaining process and to determine whether a protest was a confrontation.

COURT RESUMES

STEPHEN BANTU BIKO, STILL UNDER OATH

CROSS-EXAMINATION BY MR. ATTWELL, CONTINUED: *Mr. Biko, you were a member of which branch of BPC before your restriction?* ——Durban Central.

Now, Mr. Biko, I can't take copious notes while you are giving evidence, but during your cross-examination my recollection is that you said something to the effect that the State had proved nothing in this case but a pile of documents, or something like that? Do you recall saying something like that? ——I had used some words like that.

Could you just expand on it again? Could I just get what you . . . ? ——I was referring to the meaning of the word "terrorism." I was saying that in the minds of Blacks, and people like myself, what happens to Black society at the receiving end of the system of oppression, and I quoted several examples, constitutes much more definite terrorism than what these men here are accused of. I said that you have brought a pile of documents from which you are trying to glean out some conspiracy which I said exists only in the mind of Security Police.

Did you express the opinion that the State had proved nothing but a pile of documents? —— No, I was just expressing a sentiment. I was not commenting on the facts of the case. I am just talking about the general impression that we as Blacks have of this case.

Do you know anything about the evidence which has been led in this case? —— Nothing except from press reports—nothing more definite.

So apart from press reports, do you know nothing more? —— Nothing more, yes.

If I may [di]gress for a moment to the Mangena trial. At the time of Mangena's trial, were you restricted? —— Yes, I was restricted.

Did BPC members and/or officials give evidence at the trial of Mr. Mangena? —— Yes, I think some BPC officials gave evidence there.

Who? —— I remember Mrs. Kgwari specifically. I can't remember the others.

But there were others, you say? —— There could have been others, yes.

Do you know whether those people were concerned with the image of BPC? When giving evidence? —— Naturally they were concerned, because part of the indictment, as far as I could interpret it, was suggesting that BPC had such problems of violence.

Now, you too are concerned with the image of BPC? —— Yes, I am.

That is why you volunteered to give evidence in this case? —— That is correct, yes.

Now, I also understood you to say that you had assisted to get funds for the Mangena defense from the Council of Churches? —— That is correct.

Why did you do that? —— It was because it turned out that just before the trial was due to start Mangena had not been able to get support from anybody for the trial, and the instructing attorney in that case, who was a Mr. Tembene, was just chatting with me about it, saying that this might limit the extent to which they can go in defending this man. For instance, if an appeal is necessary they will never be able to go that far because of the insufficiency of funds. So I thought then I would assist. I wrote to the Council of Churches to find out if they could assist in a matter of this nature.

Was such assistance forthcoming? —— Eventually, yes; it was forthcoming.

Did you have anything to do with the funds for the defense in this case? —— No, I don't even know where it comes . . .

As I understand it, as I understand your evidence, SASO and BPC are in effect opposed to White racism? —— That is correct.

How strongly are you opposed to that? —— Well, it is very difficult to refer to it in terms of degrees. I can merely say that we are opposed to it, and we do not see any possibility of adjusting to White racism.

Now, I would like your comments on the following statement I am going to put to you, Mr. Biko. Would you agree with me that it is SASO and BPC's purpose to bring about a total change in South Africa? —— I would not put it that way.

How would you put it? —— I don't think SASO has a program of bringing change in the same way that BPC has a program of bringing a change. I think there is a slight difference between the two organizations. SASO aspires to change and I think SASO does articulate, as I said earlier, on the ideology which should form the guiding light in that process of change, but their operation is limited by their very nature, mainly to the student theme. On the other hand BPC is a political organization, and because of this it does adopt programs which are meant to bring about change. You know, the facilities, the whole process of change.

The point I am trying to make is that the purpose, then, if we could confine it to BPC specifically, [is] to bring about a total change in South Africa? —— Yes.

And they want to replace the Western capitalist system? —— Yes, they have stated their particular viewpoint, which is opposed to the Western capitalist system.

That the existing wealth and property will have to be redistributed? —— Something to that effect.

In other words that the Whites are going to be deprived of their so-called privileges? —— I don't think so. I think the Whites are going to be made to BPC's mind to be like everybody else. In other words, the creation of a nonracial society without any particular minority protection. Everybody becomes equal before the law. Everybody enjoys the same opportunities.

Is it the opinion of BPC and SASO that the Whites are privileged and possess certain privileges? —— Yes, that is true.

This presupposes, I imagine, purely as a matter of logic, that they have what other people don't have? —— That is correct.

And would it then be correct to say that it is the intention to deprive the Whites of those privileges? —— I think the intention is to normalize the situation.

To deprive them of their privileges? —— No, deprive might mean for instance take away private property, which is all part of the privilege. Now, SASO has not given and BPC has not given any ruling of that nature. All that BPC has said is that they want to create a nonracial society without any protection for minority or any section of the community. Everybody becomes equal before the law. One man, one vote.

Did you say "without any protection for minority"? —— That is correct. Or to put it more straight, without any recognition of minority.

Was it the intention to apply pressure to the State and to the Whites? —— I think in the course of the political process pressure will be applied.

And to achieve this, the aim of BPC was to build up the Black Power bloc? —— I would not put it that way. I said they have opted for what they call Black Solidarity, which I have interpreted several times now before the court to merely imply a creation of themselves as the spokesman of the majority of the people. In other words they require majority backing for what they say.

Black Solidarity in the united Black voice? —— Yes, these are the words that are used. But, I mean, I am interpreting it in terms of reality. In reality, it shall merely imply majority support.

And is it correct to say that up until the time of the arrest of the accused in this case, there had been no decision as to how this change was going to be brought about? —— I think there were thoughts, but it had not been reduced to a very categorical policy.

There had been no decision, I said. —— Sorry?

There had been no decision as to how this change was to be brought about? —— Yes, there was no formal policy taken. As I say, they were all just thoughts around BPC circles all the time. . . .

Now, the accused before court at the moment were your associates? —— That is correct, some of them, yes. Some of them I have not known.

Specifically, yes? —— Yes.

And together with some or all of them you were involved in these two organizations to whose aims you certainly had fully subscribed? —— That is correct.

And if the accused should be convicted in this case and an adverse finding be drawn, this would in your view be a severe setback to the BPC and SASO? —— Not only that, but to individuals concerned.

And you volunteered to give evidence in this case? —— Yes, I volunteered to give evidence, to give assistance to the court insofar as I was involved right at the beginning of SASO and BPC.

I have no further questions. Thank you, My Lord.

REEXAMINATION BY MR. SOGGOT: *Mr. Biko, to get to perhaps an essential question, I think what was suggested to you was that the BPC —I will confine myself to BPC for the moment—by its conduct is creating a dangerous situation, that BPC by its manner of conscientizing people or the way it puts out these things, for example, is creating a dangerous situation. What is your view on that proposition, bearing in mind that you have some experience in kind of BPC and the effects on people?* —— Yes, I think I have indicated in parts of my evidence that my interpretation of the BPC approach is that BPC more than anything else was seen as giving a hope to the people. They are an interpretation of events or things happening to the Black community which is essentially common knowledge amongst Blacks. When we speak of suffering amongst Blacks we speak factually, so to speak, merely to establish a point of departure for all of us, and certainly the language used is not the kind of language which could provoke any form of reaction within Black society that is akin to hostility, because it is a summarized version, so to speak, of what Black society knows from experience. . . .

Now, have you been to actual meetings where members of the public, presumably the Black public as defined by you, were spoken to? —— Yes, I have been at such meetings.

Now, at those meetings, what was the kind of language used, and what was its effect on the people? —— As I say, it . . . depends again on the issues. If the meeting is over a specific issue, we tend to focus on that particular issue and related events. Like for instance if it is Sharpeville Commemoration, we speak of similar events. Now, the language used is, as I say, more or less fair comments on what is going on within society. It is a summarization. It is not what I referred to earlier on in my evidence as the kind of colorful language which, if one wants to, one may use to evoke a reaction. It does refer to killings if there have been killings. You refer to detentions if there have been detentions. And you pinpoint the part of the problems of Black society in an effort to get a common understanding of where we as Blacks start from.

Now, that is in the case of such things as Sharpeville Day? ——— Yes.

Can I put this question to you? Do you think that if the consequence of the speech was to inflame racial hostility or anger towards the White man, you would be able to detect that? ——— I would be able to detect it, yes.

How . . . do you imagine that would manifest itself? ——— I think one of the characteristics of Black perception is that they tie up pretty closely to how emotionally dramatized an issue is. If I want to inflame a Black audience I won't talk glibly in broad facts. I would describe details, as I said to court. Just the issue of a starving child—I can say children are starving; it will be taken as a fact that is normal in Black society. But if I want to use it now for the sake of emotional rousing, my description of that starvation will be in minute detail, describing the ribs, the protruding mouths, the protruding teeth, and so on, you know, calculated to hit the Black man where he most responds, that is, at a level of emotion. Now, I don't think the BPC language generally was of that kind. I think it was more of the broad factual kind. There is of course political exaggeration one place or the other, but this is all common amongst politicians. . . .

What I want to find out is whether in fact SASO talk, SASO propaganda, has historically—as a matter of fact I am asking you now, not as a matter of speculation—altered the attitudes of Black students towards what is perceived as White oppression? ——— No. There has been no alteration whatsoever.

Now, a phrase which was put to you was you people "foresee difficulties"? ——— Yes.

What sort of difficulties did you and do you foresee? —— You mean, difficulties with respect now to the individuals involved?

I think that the question by the cross-examiner was in relation to the organization, which would presumably involve the individuals as well? —— Yes, we speak about struggle precisely because although the program we are involved in is completely aboveboard and quite within the ambit of the law, there are certain elements within White society who would tend to feel threatened by the emergence of any clear-thinking Black leadership. We could foresee, for instance, from a long distance the possibility of banning orders, not because you have done anything illegal—just because basically the State has been made afraid of Black leadership through its history. As I said, it also operates from the basis of fear. This is part of the problem that we foresaw. We foresaw, for instance, possible disruptions of our organizational program. You might get meetings banned, you might get—and this has happened of course in history now—you might get sometimes even the organization banned, not necessarily because of anything you have done but just because of the fear within White society. These are some of the difficulties we are referring to. . . .

Were there any discussions which dealt with the top, the future of the Whites? —— I remember this debate only in the context of the SASO policy manifesto, when we were not discussing the future of the Whites per se, but the future of our society. As I said later on, I do not think it is vague at all; I think it is very clear, the policy manifesto of SASO. A student organization cannot go further than that in projecting their understanding of the future society. You will find that this is common to all student organizations. They have got perhaps one or two paragraphs to state what kind of society they believe in. The article is quite clear.

Yes. On some specific points . . . The words "liberation movement" —you explained its different meanings? —— Yes.

Now, in the way that you people used it, was it a phrase which belonged to your vocabulary or what? —— I think it is a word that is generally used by Black intellectuals these days to name in a sense the process of change resulting in ultimate freeing from present bondage. When I say freeing I am talking about freeing from oppression, so to speak. It is used widely by political scientists these days. It is used by ministers in their talks. It is used by people like Gatsha

Buthelezi, like the Labour Party, and Sonny Leon, and a whole lot of people use it. It has come to be accepted now to mean a moving away from a state of oppression to one where one is free. . . .

Now, on the question of bargaining, which has occupied a considerable amount of time, you were cross-examined on the possibilities of settlement and bargaining, and what you said at one stage was that the bargaining had already started. ———— Yes.

Can you develop that, please, as to what you mean? I know you gave us some examples, but on an overall political—a macroscopic view— how would you explain that? ———— What I mean here is that both sides—that is now, Black and White—see the need for a solution in a sense. Both sides reject the present situation.

Now, when you say both sides, that includes the Whites? ———— Yes.

Why do you say . . . What is in your thinking? That is why I am posing this question—that the Whites see the need for a solution? ———— I am referring here to White political leadership, namely, the thinking tank, so to speak, of the Nationalist Party. If you remember, there are organizations like synthesis which have already been brought up in our society which bring together elements from different backgrounds politically to try and map out the future, and people like Professor Nick Rhoodie, for instance, would be there. The government itself has started to make moves which are calculated to offer some kind of solution.

What sort of moves? ———— Moves, for instance, like Bantustans, like the CRC—all these are things which have come up in the recent past. They were not there originally in the policy of the Nationalists. And I think I see them as attempts to try and meet the Blacks some distance. On the other hand, Blacks have already started applying pressure in certain areas. I referred to sport. Now, I regard all these as elements of the bargaining process. There will be aspects of it which are rejected, you know. Blacks, for instance, still reject on the whole the Bantustan concept, but I do recognize it as an attempt by the White society to solve, you know, what they regard as an impulse presently.

And that rejection by Blacks—what can it lead to, in your thinking? ———— I think it leads to a rethink, in the first instance. It leads to a rethink; it leads to a demonstration of the minimum that Blacks are

prepared to accept, and if there is a majority decision to reject Bantustans itself, like there has been already with the Labour Party and the
Colored CRC, the government has got now to come up with something new for the Colored population, for instance. They are not going
to sit back and look upon CRC as the solution after it has been so
drastically rejected by the Labour Party and the Colored leaders as
a whole in this country.

Yes, My Lord, I have no further questions.

THE COURT: *Mr. Biko, was a protest regarded as being the same as
confrontation? —— A protest?*

Yes? —— No, I think there has been a progressive change in
thinking on this question. For instance, at the Port Elizabeth
meeting, which is the present Minutes which have just been given
in, when we spoke of Sharpeville and started talking about the
kind of programs that we were going to engage in on that day,
somebody suggested that we should pamphleteer the public to inform them about elements of the Sharpeville incident historically.
Now, there was a lot of difference of opinion at that time about
the advisability of pamphlets. We were quite clear about what was
to go into the pamphlet if we do take it up—just a factual account
of what happened at Sharpeville and similar incidents—but people
felt that, you know, the very idea of dishing out pamphlets to the
public might be seen by the police as provocation; in other words,
it might constitute consultation. Now, thinking has changed from
those days; people now are much freer with issues like pamp-
hleteering, so that now a protest would depend on how it is conducted; it would depend on other factors around it. If a protest is,
for instance, on a student campus, you know, within buildings of
the campus, we are not infringing any law. It does not constitute
what I would call confrontation. But if the protest is such that
students go and, say, occupy a police station, because one or two
of them have been arrested, such protest begins to enter into the
realms of confrontation, now, because they are illegally occupying
a police station. So it just depends on surrounding factors. . . .

*I see at this meeting you people also decided to lay down a policy in
respect of Sharpeville, SASO Day and the Day of Compassion? ——*
That is correct.

Did you people decide to hold a Frelimo rally down in the Eastern Cape? —— No.

In September . . . —— Well, there was supposed to be a Frelimo rally in East London, but I think it was not a local decision; I think it was an instruction from head office.

Do you remember what the instruction was regarding that? —— Well, I was not involved in SASO. I just heard about this from rumor. I was not personally involved.

I really wanted to know whether the instruction came from BPC or SASO? —— No. There is a SASO office there, so the instruction would have come from the SASO head office.

You said that BPC was not exactly the same as SASO because BPC had programmed. Now, did the existence of a program make any real difference? —— No, I am saying, My Lord, they had a political program, in other words they were directing themselves at effecting political attitudes, and this was their total occupation. On the other hand SASO really is a student organization. They have got a political outlook, which is not all what SASO is composed of.

It is a part of their objectives? —— That is correct.

Now both these organizations [SASO and BPC] regarded themselves as being part of a struggle for a total change? —— That is correct.

And both these organizations were out to see that each and every Black man was committed to this struggle? —— As I said, the interpretation of that is that they wanted to get majority backing; they merely spoke of Black Solidarity in terms like that, but these were political terms, the practical reality of which was merely to attain a majority backing.

Yes, that I follow. But now, I think I did get the impression from the documents that where the interests of students flagged, the attitude was that they were not committed to the struggle and something had to be done to get them properly committed to the struggle? —— That is true—that as SASO we did shape the political thinking of students.

But now, how did you propose getting people committed to the struggle? —— I think, My Lord, if one has to take all the aspects of Black Consciousness and the whole belief we have in our humanity and political approach, we believe that through togetherness we can be a sufficiently important pressure group.

Now, that I follow, but now how were you to set about to get people committed to that philosophy? ——— It is through meetings, private discussions and so on, where we examined as I said initially our common problems to try and convince the people concerned of the need to overcome those problems, firstly by readjusting their own internal thinking about themselves, and secondly by availing themselves to be with other people within an organization like BPC. In other words the whole membership recruitment centers around those two questions; they call on people to readjust their own thinking, not to regard themselves anymore as slaves, not to regard themselves as unimportant—they are very important. . . .

No further questions.

Appendix

I Write What I Like:
Fear—an Important Determinant
in South African Politics

by Frank Talk

It would seem that the greatest waste of time in South Africa is to try and find logic in why the White government does certain things. If nothing else, the constant inroads into the freedom of the Black people illustrates a complete contempt for this section of the community.

My premise has always been that Black people should not at any one stage be surprised at some of the atrocities committed by the government. This to me follows logically after their initial assumption that they, being a settler minority, can have the right to be supreme masters. If they could be cruel enough to cow the natives down with brutal force and install themselves as perpetual rulers in a foreign land, then anything else they do to the same Black people becomes logical in terms of the initial cruelty. To expect justice from them at any stage is to be naive. They almost have a duty to themselves and to their "electorate" to show that they still have the upper hand over the Black people. There is only one way of showing that upper hand —by ruthlessly breaking down the back of resistance amongst the Blacks, however petty that resistance is.

One must look at the huge security force that South Africa has in order to realise this. These men must always report something to their masters in order to justify their employment. It is not enough to report that "I have been to Pondoland and the natives are behaving well and are peaceful and content." This is not satisfactory, for the perpetrators of evil are aware of the cruelty of their system and hence do not expect the natives to be satisfied. So the security boys are sent back to Pondoland to find out who the spokesman is who claims that the people are satisfied and to beat him until he admits that he is not satisfied. At that point he is either banned or brought forward to be tried under one of the many Acts. The absolutely infantile evidence upon which the State builds up its cases in some of the trials does suggest to me that they are quite capable of arresting a group of boys playing hide and seek and charging them with high treason.

This is the background against which one must see the many political trials that are held in this country. To them it looks as if something would be dangerously wrong if no major political trial was held for a period of one year. It looks as if someone will be accused by his superior for not doing his work. The strangest thing is that people are hauled in for almost nothing to be tried under the most vicious of Acts —like the Terrorism Act.

It is also against this background that one must view the recent banning and house arrest imposed on Mr. Mewa Ramgobin. No amount of persuasion by anyone can convince me that Ramgobin had something sinister up his sleeve. To all those who know him, Mewa was the last man to be considered a serious threat to anyone—let alone a powerful State with an army of perhaps 10,000 security men and informers. But then, as we said, logic is a strange word to these people.

Aimé Césaire once said: "When I turn on my radio, when I hear that Negroes have been lynched in America, I say that we have been lied to: Hitler is not dead. When I turn on my radio and hear that in Africa, forced labour has been inaugurated and legislated, I say that we have certainly been lied to: Hitler is not dead."

Perhaps one need add only the following in order to make the picture complete:

"When I turn on my radio, when I hear that someone in the Pondoland forest was beaten and tortured, I say that we have been lied to: Hitler is not dead. When I turn on my radio, when I hear that someone in jail slipped off a piece of soap, fell and died I say that we have been lied to: Hitler is not dead, he is likely to be found in Pretoria."

To look for instances of cruelty directed at those who fall into disfavour with the security police is perhaps to look too far. One need not try to establish the truth of the claim that Black people in South Africa have to struggle for survival. It presents itself in ever so many

facets of our lives. Township life alone makes it a miracle for anyone
to live up to adulthood. There we see a situation of absolute want in
which Black will kill Black to be able to survive. This is the basis of
the vandalism, murder, rape and plunder that goes on while the real
sources of the evil—White society—are suntanning on exclusive
beaches or relaxing in their bourgeois homes.

While those amongst Blacks who do bother to open their mouths
in feeble protest against what is going on are periodically intimidated
with security visits and occasional banning orders and house arrests,
the rest of the Black community lives in absolute fear of the police.
No average Black man can ever at any moment be absolutely sure that
he is not breaking a law. There are so many laws governing the lives
and behaviour of Black people that sometimes one feels that the police
only need to page at random through their statute book to be able to
get a law under which to charge a victim.

The philosophy behind police action in this country seems to be
"Harass them! harass them!" And one needs to add that they interpret
the word in a very extravagant sense. Thus even young traffic policemen, people generally known for their grace, occasionally find it
proper to slap adult Black people. It sometimes looks obvious here
that the great plan is to keep the Black people thoroughly intimidated
and to perpetuate the "super-race" image of the White man, if not
intellectually, at least in terms of force. White people, working
through their vanguard—the South African Police—have come to
realise the truth of that golden maxim—if you cannot make a man
respect you, then make him fear you.

Clearly Black people cannot respect White people, at least not in
this country. There is such an obvious aura of immorality and naked
cruelty in all that is done in the name of White people that no Black
man, no matter how intimidated, can ever be made to respect White
society. However, in spite of their obvious contempt for the values
cherished by Whites and the price at which White comfort and security is purchased, Blacks seem to me to have been successfully cowed
down by the type of brutality that emanates from this section of the
community.

It is this fear that erodes the soul of Black people in South Africa
—a fear obviously built up deliberately by the system through a

myriad of civil agents, be they post office attendants, police, C.I.D. officials, army men in uniform, security police or even the occasional trigger-happy White farmer or store owner. It is a fear so basic in the considered actions of Black people as to make it impossible for them to behave like people—let alone free people. From the attitude of a servant to his employer, to that of a Black man being served by a White attendant at a shop, one sees this fear clearly showing through. How can people be prepared to put up a resistance against their overall oppression if in their individual situations, they cannot insist on the observance of their manhood? This is a question that often occurs to overseas visitors who are perceptive enough to realise that all is not well in the land of sunshine and milk.

Yet this is a dangerous type of fear, for it only goes skin deep. It hides underneath it an immeasurable rage that often threatens to erupt. Beneath it, likes naked hatred for a group that deserves absolutely no respect. Unlike in the rest of the French or Spanish former colonies where chances of assimilation made it not impossible for Blacks to aspire towards being White, in South Africa whiteness has always been associated with police brutality and intimidation, early morning pass raids, general harassment in and out of townships, and hence no Black really aspires to being White. The claim by Whites of monopoly on comfort and security has always been so exclusive that Blacks see Whites as the major obstacle in their progress towards peace, prosperity and a sane society. Through its association with all these negative aspects, whiteness has thus been soiled beyond recognition. At best therefore Blacks see whiteness as a concept that warrants being despised, hated, destroyed and replaced by an aspiration with more human content in it. At worst Blacks envy White society for the comfort it has usurped and at the centre of this envy is the wish—nay, the secret determination—in the innermost minds of most Blacks who think like this, to kick Whites off those comfortable garden chairs that one sees as he rides in a bus, out of town, and to claim them for themselves. Day by day, one gets more convinced that Aimé Césaire could not have been right when he said, "No race possesses the monopoly on truth, intelligence, force and there is room for all of us at the rendezvous of victory."

It may, perhaps, surprise some people that I should talk of Whites in a collective sense when in fact it is a particular section i.e. the government—that carries out this unwarranted vendetta against Blacks.

There are those whites who will completely disclaim responsibility for the country's inhumanity to the Black man. These are the people who are governed by logic for 4½ years but by fear at election time. The Nationalist party has perhaps many more English votes than one imagines. All Whites collectively recognise in it a strong bastion against the highly played-up "swaart gevaar." One must not underestimate the deeply imbedded fear of the Black man so prevalent in White society. Whites know only too well what exactly they have been doing to Blacks and logically find reason for the Black man to be angry. Their state of insecurity however does not outweigh their greed for power and wealth, hence they brace themselves to react against this rage rather than to dispel it with openmindedness and fair play. This interaction between fear and reaction then sets on a vicious cycle that multiplies both the fear and the reaction. This is what makes meaningful coalitions between the Black and White totally impossible. Also this is what makes Whites act as a group and hence become culpable as a group.

In any case, even if there was a real fundamental difference in thinking amongst Whites vis-à-vis Blacks, the very fact that those disgruntled Whites remain to enjoy the fruits of the system would alone be enough to condemn them at Nuremburg. Listen to Karl Jaspers writing on the concept of metaphysical guilt:

"There exists amongst men, because they are men, a solidarity through which each shares responsibility for every injustice and every wrong committed in the world and especially for crimes that are committed in his presence or of which he cannot be ignorant. If I do not do whatever I can to prevent them, I am an accomplice in them. If I have [not] risked my life in order to prevent the murder of other men, if I have stood silent, I feel guilty in a sense that cannot in any adequate fashion be understood juristically or politically or morally . . . That I am still alive after such things have been done weighs on me as a guilt that cannot be expiated.

Somewhere in the heart of human relations, an absolute command imposes itself: in case of criminal attack or of living conditions that threaten physical being, accept life for all together or not at all."

Thus if Whites in general do not like what is happening to the Black people, they have the power in them to stop it here and now. We, on the other hand, have every reason to bundle them together and blame them jointly.

One can of course say that Blacks too are to blame for allowing the situation to exist. Or to drive the point even further, one may point out that there are Black policemen and Black Special Branch agents. To take the last point first, I must state categorically that there is no such thing as a Black policeman. Any Black man who props the system up actively has lost the right to being considered part of the Black world: he has sold his soul for thirty pieces of silver and finds that he is in fact not acceptable to the White society he sought to join. These are colourless White lackeys who live in a marginal world of unhappiness. They are extensions of the enemy into our ranks. On the other hand, the rest of the Black world is kept in check purely because of powerlessness.

Powerlessness breeds a race of beggars who smile at the enemy and swear at him in the sanctity of their toilets; who shout "Baas" willingly during the day and call the White man a dog in their buses as they go home. Once again the concept of fear is at the heart of this two-faced behaviour on the part of the conquered Blacks.

This concept of fear has now taken a different dimension. One frequently hears people say of someone who has just been arrested or banned—"there is no smoke without fire" or if the guy was outspoken —"he asked for it, I am not surprised." In a sense this is almost deifying the security police; they cannot be wrong; if they could break the Rivonia plot, what makes them afraid of an individual to the point of banning him unless there is something—which we do not know?

This kind of logic, found to varying degrees in the Afrikaaner, the English and the Black communities, is dangerous, for it completely misses the point and reinforces irrational action on the part of the security police.

The fact of the matter is that the government and its security forces are also ruled by fear, in spite of their immense power. Like anyone living in mortal fear, they occasionally resort to irrational actions in the hope that a show of strength rather than proper intelligence might scare the resistors satisfactorily. This is the basis of security operations in South Africa most of the time. If they know that there are some 3 missionaries who are dangerous to their interest but whose identity is unknown, they would rather deport about 80 missionaries and hope that the 3 are among them than use some brains and find out who the 3 are. This was also the basis of the arrest of about 5000 during the so-called "Poqo" raids of 1963. And of course the laws from which security police derive their power are so vague and sweeping as to allow for all this. Hence one concludes that the South African security system is force-oriented rather than intelligence-oriented. One may of course add that this type of mentality, in this country, stretches all the way from State security to the style of rugby Whites adopt. It has become their way of life.

One will therefore not be surprised if it proves very difficult to accept that "There is room for all of us at the rendezvous of victory." The tripartite system of fear—that of Whites fearing the Blacks, Blacks fearing Whites and the government fearing Blacks and wishing to allay the fear amongst Whites—makes it difficult to establish rapport amongst the two segments of the community. The fact of living apart adds a different dimension and perhaps a more serious one— it makes the aspirations of the two groups diametrically opposed. The White strategy so far has been to systematically break down the resistance of the Blacks to the point where the latter would accept crumbs from the White table. This we have shown we reject unequivocally; and now the stage is therefore set for a very interesting turn of events.

The Inquest into the Death
of Stephen Bantu Biko

A Report to the Lawyers' Committee
for Civil Rights Under Law

by Dean Louis H. Pollak

Prepared for the Southern Africa Project
February 24, 1978

*Louis H. Pollak is dean of the University of Pennsylvania School of
Law and Albert M. Greenfield University Professor of Human
Relations, History and Law.*
*Dean Pollak attended the Stephen Bantu Biko inquest on behalf
of the Southern Africa Project of the Lawyers' Committee for Civil
Rights Under Law. He observed the fifth through tenth day of the
inquest, November 18–25, 1977.*

THE BACKGROUND

In death, Stephen Bantu Biko is even larger than he was in life. In
life, he was, at the age of thirty, the head of South Africa's Black
Consciousness Movement—and thus one of the emerging leaders of
his country. Yet (such is the myopia of apartheid) Biko was little
known among his White fellow citizens[1] the 4 million Afrikaners and
"English-speakers" who enjoy total political dominion over 22 million
disenfranchised Blacks, Coloreds and "Asians." But if Biko was not
well known among South African Whites generally, he was well
known to the leaders of the South African regime. In 1976 was detained by the security police for many weeks. Moreover, three years

[1]N. Ashford, "World Interest in Case Surprises S. Africans," *New York Times*, November 21, 1977.

prior to his 1976 detention, Biko had achieved the distinction of being "banned"—i.e., consigned to the legal status of isolation from the community, and indeed of virtual nonidentity, which the regime has devised for a select group of citizens perceived as especially formidable antagonists.[2]

Biko was arrested for the last time on August 18, 1977. According to a subsequent affidavit of an officer of the security police, the arrest took place at a roadblock set up when word was received that Biko, in contravention of his banning order, was driving from his hometown (King William's Town) to Cape Town for the purpose, so the security police understood, of distributing "inflammatory pamphlets . . . inciting blacks to cause riots."[3] On the following day, Biko was taken to Port Elizabeth, where he was to remain until September 11, the day before he died.

Biko was not formally charged with a crime. He was detained under

---

[2]"Banning," of course, has analogies in avowedly totalitarian regimes, but it is something of a novelty in legal systems deriving from English and Western European jurisprudence. Its character and impact were tellingly described last fall in *Time* correspondent William McWhirter's report on the banning of Donald Woods, a White newspaper editor who was one of Biko's closest friends (*Time,* November 7, 1977, p. 38):

> It was a fateful end to a special friendship between a white and a black. Donald Woods, a fifth-generation English-speaking South African and editor of the feisty *East London Daily Dispatch* (circ. 30,000), is now a "Banned person," as was his friend Steve Biko, who died in jail two months ago. It was, in fact, Woods' crusade over the mystery surrounding Biko's death that probably led to his banning in the government's massive wave of detentions and crackdowns.
>
> As one of Woods' fellow journalists has put it, isolation is a curse—and banning is the most insidious punishment in South Africa. Reserved for an elite 150 or so of the government's political enemies, it amounts to an emotionally destructive public Coventry. For five years, Woods may not meet with more than one other person at a time except for members of his family; he may not write for publication or be quoted—he has become, as a result, a public non-person.

On December 31, 1977, Donald and Wendy Woods and their children escaped from South Africa. In early February, Mr. and Mrs. Woods visited the United States; he addressed the Security Council, met the President and Vice-President, and testified before Congressional committees. See the Washington *Post,* February 6, 1978, p. B1; see also footnote 21, *infra.*

While "banning" is a recent innovation in South African jurisprudence, detention of political adversaries of the regime is not new. John Vorster, the current Prime Minister, was detained for seventeen months during World War II, since he was regarded by the government of Field Marshal Jan Smuts as actively opposed to the war against Germany. *New York Times,* November 28, 1977.

[3]Rand *Daily Mail,* November 15, 1977, p. 14.

Section 6 of South Africa's Terrorism Act, which authorizes indefinite detention "for interrogation" of any person thought by the security police to be "a terrorist or . . . withholding from the South African Police any information relating to terrorists or offenses under this Act. . . ." Capital offenses defined by the Terrorism Act include "any act in the Republic or elsewhere" committed "with intent to endanger the maintenance of law and order in the Republic. . . ." The requisite intent is presumed on proof that the act committed has, or is likely to have, any of a number of proscribed effects: e.g., "to cause substantial financial loss to any person or the State," "to embarrass the administration of the affairs of the State," or "to cause, encourage or further feelings of hostility between the White and other inhabitants of the Republic."[4]

Detention under Section 6 of the Terrorism Act is incommunicado: "No person other than the Minister [of Justice], or an officer in the service of the State acting in the performance of his official duties, shall have access to any detainee, or shall be entitled to any official information relating to or obtained from any detainee." Moreover, "No court of law shall pronounce upon the validity of any action taken under this section, or order the release of any detainee."

Biko was in good health when he was arrested on August 18. And so he seems to have remained through September 5—notwithstanding that he (a) was kept in solitary confinement; (b) complained about a diet chiefly of bread, and asked in vain for leave to buy food of his own choice; (c) was not let out of his cell to exercise (in contravention of the regulations governing his custody); and (d) was kept naked most of the time.

On September 6, Biko was taken from his cell to security police headquarters for interrogation. In the course of the interrogation, Biko—according to police testimony given at the inquest—first denied and then admitted involvement in preparation of pamphlets deemed by the police to be "inflammatory." Biko's admission was said to have come about when he was confronted with written ad-

---

[4] The effect of the presumption is to place on the accused the burden of proving beyond a reasonable doubt that the act committed was not likely to have or did not have the proscribed effect. See, generally, A. S. Mathews, *Law, Order and Liberty in South Africa* (Juta: Wynberg, 1971), pp. 146–55, 169–84.

missions by associates who were also in secret detention.

According to further police testimony, the interrogation resumed at about 7:15 A.M. on September 7, but was interrupted almost at once by a violent outbreak by Biko, who, with a "wild expression in his eyes," threw a chair at and then assaulted the five-man team of interrogating officers. Restraining Biko took several minutes, and Biko may have hit his head in the course of the melee. Major Snyman, in command of the interrogation team, reported the incident to his superior, Colonel Goosen, at 7:30 A.M. Together, Goosen and Snyman went to the office in which Biko was now shackled securely. Snyman saw that Biko still had a "wild expression" and also had a swelling on his lip. Goosen summoned Dr. Lang, the district surgeon, a prison doctor. Lang, arriving two hours later, was told by Goosen that Biko was unresponsive and might have had a stroke, or be feigning illness. Lang examined Biko and could find no organic injury: Lang was inclined to agree with what he thought to be Goosen's surmise, namely, that Biko was "shamming."

From September 7 to September 11, Biko steadily deteriorated. He had intermittent difficulties of speech and (when not shackled, naked, on a urine-soaked mat) of movement. His behavior was sometimes bizarre—as, for example, sitting clothed in a bathtub. He developed symptoms (e.g., weakness of the left arm and leg, echolalia, the extensor plantar reflex) clearly betokening brain injury. But Lang and the other doctors (Tucker, the senior district surgeon; and Hersch, a private consultant) who examined and tested Biko could not reach a firm diagnosis, although Hersch seems to have suspected Biko had suffered brain injury. On September 11, when Biko was nearly comatose, the doctors concluded that he should be hospitalized for observation. Goosen then ordered Biko shipped to the prison hospital in Pretoria—750 miles, naked, in the back of a Landrover, unaccompanied by a doctor or even by his medical records. On September 12, a few hours after being delivered to the Pretoria prison hospital, Biko died. As S. W. Kentridge, counsel to the Biko family, put it in his summation at the inquest: "He died a miserable and lonely death on a mat on a stone floor in a prison cell."

On September 13, Minister of Justice James T. Kruger issued the following statement:

> Mr. Steven [sic] Bantu Biko, previously attached to SASO[5] and BPC,[6] had been restricted to the magisterial district of King William's Town. Mr. Biko and a coloured man were arrested at a road-block near Grahamstown on August 18, after information had been received that Mr. Biko was travelling between Cape Town and King William's Town. He was arrested in connection with activities related to the riots in Port Elizabeth, and *inter alia* for drafting and distributing pamphlets which incited arson and violence. He was detained at the Walmer Police Station in Port Elizabeth since September 5. Mr. Biko refused his meals and threatened a hunger strike. But he was, however, regularly supplied with meals and water which he refused to partake of. The District Surgeon was called in on September 7 after Mr. Biko appeared to be unwell. The doctor certified he could not find anything wrong with Mr. Biko. On September 8, the police arranged that Mr. Biko again be examined by a district surgeon as well as the Chief District Surgeon and, because they could diagnose no physical problem, they recommended that Mr. Biko be sent to the prison hospital for intensive examination. A specialist examined him on the same day. On September 9, Mr. Biko was again examined by a doctor who kept him for observation. On September 11, Mr. Biko was removed from the prison hospital to Walmer Police Station on the recommendation of the District Surgeon. By Sunday Mr. Biko had still not eaten and appeared to be unwell. After consultation with the District Surgeon it was decided to transfer Mr. Biko to Pretoria. He was taken to Pretoria the same night. On September 12, Mr. Biko was again examined and medically treated by a district surgeon in Pretoria. Mr. Biko died the same night. A *post mortem* will be undertaken by the Chief State Pathologist in the presence of a private pathologist appointed by Mr. Biko's relatives. Mr. Biko's mother was informed of his death because his wife, who is separated from him, could not be traced. During his detention a magistrate visited Mr. Biko on September 2 according to law.

The *post mortem* referred to by the Minister on September 13 took place on the same day. It was conducted by the Chief State Pathologist, Dr. J. O. Loubser, in the presence of two other leading pathologists, Professor I. W. Simson and Dr. J. Gluckman, the latter repre-

[5]South African Students Organization.
[6]Black People's Convention.

senting the Biko family. The general autopsy was followed two weeks later by a detailed examination of Biko's brain, conducted (in the presence of Loubser, Simson and Gluckman) by Professor N. S. F. Proctor, an eminent neuropathologist.

On September 14, Minister Kruger "provoke[d] laughter among delegates to the Transvaal Congress of the governing National Party with remarks about the death. 'I am not glad and I am not sorry about Mr. Biko . . . He leaves me cold.' The Minister also agree[d] with a delegate who applaud[ed] him for allowing the black leader his 'democratic right' to 'starve himself to death.' "[7]

The Minister's intimation that Biko had taken his own life by means of a hunger strike was not confirmed by the reports of the pathologists. Proctor's examination of Biko's brain yielded the following "summary and conclusions":

> This brain shows several areas of damage where the main pathological features are those of haemorrhage and necrosis. On microscopical examination numerous small perivascular haemorrhages are present throughout much of the brain tissue as well as in the larger lesions visible macroscopically.
>
> The most extensive lesion is in the right parieto-fronto-temporal region in an area opposite to that of the large ecchymosis demonstrated to me by Professor Loubser. This indicates a so-called contre-coup injury of traumatic origin.[8] In this lesion, as in many of the others described above the zones of haemorrhage are superficially situated and are accompanied by bleeding into the subarachnoid space. Necrosis accompanies many of these foci of haemorrhage.
>
> In my opinion therefore the lesions present are clearly indicative of severe traumatic brain contusions and contusional necrosis. The inflammatory infiltrates, the oedema (brain swelling), myelin loss and small vessel fibrin thrombi are secondary phenomena. I would estimate that these contusions are at least of three to five days duration and probably not more than twelve to fifteen days duration.

---

[7] J. Burns, "Inquest in Pretoria Ready for Testimony on How Black Leader Died," *New York Times*, November 14, 1977.
[8] The term "contre-coup injury," as used by Proctor, signifies that the principal injury to the brain was located in a portion of the head *opposite to* (i.e. "contre") the place of impact of the triggering trauma.

On October 21, Loubser, Simson and Gluckman—after consultation
with Proctor and another colleague, Professor L. S. deVilliers—cer-
tified to their joint concurrence in findings formulated by Loubser:

> (iii) that the most significant post mortem findings in connection with
> that body were as follows:
>
> Extensive brain injury of the contre-coup type with the absence of coup
> injuries.
>
> As a result of the nature and extent of this brain injury, centralization
> of the circulation occurred to such an extent that reduction of the
> circulation to the organs, [sic] complicated by disseminated intravascu-
> lar coagulation as well as acute renal failure with uremia.
>
> Some injuries were also present on the left thorax and possibly also on
> the anterior abdominal wall.
>
> Further injuries were found comprising extensive but trifling superficial
> abraded skin injuries which—to state only reasonable possibilities—
> could have arisen from 12 hours to 8 days prior to death. All the
> aforementioned skin injuries indicate a mechanical origin.
>
> (iv) that, as a result of my observations of which I append a list I have
> decided
>   (a) that death took place in the region of 12 hours prior to my
> examination and
>   (b) that the cause of death was HEAD INJURIES.

THE HEARING

Had Biko not died, and had the cause of and circumstances surrounding his death not been in doubt, there could have been no
judicial or quasijudicial inquiry into the treatment accorded Biko
while he was in detention. For, as noted above, Section 6 of the
Terrorism Act puts detainees outside the protection of the law. It was
Biko's unexplained death which was the jurisdictional predicate of
further inquiry. Such inquiry might have taken place in a court had
the public prosecutor been persuaded that he had evidence sufficient
to warrant a criminal prosecution. Unpersuaded of this, the public
prosecutor was obliged by statute to call upon a magistrate (a civil

servant, not a judge) to hold an inquest to determine "the cause or likely cause of death" and "whether the death was brought about by any act or omission involving or amounting to an offence on the part of any person."

Presiding was Pretoria's chief magistrate, M. J. Prins. Assisting him, as lay assessors, were two pathologists of high reputation, Professor I. Gordon and Professor J. A. Olivier. They shared the bench with the chief magistrate, and asked questions but their role was wholly advisory; they did not participate in the decision.

The inquest began on November 14, 1977, and continued (except for the two intervening weekends) through December 2. It was held in Pretoria, where Biko died. The hearing was conducted in the Old Synagogue—a drab, uncomfortable meeting hall in the center of the city, which had been converted from religious to sporadic judicial use many years ago. The hearing was public, and an audience numbering perhaps two hundred, mostly Black, filled the hall at all times—notwithstanding that (a) much of the testimony was given in Afrikaans, a language not easily understood by many Blacks, and (b) the acoustics were so defective as to make the proceedings almost inaudible beyond the first two rows, which were reserved for the press.[9]

In front of the audience and the press, just inside the bar, were Biko's widow and mother and their interpreter, and one or two close friends; certain medical and other advisers sitting behind counsel; and two foreign lawyers observing the inquest. One of the foreign lawyer-observers—present for all but the first three days of the fifteen-day hearing—was Sir David Napley, past president of the Law Society, who had come at the invitation of the Law Societies of South Africa, and whose remarkably perceptive and succinct appraisal of the inquest was published a week after its conclusion. The other—present from the fifth day through the tenth day—was the author of this report, representing the Lawyers' Committee for Civil Rights Under Law.[10]

---

[9]The inquest was the subject of continuing coverage by Western European and American newspapers and television; within South Africa, both Afrikaans and English-language newspapers reported the proceedings in detail.
[10]And also representing the Section of Individual Rights and Responsibilities of the

Counsel sat at a horseshoe arrangement of tables in front of the magistrate. Presenting the witnesses for the magistrate was an advocate (barrister, in British parlance) who is Deputy Attorney General for the Transvaal, K. Von Lieres, S.A.[11] The advocate who led for the police was P. R. Van Rooyen, S.A. As noted above, counsel to the Biko family was advocate S. W. Kentridge, S. A., assisted by advocates G. Bizos and E. M. Wentzel; the Biko family's attorney (solicitor, in British parlance) was Shun Chetty. A minor role was played by advocate B. de V. Pickard, representing the doctors.[12]

Van Rooyen and Pickard, while private advocates, were representing state employees. Since Deputy Attorney General Von Lieres concurred in their presentations that their clients were guiltless, and Kentridge sought to show that the police were culpable and the prison doctors their willing instruments, the hearing was in effect an adversary proceeding pitting Kentridge and his co-counsel against Van Rooyen, Von Lieres and Pickard.

Van Rooyen represented the police with vigor and skill. Pickard represented the doctors without vigor and without skill.[13] Von Lieres performed somewhat woodenly in a role which, as Sir David Napley noted in his report, seemed professionally ambiguous, since "on occasions he intervened to support the police and doctors although they were already represented by other counsel." Notwithstanding that, as deputy attorney general, "it was his duty dispassionately to present to, and test, on behalf of the Magistrate, all the relevant available evidence."

Kentridge's representation of the Biko family was exemplary; a lawyer of extraordinary distinction, he dominated the hearing. But

---

A.B.A., and the Committee on International Human Rights of the Bar Association of the City of New York. The South African authorities declined to issue a visa to Millard Arnold, Esq., Director of the Southern Africa Project of the Lawyers' Committee for Civil Rights Under Law. Also turned down for a visa was Anthony Lewis of the *New York Times*, who wished to cover the inquest.

[11]"S.A." (State's Advocate) is an honorific bestowed on senior advocates, roughly equivalent to the British "Q.C." identifying barristers who have taken silk.

[12]Advocate W. H. Heath, representing the prison guards, had virtually nothing to do, since it was common ground that his clients' treatment of Biko was correct, within the constraints of the detention system.

[13]On one occasion, Pickard examined one of his clients (Hersch) about an article from a medical journal which the witness had not read for a long time and which Pickard had never read.

Kentridge, and the lawyers for the other parties, were largely tied to the record as made by Von Lieres for the magistrate—tied by the inquest form which gives the magistrate control over the scope of the inquiry; and tied by the fact of a system of secret detention which insures that the only evidence about the operations of the security police and supporting personnel which will be brought to public view is evidence which the senior officers of the security police take measures to uncover and disclose.

Given these constraints, it was hardly surprising that the senior officers in charge of the investigation did not show any interest in asking who or what had led their superior, the Minister of Justice, to give public currency, in the days immediately following Biko's death, to the notion that Biko had "starve[d] himself to death." The magistrate's unwillingness to permit exploration of this question at the inquest did not strengthen the credibility of the proceeding. What would arguably have been a collateral issue had the hearing been a criminal trial could, so it would seem, have been properly explored in the context of an inquest which, as the South African Supreme Court has noted, "follows an informal procedure with less rigid rules"; indeed, the court has specifically admonished magistrates to "guard against conducting an inquest as if it were a criminal trial." *Timol and Another v. Magistrate, Johannesburg* [1972(2)] 281, 291–2.

Of far graver concern than this particular ruling, however, was the general lassitude of the investigation into the activities of those officers and doctors who had been in direct charge of Biko during the crucial days from September 6 to his death. Little wonder that their testimony at the inquest—supplementing the sometimes redundant, sometimes inconsistent and frequently ambiguous affidavits—added up to a partial and unconvincing narrative. Sir David Napley has aptly characterized the police investigation of their own officers as "perfunctory in the extreme. The death of anyone whilst detained in the custody of security police demands rigorous investigation. . . . The inquest revealed . . . that the officers closely concerned with the custody and interrogation of the deceased at the relevant time were questioned by means of [mimeographed] forms, which contained a series of questions with alternative answers. They were required to strike out the reply which they considered inappropriate to their answers. . . . It is clear that an investigation conducted by experienced police officers with a little of the enthusiasm and vigour with which they customarily appear to question detainees would have elicited the truth from the security police in far less time than was necessary to demonstrate their mendacity in the witness box. . . ."

The term "mendacity" is not a mild one. And yet, as a close reading of Sir David's report makes plain, the distinguished British solicitor chooses his words with care, and with a profound respect for the record. Sir David—present, as I was not, for almost the entire inquest —has embodied in his report an extensive recital of the evidence. Believing his statement to be an admirable one, I will not canvass in detail the ground he has covered so exhaustively. I will simply recapitulate the opposing claims of fact and inference as they bear upon the matters chiefly in issue at the inquest:

1. As already noted, the magistrate's duty was to seek to determine two questions: One was the cause or causes of Biko's death; the other was whether any criminal act or omission had contributed to Biko's death.

2. On the first question, there was no room for doubt. The pathological evidence showed beyond dispute that death resulted from injuries to the brain resulting from external trauma—including at least one major blow to the left forehead, which left a bruise visible on, and photographed at, the autopsy.

3. To resolve the remaining question—whether any of the police officers and doctors who had Biko in charge bore a measure of criminal responsibility for Biko's death—the magistrate needed to make findings as to the circumstances under which Biko suffered the fatal blow or blows.

4. According to the pathologists, Biko suffered the fatal blow or blows no earlier than September 6 (the first day on which Biko was interrogated). And the latest possible time was early on September 7, since it was at 7:30 that morning that Goosen, the officer in command at Port Elizabeth, finding his prisoner incapacitated and unresponsive, called District Surgeon Lang and requested him to examine Biko forthwith.

5. The witnesses presented by Deputy Attorney General Von Lieres described only a single incident in the course of which Biko may have

suffered a blow or blows to the head. This was the incident, referred to above, in which, according to Snyman and other officers, resumption of interrogation at 7:15 A.M. on September 7 was cut off by Biko's throwing a chair at and assaulting his interrogators, an outbreak which led to a "scuffle" of several minutes before Biko was subdued. In the view of Von Lieres and Van Rooyen, this incident most plausibly explained the entire matter.[14]

6. Accepting the "scuffle" as the full explanation posed major difficulties, as Kentridge made plain in his painstaking closing address to the magistrate:

(a) Neither in affidavit nor in testimony did any of the police who participated in the "scuffle" identify with any particularity a massive blow to the forehead. (Snyman, for example, described Biko falling in such a way as to hit the back of his head on the floor; and whether he actually saw, or merely supposed he may have seen, some such medically nonsignificant occurrence was by no means clear.)

(b) How massive the triggering blow or blows must have been was underscored by the consensus of the pathologists that in all likelihood Biko would have been rendered unconscious for a time. Yet no witness described a period of unconsciousness (prior to Goosen's summoning Lang).

(c) It is true that, as Von Lieres and Van Rooyen emphasized in their closing addresses, the pathologists did not assert categorically that it was inconceivable for a person to suffer mortal head injuries without losing consciousness. But they did testify that the overwhelming balance of probability was on the side of unconsciousness. And their testimony was confirmed by the medical literature presented to the magistrate. According to Sir Charles Symonds, acknowledged to be a leading authority in neuropathology, "Loss of consciousness at the onset is the rule in all cases of severe head injury." Moreover, the exceptions to the rule—e.g., "high velocity missiles penetrating the

---

[14]Speculation that Biko might have deliberately hit his own head against the wall or floor at some point (e.g., the night of September 6) when no guard was in his cell appeared to have no substance at all. The motivation for such an act was obscure. The capacity of a shackled prisoner to hurt himself so massively was doubtful in the extreme. The likelihood that such an act could have taken place unnoticed at the time or promptly thereafter appeared very remote.

brain"—show "that the type of injury which most readily causes unconsciousness is that which subjects the intracranial contents as a whole to sudden displacement."[15] And it was exactly this "type of injury," a blow or blows to one side of the head resulting in contre-coup reaction, which caused Biko's death.

(d) The weight properly owing to Sir Charles' statement of "the rule in all cases of severe head injury" is underscored by his description of a typical clinical scenario for one suffering a "moderate degree of injury"—a scenario strikingly like Biko's clinical picture beginning on September 7:

> As our criterion for this degree of injury we may take, of course, in arbitrary fashion, failure to recover consciousness within five minutes of the injury, but with subsequent recovery of consciousness within two or three hours. The initial symptoms are the same as those described for a case of the mild degree. The state of coma, however, lasts longer, probably several minutes, and is followed by one of profound stupor in which, though purposive movements of the protective kind are possible, the patient is totally unaware of his environment and inaccessible. In this state he is at first mute, unresponsive to command, and inert. Later he begins to be restless and, while still mute and stuporous, may become resistive and violent. The first evidence of returning consciousness, as a rule, is a positive response to some simple command, such as "Put out your tongue." Later he will occasionally reply to a question, such as "What is your name?" though the basic state is that of restless confusion with an occasional relapse into stupor. During or after the period of unconsciousness there may be incontinence of urine, and vomiting. After recovery of consciousness the patient remains confused and may exhibit phases of delirium especially at night. In this state of *traumatic delirium* his behavior is unpredictable and often violent. He will frequently try to get out of bed, put on his clothes, or run out of the room, will refuse his medicines, and will fight with those who try to control him. This state of confusion with delirium (sometimes known to surgeons as that of cerebral irritation) may be transient, lasting only an hour or two, or may persist for several days. So long as there is delirium there may be relapse into stupor from time to time.[16]

[15]See Symonds' essay in Feiring, *Brock's Injuries of the Brain and Spinal Cord and Their Coverings* (Springer Pub. Co., Inc.: New York, 1974), pp. 109–110.
[16]*Id.* at p. 111–112.

In Sir Charles' scenario, the patient with a "moderate degree of injury" recovers. Biko, severely injured, progressed from stupor to death.

(e) On the next-to-last day of testimony, there came to light a document casting further doubt on the contention that Biko's first massive injury was the inadvertent by-product of hitting his head once or a few times during the "scuffle" with Snyman and others at 7:15 A.M. on September 7. The document was a telex[17] sent from Port Elizabeth by Goosen on September 16, describing to his superiors in Pretoria the events leading up to Biko's death. The telex referred to injury "inflicted" on Biko at 7:00 A.M.—injury which the telex associated, furthermore, with Biko's ensuing speech difficulties. Goosen, recalled to the stand, explained "inflicted" as "a play on words."[18]

7. In their final addresses to the magistrate, Von Lieres and Van Rooyen adhered to the position that Biko accidentally hit his head in the course of a "scuffle" he provoked, thereby setting in train the ultimately fatal pathology. Kentridge, for his part, rejected the "scuffle" theory as an adequate explanation: He did not claim to have established that the record showed exactly when and how Biko did receive the injury "inflicted" on him. But concluding that the police testimony was, in the aggregate, unworthy of credit, he argued that "the verdict which we submit is the only one reasonably open to this court is one finding that the death of Mr. Biko was due to a criminal assault upon him by one or more of the eight members of the security police in whose custody he was . . . on the 6th or 7th of September, 1977."[19]

---

[17]The Telex—never referred to by Goosen in affidavit or in his testimony in the opening days of the inquest—was disclosed to Mr. Kentridge by Brigadier C. F. Zietsman, a senior officer of the security police, at an interview which took place on the tenth day of the inquest, when Mr. Kentridge was permitted by the magistrate privately to question Zietsman and other senior officers about possible sources of the discredited "hunger strike" report and related matters.

[18]*New York Times,* December 1, 1977.

[19]Mr. Kentridge did not mince words as to the deplorable indifference the doctors—particularly Lang and Tucker—displayed with respect to a visibly deteriorating patient whose direct external injury they never noticed and whose mortal illness they never diagnosed; the most charitable view, he said, was that they turned "a blind eye" to the fate of one in custody of a police apparatus with which they were subserviently cooperative. Mr. Von Lieres argued that, by the time Lang first acquired substantial information on Biko's condition, Biko's injuries were irreversible. On any reading of the record

THE VERDICT

The taking of testimony was concluded on November 30, 1977—the day of the national elections in which the ruling National Party significantly enlarged its substantial parliamentary majority. On December 1, counsel made their final addresses. On December 2, Magistrate Prins delivered his verdict:

(a) The identity of the deceased is Stephen Bantu Biko, Black man, approximately 30 years old;
(b) Date of death: 12th September 1977;
(c) Cause or likely cause of death: Head injury with associated extensive brain injury, followed by contusion of the blood circulation, disseminated intravascular coagulation as well as renal failure with uraemia. The head injury was probably sustained during the morning of Wednesday, the 7th of September 1977, when the deceased was involved in a scuffle with members of the Security Branch of the South African Police at Port Elizabeth. Date of death: 12th September 1977.

The available evidence does not prove that the death was brought about by any act or omission involving or amounting to an offence on the part of any person. That completes this inquest. The Court will adjourn now.

ASSESSING THE VERDICT

Most English and American lawyers—even those particularly sensitive to the imperatives of a free press—would tend to look somewhat askance at a judge who granted an interview to a reporter and discussed a case he had recently decided. But Magistrate Prins did exactly this, on the afternoon of the day the inquest ended, and thus managed to deliver one of the very first assessments of the verdict he had just pronounced in the matter of the slain Black leader; "To me,

it is clear that, from September 7 through September 11, Goosen and the doctors arranged to mislead each other and Biko about the condition and the prognosis.

it was just another death. It was a job, like any other."[20]

The remark bespeaks an overwhelming callousness—the more astonishing to one who, sitting in court, had heard the magistrate put to witness and lawyer alike question after question which seemed to reflect a conscientious, if not overly penetrating, resolve to clarify the tangled factual issues confronting him.

The crucial difficulty with the verdict is, of course, that it announced the magistrate's findings without explaining them. The verdict is wholly conclusory. It adopts the Von Lieres–Van Rooyen theory that the "scuffle" was the occasion on which Biko suffered his fatal injuries. But it does not purport to clear away the weighty evidence undercutting the theory. Nor does it offer a syllable of justification for rejecting the opposed Kentridge analysis. As a matter of judicial craftsmanship, the verdict is defective not so much because it is not persuasive as because it does not undertake to persuade. It merely declares a result. Offering no rationale, it can stake no claim to advancing anyone's understanding of the matter at issue. As an aid to determining what happened to Biko, the verdict has no probative significance.[21]

A likely reason for delivering findings unsupported by reasons is that a reasoned opinion would not write—or, to be more exact, would have yielded very different findings. Proper findings, in my judgment, would have been in substance those articulated by Sir David Napley:

[20] *New York Times,* December 3, 1977, p. 2. A few hours before the verdict was announced, security police arrested Biko's brother and cousin, and others, in Soweto.
[21] The verdict has, and may be expected to continue to have, some legal significance. It is true that the prosecutor, if unsatisfied with an inquest verdict, is entitled to require a magistrate to reopen the proceedings. But there is no indication that Von Lieres is unhappy with the verdict he sought. (And Van Rooyen, on a recent visit to Washington, tried to present to an impromptu press conference in the Rayburn Building "a laborious description of how Biko was killed in self-defense." Washington *Post,* February 6, 1978, p. B3. The press conference was an attempt to counter Donald Woods' testimony before a House subcommittee. See footnote 2, *supra*). It appears that the Biko family has initiated a wrongful death action against the police and the government in the South African courts. Presumably the defendants will, *inter alia,* seek to interpose the magistrate's verdict as a bar to further litigation. From an American perspective, one would not expect the verdict to have a *res judicata* effect precluding the civil suit. And, *res judicata* aside, one would like to think that a South African judge would recognize that Magistrate Prins' verdict simply sheds no light at all on the factual issues it was his duty to determine.

It is, in my opinion, reasonable to postulate as follows: The purpose of Mr. Biko's detention was to obtain information concerning alleged terrorist activities. A recognized course for illiciting [sic] information is to condition a person, e.g., by holding him incommunicado for 20 days, subjecting him to hardship and deprivation such as that endured by Mr. Biko. Not long before the interrogation was to be resumed at 0715 hours on the morning of 7th September, he sustained an injury which proved fatal, and that injury was inflicted by one or more persons with a view to rendering him compliant. In summary the following salient facts emerged:

(1) The dishonesty of the police in stressing to the Doctors that Mr. Biko was shamming illness and the fact that they steadfastly failed even to suggest to the Doctors that he sustained a blow to his head abundantly demonstrates that they had something discreditable to hide.

(2) The fact that Mr. Biko must have had a period of unconsciousness before 7:15 A.M. on the morning of the 7th September must have pinpointed the onset of the brain damage and the way in which it was sustained.

(3) The failure by the police to mount and pursue a meaningful and vigorous investigation prior to the Inquest as to the full and true circumstances was, and could only be, attributable to a significant reluctance to uncover the truth.

(4) The demonstrable pattern of conditioning of the deceased for interrogation renders it improbable, in the face of the callousness involved throughout, that actual violence would have been abhorrent and absent.

(5) The medical evidence established that the onset of the brain damage was at least as consistent with a blow having been received prior to 0715 hours on the 7th September, as in the "scuffle" at about that time.

(6) The oral evidence of the police was unconvincing and for the most part probatively unacceptable.

(7) The police, in whose custody the deceased had been when he was held incommunicado, advanced no explanation as to how he could have sustained a blow to his forehead, consistent with the brain damage subsequently disclosed.

In short, I was left in no doubt that Mr. Biko died as a result of brain injury inflicted on him by one or more unidentified members of the Security Police at some time prior to and reasonably proximate to 0715 hours on the morning of the 7th September, 1977. A blow or blows no doubt intended only to hurt, caused brain damage which resulted in death. If, within the first few hours of sustaining the

injury, the full and true facts had been given to the Doctors, and they
had been allowed to place Mr. Biko in a provincial hospital, with all
the advantages of the excellent and experienced medical services
available in South Africa, Mr. Biko might still be alive. After the first
few hours, as the Autopsy and the medical evidence showed, the
resultant damage became irreversible.

To the extent that one credits Sir David's findings, one is forced
to recognize that there may be terrifying truths lurking in the
magistrate's postscript to his verdict, ". . . it was just another
death." Biko was the twentieth person to die in the custody of the
security police since March of 1976.[22] Another detainee—eighteen-
year old Bonoventura S. Malza—died while Biko's inquest was in
progress.[23]

The verdict was widely condemned. Within South Africa, Whites
generally may have been relieved, but such major White newspapers
as the *Rand Daily Mail* and the *Johannesburg Star* were critical.
Outside South Africa, condemnation was the norm; among those
voicing shock were the United States Department of State, the House
of Commons and Secretary General Waldheim.[24]

But the crucial assessment of the verdict came from Stephen Biko
himself. Months earlier, before he was detained for the last time, in
an interview with an American businessman, he foretold what was
likely to happen:

> You are either alive and proud or you are dead, and when you are dead,
> you can't care anyway. And your method of death can itself be a
> politicizing thing. So you die in the riots. For a hell of a lot of them,
> in fact, there's really nothing to lose—almost literally, given the kind
> of situations that they come from. So if you can overcome the personal
> fear for death, which is a highly irrational thing, you know, then you're
> on the way.

[22] *New York Times,* November 29, 1977. For a detailed inventory, see *Deaths in Detention in South Africa* (Lawyers' Committee for Civil Rights Under Law: Washington,
1977) pp. 2–3. There appear to have been no deaths from 1972 to 1975; from 1963 to 1971
there were twenty-two deaths. In a number of instances, no inquests were held.
[23] Washington *Post,* November 19, 1977, p. A16.
[24] Philadelphia *Inquirer,* December 4, 1977.

APPENDIX 297

And in interrogation the same sort of thing applies. I was talking to this policeman, and I told him, "If you want us to make any progress, the best thing is for us to talk. Don't try any form of rough stuff, because it just won't work." And this is absolutely true also. For I just couldn't see what they could do to me which would make me all of a sudden soften to them. If they talk to me, well I'm bound to be affected by them as human beings. But the moment they adopt rough stuff, they are imprinting in my mind that they are police. And I only understand one form of dealing with police, and that's to be as unhelpful as possible. So I button up. And I told them this: "It's up to you." We had a boxing match the first day I was arrested. Some guy tried to clout me with a club. I went into him like a bull. I think he was under instructions to take it so far and no further, and using open hands so that he doesn't leave any marks on the face. And of course he said exactly what you were saying just now: "I will kill you." He meant to intimidate. And my answer was: "How long is it going to take you?" Now of course they were observing my reaction. And they could see that I was completely unbothered. If they beat me up, it's to my advantage. I can use it. They just killed somebody in jail—a friend of mine—about ten days before I was arrested. Now it would have been bloody useful evidence for them to assault me. At least it would indicate what kind of possibilities were there, leading to this guy's death. So, I wanted them to go ahead and do what they could do, so that I could use it. I wasn't really afraid that their violence might lead me to make revelations I didn't want to make, because I had nothing to reveal on this particular issue. I was operating from a very good position, and they were in a very weak position. My attitude is, I'm not going to allow them to carry out their program faithfully. If they want to beat me five times, they can only do so on condition that I allow them to beat me five times. If I react sharply, equally and oppositely, to the first clap, they are not going to be able to systematically count the next four claps, you see. It's a fight. So if they had meant to give me so much of a beating, and not more, my idea is to make them go beyond what they wanted to give me and to give back as much as I can give so that it becomes an uncontrollable thing. You see the one problem this guy had with me: he couldn't really fight with me because it meant he must hit back, like a man. But he was given instructions, you see, on how to hit, and now these instructions were no longer applying because it was a fight. So he had to withdraw and get more instructions. So I said to them, "Listen, if you guys want to do this your way, you have got to handcuff me and bind my feet together, so that I can't respond. If you allow me to respond, I'm certainly going to respond. And I'm afraid you may have to kill me in the process even if it's not your intention."[25]

[25]"Biko on Death," *New Republic,* January 7, 1978, p. 12.

About the Editor

MILLARD ARNOLD, an American, is a graduate of Howard University and Notre Dame Law School. He is Director of the Southern Africa Project of the Lawyers' Committee for Civil Rights Under Law in Washington, D.C. All money earned by this book is being placed in a trust for the Biko family.